Dark Ruby

by

Lisa Jackson

A TOPAZ BOOK

TOPAZ
Published by the Penguin Group
Penguin Putnam Inc., 375 Hudson Street,
New York, New York 10014, U.S.A.
Penguin Books Ltd, 27 Wrights Lane,
London W8 5TZ, England
Penguin Books Australia Ltd, Ringwood,
Victoria, Australia
Penguin Books Canada Ltd, 10 Alcorn Avenue,
Toronto, Ontario, Canada M4V 3B2
Penguin Books (N.Z.) Ltd, 182–190 Wairau Road,
Auckland 10, New Zealand

Penguin Books Ltd, Registered Offices:
Harmondsworth, Middlesex, England

First published by Topaz, an imprint of Dutton Signet,
a member of Penguin Putnam Inc.

First Printing, March, 1998
10 9 8 7 6 5 4 3 2

 REGISTERED TRADEMARK—MARCA REGISTRADA

Printed in Canada

PUBLISHER'S NOTE
This is a work of fiction. Names, characters, places, and incidents either are
the product of the author's imagination or are used fictitiously, and any resem-
blance to actual persons, living or dead, events, or locales is entirely
coincidental.

"You, Lady Gwynn," he said in a voice that was barely audible, "are unlike any woman I've met."

She didn't know if he meant his words as a compliment or insult, but didn't care. Her heart was pumping wildly, and she couldn't drag her gaze away from the hard set of his mouth. "And . . . and you, thief, you are like no other man."

"Aye." His breath fanned her face and teased her hair, the hands gripping her arms released them only to clasp at her back and drag her even closer to him. "Oh, Lady, how you vex me," he whispered, his voice tortured. "Would I had never met you." His head lowered, and for a heartbeat, he hesitated, his mouth hovering a breath above hers.

"Damn you," he groaned, just as his mouth claimed hers.

*To all my friends and family
who have supported me through
the toughest time of my life:
I love you and will
remember you forever.*

Prologue

Glimmering in the dying firelight, the jewels in the ring winked a deep bloodred. Beckoning. Seducing. Begging to be taken by trained fingers.

From his hiding spot behind the velvet curtains, Trevin wet his dry lips, rubbed the tips of his fingers together, and tried to quiet his thundering pulse. At fifteen he was a thief and a good one, an orphaned waif who stole to survive. Never had he attempted to snatch anything so valuable as the ring left carelessly on the window ledge. But he was desperate and the jewels and gold would fetch a good price, mayhap enough to buy a decent horse since his efforts at stealing one had gone awry. Painful welts on his back, the result of the farmer lashing him with a whip, still cut into his skin and burned like the very fires of hell to remind him that he'd failed.

But not this time.

Now he would have the means to escape Rhydd and his sins forever.

He listened but the lord's chamber was quiet. Aside from the occasional tread of footsteps in the hallway, the rustle of mice in the fragrant rushes tossed over the stone floor of the castle, or the hiss of flames in the grate, there was no sound but the pounding of his heart.

Noiselessly he slipped between the drapes and stole across the rushes to the window where he plucked his prize and stuffed it swiftly into the small pocket sewn into the sleeve of his tunic for just such spoils as this. Holding his breath, he started for the door only to hear a breathless woman's voice coming from the hallway.

"In here, Idelle. Quickly."

Trevin's knees nearly gave way as he realized the lord's wife was on the other side of the oaken door. He had no choice but to duck back behind the curtain and hide himself in the alcove where Baron Roderick's clothes were tucked. *Help me,* he silently prayed to a God who rarely seemed to listen.

The door swung open and a rush of air caused the fire to glow more brightly. Golden shadows danced upon the whitewashed walls.

Trevin dared peek through the heavy velvet and watched as Lady Gwynn yanked her tunic over her head, then tossed it carelessly onto the floor. With a bored sigh, she, now clad only in her underdress, dropped onto the bed.

Trevin's groin tightened at the sight of the lacy chemise against Gwynn's skin. Idelle, the old midwife and a woman many proclaimed to be a witch, shuffled into the room and closed the door behind her. Half blind and a bit crippled, Idelle held some kind of special power and even though her ancient eyes were clouded a milky white, she seemed to see more than most people within these castle walls. 'Twas said that she had the uncanny gift of searching out a man's soul.

" 'Tis the time," she said in a voice not unlike that

of a toad. Carefully she set her basket of herbs and candles on a small table. She laid each wick upon a red-hot coal from the fire until all the beeswax tapers were lit. Once the flames were strong and flickering in the breeze, Idelle reached into a pouch in her basket and dropped a handful of pungent herbs over the table. Some sparked in the candles' flames and the scents of rose and myrtle blended over the odor of burning oak.

"Then let's get it done." Squirming upon the coverlet Lady Gwynn lifted her chemise over her legs and hips. Trevin was suddenly much too hot. High and higher the chemise was raised until the sheer fabric was wadded beneath her breasts.

Though he knew it a sin, he could not drag his eyes away from her naked body. White and supple in the quivering firelight she rolled toward the old woman.

Trevin clamped his jaw tight. He couldn't resist eyeing her flat white abdomen, the slight indentations between her ribs, and the nest of red-brown curls that seemed to sparkle in the juncture of her legs.

His throat turned to dust. So this is what a noblewoman looked like beneath her velvet and furs. Oh, what he wouldn't give to run one of his callused fingers over that soft irresistible skin.

"There ye be, lass. Now, let me see what ye've got." Idelle knelt at the side of the bed and her fingers, knotted with age, moved gently over the younger woman's smooth belly. Groping and prodding, she murmured something in the old language, a spell mayhap, as it was common knowledge that she prayed and offered sacrifices to the pagan gods of the elders, just as the man who had raised him, the sorcerer Muir had. "By the gods, 'tis no use." With a sigh, she shook her graying head. Sorrow added years to a face that was barely a skull with skin stretched over old, bleached bones. " 'Tis barren ye be, lass. There is no babe."

"Nay!" Gwynn cried, but lacked conviction.

Sadly, Idelle clucked her tongue. " 'Tis sorry I be and ye know it." ·

"And wrong you be! Oh, please, Idelle, tell me I am with child," she insisted desperately.

"Nay, I—"

"Hush! There *is* a child. There must be!" Stubborn pride flashed in the lady's eyes as if by sheer will a baby would grow within her womb. "Oh, dear God you must be mistaken!" She whispered, though her chin wobbled indecisively.

Try as he might Trevin couldn't draw his gaze away from her. She pushed her chemise upward to the juncture of her arms and for the first time in his life he saw a noblewoman, a beautiful lady, naked. He'd caught glimpses of serving wenches and whores, of course, but never before had he seen the wife of a baron. His mouth drew no spit as he looked upon the sweet roundness of her breasts. Her nipples were small and pink, reminding him of rosebuds. His damned manhood, always at the ready, became stiff.

"Touch me again. Try harder to feel the babe," Gwynn pleaded, though she seemed resigned, as if she understood her fate.

Regret drew Idelle's old lips into a knot. She laid the flat of her hand beneath Lady Gwynn's navel, closed her sightless eyes, and whispered a chant. Upon the bed, the naked woman lay perfectly still.

With a sigh, Idelle removed her spotted fingers. "There's nothing."

"What will I do?" Gwynn asked, swallowing hard.

"I know not."

"Mary, sweet mother of Jesus, help me," Lady Gwynn whispered from her bed—the lord's bed. If the baron had any idea that a poor stable boy—nay, a thief—had seen his wife naked, there would be hell to pay. Trevin would probably be drawn and quartered, his spilled guts fed to the castle hogs. He shuddered at the thought but still could not draw his wayward gaze away.

Her eyes were wide with fear and she bit into her lower lip. The candles near the bed gave off black smoke and the tiny flames reflected in tears drizzling from her eyes. Saint Peter, she was a beauty. "If I bear not a son, my husband will kill me."

Trevin's heart gave a jolt. He'd heard stories of the lord's cruelty, but to kill this woman—this beautiful wife?

"Nay, he would never—"

"Don't lie to me, Idelle." Gwynn sat bolt upright on the bed, her pointed chin thrust forward, her chemise lowering over those perfect breasts. Frightened, she curved the fingers of one hand over the midwife's scrawny arm. "There *must* be a child."

"I'm sorry, m'lady, 'tis ripe ye are, that I know. Aye, but—"

"I *will* bear my husband a son!" Gwynn's pretty face twisted from desperation to a sly expression that reminded Trevin of a wolf coming upon a wounded lamb. "I . . . I . . . slept with my husband each night before he rode to battle," she said softly, as if to convince herself, "I tried, oh, how I tried. . . ."

" 'Tis a pity, to be sure."

"And I did what you advised," Gwynn added, as if her childless state were the old midwife's fault. With one hand, she gestured to the beeswax candles dripping near the bed. "I added myrtle, oak, and rose to

candles. I drew fertility runes in the sand and lied to
Father Anthony when he caught me practicing the old
ways." Her eyes slitted and a cunning expression overcame her perfect features. "Then, to atone, I prayed
on my knees on the cold stone floor of the chapel
for hours upon hours, hoping God would answer my
prayers. I did everything I could and yet you dare tell
me there is no babe."

Idelle frowned and rubbed at the sprinkle of whiskers upon her chin. "I'll not lie to ye, m'lady."

"For the love of Saint Jude!" Gwynn hopped off
the bed and walked barefoot through the rushes to the
small window cut into the chamber wall. Moonlight
streamed through the opening and fell upon her beautiful, angry face while casting a silver sheen to her
fiery hair. "You must help me."

Idelle clucked her tongue while worrying her
gnarled fingers. "I tried. By the gods, I tried, lass. But
sometimes when a man and woman lay together, a
child eludes them."

"But why?" Gwynn asked, frowning and tapping
her fingers in agitation along the whitewashed wall.

"Who knows?"

"God is punishing me, though 'tis the baron's fault."

Idelle lifted a graying eyebrow. "His fault?"

"Aye, but he will kill me if I give him no sons,"
she said again, turning and resting her head against
the sill. Trevin cringed. If not for the shadows, she
would see him. "Was not his first wife, Katherine,
found dead in her bed"—she waved a hand at the pile
of furs on the curtained mattress—"this very bed after
six years of marriage and no children?"

"Aye, but—"

"Strangled, they say, or suffocated."

"The Lord denied it, even unto Father Anthony."

"And his second wife, Rose, drowned when she, too, was unable to give him a babe."

" 'Tis true," Idelle agreed, rubbing her knuckles until Trevin thought she might work the skin off her bones.

Gwynn sighed loudly. "Lord Roderick is a young man no longer. He wants sons and I, Idelle, will give them to him, one way or another."

Trevin bit his lip. He'd heard the talk whispered by the servants in the solar, scullery, stables, and throughout the barony. Even peasants in the village suspected that Baron Roderick had suffocated his first wife, drowned his second, and took another—this one, Gwynn of Llynwen, a woman of fifteen for the singular purpose of bearing him an heir. A son. Trevin swallowed though his throat was dry as sand.

Through the crack in the drapes, he watched as the lady's eyebrows drew together and her gaze moved swiftly over the window ledge. "My ring," she whispered, distracted for a moment as her fingers ran over the stone and mortar. Trevin's heart stilled. Guilt pierced his soul. " 'Twas here but a little while ago . . . the ruby my father gave me . . ." She bit her lip in vexation. "I know I put it here. Oh, for the love of Saint Mary, my mind is gone with all this worry about a babe!"

Trevin didn't dare breathe as she stooped to sweep the rushes with her fingers, as if the jewel had fallen onto the floor. Idelle, too, began searching and the damned ring burned a hole in Trevin's sleeve.

"How very odd . . ."

"Could ye have misplaced it, m'lady?"

"Nay. Nay. It was here. Right in this very spot. I know it!" She slapped the ledge with her palm and then her gaze inched slowly around her chamber.

Sweat dripped down Trevin's spine as she stared at the curtains. Trevin froze. Could she see him? Did his eyes reflect in the dim candlelight? Had he moved and caught her gaze? He closed his eyes to slits, mouthed a silent prayer to a God he didn't trust, and swallowed a lump as large as an egg that had formed in his throat. Sweat rolled down his muscles though the autumn breeze rushing through the window was cold and caused the embers in the fire to glow a scarlet hue that cast bold red shadows upon the walls. Christ Jesus, how had he ended up here—trapped like a cornered fox?

Lady Gwynn sank to the floor. "I cannot worry about the ring right now," she said, her voice soft and forlorn. "Not when I need not a ruby but a babe."

"Would that I could conjure up a child, but . . ." Idelle shook her head and scratched at the hairs sprouting upon her chin. " 'Tis not possible."

Standing, Gwynn turned her thoughtful gaze back to the midwife. "You could be mistaken."

"Oh, m'lady, would that I were."

"My time of the month is not for a fortnight yet. Only then will we know for certain."

"But—"

"Leave me," Gwynn ordered, dashing away her tears and plopping back on the bed. She tossed her long auburn curls in spoiled disdain. "I'll hear no more of your heresy, old woman. I'm with child, I tell you as sure as there is a God, I am carrying the son of Roderick of Rhydd."

"Would that it were so."

"It is, I tell you. Go." Gwynn hitched her chin to the door and there was nothing for the midwife to do but gather her basket of herbs, candles, and knives and start for the hallway.

However, at the door, Idelle hesitated and shivered as if the cold touch of winter had invaded her soul. "Lady," she said, casting a worried glance over her shoulder, "do not contemplate that which is forbidden."

"Forbidden?"

"I see it in your eyes, child," Idelle said, her voice a worried whisper. "If you consider trying to trick him—"

"Hush!" Gwynn said, her cheeks flaming. "You speak nonsense and what can you see, half blind as you are?"

"My sight is from the soul. Be not foolish," the old woman cautioned, as if she could read the dark turn of Lady Gwynn's thoughts. She cleared her throat and added, "If ye be so troubled, I could send for the priest."

Gwynn let out a breath of disdain and waved Idelle's offer away. "Father Anthony and his prayers and penance are not what I need. Why the man asks to be flogged so hard that blood stains his shirt in order that he appear a servant and martyr of God I understand not."

"Mayhap he has reason to repent."

Gwynn sighed. "He is a man of the faith."

"Aye, but even a man who speaks the words of the Father is made of flesh and bone."

"Be that as it may, I'll not speak to him of this. 'Twould but cause him to stutter and gulp so hard his Adam's apple would bob as fast as a hummingbird's wings in flight." Gwynn's smile wasn't kind. "Please, leave me now."

"As ye wish, child, but take care."

Eyes squeezed shut, Trevin counted out his heartbeats as he heard Idelle shuffle from the room. The large door creaked open only to close with a thud and the chamber was silent aside from the hiss and pop of the fire.

Now, if only the lady would lie on the bed and fall asleep, he could make good his leave. The ring would be his and he would leave Rhydd and his past far behind him.

"Come here."

Her voice seemed to echo through the room.

Trevin's muscles turned to stone.

"Come here," Gwynn ordered again and Trevin prayed there was a cat lurking in the shadows somewhere that she was calling. "You there, boy, behind the velvet. I know you're there."

Holy Mother of God.

He dared open his eyes to stare straight into hers as she was standing before him, her face looming in the crack of the curtains.

There was nothing he could do but slowly edge away from his hiding spot and stand before her in his bloody, mud-stained tunic. She was a small thing, inches shorter than he, but she held herself erect and stiff, as if she were looking down on him with all the power of the barony. "You heard me speaking with the midwife."

It wasn't a question.

"You know of my . . . difficulty."

Sweet Mary she was staring up at him with eyes the color of the forest at dawn. "Aye."

"And I know who you are. The thief who was bold enough to steal my ring from my chamber."

His jaw grew tight and hard.

"This blood—" She touched his shirt with a long finger and eyed the scar that ran along his hairline. "Yours?"

"Some, mayhap."

"Another man's as well?"

He didn't answer. Wouldn't incriminate himself.

"Did you kill him?"

He remembered the ire on the nobleman's face, Ian of Rhydd, Roderick's brother, when he'd realized that his bejeweled dagger had been stolen on the streets of the village. He'd spied Trevin pocketing the prize, caught him by the collar, and slapped him hard.

"You'll not best me, you filthy urchin!"

"Won't I?" Trevin had flipped the knife into his fingers and Ian had turned his wrist, the sharp blade slicing down the side of Trevin's face and neck.

Blood had gushed.

With all his strength, he'd kicked Ian of Rhydd in the groin. The older man had let out a bellow like a wounded bull and Trevin, blinded by the blood running down his face had lashed out with his newfound weapon, taking off a piece of the nobleman's ear. Then he'd run as far and as fast as his legs had carried him. He'd dashed through the muddy, dung-strewn alley, dodging carts, peddlers, and such, reeling off corners and wiping his eyes as the blood had dried. He'd ended up here deep within the castle walls where no one would think to search for him. No one but the lord's comely wife.

Now, Gwynn's lashes thinned a bit. Stepping away from him, she said, "My husband would flog you and throw you into the dungeon to rot for your sins. And," she held up a finger, "if he thought that you'd been spying in his chamber and had seen his wife without her clothes, he'd whip you within an inch of your life, then gut you and spill your innards for the dogs while there was still a breath of life in your body."

Again, the truth. Trevin's insides turned to jelly but

he didn't flinch, just held her gaze steadily. "Is that
what you want, m'lady?" he finally asked, unable to
still his sharp tongue.

"What I want is a babe."

She looked at him and he sensed an idea forming
in her mind—an idea that, he was certain, would scare
the liver from him. "So what are we going to do with
you?" she asked.

His heart was a drum. If he made a run for the
door, she would scream and call the guards and the
window was far above the ground; he would break
both his legs if he attempted to jump into the bailey.
There was no escape unless he were to grab her swiftly
and cover her mouth with his hand. And what then?

She smiled and tapped a fingernail to a front tooth
that slightly overlapped its twin. "Thief," she said,
nodding in self-approval as her idea took shape. "I
have a bargain for you."

"A bargain?" He'd been in enough tight spaces to
smell a trap when one was being offered and yet he
had no choice but to listen.

" 'Twill not be unpleasant," she said, clearing her
throat as if her plan scared her a bit. "I . . . I want
you to spend the next three days here in my bed,
getting me with child." Her face flushed a deep shade
of red and she avoided his eyes as if suddenly
ashamed. "No one will know you are here, trust me,
and on the third night, I will see that you are able to
leave Rhydd with a fine horse, a purse full of gold,
and a new name. Nary a soul will know what became
of you unless you are foolish." Again she narrowed
those dark-lashed eyes thoughtfully as if weighing
each part of her plan, testing it carefully, wondering
if she, a lady of noble birth, could trust a man who
had entered her chamber only to rob her.

His heart was pounding wildly, his erection was full and hard, yet he knew that bedding her was a mistake he didn't dare make, that to touch even one hair of her gorgeous head was as dangerous as stepping through the very portals of hell.

"Come, boy, please," she entreated and for a second she seemed a scared little girl, one he would love to protect. "All I ask is that you lay with me, and . . . and . . . afterward you'll leave here a free man." She reached forward, wound warm, soft fingers around his wrist, and drew his hand to her breast.

He felt the smooth flesh through her chemise and a bud of a nipple against his open palm. *Oh, Mother Mary, what was this tormented ecstasy! This was wrong . . . so wrong.* His chest was as tight as if barrel staves had surrounded it.

" 'Tis a sin," he said, his voice low and rough, not sounding at all as if it belonged to him.

She closed her eyes a second and bit her trembling lower lip. Squaring her shoulders, she nodded solemnly. "Aye, 'tis a sin, and we know that you would never sin, eh, thief?"

"Sweet Jesus."

"This is not the time for prayer."

"But—"

"I'm asking you to help me," she said simply and innocence overshadowed her display of cunning. She was one moment a vixen, the next a frightened girl.

And he, damn it, was only a man. A weak man.

Gaze locked with hers, he let out his breath. Slowly he ran his thumb over the hardening bud of her nipple and heard her sigh, as soft as the wind rustling through the dry leaves still clinging to the trees.

"This is wrong."

"But it will save my life and yours." She smiled

slightly, sadly, as tears again filled her hazel eyes. " 'Tis no choice we have, thief. Come to the bed. Save your soul as well as mine."

"God help me."

She lifted her arms and circled his neck in an embrace he couldn't avoid. Oh, God, how he ached. Desire pounded through his head. Need pulsed hot in his veins.

Tilting her head she offered him the seductive white column of her throat. "Please."

He could resist no longer. A groan of surrender escaped from his throat. His mouth crashed down upon hers eagerly, as if he'd expected this moment in time to be his forever, as if destiny had claimed him.

Her lips parted willingly.

His blood was liquid fire. Hot. Dark. Wanting.

She quivered.

Could it be that this beautiful lady actually wanted him?

Trembling, he lifted her from her feet, carried her to the bed, and fell with her onto the fur coverlet. His hands found the hem of her chemise, his cock was thick and ready to burst, and he never stopped kissing her as she unlaced his breeches and peeled off his tunic.

This is madness, Trevin! Stop before you cross a bridge that leads to damnation.

Anxious fingers skimmed the muscles of his shoulders, the few hairs on his chest. So hot he was sweating, he kissed her hard, his tongue probing, his hands upon the laces holding her chemise closed.

His tunic slid to the floor and the ring, gold and deep dusky scarlet, rolled into the rushes.

"I knew it," she whispered. "You're a bold one, thief."

And stupid to be contemplating bedding the baron's wife. But his head was thundering with want, his flesh ready and as he shoved the chemise up her body, he parted her legs with his knees, shed all doubts, and thrust deep into her warmth, only to feel resistance, then a rending.

She let out a soft cry of pain.

He didn't move for a second. Lust thundered through his body and yet something was wrong. Very wrong. "For the love of . . . you . . . you are a virgin," he whispered, his voice raw, his mind screaming at him that he'd been played for a fool.

A tiny pool of blood stained the furs beneath them. Firelight played in eerie shadows against the walls.

"Aye." Again tears starred her lashes.

His mind was swimming in murky waters as he stared down at her vexed face, her skin glowing gold in the flickering light. "I heard you tell the old woman that you thought you were with child." Oh sweet Jesus 'twas all he could do to concentrate to not move and feel her feminine warmth rubbing against him.

She didn't say a word, just stared up at him through her tears and, swallowing hard, scaled his ribs with warm fingers.

"The baron will—"

"Never know of you. Trust me," she begged. " 'Tis my worry, not yours."

"How could he—?"

"Shh. There are some secrets between a man and a woman that are not to be shared with another. Come, thief, do not stop now." She touched him so gently he wanted to believe in her forever. Slowly, she rubbed her smooth skin against him, lifting her hips, and touching his flat nipples with her thumbs. "Love me."

"Nay, I—"

"Love me, please."

Oh, glorious torment, he couldn't resist. Moaning in surrender, he caught her rhythm and was unable to keep from delving into her sweet heat again and again, faster and faster as the world caught fire behind his eyes. With a primal cry, he spilled his seed into the most secret part of her.

"Yes, thief, yes," she whispered, suppressing a sob. " 'Tis good you be."

And a fool like no other!

Falling against her, crushing her breasts, feeling her arms wrap around his sweaty torso, he found no joy. No satisfaction. For deep in the marrow of his bones he knew with a deadly certainty that this single act would be his undoing. Though Lady Gwynn had seduced him, the truth was that he, an orphaned stable boy who had been raised by a magician with a lust for wine had become a thief and had, in his most bold and stupid act stolen not only the lady's ring, but Baron Roderick of Rhydd's wife's virginity.

'Twas no doubt, there would be hell to pay.

Chapter One

" 'Tis bad news I bear." Muir, self-proclaimed sorcerer and often times the village idiot slipped, like an eel through clear water, over the threshold of the countinghouse. Carrying a cane that was more for appearance than use, he cast a furtive glance over his shoulder, as if sensing he was being followed into this private room so near the lord's chamber.

Trevin was not amused by the elder man's theatrics. Muir was known to overplay a part; his dramatics were a bit of his questionable charm. Seated at a small, scarred table near the single window, he looked up from the feeble accounts the treasurer of Black Oak had recorded. "Come on in, Muir," he suggested, leaning back in his chair until the front legs were elevated from the floor. "Do not be shy."

"Ye mock me, boy," the old one grumbled.

"You mock yourself."

"Ah, 'tis a sorry orphaned lad I raised into the lord of this fine castle, one who minces words with me."

Trevin let the chair fall back to the floor, the legs banging and startling Muir.

"But I lose myself. There is news from Rhydd."

Rhydd. The bane of his existence and the beginning of his journey to a barony he'd never wanted and now was forced to rule. Trevin's jaw grew tight and the blackness that forever darkened his heart seemed only to deepen. The quill snapped between fingers that ached to do something, *any*thing other than oversee the daily routine of a castle he'd won by a lucky roll of the dice. He was sick to the back teeth of grumbling peasants, lazy servants, crumbling walls, and a treasury with no coin. "Bad news?" he asked in a slow, angry whisper. "Is there any other kind?"

"I take it the ledgers bode ill." Muir leaned heavily upon his crook and fastened his good eye on the man he had raised from a whimpering blue-lipped babe. He was the only man within the walls of the keep who had no fear of Trevin's black rage.

"Aye, the ledgers bode ill. Very ill. As they always do." Trevin rubbed the ache from his shoulders, then, disgusted, slammed the ledger book closed. A cloud of dust swirled upward. "But tell me of Rhydd."

"I've seen a vision."

"Ah." Trevin folded his arms over his chest and tried not to notice the stale odor of wine that was forever Muir's companion. After all, he'd grown up witnessing the old man's fondness for the cup. "A vision of Rhydd. What this time?"

"There is trouble brewing in the keep."

"At Rhydd?" After thirteen years he could not hear the name of that castle without thinking of the nights he'd spent in Lady Gwynn's bed and the fact that nine months later she'd borne a son. His son. A boy he'd allowed to be named after another, all for the price of a ruby ring, jeweled dagger, and a few gold coins.

"The Lord Roderick returns."

Trevin's head snapped up. His muscles tightened. "He's been locked away at Castle Carter—"

"I know, I know. For as long as there has been peace, but now he's escaped and is returning to Rhydd."

"You *saw* this?"

"Aye." Muir nodded. "In a dream."

"A dream you had after falling asleep from too much ale?"

"Nay, m'lord—"

"Don't call me that." Trevin found it bothersome that the man who had raised him would refer to him as lord, sire, baron, or any such nonsense.

"But ye be the ruler here now."

"Aye, because I was lucky with the dice and won the castle from an addled old man who'd been far too deep in his cups. But we stray from the point. Many of your 'dreams' and 'visions,' Muir, have come to mean naught."

"In the past, aye, I know." He bobbed his bald head eagerly. "But this time 'tis true. If ye do not trust me, then be so good as to speak with Farmer Hal who came from Castle Carter with the news of Roderick's escape as well as a cart of fodder corn and seeds for the planting season."

Trevin couldn't help but raise a disbelieving eyebrow. "The good farmer comes with the news to Black Oak just as you see your 'vision,' Muir? 'Tis lucky timing, is it not?"

"You doubt me? Me who raised you from a sniffling, scrawny babe?"

"Never," Trevin said and would have smiled at his mentor's furrowed pate if he were not disturbed by the news. He snatched the book of ledgers and placed it in an oak and iron chest, then hesitated and, for an unknown reason, picked up a small faded pouch wherein a ring was hidden—the darkly jeweled ring he'd stolen from the Lady of Rhydd. Though in need of coin or food or a steed many times over the years, he'd never sold that little bit of his past that reminded him of her. Fool. He slipped the ring into a pocket, then locked the chest securely once again.

This was not the first time Muir had predicted a shadow over Rhydd, but in this instance, the old man seemed more sure of himself. "Let us see what the farmer has to say." Swiftly, he ushered the magician out the door and turned the key in the lock.

Muir, despite his claims of pain in his knees, nearly flew down the stairs, the skirts of his sorry-looking tunic sailing behind him, the eyes of the ever-vigilant dogs watching him as he hurried past their resting spot on the landing.

One let out a short "woof," then hung his head as he spied Trevin.

Hal, the farmer, was in the bailey arguing over the value of his seeds as he measured them for the steward. " 'Tis the best beans in all of Wales, you can be sure," he was saying, but paused in his boasting as Trevin approached.

"Muir tells me you bring news from Castle Carter," Trevin said and, as the old man had predicted, the farmer told him of Roderick's escape from the dungeon.

". . . yea, the baron is expected back at Rhydd within a few days," Hal said as the first few drops of rain fell from purple-bellied clouds scudding slowly across the sky. " 'Tis a pity, if ye ask me, m'lord, for 'tis no secret that Roderick is a hard ruler." Hal shook his head. "Thank our Lord that the lady was able to bear him a son, elsewise I fear she would have met the same fate as those who had wed the baron before her."

The muscles in the back of Trevin's neck twisted into tight, painful knots.

"Now, no doubt, he'll want more sons."

"No doubt." Trevin left the farmer and the steward to argue over the price of seeds and walked across the mashed grass of the bailey. Fingering the hilt of his dagger he silently cursed the fates that had caused him to steal Lady Gwynn's ring so many years ago. As he had promised her on their parting, he should have forgotten that he had sired a son, that the boy now residing at Rhydd was his own flesh and blood. He could not cast that memory aside. Nor had the years diluted his need to see his boy, to claim him. If anything, his desire to give Gareth of Rhydd his name was stronger than ever.

There had been a time when he'd believed that he would father more children, that this very castle would be filled with so many of his sons and daughters he would rarely think of his firstborn, conceived in sin, raised as another man's heir. But time and fate had played their cruel tricks upon his plans and now, he was certain, Gareth of Rhydd would be his only child; the only son he would ever spawn.

For nearly a year he'd struggled with himself, remembering his bargain with Gwynn, his promise of silence about the boy's begetting. He'd kept the secret for years, secure in the knowledge that Roderick, bound forever a prisoner by Baron Hamilton of Castle Carter, would never guess the truth, never put the boy in danger.

"Lord Hamilton was never one to be trusted," Muir said as if reading Trevin's mind and flipped the hood of his tunic over his head as the rain pelted from the sky. His one good eye stared without blinking at Trevin. The old man had always had the disturbing ability to see into his young charge's soul at the most dire of times. 'Twas a constant battle to keep the sorcerer from looking too closely and spying Trevin's weaknesses. "Ye, m'lord, have a duty to protect yer—"

"Devil be with you, Muir," Trevin grumbled as the wind slapped against his face in icy gusts. "And don't call me lord."

Muir waved off his protest. " 'Tis only ye who has to deal with the darkness in your soul. Only ye who have to face yer Maker and—"

"Oh, for the love of Christ!" Squinting against the rain that ran down his face and neck, Trevin threw an irritated glare up at the menacing heavens. His old bargain with Gwynn be damned. He'd pay her back tenfold, but by the gods of good and evil, he was going to claim his son.

"Holy Father forgive me, for I have sinned . . ." Gwynn whispered her prayers in the nave, hoping that her request wouldn't fall upon deaf ears. Surely God wouldn't forsake her now—or would He? She thought of all the spells she'd tried to weave, the runes she'd drawn, the pagan chants she'd murmured in the vain hope that her husband would never return. She'd lain with another man, deceived everyone in the castle, claiming her son was Roderick's child.

Selfish, selfish woman. Creating a child so that you could live and now you have a son more precious than life itself.

Raindrops pounded upon the ceiling and the wind rushed noisily outside as Gwynn prayed.

For thirteen years she'd been favored. Her husband

had been wounded in battle and held prisoner at a castle to the north without ever setting eyes upon the son she'd sworn was his. The ransom that Ian, his brother, had offered had been turned down by the Baron Hamilton of Castle Carter, the ruler who seemed to find some perverse pleasure in holding Roderick as his prisoner.

There had been, at the behest of Ian a few failed attempts at freeing Roderick. The attacks on Castle Carter had been futile, costly in men and arms and Ian had finally given up. Gwynn had fervently hoped that she would never have to see the man she'd married again, never have to lie about Gareth's conception.

Gareth. Her son. The boy who would someday rule Rhydd. Spawned by the thief so many years before and passed off as the heir to a heartless man who had murdered his first two wives.

Oh, cruel fate that Roderick was now returning.

As it had so many times in the past, guilt seeped into her soul but she steadfastly swept it aside. Had she not lain with the outlaw, had she not spent three days of bittersweet passion in the lord's bed with him, she would never have conceived Gareth, her sole joy in life, her reason for living. "Our Lord, please hear my prayers," she intoned as the stones of the floor pressed hard against her knees. Stiffening her spine and bowing her head, she closed her eyes. She wouldn't feel any more guilt for bearing a child as bright and true as her son.

"You appear troubled, child."

Gwynn nearly jumped out of her skin. Her hand flew to her chest, as if to hold her heart in place. She'd thought she'd been alone in the chapel and hadn't heard the scrape of Father Anthony's leather shoes on the worn floor or the sound of his wheezing breath as he'd approached.

Her prayers forgotten, Gwynn scrambled to her feet.

"What bothers you?" Father Anthony's gentle voice seemed to reverberate from the rafters though, in truth, he barely moved his thin, white-rimmed lips.

"Oh, Father Anthony . . . you . . . you startled me."

" 'Twas not my intention."

"I . . . I was in need of . . . of solace," she said and saw his bloodless lips curve into a knowing smile.

A tall, thin man with stooped shoulders and a ring of blond hair around a bald pate, he nodded, as if he, too, felt a need for the cleansing of his soul. He laid a long-fingered hand upon her shoulder. "Do not let me disturb you."

"Nay, I was finished," she said and hoped that her cheeks were not as red as they felt. 'Twas unsettling the way he could sneak up on a body.

"You were praying for the b-baron's safe return." Father Anthony's eyebrows raised in silent question and his Adam's apple started to wobble, betraying his anxiety.

"Aye." The lie tripped over her tongue and she cringed inside. 'Twas one thing to stretch the truth to suit one's purposes but quite another to lie baldly to the priest in the very chapel itself. "Thank you, Father," she said.

"Rest well."

As if she could.

"And, please, Lady, do not heed old Id-Idelle and her dark ways. She means well, b-but—" He spread his fingers wide, palms upward, as if he were imploring heaven to understand some great mystery. "She is b-but a woman and a weak one at that. The d-d-devil is always looking for those who are not strong." His gaze held hers. "Do not let Satan fool you, even if he dresses in the guise of a midwife."

"Idelle is no devil."

"I said it not. Just be careful, m'lady. Lucifer dons many masks."

"I know my heart, Father," she said, though she couldn't admit what was in the depths of her soul. Clutching the folds of her tunic, she nodded and slipped out the doorway to the corridor where the candles flickered and smoked.

The thought of seeing Roderick again was like a vile poison seeping through her blood and curdling in her innards. She'd never loved him, had been betrothed by her father, and had spent only two weeks with the older baron before he'd ridden off to battle nearly thirteen years before. Since then she'd been the lady of the castle and had only to deal with Roderick's brother, Ian. She shivered at the thought of her brother-in-law. He was a huge man with meaty hands that were covered on the backside with the same sable brown hair that darkened his jaw.

Though educated, he had a crude manner of speaking and there was no light of kindness in his eyes. Often times when he'd sipped from too many cups of wine, his eyes had narrowed and he'd stared at his sister-in-law in silent, evil regard. His own wife had died two years before. A small slip of a woman with pale skin and eyes that were red from disease and painful tears, Margaret had given up her soul in her husband's bed, leaving him, like his only brother, without any issue. Since Margaret's death, Ian's interest in Gwynn had been bolder than ever and his brooding gaze had grown evermore filled with a hideous lust that made her skin crawl.

At the thought, Gwynn's stomach roiled. She hustled through a door and across a short path to the kitchen where the cook, a tiny freckled man named Jack, was scolding two boys turning the spit on which an ox was roasting. Fat that streamed from the carcass sizzled on the coals and smoke rose up a wide chimney where slabs of meat were hung to cure.

"Faster, faster, you lazy swine," Jack growled, boxing one of the lad's ears. The boy yelped in pain but spun the roasting beast at a snappier pace. His partner, on the other side of the spit, avoided the cook's eyes and put all his muscles behind rotating the cross bar. "That's better . . . much better. See that ye keep it so." Jack's hands fisted and rested upon thin, bony hips. "We wouldn't want to disappoint the lord when he returns, now, would we?"

Both boys shook their heads vigorously while a kitchen girl grinding spices with a mortar and pestle at a nearby table smothered a smile. Finally the cook, turning slightly, realized he wasn't alone with his lazy charges. "Oh, m'lady," he said, showing off uneven teeth and gesturing expansively to the bustle of his workers in the kitchen. One girl was paring winter apples, another plucking the feathers from a pheasant just outside the door. While boys carried bundles of firewood or buckets of wriggling eels, girls toted baskets of goose eggs. "As ye can see we're making ready for the baron's return."

"Good, good," Gwynn said, feigning interest, her fingers fumbling with the cross that dangled from the chain of gold encircling her throat.

" 'Tis an intricate sugar castle we be making and the huntsman has brought us fine pheasants, six crane, and a stag." The wiry man beamed at the thought of his feast. "We've eels from the pond and salmon and—"

"—'tis pleased my husband will be. Carry on," Gwynn interrupted, holding up a hand and heading toward the door leading to the bailey. All this talk of Roderick's return was bringing an ache to her head and pain in her stomach. What was she to do? When he took one look at Gareth . . . *Sweet Mother of the Lord, please help me.* Ever since the messenger arrived with the news that her husband had escaped, Gwynn had been questioning herself, certain that she should have sent her boy to her sister, Luella. As the lady of Castle Heath far, far to the south, Luella would have seen to Gareth's upbringing as well as to his safety. He would have become a page and a squire, learning the skills necessary to become a knight. He would have been safe. Gwynn could have sent word to Luella that Roderick was returning to Rhydd.

Oh, what a foolish, foolish woman she'd been! Had she really thought her husband would be imprisoned forever, or that he would die rotting in that dungeon? In thirteen years she'd become complacent, living within the comfort and safety of Rhydd's thick stone walls, acting as if she were the baron, loving her son with all her heart, her only problem keeping her brother-in-law at arm's length.

Since his wife's death, Ian had become more impossible and bold, trying to corner her alone in dark corridors, brushing against her as they passed, staring at her with narrowed, sinister eyes that sent a chill racing through her blood.

But she would gladly face Ian a thousand times over if only Roderick would never return.

Her soft shoes sank into the mud as she dashed along the path winding through the bailey. Geese

honked noisily, flapping their wings and losing feathers
as they scattered toward the eel pond. Two boys hauling a dead boar veered out of her path as a young
girl lugged a basket of wet laundry away from ropes
strung near the north tower. Gwynn barely noticed as
raindrops splashed against her tunic. She had to find
Gareth and explain to a boy of barely twelve years
that his life was in danger from the man who was
supposed to be his father. When she'd hastily con-
cocted her plan to conceive a child other than Roderick's, she'd thought that the baron wouldn't know the
babe was not his. Only later, after years of loving and
doting on the lad would he suspect that the child
might not have been his issue. By then he would have
accepted the boy as his own or, should he suspect
otherwise, not voice his fears as he would appear a
stupid cuckold fool.

Oh, Lord, she must've been daft to think she could
get away with her plan. But had she not lain with the
thief, she would not have had her son. Nor would she
have had years of memories of lovemaking. Even now,
over a dozen years later, she could still remember the
warmth of his touch, the sense of his tongue against
her skin, the moist heat his kisses had inspired . . .

"Looking for your son?" Ian's voice echoed through
the bailey, ringing off the stone walls and thundering
in her heart. She blushed, wondering if he could guess
the turn of her wayward thoughts. 'Twas silly and a
waste of time to think of the youthful thief who had
slipped out of the castle and her life just as she'd
asked.

Now, Ian stood, fingering the blade of his knife as
he watched a group of boys, Gareth among them,
playing with wooden swords they'd constructed. Gareth, taller than the rest, was the most agile. A tight-

muscled youth with black curls, sharp blue eyes, and quick reflexes, he was able to leap onto barrels or slide swiftly under a hayrick to avoid the advances of the thicker, clumsier boys.

Tom, the butcher's son, lunged forward with his wooden sword, but Gareth ducked low, spun on one foot, and rolled beneath a peddler's cart. "Clever lad." Ian clucked his tongue and shook his head. "Much more clever than his father."

Gwynn's heart nearly stopped. "Is he?" she replied, lifting her chin though she felt the breath of doom against the back of her neck. She'd learned over the years that the best way to deal with Ian was to defy him openly and not allow him to see any hint of fear.

"Aye." Ian's pale gold eyes became slits and he rubbed the blade thoughtfully over the graying stubble of his beard. He was tall and muscular with a thick neck and sharp-edged teeth. "He'll grow, though, given the time. Surely he'll make his father proud." He chuckled deep in his throat. " 'Tis time Roderick met the lad."

Never. Never will it be time. Despite the cool drizzle, Gwynn's palms began to sweat.

" 'Twill not be long now."

God, please no! "Gareth, come!" she said, ignoring her brother-in-law as the boy spun and withdrawing a rock from the band of his pants, sent the pebble sailing, hitting one boy square in the buttocks. The lad sent up a howl and Gwynn had to shout over his cries of pain. "Gareth, please. Come along. Let us prepare to meet your father."

Distracted from his game, her son looked up and was tagged by Tom whose wooden sword caught him between the shoulder blades. "Nay!"

"Got ye!" Tom said, laughing in a way that reminded Gwynn of an ass braying. He wound up again, ready to deliver another blow, but Gareth feigned to the left before diving right and catching not only Tom with the tip of his blade but two other boys as well. Sheathing his weapon in his belt, he hurried to his mother and she, feeling Ian's keen eyes upon her back, ushered him into the keep. " 'Tis time I had a real sword," he said. "I be near my twelfth—"

"We'll talk of this later."

"But, Mother—"

"Later, Gareth." He was changing, becoming a man before her eyes. 'Twas only right that he would want his own weapons. And, considering all that was to happen, mayhap she should have given him more than the small dagger she'd bestowed upon him years earlier. "Remember how I told you that 'twould be better if you went to live with my sister and her husband?" she asked when they were in the chamber where her son slept, he distracted by a pair of dice he'd won from Alfred, the foolish servant whose only talent was to train and keep the hunting dogs fit.

"Aye." Gareth watched her as she threw his favorite tunic, hose, and mantle into a leather pack. Quickly she opened the purse at her belt and withdrew a few coins and dropped them, along with a gold cross she wore at her neck and two rings into the bag.

" 'Tis time that you—"

"What?" As if finally understanding, he paled. "Time I left?"

"Long past time for your training—"

"Nay!"

"Do not argue, Gareth."

His eyes thinned suspiciously as they had more often than not lately. Oh, he looked so much like his father. "But why now, Mother?" he asked.

She laughed, hoping to sound amused, but her voice was hollow from the fear that tore at her insides. "I've been selfish, Gareth, keeping you here when all boys your age and younger are sent off to be pages and—"

" 'Tis because father is returning." He stared at her with eyes as blue and clear as a summer sky. So like the thief.

Gwynn swallowed hard. What could she say? The truth? Admit her lie? Tell her son, the very reason for her life, that she'd lain with a common stable boy-turned thief in order to conceive a child and deceive everyone, including the very child she'd borne? " 'Tis not the time for questions, Gareth, now come along and—"

" 'Tis a sin to lie. You say so. Father Anthony and old Idelle who agree on nothing say so. Yet you are lying, Mother. I can see it in your eyes."

From the age of three Gareth had been able to read his mother's expression with an uncanny observation, though he'd never guessed at the lie that was his birthright.

" 'Tis a difficult time, son. Here, wear this." Gwynn tossed him his heaviest mantle lined in squirrel fur.

"You are afraid."

Sighing, she set the pack on a stool in the corner and shoved a wayward strand of hair from her eyes. "Yea, son. Sit down." She pointed to the bed and for one of the first times in his young life, Gareth obeyed. Firelight played in his black hair and cast shadows on the walls and coved ceiling though it was barely noon. " 'Tis difficult for me to say this," she admitted, tempering her words carefully. "Lord Roderick is not a kind man."

Gareth snorted. The absent baron's cruelty was common knowledge within the steep walls of Rhydd and, over the years of his imprisonment, the stories of his wretchedness had become legendary. Nary a child born within the keep did not know the mysteries of the lord's first wives' deaths.

The tales had been embellished with the passing of time and the gossip circulating from one mouth to another seeped like venom from the inner walls of the castle and through the gatehouse to the village. Few in Rhydd looked upon the baron's return as a blessing.

"I fear him not."

" 'Tis foolish, for I—I worry for you." There, it was said.

"Why?"

"Your father—" Oh, how her tongue tripped on that deceitful word. "—he, he might be displeased to know that you were not sent away as planned, that you are behind in learning to become a page and a knight."

"Bah. If only I had a true sword I could—"

"You will have your bloody sword," she assured him, to stave off the argument and with the final reality that he might, indeed, need a strong steel blade.

"Truly?" He was awed. A smile split his chin and he let out a whoop, reminding her that he, though starting to look a man, was still a boy.

"Aye, aye. But you must hurry now, don your mantle."

"I can learn everything I needs know here," Gareth wheedled, anxious to take advantage of her giving mood.

"Not if you want the weapon," she said, bartering with the youth who had become a master at getting what he wanted from her. "Come, we have no time to waste. Idelle told the stable master to prepare a horse. Charles will ride with you to Heath. Hurry, now, don't tarry."

"There is something more."

"What?" she asked sharply, feeling that with each passing second her son's chances for safety were fleeting. "No, never mind, now come along!" With one hand she grabbed his upper arm, hauling him to his oversized feet, and heading toward the door. She scooped up the pouch holding his few belongings and slung his mantle over her arm.

"Do not send me away," Gareth insisted, his forehead furrowing. "I should stay with you and protect you."

"Protect *me*?"

"If Father has killed his other wives—"

"I will deal with him. Now, do not think such things. Maybe at Heath you'll learn to treat your mother with some respect! Hurry!" There was no time for argument. She shepherded the boy down the backstairs, past the solar, and along the path between the kitchens and keep.

The smells of baking bread and crushed garlic filtered through the alley as they half ran to the armorer's hut where Gwynn procured a fine long sword, sheath, and belt that Gareth, grinning ear to ear, slipped around his thin waist.

"Now, let us be off," Gwynn insisted, her worries growing with each second that passed. Clouds stole the sunlight as the mist turned to thick drops that peppered the ground to collect in muddy puddles. "Come," Gwynn whispered as they ducked behind a grain cart and dashed to the stables where Charles, holding the reins of two of the best destriers in the castle, stood with his back huddled against the rain.

Gareth glanced at his mother for he'd never before

been allowed to ride any horse other than a bay palfrey with an even temperament and no speed.

At the lift of his young eyebrow, Gwynn said, "Well, you don't expect me to send you to Heath looking as if we're poor, do you? What would my sister think?" She hugged her son fiercely and fought tears that suddenly filled her throat and burned the back of her eyes. Would she ever see him again, this, her only child?

Finally, she released him and, as if he finally recognized her fears, Gareth stared at her. "Fear not, Mother. I will return."

"Of course you will." She sniffed and cleared her throat.

"Soon."

Oh, her heart tore into small pieces. "Aye. Now. Off with you!"

The black charger, a fiery beast named Dragon, snorted and half reared as Gareth quickly threw on his mantle, grabbed his leather bag, and tried to mount. The huge animal tossed his great head and sidestepped, rolling one dark, distrusting eye at the young man who dared tried to climb upon his back.

"Easy, there," Charles murmured to the horse.

Gareth swung into the saddle and a prideful smile cut across a square jaw where a few early whiskers were beginning to sprout. " 'Tis a grand animal you be, Dragon," he said, taking up the reins.

"God help us," Charles said under his breath. He was quickly astride the other charger, a red-brown animal with three white stockings and a barrel chest. "Let us be off."

"Take care of yourself," she said, raising her hand.

But as the words were uttered Gwynn heard the ominous blare of trumpets. *Oh, God, no!*

A shout rang through the bailey.

Gwynn's knees grew weak. *No! No! No!*

But deep in her heart she knew all her plans were for naught. Her chest constricted and despair clutched at her heart.

"Mother?" Gareth asked, his fingers clutching the reins.

She bit her lip. "God help us," she whispered as the wind whipped her skirts and rain fell mercilessly from the dark heavens.

The guard shouted down to the keeper of the gate. "Open the portcullis and give praise to the Holy Father! Lord Roderick has returned."

Chapter Two

"No tears of joy for your husband?" Ian asked.

Gwynn ignored his evil grin and watched in despair as a mangy gray horse galloped through the castle gates. Astride the bony nag was Roderick of Rhydd, or what was left of him. Never a particularly handsome man, he had aged horridly in the thirteen years of his imprisonment. Bareheaded in the rain, his once-reddish strands had become gray and scraggly to match a beard more silver than russet. His shirt was in tatters, his mantle a ragged and dingy green.

All work within the castle walls stopped. Carpenters, masons, and alewives abandoned their tasks to stand in the open doorways of shops. The beekeeper, farrier, and candle maker clustered near the north tower while boys lugging stones and girls washing wool turned to stare through a curtain of rain at their lord, a man many had never before set eyes upon.

Gwynn swallowed hard and crossed herself quickly at the sight of the pathetic creature who could, despite his shabby appearance, instill a gnawing fear in her heart. Roderick was hollow-cheeked and gaunt of frame, his skin sagging on his bones.

As the horse slid to a stop, he winced as he climbed from the saddle. A pasty-faced boy named George whose skin was marred with blemishes raced across the grass to catch the reins of the master's steed. Another page scurried from the kitchen with a cup of wine.

Roderick drank heartily, red rivulets trailing through his beard, then flung the cup back to the boy. He swiped the back of his hand over his lips. "Bring me more," he ordered, seeming to enjoy casting out a command. "I'll have the wine, along with pheasant and a joint of boar in the great hall."

"Aye, m'lord." The page, ducking his head against the rain, ran toward the keep.

"Brother!" Ian stepped forward while Gwynn tried hard to find her tongue. " 'Tis good to see you again."

"Is it?" Roderick's eyes, the color of ale appeared murky and haunted. "Why did you not pay a ransom and have me returned?"

"Baron Hamilton did not ask for ransom, would not consider payment."

"Bah! Then why not help me with my escape, eh?" Roderick asked, his nostrils beginning to quiver in rage that had festered for longer than a decade.

"We tried. Thrice within the first two years of your capture. But Castle Carter is strong, the walls impossible to scale, and Hamilton seemed to know whenever we planned an attack." Ian's excuses sounded feeble, even to Gwynn.

"Hamilton is a black-hearted bastard, but his fortress is not secure. I escaped without your help."

"Aye and how did you—"

"A traitor to Hamilton, one in his army rode in the opposite direction to mislead the guards, but he will come through our gates and when he arrives, he is to be brought to me and paid handsomely." Roderick smoothed his mustache with one finger. "You may remember him, Ian. He is called Sir Webb these days. He has ridden with you before. Long ago."

Ian lifted a shoulder and shook his head. "Webb? Nay, I recall not."

Roderick crackled, his laugh ending in a rattling cough. "He was Sir Hamilton's trusted knight, but I persuaded him that he would better serve me."

"You bribed him?"

Roderick grinned. "Aye, and he will lead the rest of Rhydd's soldiers for he, as only one knight, managed to do what, so you claim, my entire army was unable to do. He, alone, freed me."

"But, Roderick, do you think that a stranger will be able to—"

"Enough! We will discuss this later. Now—let me savor this moment." Roderick surveyed the high stone battlements and the north tower where a knight was raising the flag, showing off the green and gold standard announcing that the lord of the manor was home. For a second Roderick's throat worked, then his tired eyes took in the rest of the keep—old familiar walls and turrets as well as huts and buildings added while he was away. "Rhydd has prospered in my absence," he said, as if to himself.

"Aye." Ian clasped him on the shoulder as mist rose from the grass and a dampness seeped through Gwynn's clothes to chill her heart. "But 'tis good you return."

One of Roderick's red-gray brows lifted and he scratched at his beard as his gaze moved past several knights to land full force on Gwynn.

Dear Jesus, help me.

"Wife."

"Husband." Her voice was firm though it tripped over the hated word.

Roderick's murky eyes narrowed as icy fingers of the wind plucked at Gwynn's cloak. "I have thought of you often these past years."

"As I of you," she said.

"As so you should." He eyed her as a man would were he purchasing a new horse. "Tell me, where is my son? I have waited many years to meet him."

Her spine stiffened as if it were suddenly starched. "Gareth," she called, but the boy, always inquisitive, had already slid off Dragon's broad back and had walked, squishing in the mud, toward the man he thought had sired him.

A smile teased the corners of Roderick's mouth for Gareth, not quite as tall as he, was a proud boy with an arrogant tilt of his chin and eyes that missed nothing. Rain flattened his hair and ran down his nose. "Father."

Gwynn's heart ached.

Roderick glanced at the horses and leather pouch. "He was leaving?" Silvering red eyebrows slammed together.

"Aye." The lie was already in place. " 'Tis long past time for his training as a page and squire. I had sent a messenger to Luella at—"

"Had you not heard I was returning?"

Gwynn nodded. "Only this morn, m'lord."

"And yet still you would send my boy away?" His nostrils flared slightly and quivered as if suddenly stung by a foul odor.

"Luella was expecting him—"

"Hush!"

At his harsh command, Dragon snorted loudly and pawed the sodden ground. Charles, who had dismounted and again held the reins of both horses, offered soft words to the animal while Gareth stopped directly in front of Roderick. He did not bow, nor change expression, just stared hard at the older man in the ragged clothes as the heavens poured and gusts of wind tossed damp leaves in the air.

"You are called Gareth."

"Aye."

Roderick's sallow skin suffused with sudden color as he glanced at the peasants and servants gathered in small clusters within the bailey walls. The silence was suddenly deafening. Even the cattle and sheep, penned on the other side of the inner gate quieted.

"So. You are my son." The baron's gaze moved from the boy to Gwynn.

Gareth nodded, but didn't say a word.

"Then 'tis long past time we met." He placed a gnarled hand upon the lad's shoulder and Gwynn let out a long sigh of relief. Mayhap he was vain enough and his memory addled so that he would not recognize that the boy wasn't his.

"You will not be going to Heath."

"Husband, please, 'tis time," Gwynn insisted.

He waved her arguments away with a flick of his almighty wrist. "We will speak of this later." His gaze again centered on Gareth.

Gwynn's heart hammered in her chest and she saw all the differences in her son and the baron. Gareth's skin was darker, like that of the thief, his hair as black as a raven's wing, his eyes clear and blue. As had been Trevin's. Though Gareth was but a boy, his features were already showing signs of becoming sharp and rough-hewn.

"Saints be praised." Father Anthony's voice rocked through the bailey.

"Christ Jesus," Roderick swore as the priest, robes

flapping behind him ran through the wet grass and mud of the bailey.

"M'lord," he intoned and Gwynn thought she saw tears gather in the holy man's eyes. Surely she was mistaken. 'Twas only the rain that ran down his cheeks. "I thought . . . er, I f-feared I would never see you again, that you would never . . . oh, we must thank the heavenly F-Father for your return." He bowed his head and crossed himself swiftly.

A flush stole up Roderick's neck. "Good Father Anthony," he said quietly, " 'tis comforting to know that you were here, asking for blessings of Rhydd."

"My prayers and thoughts were with you." The priest, blinking rapidly, composed himself. "Perhaps we should share a prayer now, thanking the Holy Mother and—"

"Later." Roderick shook his head and wiped the rain from his face. " 'Tis freezing, I am. Now I needs clean myself and eat." He touched Gwynn's arm. "I trust that all has been prepared?"

"Aye, m'lord. Water has been heated and scented, a meal of thanks will be served at your command, and fresh clothes await you."

"As did you." His smile was as cold as the sleet in winter.

Gwynn's teeth ground together. "Aye." *Oh, Sweet Mary, how would she ever lay with him again?* Share a bed and have him reach for her only to touch her with icy fingers and an even colder heart?

"Good." He clapped his hands. "Everyone, go back to work." His mirthless smile curdled Gwynn's blood as he stared one long heart-stopping minute at Gareth again. "There is much to learn. Much that has happened."

"Amen," whispered Father Anthony.

"Aye. Amen." Ian didn't bother hiding the amusement that glinted in his eyes. He's enjoying this, Gwynn thought.

"You, Wife," Roderick added as he started toward the great hall. There was a fierceness to his tone, an edge underlying his words that made Gwynn's insides turn to water. "I will have words with you about our son."

"As you wish," she said weakly. Roderick, seeming to gather strength with each moment he was within the walls of the castle, strode ahead while curious servants and peasants parted whispering among themselves and allowing him a path. Sheep bleated in nearby pens, a raven, cawing wickedly, flew overhead and fat pigeons cooed from their roosts.

"The boy—he looks not like me," Roderick said thoughtfully, his gait increasing.

"He—he takes after my older brother Neal."

"Does he?" Roderick began climbing the steps to the great hall. "A pity Neal died young and no one remembers him."

He knows! she thought, her heart thundering. Of course he knows for unless he's become addled and his memory gone, he knows that he did not get you with child. How could he have? She swallowed back her fear and only hoped that he would rather pretend that Gareth was his son than suffer the indignities of admitting to an unfaithful wife who might charge him with being unable to lay with a woman.

The dogs, ever vigilant, sat on the stoop and with rain turning their gray coats to slimy black, growled at Roderick's approach.

"I'll not have my own beasts distrust me," he said, frowning at the hounds. With a hand, he motioned to the guard near the heavy door. "Kill them and get new ones—young ones who will obey me."

"Aye m'lord," the guard agreed and started for the growling beasts.

"Nay!" Gwynn, who was a step behind her husband, hurried to catch up with him as he walked into the vast open chamber. Closing his eyes, Roderick drew in deep breaths of air, as if his lungs, so long imprisoned, needed to be cleansed with the smoky air within the walls of the keep.

"Please, do not harm the dogs. They have been loyal and have lain in front of the door to my chamber, keeping watch."

Roderick's eyes flew open. "What know you of loyalty!"

"Husband, please—"

"Husband," he repeated with a sneer. "And what should I call you? Wife?" He glanced at the guard, then leaned closer to her, so that only she could hear. "Mayhap harlot would better suit."

Her heart turned to stone.

"Send the dogs back to the kennel," he ordered to the castle at large. "I will decide what to do with the curs later. As for you, *wife,* there is much we needs discuss, but 'twill have to wait. I'm tired and hungry." He shoved the wet strands of his hair from his eyes and surveyed the great hall. Tables and benches filled the fore part of the chamber while tapestries splashed color on the whitewashed walls. Candles burned brightly and the fire hissed as it blazed, warming the shadowy interior. " 'Tis as I remember it," Roderick said, his voice softening slightly. "Ah, Rhydd." He rubbed the tips of his gnarled fingers against the wall in a loving gesture. "I feared I might never return."

Gwynn felt a moment's regret for the man who had

been imprisoned for nearly thirteen years, but she quickly reminded herself that he was capable of murder, that his previous wives had died, and that she was fearful for her son's life.

As Roderick stepped onto the dais and sat for a minute in his chair rubbing the worn wooden arms with his palms, she wondered how she could convince him that Gareth was his son. "Go now," he ordered Gwynn. "I will speak to Ian now and later we will talk. Privately. Of your son."

"Our son."

His tired, murky eyes accused her of the lie. "I'll hear no more of your blasphemy."

Panic squeezed Gwynn's heart. So his mind was not addled—he realized that they had never lain together as man and wife. "Do not blame the boy—"

"I know where the blame lays." He propped an elbow on the arm of the chair and rested his grizzled chin in his fingers. "With you."

"Nay—"

"And whoever it was who got you with child."

She gulped. "Nay, Roderick, the boy is yours. As I live and breathe—"

"Hush, woman!" Roderick was on his feet in an instant. He rounded on her, his muscles tense, his gold eyes suddenly ablaze. "You and your boy have made a fool of me within my own keep. Think you not that the servants and freeman can see what I myself have witnessed?"

"If you will but listen—"

"Listen? *Listen?* To what? More lies. You and . . . *that boy* will not cause me the disrespect of all whom I rule."

"He is but a lad—"

"Enough!"

" 'Tis not his fault that—"

Roderick leaned close and very slowly curled his fists in her hair. "If you be not quiet, m'lady," he snarled in a hushed whisper meant only for her ears, "you'll have no room to bargain." His fetid breath surrounded her in a thick, sickening cloud and she could but nod. To disobey him now would only enrage him further and though she had no fear for herself— those days were long past—she knew that he could harm Gareth, her one weak spot. She needed time to see that her son was safely away and if she had to put up with his scathing tongue, or brute strength, or even lay in the bed with him, so be it.

His fingers unwound from the tangle that was her hair, and then, as if sensing the servants' eyes upon him, he grabbed the crook of her neck, dragged her face close and kissed her so hard she thought her lips would be forever mashed against her teeth.

Yanking back his head to a chorus of laughter and well wishes from those observing, he flashed a triumphant smile—the martyred ruler returning to his bride and keep. Gwynn's stomach turned over and 'twas all she could do not to spit on him. Instead she forced back the bile rushing up her throat, managed a poor excuse of a curtsy, and turned on her heel.

Heat climbing up her neck, she heard the jeers, men's raucous jokes, and a few nervous twitters at her expense. Her fists balled and her chin inched upward defiantly as she picked up her skirts and took the stairs to her chamber two at a time.

Only when she was inside the room, the door closed and pressed hard against her spine, did she wipe the filth of his kiss from her lips. No longer could she hold back nature and she retched violently, losing the contents of her stomach in the rushes at her feet.

What was she to do? How could she save Gareth?

There was a soft knock upon the door and Idelle, her stiff, steel-colored hair bristling around her wimple, swept into the room. "By the gods, Gwynn, look at this." Through her clouded eyes, she saw more than many. Clucking her tongue she whipped a rag from a pocket in her apron and began cleaning the soiled floor. "I fear for your life," she said as she gathered the fouled rushes and threw them into the fire. Angry flames snapped and sputtered in revolt. "Roderick is not a forgiving man."

"Nor a kind one."

"Aye." Idelle straightened. Her wise milky eyes met the fear in Gwynn's. "He sees as plainly as I do, lass, that the boy is not his."

"I know." 'Twas in this very room where Gareth was conceived, where she'd lain with the thief so many years before. She swallowed hard and chewed on the corner of her lip. She was not a woman to whimper and whine. She believed that for every problem that arose, there was a solution.

Idelle gave the floor a final swipe with her rag. "You should have confided in me, m'lady. Mayhap I could have helped."

"I—I thought it best to—"

"Lie," Idelle accused.

"Aye. 'Tis no use in arguing about it now. What's done is done. We must but find a way to keep Gareth safe."

"Mayhap ye should tell his father. The one who helped create him."

Gwynn shook her head and began pacing, trying to come up with a plan for Gareth's escape. " 'Twould do no good. I know not what became of him. He was

but a thief who lingered too long in my chamber."
Sighing, she shook her head. "He may be long dead."

"So think ye?" Idelle asked and again clucked her
tongue in a manner that Gwynn found irritating.
"Well, wrong ye be, m'lady, for I know of him."

Gwynn stopped dead in her tracks and pinned the
older woman with a glare meant to freeze blood. "I
believe you not."

"Trevin the thief, raised by Muir, a befuddled sorcerer who knows the old ways. With the jewels ye
gave that boy and those he stole off other trusting
souls he began his fortune and, in a game of dice, was
lucky enough to win Black Oak Hall from the old lord
who'd had too much drink and too little luck."

"Nay, ye deceive me." Gwynn sagged against the
bed. She'd heard the story, of course. Who had not?
Black Oak Hall had a history of darkness surrounding
it, of trouble within the castle walls.

Baron Dryw, a fool of a man known to enjoy drink
and gambling, had drunk too much wine one evening,
invited some of his knights to join him in a simple
game of chance, and had wagered his keep only to
lose it. Some had said the game was crooked, that the
soldier who won had cheated but that he was a fierce
one whom no one had dared challenge. Worse yet,
the baron had died, and it was oft speculated that the
dark knight who took the rule of Black Oak so callously had killed the older man. Gwynn had listened
to the gossip with only half an ear, for she cared not
what happened in other castles, nor did she know
Dryw of Black Oak. "Did . . . did not the new baron
wed the old man's daughter?" she asked, her interest
piqued as she twisted her wedding ring. Was it possible? The stable-boy-turned-thief had become a baron?
A neighbor? One who had never violated their pact

upon his leaving so many years ago? Her wretched heart twisted knowing that he was nearby.

"Aye." A shadow passed through Idelle's cloudy eyes. "Faith was Dryw's only issue. The poor lass died in childbirth and the babe was born without drawing a breath." Idelle sighed. " 'Tis much trouble they've had at Black Oak. Some say the castle is cursed."

Gwynn had heard as much for gossip ran swift and eagerly through the land. Had she but listened more carefully to the rumors flowing between castles, she, too, might have divined that Trevin the thief was the black knight who had by less than honest means become baron of a nearby castle, that the father of her son was within three days' ride. That thought should have given her solace. Instead she shivered, as if an ill wind had passed through her body and rattled her bones. "I cannot believe that—"

" 'Tis the truth I tell as always."

"But—"

"Have ye ever known me to lie?"

Gwynn shook her head and rubbed her arms.

"M'lady, please," Idelle entreated as she tossed a final handful of soiled rushes into the fire, then wiped her hands on her apron. "I know 'tis said that Trevin killed Dryw, though no one saw him push the baron from the curtain wall. But I believe it not."

"You trust him?"

"More than I trust your husband."

Gwynn could not disagree. "Why tell me this now?"

" 'Tis a feeling I have deep in me bones. Trevin of Black Oak will come and claim his son."

"Why now?" Gwynn asked, her heart beating a little faster at the thought of seeing him again. "I have his word—"

"The word of a thief and outlaw."

"He has not come forward afore."

"Roderick was not on his way home." Idelle frowned deeply. " 'Twill be evident to him that Gareth is not of his flesh. What then? Will he accuse ye of betraying him? Betraying the castle? I mean not to frighten you, but I worry."

"And what would you have me do?" Gwynn demanded, her head reeling.

"Be careful," Idelle warned, then offered an enigmatic smile. "And trust only your heart, for it is true."

Though a fire blazed in the grate, candles flickered and smoked, the scents of cinnamon, apples, and roasted meat still lingered, the great hall was cold as death. Roderick, clean-shaven and washed, fresh tunic and hose upon him, appeared stronger than he had when he'd first arrived at Rhydd. He sat in his chair with the carved-wood arms as if he'd never left, as if he had every right to rule all those who resided within the curtain walls.

The hall had reverberated with laughter and good cheer, though beneath it all had been a silent tension, dark looks, distrustful glances, and thinned lips.

Toasts had been offered, much wine consumed, and Jack the cook had outdone himself. The sugar sculpture in the shape of a castle had caused a collective gasp from those at the tables below the salt and a smile to light Roderick's grim countenance. Musicians, acrobats, and the jester had entertained them with stories, song, and bawdy jokes. Though she'd sat at her husband's side, Gwynn had barely eaten or spoken. While Roderick had feasted on eel, jellied eggs, pheasant, venison, beef, and plum tarts, she'd not been able to swallow, hadn't so much as dirtied her fingers on her trencher or picked at a bite of bread.

Gareth sat on the far side of Roderick. He had eaten hungrily, without many manners, suspiciously eyeing the man who was supposed to have spawned him. They had barely said a word throughout the meal though Ian, near his nephew, had appeared amused, his cold eyes laughing, his lips curved in a smile that had not been inspired by the musicians and jesters who had entertained them.

But now the great hall was nearly empty, the tables cleared and stacked as Roderick had ordered everyone back to his tasks. Everyone but family members and Sir Webb, the knight who had helped the imprisoned baron to escape. Webb had ridden from Castle Carter and now stood at the fire warming the backs of his legs. Smelly steam rose from his dark, damp tunic. His brown hair was lank and straight, his face flushed from hours riding in the cold weather. He was a man who did not hide his evil in masks of civility, a soul, Gwynn was certain, who had not one redeeming quality. If ever there was a devil, Webb of Castle Carter was sure to be Satan Incarnate.

"Is there something you would say to me, Wife?" Roderick finally asked, picking at his teeth with the nail of one thumb and watching her every move.

Her heart stilled. Her fingers twisted in her woolen skirt. "Just that I am glad you are safe."

"In what? Twelve, nay, nigh onto thirteen winters, you have no other words?" He reached for his mazer of wine and scowled at its contents.

"Nay, my lord," she said pleasantly though each muscle in her body ached with the strain.

"About the boy?"

Dear God, help me, please. " 'Tis not the place."

"Ah, but it is, Wife," he insisted, rolling the cup between his palms. "You betrayed me."

"Nay—"

Gareth's head snapped up. "Mother—?"

"Do not heed your father. He has traveled far and been through a great ordeal." She held Roderick's hateful gaze. "Husband, I implore you to think before you speak. We should discuss Gareth and his training to be a knight later, when you are not so tired or have not had so much wine or—"

"—or when the boy cannot hear the truth, is that it?" Roderick demanded, leaning closer, the pupils of his eyes wide. "I speak not of his training, for he will have none. Does he not know that his mother is a common whore? A woman who would sleep with another man and pass him off as her husband's?"

"Nay!" Gareth's face flushed red, his entire body shaking.

" 'Tis true. Tell him," Roderick ordered, grabbing Gwynn's arm with fingers that were calloused, stained, and surprisingly strong. "Tell him that he is the son of—whom? Now that is the question, is it not?" He pinched her harder, his jaw set and hard as he spat out his words. "Who slept in my bed and got my wife with child, eh? Whose little bastard is he?"

" 'Tis enough of your lies I've heard!" Gareth said, jumping onto the table and snatching up the sword Roderick had left by his chair. "Leave Mother alone!"

"Gareth, stop!" Gwynn said, her heart pounding with dread.

"Bastard." Webb's sword was instantly unsheathed.

"Nay, do not spill blood!" she cried attempting to yank her arm from her husband's grasp.

"You dare defy me?" Roderick's nostrils flared and a sickening grin settled onto his lips.

"Leave her be!" Gareth ordered. He was on top of

the table, Roderick's sword raised as if he intended
to cleave him in two.

Fear clawed at Gwynn's soul. "Gareth, please, do
not—"

"The boy has balls," Ian said as he reached forward
to grab his nephew. "But not many brains." Gareth
nimbly ducked from his uncle's outstretched arms and
knocked over a mazer of wine that had not been
cleared. Red liquid ran like blood and Ian's face
clouded.

"No brains at all," Webb agreed.

"I said, 'leave her be!'" Gareth ordered, the blade
of Roderick's upraised sword glinting malevolently in
the shifting light from the fire.

"Get down!" Gwynn screamed, scrambling to get
away.

"Hush!" Roderick tried vainly to restrain his wife.

"Let me go, Husband," she hissed, fear taking hold
of her tongue. "And you, Gareth, do not do anything
foolish!" She stumbled backward. Roderick lost his
grip.

He raised a hand.

"No!" Gareth cried.

Slap! The sound of Roderick's hand smacking
against her cheek ricocheted off the walls and ceiling.
"Scheming, whoring, daughter of Satan!"

Gwynn spun backward, tripping over chairs and the
table. Roderick pounced on her and shook her as she
kicked and clawed. "I'll see that you get the punishment you deserve, Jezebel." He raised his hand and
hit her again. Pain exploded behind her eyes.

"Nay!" Gareth screamed.

The room spun but Gwynn managed to draw some
moisture and spit upon the dog who was her husband.

"A pubic flogging until you faint, then I'll revive you and use the whip again!"

"Die!" Gareth swung the heavy sword downward and Webb jumped onto the table.

"NO!" Gwynn's shriek exploded through the chamber.

The blade glanced off Roderick's shoulder and rammed into the dark knight's arm. Blood spurted. Roderick howled. Webb swore and fell back, clinging to his wound, blood running through his fingers.

"Bastard! I'll kill you!" Roderick rounded on the small imposter, reaching into his belt for his dagger. Webb shot forward, Ian hoisted his sword aloft, but Gareth, atop the table, dodged and ducked, swinging wildly with his deadly blade.

"Miserable cur!" Webb spun and sliced.

Gareth lithely jumped above the sword. Webb jabbed, Ian flung himself onto the table. Gareth rolled away from both men.

"Run!" Gwynn yelled as she climbed to her feet. Her face throbbed but she grabbed a table knife and before Webb could deliver another blow toward her son, she flung the blade at him. It caught him on the thigh and he winced, throwing off his mark.

"Aaaggh!"

Roderick grabbed for Gareth's legs, missed, flailed wildly with his knife, cutting Gareth's knee, sending a spray of blood from an ugly gash as the boy spun, slashing downward, his weapon imbedding in Roderick's side.

With a horrifying wail, Roderick fell across the table, his blood spilling into the pool of wine, the sword imbedded deeply in his body.

"Nay!" Father Anthony ran into the great hall, his vestments unfurling behind him. His face was white with terror, his eyes wide at the carnage. "For the love of all that is holy, stop! M'lord, m'lord!" Crossing himself and mumbling prayers, he flung himself upon Roderick who lay, half sprawled over the table. With a strength borne of desperation, he withdrew the bloodied blade and dropped it onto the floor. "Bless this man, keep him safe." The priest's face was twisted in a grief so deep it tore at the man's soul. "Do not let him die, Father, I beseech thee! Now that he has returned to us, do not take him away!"

Gwynn, still stunned, reached for her boy, pulled him off the table, and whispered into his ear. "Run for your life. Find Idelle or Sir Charles—"

"He will go nowhere!" Ian's voice boomed through the castle. He stood next to his brother who lay slumped over the table. "Guards, grab the boy. He is an imposter. His mother betrayed Rhydd and, therefore, as I am Roderick's only brother, I will rule."

"No!" Gwynn was frantic. Knights appeared from the hallways and several looked to Gwynn. "Leave Gareth be."

Gareth was still wound in her arms and she clung to him as if to life itself.

"I said, 'grab him.' And his lying mother as well," Ian ordered.

Webb staggered forward, swiping the air as if to take her child from her. With only thoughts of saving her son, Gwynn pushed Gareth toward the door and tripped the black knight. "Run! Gareth, *RUN!*"

The boy took off, only to be blocked by three guards, all men Gwynn had once trusted, the heaviest of which grabbed her son and plucked him, swinging and kicking, off the floor.

"Let him go!"

" 'Tis too late, m'lady," Ian said, his face spattered with blood, his expression fierce.

With a last rattling breath, Roderick of Rhydd gave up his soul and slumped to the floor.

"Oh, no. No, no, no!" Gwynn said as hands, some-one's hands who was behind her, an enemy she could not see, tried to restrain her. Blood smeared over her sleeves and she realized Webb was holding her fast.

"He's dead! The baron is slain!" the priest pro-claimed with tears running down his face. "Oh, Father, who art in heaven . . ."

"You did this, woman!" Ian pointed a long, sancti-monious finger in her direction. "With your whoring ways and evil treachery, you brought death upon your husband. You and your son be murderers."

"Nay!"

" 'Twill be." He glanced around the chamber, as if to see if anyone would dare disagree with him. Ser-vants, peasants, and soldiers had gathered, circling the carnage, their faces ashen.

Pleading, fearful eyes gazed at the corpse of a leader most had never seen. Many made quick signs of the cross upon their chests and whispered prayers while others appeared unable to move.

Ian climbed onto the table, his sword at his side. "Make no mistake," he said to everyone within ear-shot. "As Roderick's brother, I am baron now. The lady has proved herself to be nothing more than a lying harlot who betrayed my brother by pretending that another man's son was his. The boy"—he swung his bloodied sword in Gareth's direction—"was no issue of Roderick's."

Some of the servants dared speak, but only in low tones, and only among themselves. Gwynn saw them all—Jack, the cook, the beekeeper, Alfred who handled the hounds, the candle maker, tailor, and dozens more, standing transfixed in the great hall, as if rooted to their places.

She tried to pull away but Webb's meaty, stained fingers only gripped her tighter, squeezing her flesh, causing pain to scream up her arms.

"The boy will be hanged at nightfall tomorrow," Ian proclaimed and Gwynn's heart was pierced as though by a lance. She let out a wail that trilled through the turrets. Tears blurred her vision and ran down her cheeks in hot rivulets. "Nay, Ian, you must not. Do what you will to me, but leave Gareth go free."

"He is a traitor—"

"Nay, a boy. A lad who knew nothing. 'Twas I who sinned, I who betrayed Roderick and Rhydd, I who should be punished." Despite the heavy hands restraining her, she flung herself at her brother-in-law, groveling on her knees for her boy. "I will do anything," she vowed, "suffer any punishment, but please, please, let Gareth go free."

From his perch on the table, Ian studied the woman trembling at his feet. Lust, ever his enemy, burned bright in his loins. He'd wanted Gwynn for thirteen long years, had lain awake at night thinking of her, letting other whores touch and kiss his member when it was she he wanted, only she who could quell his passion. Now, through the fates, she would willingly give herself to him. But for how long? Only until the boy was safe, then, he was certain, she would rather die than lay with him. She was a beautiful, prideful woman; one unlike any other and he was moved by her passion for her boy.

And then there were the servants and peasants to consider. Most of them seemed to adore her, many of the soldiers were loyal to her. Were he to marry her, they would swear their allegiance to him. 'Twas a gamble, either way, but he thought the odds weighed heavily in allying himself with this woman. Asides, having her warm his bed was oh, so inviting. "So be it, then, if you agree to marry me and bear me my own sons, Gareth will go free." She looked up at him with hope in her lovely, damp eyes. "If, however, you betray me as you did Roderick, or withhold your favors from me, or displease me in any manner, your son will be hunted down like a dog, hanged, and drawn and quartered. Do you understand?"

"Aye." She nodded gravely, terror distorting the fine features of her face at the thought of her only child so treated.

"Then, Gwynn, arise and stand by my side." He hopped to the floor and glared at the guards. "Let the boy go. He is to be banished from Rhydd, but no harm to come to him."

Gareth's face was white as snow. "Mother, nay—"

"Hush!" Her voice was harsh. "You are to do as Lord Ian says."

"But—"

"Do it, Gareth, and do not argue!" she said firmly though tears again rained from her eyes. The boy had no choice. At a nod from Ian, he was hoisted away and she, pale as death, seemed certain she would never see him again, which, of course, was true. Ian turned to the priest who was still mumbling prayers and crying over Roderick's body. "Get up, Father Anthony, and quit your insipid grieving. You have much to do. Not only have you my brother's body to lay to rest, but you must perform the marriage rites for Lady Gwynn and me.

"Now?" she cried, "But the bans have not yet been—"

"Hush! I am baron and as such I say we are to be wed this day. There will be no postponement." He wouldn't give her even a minute to change her mind. "The boy is not yet out of the castle, so what say you, Bride?"

She swallowed hard, but her small backbone seemed to solidify and her chin, once wobbling, became strong as steel. "Aye, m'lord," she agreed without any further trace of emotion. "Let us be wed."

Chapter Three

The vision came quickly on the third day of the ride. One second Muir was riding upon his gray palfrey, the horse cantering easily toward Rhydd, the next he was in a dark forest, with mists rising up from the ferns and bracken and blood running like sap from the trees. "What devilment is this?" he asked, the pain in his bad eye excruciating as he stared at his feet.

In a misting fog, he saw a snake slithering through the undergrowth. The viper crawled up his back and coiled at his neck, then, with a hiss, it changed, biting its own tail and turning into a chain. Cold, lifeless metal cut into the folds of skin at Muir's neck and blood—was it his?—began to flow as the links snapped, one by one, allowing him to breathe, staining his beard and tunic and disappearing.

"Muir! For the love of God, man, wake up!" Trevin reached over from his horse and shook the older man's shoulder. On the palfrey Muir sucked in his breath and leaned forward in the saddle.

"Be gone, Devil, and take this pain with ye!"

Trevin yanked hard on his mount's reins and the horse, lathered and muddied from hours upon the road sidestepped, nearly bumping into Muir's animal. The five soldiers behind them slowed their mounts to skidding stops. "What is it?" Trevin demanded as the horses snorted and pawed, their ears twitching, their nostrils quivering nervously.

" 'Tis trouble at Rhydd."

"You told me of this before," Trevin muttered, looking at the darkening sky. It was nearly nightfall and soon there would be no daylight. With the clouds as they were there would be little moon glow or starlight to guide them. "We must be off if we are to make the castle gates before 'tis dark."

"Nay, nay." Muir held a hand to his bad eye, the one that saw nothing, yet somehow foretold the future. " 'Tis blood I see, blood flowing in rivers."

"At Rhydd?"

"Aye. Aach, this pain."

" 'Tis bad, eh?"

"Worse than you can imagine. 'Tis like the bite of a viper that never ends, or the burn of flesh, yet there be no fire. Oooh. By the gods, 'tis a curse, I tell ye."

"For all of us," Trevin said dryly.

Muir scoffed and yanked on the hood of his cloak. " 'Tis no time for humor. There is much trouble at Rhydd, more than I saw earlier." He closed his one good eye and flinched as if a bolt of lightning had been flung from the sky to skewer him. "As I live and breathe," he whispered and jolted again. His horse shied and shook his gray head, rattling the bridle and bit. " 'Tis more than trouble at this castle, m'lord."

"Don't call me—"

" 'Tis a chain I spy, one of links that are bound together. Father to son and son to father, cursed to fight and kill each other."

" 'Tis nonsense you speak."

"Nay, Trevin," the old one disagreed. He tore off the hood of his cloak and glared at the heavens with that unblinking, sightless eye. "God or Lucifer, I know not which."

"I have no time for this." Trevin kicked his destrier and the muddied horse took off again while Muir's smaller mount and those of the other soldiers struggled to keep up as they galloped through the mud.

"I fear there is danger lurking about," Muir called after him.

"You always fear danger."

"Aye. And ye embrace it."

Trevin's mouth lifted in a grim smile. How often had he been called reckless or fearless or just plain stubborn? Too many times to count. Near the river, the road curved and the thickets of oak and pine opened to grassy fields that surrounded the bluff on which the castle had been built.

Gray stone walls surrounded the keep and rose sharply from rocky cliffs overlooking the surrounding woods. High turrets and watchtowers spired from wide battlements and appeared to scrape the underbellies of the dark clouds that rolled restlessly through the heavens. An emerald-and-gold standard snapped in the wind and the portcullis was open wide, inviting visitors inside.

Through the sheeting rain, Trevin pulled up on his mount's reins and gazed upon the fortress where he had become a part of Lady Gwynn's plot. He'd been young and foolish at the time—and willing, oh, so willing. Sleeping in the lady's bed had been sweet sacrifice indeed and he'd never forgotten the feel of her skin against his rough fingers, the way she'd trembled when he'd kissed her, the pure, unashamed wanting within her. Deep within him, a dark, unbidden desire flowed again and he forced it back.

Was she naught but a rich, scheming female whose

only ambition was to save her own beautiful neck? Had she not conceived a child, lied to her husband, committed willing adultery all for her own gain?

And what about you? Did you not aid her, do all that she did, to save your skin?

Aye, he was as guilty as she. And now a boy—their son—was in jeopardy.

Turning in the saddle he gave orders to his small group of soldiers. He would enter the castle alone and if he did not return with the boy or get word to his men by the time the guard in the watchtower changed, he told Gerald to return to Black Oak for reinforcements. The others were to sneak into the castle as spies.

There were already those within the keep's well-guarded walls who would aid them for Trevin of Black Oak had men loyal to him, men with pasts blackened much as his own was, hidden within the surrounding keeps, including Rhydd. Those men, traitors to their own barons, were paid to keep him informed and warn him of any attack to be waged against Black Oak Hall.

His plan was simple. He would sneak into Rhydd and meet with Richard the carpenter and Mildred the alewife, both of whom were paid to keep their eyes and ears open. Only then would he speak to Gwynn alone before he started bartering with her husband. He owed her that much for breaking his part of their bargain. His conscience twinged a little for he had a code of honor such as it was. His word was usually good and he had promised Gwynn to keep their secret.

"I like this not," Muir muttered as the men dispersed into the woods.

"Trust me."

"Bah."

Trevin placed a hand on the old man's shoulder. "If my plan goes awry, 'tis your duty to take care of the boy, Gareth."

"Take care of him?"

"If something happens to me, take him to the cave. Wait for me there but two days."

"And then what?"

Trevin shook his head and offered Muir an evil grin. "Then conjure up some spells for me, old man, for 'twill mean that something ill has happened."

"Just as I have foreseen."

"From the bottom of an ale cup."

Muir shook the rain from his cowl. " 'Tis not the time for jest."

"Trust me, old man, all will be well." Trevin turned his steed toward the yawning castle gates and leaned forward, nudging the beast's ribs. The horse responded, tearing off and flinging mud and pebbles behind him.

"I pray it so," Muir called after him, his old voice growing fainter. "I pray it so."

"In the name of the Father and the Son and . . ."

Gwynn, kneeling in the chapel next to her new husband and the Lord of Rhydd, didn't hear the rest of the priest's prayer. She was married. Again. To another man she didn't love, nay a man who she was sure was as black-hearted as his brother.

But Gareth would be safe. Banished from the castle forever, the boy would be alone in the world and she would never see him again, but he would live and he was almost a man as it was. Tears touched her eyes and her heart was heavy, but she knew she had no choice.

Father Anthony, his face a pasty white, his voice

dull and without life, had finally stopped speaking. It was over. Doom settled like lead in her heart. Oh, cruel, cruel fate. She crossed her bosom quickly.

"Come, Wife," Ian said with a wicked grin as he helped her to her feet. His hand upon her arm was hard, his fingers viselike and sickeningly possessive.

Never had she wanted to be any man's bride and now she was married to a man she despised.

"Wait for me in your chamber as I have some business to attend to." His eyes gleamed with an inner satisfaction that caused her insides to curdle like sour milk. " 'Tis a long time I've waited for this night."

Her stomach heaved, but she managed a thin, sickly smile. She could endure anything as long as she knew Gareth would come to no harm. She started to turn, but he didn't release her. "Gwynn," he said in a whisper. "I know of your temper and your schemes. Make no mistake, you are naught but my wife and can act no longer like the baron. While Roderick was alive, you ruled the castle, but he is now dead. I am your husband and as such I will expect your complete obedience, elsewise Gareth will be hunted down, found, and brought back to be hanged." His fingers tightened over her arm. "Do you understand me?"

"Aye," she said through clenched teeth.

"You will never defy me." He stared at her face and she knew he saw the shadow of a bruise on her cheek, a painful reminder of her last husband's hand.

"Never, my lord," she lied, forcing the hated word over her tongue.

"Good." He smiled smugly, then drawing her near, brushed a kiss across her lips, his beard prickly against her skin. Her stomach roiled but pulling up inner strength, she endured his attempt at tenderness. "Go to your chamber and wait for me."

"I will."

She half ran down the shadowy corridor and tried to convince herself that she could live through anything as long as she knew that Gareth was free and safe.

As she opened the door to her chamber, she found Idelle pouring clean water into the basin. Fresh rushes gave off a heady fragrance and new candles had been lit, their small flames giving off pools of light that caused the colors of the tapestry hanging on the wall above her bed, crimson, gold, and purple to seem deep and comforting.

"So it is done?" Idelle asked as she shook the final drops from her bucket.

"Aye," Gwynn said with an angry sigh. "It seems my curse to be forever wed."

"To the wrong man."

"To any man." Pausing at the basin, she splashed cool water onto her face and tried to think. She could leave. As soon as she knew that Gareth was safely away from Rhydd, she could pack a few things and ride as far away as possible—mayhap to stay with Luella or . . . oh, 'twas foolish to think so. Ian would never let her go. Had she not promised him a castle full of sons? Did he not just vow to hunt Gareth down like a beast in the forest and see him hanged if she were to cross him?

The only way to be certain that Gareth remained safe was for her to pretend to be faithful to Ian. Each day she pretended to obey her husband would give her son that much more time to flee as far away from the castle walls as was possible. He would have to take the fastest destrier in the stables and ride to the sea where he could board a ship for some faraway port.

Oh, if she only had more time to make arrangements. "I must see my son," she decided.

"But Ian said you were to stay here."

"I am but his wife. Not his slave."

"There is not much difference." Idelle's lips pursed into a frown.

"I will see Gareth, Idelle, and I will see him now," she said, the fingers of one hand curling into a fist of determination. "But Ian is not to know."

"M'lady, please, do not anger the lord."

"I will not." She shot Idelle a conspiring look. "Do not say a word to anyone but Gareth."

"I like this not," Idelle worried aloud.

Gwynn flung her favorite cloak over the damask dress she'd worn to become Ian's wife. Ignoring the old woman's warnings, she took the backstairs and avoided the sentries who, thankfully, were dozing at their posts, their heads nodding in time with their snores.

Hiking the hood of the cloak over her head, she ducked out the back door, sending a pair of geese scurrying into the wet grass. Darkness had fallen over the land and aside from the firelight shimmering in the doorways and windows, there was no illumination. Not that it mattered much. Gwynn knew the keep well and as her slippers slid in the mud and wet grass, she dashed along a wide path leading past pens of sheep and pigs to the stables.

Once inside, she lit a candle and was careful to place it on a metal shelf far from the straw that covered the floor. A moist wind caused the flame to flicker and dance and mingled with the scents of horse dung, sweat, leather, and straw.

Wrapping her arms about herself, she sighed and waited.

"So, m'lady, you have found yourself another husband and the first one is not yet buried."

Gwynn jumped. Her heart jolted. The deep male voice came from the shadows behind her. She reached for her dagger.

"Who goes—oh!" Strong, callused fingers covered her mouth and a man's head was suddenly next to hers, looking over her shoulder, his breath hot against her ear. The hand that had scrabbled for her little knife was caught by his other hand. "Fear not. 'Tis naught but a thief."

Trevin? Her legs were suddenly weak as the scent of him—an odor she remembered from their lovemaking—enveloped her. Slowly he removed his hand from her mouth and she licked her lips. Could it be? Was he really here?

Still holding onto her wrist he moved soundlessly into the small pool of light cast by the candle. For the first time in thirteen years, she stared into the disturbing eyes of the thief, the father of her only son. A familiar ache squeezed hard upon her heart.

"You—you scared the devil from me!"

He didn't smile, nor did his fingers unclasp her wrist. His mirthless chuckle was positively wicked and as such disturbed her all the more. "I doubt that's possible."

"What are you doing here?"

"Waiting for you."

Her stupid heart missed a beat.

"We needs talk."

"Must we?" She glanced over her shoulder and tried to pull her arm away. His fingers tightened ever so slightly and she realized that she was trapped. He was much stronger than she, much more agile, much larger.

"What want you?"

"My son."

There it was. Dear God, now what? A weight settled heavy on her shoulders. "We had a bargain."

"I will keep him safe."

"You? The thief?" she mocked. "An outlaw, a swindler who won your barony from a befuddled old man in a crooked game of dice? You will keep him safe?"

"Without a doubt, m'lady," he said with confidence.

Dear Lord in heaven, was that her heart knocking so wildly? She hazarded a quick glance through the doorway again, hoping that Gareth would not come upon them now, but wait until she'd dispensed with this . . . this interloper. What would she tell her son when he ran through the open door? What could she say? This man hiding in the shadows, the purported baron of Black Oak Hall and known criminal was the man she'd chosen to betray her husband?

"I came to claim my son," he said, as if she might not have understood his intentions.

"Now?" She shook her head. "For the love of God, Trevin, do you not know what would happen to the lad if it were known that his father was . . . was—"

"Not Roderick?" at last he dropped her hand.

With a sigh, she shook her head. "That much he knows."

"But you did not tell him of me?"

"I knew not that you were the baron of Black Oak Hall."

He studied her for a few seconds, as if she was a puzzle he couldn't quite piece together. "Had you known?"

"I would not have told him. He's but a lad—too young to understand."

"Let me be the judge of that."

"On your honor, you swore that you would never breathe a word."

"I changed my mind."

"We had a bargain," she reminded him, the stables seeming suddenly close, the night air difficult to breathe. Thirteen years seem to fade away and he was once again her lover, the one man who had heard her moan in pleasure, seen her stretch against him with the dawn, felt the deepest, most intimate parts of her.

"Aye, and for a few baubles I gave up my son." His voice was low, seductive.

"For a few baubles and your freedom," she said, stepping backward, trying to break the spell of being so close to him. "If—if you had been caught you would have lost your hand, mayhap your life."

"I had no choice," he said simply and she felt a horrible misgiving. "For you, m'lady, would have gladly turned me over to the sheriff. Yours was the perfect seduction."

She blushed at the memory. At the time he was barely a man, but now, so close that she could smell the scents of leather and musk around him, feel his heat, see the dark shadow of his beard there was no mistaking he was a male, hard and virile and strong.

No longer was he the dirty, misbehaved thief she had forced to do her bidding. No trace of that boy lingered. In his stead, standing in the dusky shadows was a man, a severe-appearing man, with harsh features. Black stubble shaded a rock-solid jaw, ebony brows and spiked lashes guarded eyes a dark, intense blue that followed her every move, and lips, once supple with youth, were now thin as the blade of a dagger. Dressed in black from his muddied cloak to the tips of his boots, he appeared as Stygian as any devil who had found a way to escape from the very depths of hell.

"Roderick is dead, is he not?" he asked suddenly.

"Aye, but—"

"And you've already found yourself a new husband."

" 'Twas part of a bargain," she said, instantly furious. No longer intimidated, she stepped closer to him and tilted her face upward defiantly.

"Ah, and you, mistress, seem to have a way with such arrangements."

"I keep my word," she said haughtily.

"As I have kept mine."

"Until now."

"As I said, I was cornered as well as young and foolish."

She wouldn't give an inch. Couldn't. Too much, even Gareth's very life, was at stake. "You gave me your word."

"You believed a thief?"

"I had no choice—" she said, hearing his own words coming from her lips.

"Bitter irony, is it not?" he mocked. "No, m'lady, 'tis time I claimed my son."

A horse nickered softly in the blackness and there was the rustle of straw as the animals shifted on the other side of their mangers. Gwynn felt desperation claw at her throat. She needed time to think, to lay plans. "Does Lord Ian know that you're here?"

She felt, rather than saw, him tense. "I've not yet approached the lord," he said, leaning one shoulder against a post supporting the roof. "I thought it best to first speak with you."

"And so you've done," she said, unnerved.

"Tell me, how is it you're married to him before

your other husband is in the grave? What kind of bargain is this?"

"One that was necessary," she said, unwilling to give him any further information. "Now, if you will leave—"

"Not without my son."

"He is in enough trouble as it is," she said. "If Ian finds you here, it will only cause more."

"What kind of trouble?"

Gwynn hesitated. "You have heard that Roderick was killed by Gareth?"

"I knew only that the baron was slain." Trevin said, his voice sober.

" 'Twas terrible. Roderick returned and met Gareth for the first time. He realized the boy was not his son and accused me of . . . well, many things. None of them good." She cleared her throat and remembered the clang of swords, the screams of pain, spray of blood, and Roderick's last, rattling breath. "There . . . was a fight and Gareth, in an attempt to defend my honor and, I suppose, my life as well took up Roderick's sword and killed him."

"Jesus, son of God."

"Ian saw it all and accused Gareth of murder. Sentenced him to be hanged."

"Not as long as I breathe."

For some reason, Gwynn felt reassured, though, in truth, what could Trevin do? Was he not assumed to be a murderer himself? She placed a hand upon his sleeve. " 'Tis why I am married again. Ian . . . he only agreed to spare Gareth's life if I would agree to marry him."

With one strong finger, he lifted her chin and gazed at her with night-darkened eyes. "Think you I believe that you sacrificed yourself?"

"I did only what I had to." She licked her lips nervously and his gaze lowered to her mouth. Her pulse jumped as she realized how alone they were, felt a tingle where his finger pressed against the sensitive skin at the underside of her jaw, sensed a dusky yearning in his touch. A flame of desire flared in his eyes and she swallowed hard. Oh, God, what was she doing here with him? Why could she not step away?

"Where is Gareth now?"

"He . . . he has not yet left the castle." With all her strength, she stepped away from him and his hand fell away from her chin as she released his arm. "I await him now."

"Good." Trevin folded his arms over his chest and leaned one shoulder against a post supporting the roof. "Then, m'lady," he said. "I will wait as well."

The ferrets scrambled in their kennels, growling softly, their claws clicking nervously on the wooden floor.

"Quickly, over here!" Ian's voice was but a whisper as he led the dark knight through the herb garden. Webb hobbled slightly, his wound, now stitched and bound still bothering him. They stopped at a corner of the keep, in a sheltered spot near the dove cote where the wind, damp and chill, was not so strong. "Roderick trusted you."

"Aye." Webb nodded and blew on his hands. "He promised to pay me well."

"And you shall be."

To ensure the man's trust, Ian untied a small leather pouch from his belt, opened the bag, and poured the coins into his gloved palm. "For your service to Roderick and your allegiance to Rhydd." He dropped the coins into the pouch again and drew the string. The coins clinked softly—such sweet, sweet music. "You will take the boy tonight and ride for three days, then kill him as quickly and as painlessly as possible."

" 'Twill be my pleasure," Webb said. There was a muffled woof from the direction of the dog kennels a few feet away. "What was that?" Webb demanded, turning swiftly on his heel and reaching for his sword.

"Nothing. Just a nervous cur. You're jumpy, my friend."

"Mayhap from being hacked with your brother's sword." He turned around again and sheathed his weapon, his face paling with the effort. " 'Tis an ill wind blowing through your keep tonight, m'lord."

"A poet be you?"

"Nay, just a soldier for hire."

"You have a job." Another dog started howling and the hound master yelled sharply at his charges.

"Shut up ye bloody mutts, er I'll teach ye a lesson ye'll not soon forget!"

Ian waited a few tense seconds as the dogs quieted. When he spoke it was in the barest of whispers. "You must make it look as if you were attacked by outlaws. You'll say that the boy's brash ways got him into trouble as he tried to elude the robbers rather than give them any of his money." Ian snapped his fingers as he thought. "Take Sir Charles and Sir Reynolds with you. They, too, must be killed, of course, and their corpses returned as well."

"Aye."

"Can you take care of all of them?" Ian wasn't certain for though Webb had proven himself to Roderick, he was wounded.

"I have friends, m'lord. They be only too willing to slit a man's throat for a few coins."

"Good. Good." Ian ignored his twinge of conscience. He was baron of Rhydd now. His word was

law. He had to do that which was best for himself as
well as the rest of the castle. "My faith is with you."

The dark knight snorted and spat into the garden.
"As well it should be, m'lord."

Ian licked his chapped lips. He was no stranger to
violence, but 'twas not the lad's fault he was born a
bastard, and the boy had killed the one man who
stood in Ian's way of ruling Rhydd. In truth, Gareth
had saved Ian the trouble of murdering his brother.
Now, however, the boy, too, had to be done away
with. "His mother must believe that you were laid
siege upon. 'Twould be good if you were to have suffered a wound."

"Another?"

" 'Tis well paid you are."

"Do not worry, *m'lord,*" Webb sneered. "I will be
sufficiently cut."

"Your sacrifice will be rewarded." Ian sighed in relief and picked at the skin flaking from his lips. "No
one is to know otherwise. 'Tis between us only."

"Aye, Lord Ian. The truth is that the boy, Charles,
and Reynolds were all killed by outlaws who showed
no mercy. They left me, too, for dead. No torture or
inquisition will ever make me say elsewise."

"Ah, you be a good and loyal man, Sir Webb," Ian
said, wondering if this man would sell his allegiance
to another for a higher price. He'd met him years ago
before Webb had become a knight. Then, he was but
a mercenary who had, for a while, ridden with Ian
while Roderick ruled Rhydd and was married to his
first wife. Ian hadn't trusted the man then, but now,
through a twist of the fates, he was forced to depend
upon the dark knight. "When you return, you will be
paid again, thrice what we agreed upon. Also, lest you
think your deeds go unappreciated, I will make you my

most trusted knight upon full recovery of your wounds."

"See that I do recover," Webb warned, his voice low and without a trace of jest. "Elsewise the outlaws who be my friends will come for you and your wife."

"Do not fear." They clasped hands firmly and Ian felt the strength in Webb's fingers—stronger than steel.

"So be it." Webb tied the purse to his belt and winced at a jab of pain in his thigh, as if his wound was throbbing.

They parted ways and did not notice the two sets of eyes watching them from a hiding space under the dog kennels. Gareth held the half-grown pup his mother had given him this past boon day, during the harvest season. While trying to keep the playful dog quiet, he had heard each bone-chilling word exchanged between the man he'd thought was his uncle and the knight he'd maimed this afternoon. Ian meant to kill him and Webb was only too glad to do the deed. All of Gareth's bravado evaporated in the frigid night and he shivered as he cradled the clawing, wild hound to his chest. He could not waste a second, for with each beat of his heart he came closer to being discovered and murdered.

He had the coins and rings his mother had dropped into his pack earlier as well as the cross, a dagger, and black cloak. He didn't dare make his way to the stables for fear he would be caught. Though he would love to ride Dragon at a breakneck gallop through the main gate and across the moat bridge to the forest, he couldn't take the chance of running into Webb or Ian. Asides, he would be able to buy a good horse with his small cache should he need one, but, for now, he had to run as far from Rhydd as possible.

"Come, Boon," he ordered softly. He pocketed apples from the storage bin and a loaf of day-old bread being saved for the beggars, then whistled softly to the speckled pup who had more energy than brains.

Not for the first time in his twelve years, Gareth opened the sally port near the kennels, cringed as the huge door creaked on its ancient hinges, and let it swing open behind him as he, still holding the scrambling dog, dropped the six feet to the sodden ground.

He landed hard, twisted an ankle, but took off at a dead run through the swampy grasslands and into the black moat. The water was cold as ice, but he swam the brackish span, his skin turning blue, his body chilled to the marrow of his bones.

Boon, with only his head above the water line, splashed and swam enthusiastically at his side.

Teeth rattling, Gareth climbed up the opposite shore and ran, hobbling across the grassland as Boon shook the water from his coat.

"Come!" Gareth ordered in a hoarse whisper. Sometimes the dog had not a brain in his head! He whistled softly and Boon bounded to his side.

In the forest it was black as the very depths of hell. Gareth could barely distinguish the gnarled, twisted shapes of the trees or the path that veered through the thicket. Still he ran with the pup at his heels.

Vines tripped him. Branches slapped his face. Cobwebs clung to his skin. Thorns tore at his breeches and his boots were so wet they sloshed, but he sped along the twisting trails, faster and faster, the burn in his ankle cutting like a knife, his young heart pumping, his lungs burning, tears blinding his eyes. He knew not where he was going, but fear chased him on.

"Come, Boon, blast you!" he said, gasping as the

dog stopped short and growled. "Hurry! The devil will have us both if Sir Webb catches up to us."

"Who be you?"

The voice rumbled from the darkness.

"Ahh!" Gareth screamed as a hand, seeming to snake out of the very soul of the forest, clamped around his wrist in a death grip. "Hush!"

The dog lunged, but the voice commanded, "Stay, beast!" Boon stopped cold.

The fingers around his arm tightened as if drawn by an invisible string and yet he saw no one in the dark, gloomy night. "Now, boy, who be ye and what are ye running from?"

'Twas Satan, Gareth thought wildly, his blood pumping through his veins. Lucifer had come up from hell to capture him. He tried to speak, but his voice was lost and for a second he thought he might wet himself. "I—I—" Should he lie? What if this man, nay this demon, was one of Webb's outlaws, the men who wanted to slit his throat.

"I know who ye be. Y'er Gareth of Rhydd, are ye not?"

Gareth's tongue wouldn't work and he reached for the knife at his belt with his free hand. He'd kill this bastard from Hades before the creature had a chance to slay him.

"Do it not, boy," the voice commanded, "or, 'tis certain ye and this mutt ye call a dog will both meet yer doom."

Chapter Four

"Something's wrong." Gwynn peered through the darkness and wrapped her arms around herself. She couldn't stand another second waiting for Gareth, of feeling the weight of Trevin's enigmatic gaze as it bored into her back. "He should have been here by now."

Somewhere near the kennels the dogs put up a racket and were rewarded with a stern command from Alfred, the simpleton who had a way with animals but could not communicate with another human being if it were to save his soul.

"You're sure the old woman can be trusted?"

"Idelle? Aye. With my life." Gwynn fingered the worn handle of a pitchfork hung near the door. The bailey was dark, few patches of light glowing from the windows of the huts surrounding the great hall. Only the farrier's forge glowed bright in the night. She shook her head. "Something is amiss."

"Then we must go find the boy."

"Not yet." Thoughtfully she chewed on the corner of her lip. Where could the boy be? Not in his chamber or Idelle would have found him and sent him to the stables. Sometimes he hid in closets and crevices within the castle walls, watching for a game of dice. As she had learned the runes and spells of the old ones growing up, Gareth had learned how to wager at games of chance—so like his father.

She glanced again at Trevin and cursed silently that he should arrive this day, at the very time when Gareth was in jeopardy. A spell came to mind, one that would make an enemy disappear, but she held her tongue because, in truth, she didn't know whether the man before her, the only man to have made love to her, was friend or foe. Her mind told her not to trust him, her wayward heart wanted desperately to believe in him.

"I must go." She started to step through the door, but Trevin wrapped determined fingers around her arm.

"Careful, woman," he said into her ear and his breath caused goose bumps to rise on her skin and oh, so, heart-stopping memories to roll through her mind. "Do not cross me."

"I would not—" she said, but knew the words to be a lie.

"Good, because I have many friends within the walls of Rhydd, men with weapons who would come to my aid." He hesitated, then said, "If there be trouble, seek out the carpenter. Richard."

"The carpenter?"

"Aye, he is a friend."

"And a traitor to Rhydd."

"As you were, m'lady, when you slept with a man other than your husband."

She stiffened and tried to ignore the warmth of his fingertips through her cloak. "The people of Rhydd are loyal to Roderick and—"

"Roderick's dead."

"—his wife—"

"You, m'lady, are now married to Ian."

"Oh, bother!" How had her life become so complicated? "Everyone knows I only married Ian to save Gareth's life."

One of the horses nipped at another and the second neighed and kicked in defense.

"Shh!" Trevin commanded and he yanked her hard against him. He blew out the candle and the stables were instantly dark. Through the open door she saw movement as a guard, watching from the north tower, held a torch aloft and called down to the gatekeeper.

"Who goes there?"

"Wha'?"

Gwynn froze and silently prayed that she wouldn't be found hiding in the stables in the arms of the outlaw baron of Black Oak Hall. Hard, inflexible muscles surrounded her and the smell of him, all male and leather reminded her of lying naked in his arms so long ago.

"Hush," he whispered, his breath, warm and inviting as it teased the rim of her ear.

Through her clothes her buttocks were pressed hard against his thighs. He shifted slightly and taut muscles pressed against the curve of her spine. Desire unwanted, raced through her blood though she had no time for such nonsense.

Trevin and his lean body be damned, she had to think of Gareth. Barely able to breathe, she tried to concentrate on anything other than the splay of his fingers over her abdomen.

"I say, 'who goes there?' " the guard yelled again.

Sweet Jesus, let me out of here so that I can find Gareth. Her breathing was shallow and soft and her mind spun in images of Trevin and Gareth, father and son, so alike and yet so different. With each of her breaths, his arms tightened, fingertips brushing the underside of her breasts.

Somewhere in a nearby pen, a cow lowed and the dogs began baying again.

"No one's about, ya ninny." The gatehouse guard walked into the bailey and took a cursory look at the darkened grass. Cupping his mouth, he turned his head upward and shouted, "Stand yer watch and mind yer own business."

"Christ A'mighty, y're in a foul mood."

"Yeah, well, ye got the dogs all worked up again, now, didn't ye?" Grumbling under his breath the guard returned to the gatehouse and the sentry on the wall walk made his way to the tower, his torch a moving beacon.

"Now," Trevin said, his lips brushing against her nape, "go you to the castle and find the boy. Bring him here to meet me."

"I cannot."

"If you do not," he promised, agitation evident in his voice, "I will search him out myself and tell him the truth. 'Tis time he knew whose blood is flowing through his veins."

"That of a thief."

"And worse," he admitted and she thought of the rumors surrounding him. A black-heart. A rogue baron. A murderer and, as always, an outlaw.

"I'll go," she finally agreed as she couldn't stand another minute in his arms. Her blood was heating, her traitorous heart pounding out a wild cadence, and her fears for her son were distracted by visions of lying naked in his arms, letting desire run its wayward course as she felt his weight upon her.

Swallowing hard at the memory, she slipped through the doorway and, without making a sound, darted through the blackest shadows of the bailey. Smoke from the fires of the day lay low and sifted through the damp air as she slogged through the bent grass and mud toward the great hall.

Puddles had collected on the path dampening her skirts and shoes. She had to think, to come up with a plan to save her son. Trevin and his wants be damned. 'Twas Gareth who was in danger.

A scheme was forming in her mind as she rimmed the eel pond and a fish jumped near her feet. 'Twas just a thought at this point, but swirling into a more definite notion. She would bribe the soldiers that were to ride Gareth to the outer reaches of Rhydd. Surely one would take the boy to Heath Castle where Luella would see that he was hidden safely away. Then, much later, would she join him. Somehow, someway she would be with her son again.

But you are married to Ian. At that thought she shriveled inside. How could she lay with him? Sleep in his bed? Pretend that she did not despise him? Her stomach turned over at the thought and she slid out of her slippers to climb the stairs of the keep.

The candles were burning down, their light muted, the smoke hanging in the corridors. Surely Ian had missed her by now and he would want to know where she'd been. She would lie, of course, claim that she'd been restless and had to walk to clear her head of all the pain and suffering she'd witnessed this day. Surely, Ian would expect her to mourn Roderick's passing as well as worry about her son's banishment.

She shoved open the door to her chamber.

She shopped short.

All the spit dried in her mouth.

"Wife." There was no hint of a smile on Ian's wicked face. He sat on the edge of her bed, leaning backward on one elbow, as if he owned the very place where she slept.

Webb, the abomination of a knight, stood near the fire. Blood, black, and caked, stained one leg of his breeches and his eyes, above his beard-darkened jaw glinted with an evil light that scared the liver out of her.

"Where is he?" Ian demanded.

Gwynn's breath stopped. "W-who?" she forced out and willed her feet to keep moving into her room. Being in the chamber alone with these two men caused fear to eat at her innards, but she managed an outward calm. "Who are you looking for?"

"Your son, Wife."

Sweet, merciful Lord in heaven. "Gareth? He is not in the castle?"

"Nowhere in the keep."

"But he must be." Silently she prayed that Idelle had snatched him away and that even now he was riding like a demon to castle Heath.

"We've searched everywhere."

"Everywhere," Webb repeated, then spit into the fire. The flames crackled.

"But the castle is large, with many hiding places. You know how Gareth is, still a boy. Always teasing and playing."

"He's gone." Ian's voice was flat.

"Nay. I do not believe that—"

"The sally port was not barred or locked. A guard found it creaking open and he's certain it was secure when last he passed it. Also, the pup that you gave the boy is missing."

Gwynn's knees weakened. Was Gareth with Trevin? Had they escaped together? The sally port, usually guarded, was the back door of the castle, positioned high above the moat, a means of escape if ever Rhydd was under siege. She shrugged. "I know not where he is."

With a snort of contempt, Webb limped to the window and regarded her silently.

"You can do better than this, Lady," Ian said, scratching his beard. "Do not lie to me. Tell me where he is."

"I swear to you on my life, I know not."

"So be it." Never taking his eyes off his wife, Ian pushed himself lazily to his feet. As he approached Gwynn she was aware of how much larger he was than she. Sighing he reached for his belt and began to slowly unbuckle the leather strap. Fear scraped down her insides. "Now, Wife," he said as the buckle gave way and the belt slipped into his fingers, "my patience is gone. 'Tis time to tell me where you have hidden the boy. I want not to harm you, but, if needs be, I am willing to do what I must to rule this castle."

"And that includes flogging me?" she demanded, refusing to show him any of the dread that was strangling her.

"It only means that I am not afraid to make anyone, even my new bride, bend to my will." He fingered the strap. "Pray that I won't have to use force."

"Do what you will," she said meeting his gaze. "I fear you not, Ian. Nor will I ever."

"Who the devil are you?" Gareth demanded as he tried to yank his shoulder away from the claw holding it firmly.

"Know you not?"

"Be you Lucifer?"

"By the gods, boy, would Lord Trevin have sent you to the devil?"

"Lord Trevin?" Gareth tried to view the man—for he appeared to be a man rather than a forest monster—who held him fast, but it was too dark to see much except his white beard and the moving hole that was his mouth. "You talk in circles. Now leave me be."

"Not yet, m'boy. 'Tis my duty to keep ye safe, so I'll have no more of yer sass."

"Your *duty*?"

"Aye, to Trevin of Black Oak."

"Speak you of the outlaw who stole the castle?" Though shivering Gareth spat on the ground. "I've heard of him. Old Bart said he is a cheat."

"Mayhap."

"One who bested an addled, drunken old man who was foolish enough to bet his barony in a game of dice."

"Well—"

"Then, Bart says, when the lord recognized what he'd done, this Trevin, who was but an outlaw knight, ran the lord through and tossed him into the moat!"

"Nay, nay, nay. Who is this Bart?"

"The best huntsman in all of Rhydd . . . well, he was until he lost his fingers to a wolf."

"Bah! He knows only half the truth."

"Nay, Matilda—she scrapes the hides from the huntsman's kill, she, too, says Trevin of Black Oak is a murdering thief."

"Well, she is a liar and the old man—Bart or whatever is his name, he be a fool. Don't ye know better than to listen to women? They be the bane of a man's existence, let me tell you. Now, come along."

"Bart is not a woman."

"Ah, well, some men, too, they are not to be trusted."

"I'll go nowhere." The man not only spoke like he was truly daft but he reeked of sour wine.

"I've food and a warm fire, lad, now come along afore whoever it is y're runnin' from finds ye."

"Leave me be!" Gareth started to struggle and it took all of Muir's strength to hold him down. The dog yapped wildly again and jumped up and down, snapping his ugly jowls. "You—beast—get back!"

"Nay, Boon, attack. Attack!" Gareth kicked and landed a blow to Muir's shin.

"Miserable brat. If ye were not the son of—" He bit down his tongue though his leg smarted. "I'm here to help ye, if ye would but calm down."

"Help me?"

"Aye. To save ye from those that would rather see ye in yer grave before ye reach thirteen years."

The clawing, scratching, and kicking stopped. "You know of them?" he asked.

"Aye. Down, ye little cur!"

"Boon, stay!" Gareth commanded as he eyed this bearded man who held him in his aged hands. He was a short man with an expanding girth, flowing beard, and gravelly voice. His breath stank of sour wine and, even in the blackness, Gareth sensed that his clothes were those of a pauper and there was something not quite right with his face.

"Why be ye here in the forests of Rhydd?"

"Waiting for you, of course."

"Of course," Gareth mocked and the old man sniffed in disdain.

"We must be off. If ye've escaped, then there's trouble brewin' just like I saw in my vision."

"Vision? What be ye? A wizard?" Gareth doubted it. The old man was a drunk, little more. Any vision he saw came from the bottom of a cup of ale unless Gareth missed his guess.

Muir sighed theatrically. "Right now it seems I'm a pitiful man with a boy who asks far too many questions and a dog that would like to bite out my throat. Hurry along this way, would ye, and be quick about it."

Gareth whistled for the pup.

"Oh, do be quiet," Muir grumbled in irritation. He'd never much cared for lads of this age. Too old to be innocent and too young to know anything of any substance, they were trouble through and through. Trevin, at twelve, had been more difficulty than he was worth. Muir had been forever getting that one out of trouble.

"Where are we going?"

"Someplace safe."

Gareth fell into step with the old man who held on to a cane, but never used it, and found his way to a horse that was tethered to a small sapling. Bridle jangling, the palfrey was trying to pluck a few meager blades of grass in the darkness.

At that moment the pup gave out an excited yip and there was a baying of hounds in the distance.

"Saints be damned." The dogs of Rhydd would be released to hunt him down like a wound stag. "Climb up, then," the drunk insisted and Gareth had no choice but to follow this crippled old man who mounted the horse with surprising ease. He clucked to the beast and though the forest was dark as pitch the palfrey clipped at a fast walk.

Again the dogs let out a chorus of baying that paralyzed Gareth. His teeth chattered and he closed out his mind to memories of slicing through Roderick's flesh with his sword. 'Twas far different from the games he played with Tom, the butcher's simpleton of a son. The feel of metal piercing skin and scraping bone was sinister and cold. He held tight on to the pup, feeling the dog's warmth and wishing that all this trouble had never started.

If only Lord Roderick, the man he'd thought to be his father, had never escaped.

"Hurry along," the magician urged to the horse.

Their path was crooked and doubled back upon itself several times, enough that in the thick rain-washed night, Gareth, who knew the forest as well as the back of his hand, was completely turned around. Finally the old man guided the beast through a glen and around a small lake. On the far side, in a copse of dense bracken and fir trees, he dismounted and showed Gareth the thin slit of an entrance to a cave.

"This is the safe place?" Gareth whispered. He could have done better by himself.

"Trust me."

"I know you not, old man." He was suspicious. Why should he trust this old coot? Was there anyone he could believe in?

He watched the would-be magician pat the horse and tie him to a scrawny tree. "Come you, boy. 'Tis time to eat."

Gareth's stomach grumbled as the ancient man paused to light a single torch from a stash near an outcropping of rock. The ancient one's back was to the boy and Gareth saw nothing but a ragged black cape with a dusty hood and boots that were in sorry need of new heels and soles. Holding the torch aloft, he led Gareth down a dusty trail inside the cavern.

"Be there bears in here, or badgers?" Gareth asked, wishing he'd been clever enough to pack his quiver and bow with him as he strained to see into every nook and cranny of the cavern. His only weapon was a dagger and it seemed small at the thought of snarling wild creatures with sharp fangs.

Boon wasn't much help. The pup whimpered and followed close on Gareth's heels.

"Nay. Naught but a few bats."

"But—" He swallowed back his fear. Droppings and bleached dry bones from several beasts littered the floor. Overhead the rustle of wings was ever-present. Gareth had to remind himself that being here with the old man was surely better than being alone in the forest certain that at any second Sir Webb would leap from the darkness to slit his throat.

" 'Tis empty, I say. Would I bring ye to face some hideous, fanged beast if 'twas my bidding to keep ye safe?"

"Nay, but—"

"Hush. All yer questions rattle around in my brain and cause my head to ache. Here we go now—" He placed his torch to a pile of dry sticks already laid in a circle of well-worn stones. With a crackle and spark the fire caught, flames and smoke rising over upward. Gold shadows played upon the uneven rock walls and the ceiling where roots tangled and weaved.

In one corner were two pallets and upon them furs that were old and dusty. The dog sniffed around the darkened corners, his breath moving the dust and dirt of the cavern's floor.

"Here we be, home sweet home," the cripple muttered and turned to face his young charge.

A scream died in Gareth's throat.

The old man was hideous. He had but one eye and his face was disfigured.

The magician smiled and showed off a few remaining teeth. "This," he said, motioning to his face, "is what happens when a lad gets too cocky and thinks he can best a stronger foe."

"But—but you have only one eye."

"Nay, son, I have two. One that sees as the rest of the world does and one that has visions that no one else views." He settled onto a large rock and placed both gnarly hands around his cane. " 'Tis a curse. Until I was blinded and bleeding, I was no different from the other men in the town. But I was caught robbing a rich man . . . well, there is more to the story but 'tis best if ye hear it later, if at all. The long and short of it is that I was nursed back to health by an old woman who taught me of my magic."

He frowned at the memory. " 'Twas then I learned to use my other faculties. My ears and nose became my eyes. My fingers gave me sight as my vision failed me and when at last the bandages were removed, only one eye saw the light of day. The other, though, came to behold that which others could not see—the dark of the night."

Gareth's skin crawled. "Who are you?"

"I be called Muir."

"Of Black Oak?"

The old man smiled that crooked grin. "For now I belong here, in this cave. Take off your wet clothes, place them near the fire here, and warm yourself in the bed. 'Twould be my hide if I were to deliver ye to Trevin and ye be ill. Go on now—" He waved Gareth toward the pallets, but the boy didn't move.

"What does this Trevin want of me?"

Muir hesitated. "He'll have to tell ye himself, boy, but trust me that he is no friend of Ian of Rhydd's."

"Where is he now?"

"That. I'm afraid, I know not." The old man scowled, then eyed Gareth's pack as the pup turned several circles before settling his head on his paws and watching the boy. "Did ye think to bring anything to drink with ye?"

"Nay."

Muir sighed and rolled his good eye toward the ceiling. "I thought not. 'Tis my lot in life to forever have a dry throat and parched tongue."

Gareth, taking off his shirt, didn't believe the old goat for a minute. However, for now, he had no choice but to trust him and hope beyond hope that Webb or any other of Ian's soldiers didn't find the cave. For as safe as the old man thought it was, the cavern was a trap as it had only one entrance.

If they were discovered, they were doomed.

She had betrayed him. As surely as the moon was hiding behind the clouds, Gwynn had double-crossed him. Silently cursing himself for being a fool, Trevin slunk through the shadows and made his way to the keep. He heard the sounds of the night, the river flowing wildly on the other side of the castle walls, an owl hooting in the forest, and pigs grunting and rooting in their sties.

Why had he trusted her? Had she not used him before? Seduced and bartered with him? Traded him his freedom for a few nights in her bed? The wench had no heart, no morals and certainly no loyalty.

Except to the boy. She seemed genuinely concerned about her son and his safety. *His* son, he reminded himself as he skirted the fish pond and slid noiselessly into the keep. Something was amiss, he was certain of it. The dogs in the kennels were restless, the doves in the dovecote disturbed, and Gwynn had been gone far too long.

He'd seen her enter the great hall and followed her

path, his boots muted on the rushes. Several knights dozed at their posts; another two were engrossed in a game of chess, still one more was lifting the skirts of a maid near the doorway to the chapel. The image of the woman's legs wrapped so eagerly around the knight's torso burned deep into Trevin's brain. It had been long since he'd been with a woman and holding Gwynn so tightly a short while earlier had brought his cock to attention.

Not since his wife had died had he bedded a woman, nor had he wanted one.

Until tonight. The smell of Gwynn's hair, the feel of her ribs rising and falling beneath firm breasts, the nip of her waist in his palm and her rump, round and yielding against his legs had been too much too bear. He had not time for the distraction of a woman, any woman, least of all Gwynn and yet here he was, climbing the stairs to her chamber, hiding in the shadows, his heart thudding expectantly.

There had been many women since he'd first made love to Gwynn all those years ago, but never had any touched him with the same primal, aching passion. He'd told himself it was because she'd been his first lover, a forbidden fruit, but now, as he made his way to her room, he felt the same breathless pang of desire squeezing his innards as he had so long ago.

He crouched near her door and heard her voice through the oaken panels.

"I swear to you, Lord Ian, I know not where Gareth is."

"Liar!"

"Nay, do not—"

Slap!

Trevin sprang to his feet. He kicked hard. The door gave way.

Sword drawn, he leapt into the chamber.

"What the devil?" Ian demanded, his gaze moving from his beautiful wife, standing proudly before him with her fists clenched, to the doorway. "If it isn't the thief." He held his belt securely in one hand while the other was raised as if to strike again.

"Leave her be," Trevin ordered and noticed a dark knight in the corner.

"She is my wife."

"And you, Lord, are destined for hell if you do not lower your hand." Trevin's voice was deadly and he glared at the new baron of Rhydd in seething, barely leashed fury. "Gwynn, leave."

"Nay, Trevin, this is not your battle." Gwynn tossed him an anxious glance, silently begging him to hold his tongue.

"Isn't it?" He sheathed his sword but kept his gaze fixed on the two other men in the room—both now his sworn enemies. "I know you." Ian's lips curled. "You're the pathetic little cur who stole my dagger."

"Aye, and sliced your face."

Ian's right hand flew to his cheek and he touched a scar that ran near his hairline.

"Get out of here now, Gwynn," Trevin ordered, smelling a fight that was soon to erupt. From the sheath strapped to his belt he grabbed the dagger.

"I see you have it still."

Trevin grinned wickedly. "Here." He tossed the bejeweled knife at Ian. Rubies, emeralds, and sapphires glimmered in the firelight as the little knife sailed across the chamber to land in the lord's outstretched palm. "I was but borrowing your weapon."

"Ye be Trevin of Black Oak." Webb's eyes were mere slits, visible only as they reflected the light of the fire. "Ye killed Baron Dryw."

"What business do you have here?" Ian asked, slowly circling Gwynn, his eyes never leaving Trevin. His fingers tightened around the knife's hilt.

"I come for my son."

Gwynn sucked in her breath and shook her head. "He knows not what he says."

"Your son?" Ian asked. "Your son?"

Trevin nodded.

Gwynn was frantic. "He knows not—"

"The boy, Gareth?" Dark eyebrows raised in surprise and he barked out a jaded laugh. "*Your* son? You, a lowly thief, a mere boy yourself at the time, you fathered the lad?" Disbelieving, Ian looked at Gwynn, saw the stain on her cheeks, her eyes snapping fire. "For the love of God!"

"Where is he?" Trevin demanded.

Ian fingered the dagger. "You slept with Roderick's wife while he was away at battle?"

"You suspected Gareth was not my husband's issue," Gwynn interjected, her voice trembling slightly.

"But I knew not that you were whore enough to sleep with a common thief, a man not worthy of polishing Roderick's shoes."

"What does it matter who is Gareth's father?" she said while Webb rubbed his leg and slid his sword from its sheath.

Ian's lips curled into a snarl. "I hoped that you had better taste, Wife. That at the very least you could have done your whoring with a nobleman."

"Where is the boy?" Trevin asked as Webb, sensing Ian's intent, began circling the other side of Gwynn.

"A good question." Ian rubbed the whiskers upon his chin and the scar running along his hairline seemed suddenly more distinct. "I was just asking the same of my wife."

"By beating his whereabouts from her?" Trevin's fingers tightened over the hilt of his weapon. Sweat collected at the roots of his hair.

"The boy killed my brother, the baron. His punishment is to be forever banished from Rhydd."

Trevin lifted a shoulder. "Then, mayhap, he has saved you the trouble by leaving himself."

"Nay! He would not have left without talking first to me," Gwynn insisted, desperation echoing in her voice.

"Make your leave, lady," Trevin warned.

"Stay!" Ian ordered.

"Now!" Trevin yelled and Gwynn fled to the door. Ian hurled his dagger at Trevin, but the younger man ducked and spun. Thunk! The knife buried itself in the oaken planks of the door.

Webb rounded on the interloper. His sword sliced the air. Trevin drew in his stomach but the tip of Webb's weapon slit his cloak and cut his flesh. Gwynn wrenched the dagger free and flung it at Webb. The blade lodged in his shoulder and he shrieked like a gutted pig. Blood oozed down his arm as he yanked the hated dagger from his flesh.

"Run!" Trevin yelled and this time she flew through the door. Trevin, backing up, carving the air with his sword, followed, only to hide in a corner as Gwynn fled down the stairs. Crouching, he waited and as Ian dashed down the stone steps, he readied his sword.

"Guards! There is a traitor. A criminal! Catch him!" Ian rounded the corner. Trevin swung. His sword sliced and held in shinbone. Shrieking in agony, Ian rolled down the stairs.

Trevin raced upward, through the solar and onto the ledge of the window. With a leap, he flung himself through the air, caught hold of another window ledge, then slid down the stone walls, scraping his fingers and body until his feet hit the thatched roof of the carpenter's shop. His bones jarred. He bit his tongue. Pain screamed through his body.

"For the love of God, man," Richard cried as Trevin rolled down the thatches to the ground, "are ye truly daft?"

Trevin's body ached and blood seeped through his tunic and cloak, but, as arranged, Richard handed him the stolen guise of a soldier of Rhydd. "Where's the boy?"

"Already gone, it seems." Trevin stripped and with Richard's help, donned the armor. The smells of sawdust and wood were cut off as the helmet was forced upon his head. Dogs barked, soldiers yelled, horses neighed nervously, and the ring of boots upon stone thundered.

"And the lady?"

"Did she not come here?"

"Nay. I've seen her not."

"Then I must stay."

"You cannot."

Could he leave Gwynn? Trevin remembered her cheek, bright with the pain of Ian's hand, and for what? Not telling him where her son was? Now she had betrayed him, gone against his word. The torture Ian would inflict upon her would be merciless. Damn that woman.

"I cannot leave."

"You will be killed, and I as well. In our effort I have detained one of Ian's soldiers, mayhap have killed him." Richard's voice was harsh. "My family will suffer and my wife is with child again."

"I will not leave her."

"You must, Trevin, or I will turn you in myself."

Richard's face, skeletal in the dark, was set with a fierce determination Trevin recognized. "I will see to the lady."

"There is no need," a hushed voice said as Idelle slipped through the doorway. "She is safe."

"Here at Rhydd?"

"Nay."

"She's left the castle?"

The old midwife ducked into a corner, behind a stack of posts. "Do not worry over her, Trevin of Black Oak. You have your own dark heart to mend."

"How am I to know that she is safe?" he asked.

"Trust in the Lord."

"This from you—the woman who is known to cast spells and conjure demons?"

"The lady is well. She bid me tell you. Now, go, or Ian will have your hide and ours as well."

Trevin felt a lie brewing in the air. "You be certain?"

"On the lives of the lady and her son, I swear to you Lady Gwynn is safely away. Now, you, too, must leave."

Trevin didn't bother to argue. He had to trust the old woman. But, he swore under his breath as he joined the other soldiers grabbing their mounts from the stable master, if he ever saw Gwynn of Rhydd alive again, he'd personally shake the living devil from her.

Or, he thought angrily, make love to her until neither of them had an ounce of strength left in their bodies.

"Let us pass, 'tis the Lord's bidding," Father Anthony ordered as he led the ass and a cart laden with caskets. Wheels protested under the dead weight of the load and the donkey brayed loudly, protesting his dark task.

Deep within one coffin, Gwynn squeezed her eyes shut and silently cursed Idelle's morbid scheme for her escape.

"Now?" the guard asked. "But there be—"

" 'Tis Lord Ian's request," Anthony insisted as Gwynn, hearing the argument dared not move. She was pinned beneath the cover of a dead corpse, a thin peasant woman who had worked spinning and dying wool until the cough that had rattled deep in her lungs and become so persistent and painful, it had finally taken her from this world.

"I heard not of this."

"You hear of it now," the priest insisted.

'Twas all Gwynn could do not to scream or retch, but she closed her mind to the brittle woman lying atop her and remembered that she would soon see her son again. She had no more life at Rhydd and, if only she could escape, she would be able to find a way to Heath Castle, which was only a fortnight's journey to the south on foot. 'Twould be treacherous, but she had enough jewels and coin with her to hire a horse and guard, if only she survived this horrid part of her journey. Why must the sentry be so stubborn? Though the night was as cold as death, she began to sweat.

"I was told not to let anyone pass." The guard sounded certain and Gwynn's heart sank.

"Even against the Lord's bidding?"

"Who've ye got?"

"Bartholomew, the miller."

"Aye. He keeled over this morn."

"Then the girl, Kate, who drowned in the mill pond,

and Brenna, one of the women who worked with the fleece."

"Well, ye won't mind if I have a look, now, will ye?"

"You t-t-trust me not."

" 'Tis my job, Father." There was the stomp of feet and the cart jostled with the guard's weight. *Dear God in heaven, please save me.* With a wrenching squeak one of the coffin lids was raised. Golden light shined through the knotholes of Gwynn's box.

Sweat soaked Gwynn's skin. Breathing was nearly impossible.

"Yea. 'Tis Bartholomew, poor old sod. A better miller we'll never have."

"Aye, 'tis true," Anthony replied, his voice nervous as the sound of horses and soldiers reached her ears. Shouts, jangles of harnesses and armor, the anxious whinnies of steeds being mounted.

The second coffin was pried open and the guard sighed. " 'Tis hard to see a child so. I saw her just yesterday chasing the piggies."

"Listen, man," the priest said solemnly. "Th-thi-this is enough desecration of the d-dead!"

"As I said, 'tis my job. 'Tis not that I want to look upon the dead, believe you me." The guard's bar squeezed through the lid and box of the coffin and creaking, the top popped open. Gwynn felt a rush of cool, welcome air. She closed her eyes but could see through her lids some flickering orange light as the sentry held his torch aloft.

"Ahh, Brenna. We'll miss ya, lass."

Do not let him see me, please God. Gwynn held her breath and the seconds stretched endlessly.

"Hurry, man."

With a thud the lid was in place again. "Ye may pass."

Thank you, Gwynn said silently. The cart started rolling forward again and Gwynn suffered the stale air and close quarters gratefully as the scrawny woman's cold hand brushed against hers. In the dark, she heard the portcullis clanking open and the echo of the ass's hooves as it pulled the heavy load over the bridge crossing the moat.

Only a little while longer would she have to endure this misery. However it seemed forever until the priest ordered "Whoa," and the wagon stopped its uneven movement.

"God forgive me," he muttered as he pried the lid open and yanked Brenna's breathless body off Gwynn. Without wasting a second, Gwynn scrambled free and bit her lip to keep from retching as she climbed out of the coffin and down the side of the cart.

"Thank you, Father," she said, shuddering as he gently replaced Brenna's body into the casket. "And, Idelle, thank her for me as well."

He frowned. "Idelle. 'Twas her idea."

"But it would not have worked had you not helped."

He sighed and glanced at the castle walls. "Be well, m'lady. And, p-p-please, think fondly of R-Roderick."

"And you, Father Anthony."

"Aye, now be off before we both be caught and end up praying for our souls at the gallows."

"Bless you." Lifting her skirts, she hurried through the cemetery, dodging graves and their tombstones as she made her way through wet grass and weeds to the forest.

No matter what else she encountered, she would find her son.

And what of his father?

She felt a little guilty about leaving Trevin in Rhydd but knew deep in her heart that he would find his way safely free. She fingered the pouch of jewels she'd put in the pocket of her cloak. She couldn't think too much of Trevin. 'Twas dangerous.

After thirteen years she'd thought any emotion she may have felt for him would be long dead. Oh, how very wrong she'd been. As she thought of his body pressed so closely to hers in the stables, her thoughts spun out of control. Her heart began to beat wildly, as if in anticipation of his kiss.

Foolish, foolish woman! What think you? You know better than to give your heart to a thief, for, if you do, you can be certain he will surely steal it.

Chapter Five

Curse and rot his foolish hide, where the devil was Trevin? Muir paced through the mist, his good eye trained to the east, his patience wearing as thin as the dew-soaked spiderwebs glistening with the coming of the dawn. Three nights he'd waited, two long days, expecting Trevin to appear, only to be disappointed and stuck with the lad and his incessant questions.

"Why must we wait for him?"

"Is he naught but a murdering thief?"

"What does he want with me?"

"Come, old man, let us be off."

Chatter, chatter, chatter coupled with the half-grown hound's yipping caused Muir's head to pound. The dog was always running off chasing birds and rodents and anything that dared move within his earshot. Oh, 'twas a pitiful lot old Muir had been handed and not a drop of ale or wine to help ease his burden.

"So where is this thief-baron?" Gareth asked, stretching his gangly arms over his head and blinking from recent sleep. The damned cur was beside him, yawning and showing off clean white fangs.

"He'll be here." Or would he? Had he not said wait but two days?

Gareth scowled. "How do you know?"

"Because he keeps his word."

"Oh, I'll just wager he does. The murdering, thieving, cheater who stole his castle from a half-daft old man? *He* keeps his word?" Gareth shook the dust from his hair. "Bah!"

"Ye must have faith, boy."

"Why? I needs be off."

"Do ye now? And what will keep ye from fallin' arse over crown into the hands of Baron Ian's soldiers?"

"I fear them not," Gareth said boldly.

"Then a fool ye be, for they'd just as soon slit your throat as speak with ye."

The boy had the brains to shudder and look over his shoulder as if he expected the soldiers of Rhydd to be hiding in the thicket of oak trees guarding a small pond. Oh, he was like his father, he was, and, a bit like his grandfather though that thought rankled Muir and, as always, he held his tongue. Trevin's ancestry was a secret he would keep with him to the grave.

Muir had raised Trevin from a babe, taught him the ways of the streets, turned his blind eye as all too easily Trevin had learned how to slide a penny out of a rich man's purse. As a lad, he'd asked often enough about his mother, but Muir had kept his promise and had lied to the boy, telling him he knew not who had borne or spawned him, that Trevin, as a swaddled babe, had been left on the doorstep of his hut. Over the years, as Trevin had grown working as a stable boy before he'd decided thievery was an easier lot, he'd quit questioning his birth.

So now, what to do? Muir and the boy could not stay here much longer. The lad and pup were growing restless, the horse needed more feed than the forest offered and the few stores he had with him—smoked meat and bread—were about gone. Eventually, should they stay, they would be discovered. However, they could not return to Black Oak for a while for fear they might encounter Ian of Rhydd's soldiers along the road.

He considered using a spell or two, then discarded the idea. What he really needed was a cup of ale. Mayhap more than one.

The sun peeked over the eastern hills, sending forth a blaze of light that burned through the mist and caused long shadows to fall over the damp ground. Muir took the sunlight as a good omen. They would wait one more day and then, by the gods, they would break camp.

And go where?

For the love of Myrddin, 'twas a vexation.

In the middle of the first night, wearing the colors of Rhydd, Trevin had let his horse lag behind the rest of the mounted soldiers, then turned his steed into the forest. He'd ridden far to the east following the course of the river, crossing the swift-moving current where the waters were shallow. Once on the far bank, he'd avoided the main roads, traveling on deer trails and shepherd's paths that slashed through the hills and cut into the dense forests.

He'd urged his horse onward mostly at night, hidden and rested his steed during the middle of the day and used his own sense of direction as well as the pale light of the moon and stars whenever the heavens were clear.

Finally, convinced that he'd created a cold, endless trail for his enemies, he'd forced his horse to swim across the river again a few miles downstream from the cave.

He'd hoped to miss the search party. However, the new Baron of Rhydd's soldiers were nothing if not dogged. They had not given up their search. Twice Trevin had spied groups of warriors, search parties of trained huntsmen and hounds who had fanned through the forest. The dogs had galloped wildly, sniffed, bayed, and turned in circles of confusion, causing their keepers to order them onward and snap whips at their backsides. Each time Trevin had eluded his pursuers, but his luck would not hold forever and, he feared, Ian of Rhydd would never give up.

Now, 'twas dusk again and, with his stomach growling from lack of food, he'd renewed his journey. He had to make his way to the cave and find his boy. Ian had not had enough time to mount a siege of Black Oak Castle, but 'twas only a matter of days.

What if Muir had not found Gareth? What if the boy was again in Ian's cruel hands? What of Gwynn? Had she escaped the walls of Rhydd or was she again facing the brute who was her husband? Trevin's back teeth ground together at the thought of Ian's hand slapping her, his foul mouth kissing her. Though Gwynn was legally Ian's wife, Trevin couldn't accept the thought of the older man bedding her.

'Twas he who should make love to her as he had in the past. 'Twas he who should feel her lips move sensually upon his skin, he who should taste the sweetness of her and watch her silver-green eyes widen as he entered her. Ah, sweet Christ, how he would love to entwine his body with hers.

Bitterly he thought that laying with her might be a way of savoring a dark revenge against Ian, but he discarded the idea quickly. Though Gwynn was no saint, he would not use her so cruelly. Nor did he dare care for her. He'd made a vow . . .

Did Gwynn not lay with you for her own purposes?

He swore under his breath. Gwynn, damn her, was sinful vexation! Where was she and how had she, in so few hours, become his concern? 'Twas his boy he was after, not the woman who bore him. Yet she filled his thoughts, day and night. Be careful.

For years he'd considered her spoiled and vain. Hadn't she bargained and lain with him to bear a child and pass the boy off as Roderick's to save her own pretty neck? Beautiful, she'd been, and passionate. The days and nights lying with her had been pure heaven though she'd been coldly plotting to achieve that which suited her.

The years, rather than ravage her beauty, had been kind and bestowed upon her a depth, a nobility, that he hadn't expected to find. No longer was she a scheming vixen. She appeared to be willing to do anything, even marry Ian of Rhydd to save her son—*his son*—from the hangman's noose. As beautiful as ever, she now possessed a spark of pride that he couldn't trust. Nor did he want to.

His dark thoughts chased through his head as he turned onto a little-used road leading through thickets of bare-branched trees to an old, abandoned mill he'd used as a lair when once, long ago, he'd been an outlaw. A smile toyed upon the corners of his lips for he missed those bawdy irreverent days when he along with others much like him had banded together. He was much better suited as a criminal than a nobleman, he thought and wondered at the turn of events that had led him to rule Black Oak Hall. 'Twas a joke.

He drew up the reins and his horse slowed near a stream that splashed over rocks and pooled near the ruins of a toppled stone tower. A rotted water wheel moved listlessly, broken paddles causing the axle to creak and lurch as it turned slowly with the current.

". . . and keep him safe."

Gwynn's voice floated on the breeze as if from a dream.

Trevin slid out of his saddle quietly and, leading his horse made his way through a patch of undergrowth to a shady glen where Gwynn, her back to him, drew the three-clawed rune that looked like a rooster's foot, then tossed dust into the gathering darkness. A small twig of mistletoe—a herb for protection—was laid at the base of an ash tree.

Christ Jesus, she was beautiful.

In the coming night, the wind caught in her skirts and played with the long, fiery strands of hair that had escaped her hood. She turned her face to the sky and murmured words he didn't understand from lips he'd kissed so long ago, lips he'd never forgotten. He'd heard from his spies at Rhydd that she'd practiced the dark arts she'd learned from old Idelle, but until this moment, he hadn't believed the rumors.

She fell to her knees and bent her head, whispering a prayer to the Christian God over her pagan scratchings in the dirt.

His lungs constricted, as they seemed to each time he looked upon her. As he watched, her lips moved soundlessly yet he knew she was praying for the safety of their child. A boy who was not with her. Pagan rites and Christian prayers, whatever was necessary to keep Gareth safe.

Her mount, a sorry-looking beast favoring his right foreleg, flicked his dark ears then let out a whinny. Gwynn turned quickly, her face set as she reached to her belt where a small dagger was sheathed. "Who goes there?"

"Shh."

Her eyes widened in fear for a second before they found his. "For the love of God, Trevin, you nearly scared the life out of me! You wear the colors of Rhydd." Relief stole over her features. "I thought you were one of Ian's men."

" 'Tis but my disguise for my escape."

"So you are alone?"

"Aye."

"Where's Gareth?" she asked hopefully.

Trevin's stomach tightened into knots. "I had hoped he be with you."

"Nay," she said and again worry caused lines to purse her lips and etch her forehead.

"Have you not seen an old magician in the forest?"

"Magician?"

"Yea, a sorcerer who has little hair, a thick white beard, one good eye, and a lust for wine."

Slowly she shook her head and her eyes narrowed in suspicion. "Tell me not that you are trusting this . . . this drunk of a wizard with my son's life."

"Gareth will be safe with Muir."

"Oh, for the love of all that is holy!" She threw up her hands and stared at the dark heavens as if hoping for divine intervention. Her cheeks were a sweet pink hue, her lips darker still. He felt an unwanted tightening in his groin and silently called himself every kind of fool. " 'Tis a madman you are, Trevin of Black Oak," she chastised with a tired sigh. "An old man with one eye and a need for drink?"

"A good man he is."

"Aye, and probably spends his days trying to turn water into wine."

"I think he leaves that for the Son of God," Trevin replied without hiding any of his sarcasm. "And who be you to judge, lady. Did I not catch you chanting a spell?"

"For Gareth's safety."

"Aye."

"And for my horse who is lame," she said with a scowl. "I bought him from a farmer who assured me he was sound, but—"

"Let me look." Trevin approached the animal and watched the gelding's muscles quiver and ears flatten in distrust. " 'Tis all right," he said softly and ran practiced hands over the beast's muscles, encouraging the bay to lift his leg. The horse snorted, but complied.

In the darkness, Trevin bent the animal's leg and caught it between his thighs. Gently prodding, he found a stone, lodged deep in the center of the gelding's hoof and as he touched the embedded pebble, the horse let out a whinny of pain and tried to pull away. "Don't move, you devil," Trevin commanded, but could not dislodge the sharp little rock.

" 'Twill have to wait till morn," he said as he allowed the palfrey to stand on its own again.

"We cannot. We must find Gareth."

"With a lame horse?"

"If we must walk—"

Voices, muted and distant, reach him. As quickly as lightning striking, he grabbed Gwynn and clamped a hand over her mouth.

"Wha—" She struggled against him until she, too, heard the thud of hooves and jangling bridles that rippled through the forest. Gwynn froze. All protests died on her lips. Through her small body, he felt her heart pounding in fear.

Torches winked with an eerie golden light from the main road, two single rows of eight flames blinking behind the trees, but moving ever steadily toward the old mill.

"Come," he whispered into her ear.

In silent agreement, they took up the reins of both their mounts and dashed swiftly through the creek. The horses splashed but didn't give out a betraying neigh. Water, cold as a January snow seeped through his boots and worry gnawed deep at his soul. He would not let them find her, would die rather than let her be taken by Ian of Rhydd's men.

That thought jolted him. Why did he care? Aye, she was Gareth's mother, but nothing more. Comely, yes. Smart, aye, but worth giving up his life?

Gwynn slipped but didn't cry out.

Trevin caught her arm before she fell and was completely immersed. He didn't let go, but pulled her through the water and helped her up the slick mud of the far bank.

Noiselessly they ducked into a dense copse of pine trees just as the small company of soldiers reached the clearing surrounding the mill.

"We'll camp here," a strong male voice that caused Trevin's innards to congeal ordered. Webb, huge and imposing, swung off the back of a sturdy black destrier with a crooked blaze. Landing with a curse, Webb limped to the gaping door of the mill and rubbed his arm. "Bastard of a boy. I can't wait to get me hands on that one."

Beside Trevin, Gwynn tensed, her face as pale as death.

"He'll learn who to slice with a sword or the devil will take my soul," Webb vowed.

Gwynn gasped and would have jumped forward to defend her son, but once again Trevin held her fast. One hand clamped over her lips, his other arm banded

her body as she strained against him. "Later," he
mouthed against her ear, for he understood her need
to do bodily damage to the man who threatened their
child. 'Twas all Trevin could do to restrain himself
and the furious woman in his arms. "Leave him to
me." His lips curled, his eyes slitted, and every muscle
in his body coiled as if for a fight. He would have
liked nothing better than to slam his fist into Webb's
ugly jaw, but now was not the time.

Patience, as ever, was a virtue.

Carrying a torch aloft, Webb hitched himself into
the mill. Trevin tracked his enemy's movements within
the building by the shafts of light that spilled through
the cracks in the mortar and the few windows.

The small army was going to settle for the night.
Soon all but a sentry or two would be asleep. "Come,"
Trevin whispered into Gwynn's ear and, thank the
saints, for once she obeyed.

He led her and the horses along a dark trail away
from the clearing and up a steep hill. As night settled
around them and the dense forest grew black as pitch,
they plodded slowly, inching their way forward
through overgrown branches or stumbling over exposed roots and mole holes. Winding ever upward, the
path was steep and Gwynn's gelding plodded reluctantly, limping on his foreleg and pulling against the
bit.

"We must make our leave," Trevin said as they
reached a knoll unfettered by trees. Wind raced across
the hill, bending the grass, smelling of rain. "But we
go too slowly afoot, your horse is lame and my mount
is tired." He rubbed his chin as a plan formed in his
mind. 'Twas a risk, but one worth the price. He smiled
to himself. "I think it best if we borrow a few horses
from Sir Webb."

"What?" Gwynn said and in the moonlight he saw her beautiful eyes round as she understood his meaning. "Nay, Trevin, 'tis too dangerous. Webb would like nothing better than to have the excuse and opportunity to kill you."

"I thought you wanted to slit his throat yourself."

"I would if I could save Gareth, but Ian will only send more men and then, I, too, would be found guilty of murder." She scowled in the darkness, her face puckering in worry. Aye, she was as beautiful as a goddess and just as scheming.

"No harm will come to my son," Trevin pledged. "Trust me." He handed her the reins of his horse and slid the bridle from the lame gelding's head. "Release this one," he ordered, "and ride mine ever south. I will catch up with you."

"No, I don't—"

"Listen, woman, 'tis our only chance."

"And if you do not return?" Her chin jutted proudly forward, her eyes held his. Oh, how he wanted to reach forward and stroke the smooth skin stretched upon her jaw, but he didn't. He had no time to lose himself in her, no time to contemplate his baffling fate of caring for her, no time to think of a promise he'd made long ago, to another woman.

"I will be back."

"Brave words from a foolish man. What happens if you are captured?" Her chin wobbled slightly, as if she were afraid for him, as if she cared a bit. But surely he was imagining things; she thought only of herself and her boy. "How shall I find this Muir and my son?" she asked sharply.

"Muir and Gareth will find you."

"So now I am to trust some half-blind drunken sorcerer and a boy."

"Nay," he said and gave into a foolish impulse. Though he knew it was a mistake, his arms folded around Ian of Rhydd's bride and he lowered his head, his chilled lips claiming hers in a kiss that brought back memories from another time, another place. She jerked back, only to sag against him and sigh, her resistance fleeing upon the wind. A tremor slid through his body and desire, unwanted and wild, stormed through his blood. He pulled her roughly to him and kissed her until his head was spinning. "You are to trust only me, m'lady," he said into her open mouth. "Only me." He released her swiftly and she nearly fell. Dear God, what had he been thinking?

"Trevin—?"

He turned on his heel. "I will find you," he promised and damned himself. Memories crowded into his mind.

Vow to me, Trevin, that you'll never love another woman. Swear it. His dying wife's words haunted him still.

His response rang hollowly through his soul. I swear. On my life, Faith. I will never love another.

By the time Trevin reached the encampment, the torches had burned low. Two soldiers guarded the tethered horses and though he'd hoped to find the sentries asleep, they stood together, talking and joking and seeming as if they would never nod off. One was a burly man whose laughter was but a rasp, the other was gaunt and tall, the kind of man who was little more than a skeleton sprinkled with a few pounds of flesh and skin. He held the other guard's attention, telling bawdy tales that came to Trevin's ears in bits and pieces.

". . . a sweet plump arse she had, that one . . . lifted

her skirts for any man who would buy her a pint . . .
her friend was a shrew, cackled like a mud hen . . ."

In the shadows of the trees Trevin slid his dagger
from its sheath and held it between his teeth as he
crept between the horses' legs. His plan was simple:
Slide the bridle he'd brought with him over the head
of the strongest of the lot, cut the line holding all the
animals together, slap as many as possible on their
rumps and as the steeds squealed, wheeled, and reared
in panic, steal away in the ensuing melee. By the time
all the beasts had been rounded up and it was discovered that one was missing, he and the horse would be
long gone.

". . . I tell ye, mate, a better little ride ye'd never
find this side of . . ."

Smiling grimly to himself, Trevin found the horse
he recognized as Webb's charger—a strong black stallion with a crooked white slash running down his nose.
Carefully, his gaze fastened on the two guards, Trevin
laid a hand upon the destrier's thick neck. Hot flesh
quivered beneath a smooth coat. The horse sidestepped and snorted and Trevin ducked as one of the
guards' gaze swept toward him.

"Quiet," the big man growled and for a few seconds
there was no noise save the breathing and stomping
of hooves. The charger shifted and a heavy hoof
landed on the toe of Trevin's boot. Pain screamed up
his leg and he nearly dropped the knife from between
his teeth.

An owl hooted and again the horse shifted. "Oh,
bugger," the guard said. " 'Tis only a silly bird. One
I'd shoot with me arrow, if 'tweren't so dark." He
turned back to the other sentry and slowly Trevin let
out his breath. He was sweating, his muscles so tense
they ached.

Without so much as the clink of the metal fasteners, he placed his bridle over the black's head. The charger rolled a white-rimmed eye, snorted, and kicked. Another horse shrieked in pain.

"Say, wha—?"

Trevin didn't wait. He grabbed the knife from his mouth. With one swift stroke, he severed the rope binding the herd together.

"Did ye hear somethin'?"

"Oh, Holy Christ!"

Trevin hoisted himself onto the black's back. The horse reared. Other animals screamed, bucking and rearing. Tethers snapped. Leaning low on his mount, his head pounding, Trevin slapped several stallions on their rumps with his reins.

Hooves thundered.

Frightened neighs rang through the woods.

"Halt! Who goes—oh, fer the bloody love of Saint Peter!"

Horses scattered wildly. Hoofbeats rumbled through the forest. Branches snapped. The guards yelled.

Trevin clung to the back of the destrier, ducking low, heading him toward the creek.

"Sir Webb!"

"Wake, ye bloody fools!"

"What in the devil's name?" Webb's voice boomed through the night. "Get them! Damn it all to hell, catch them!"

Trevin spurred his mount toward the creek.

Horses shot through the trees.

Guards chased after them.

"Move, damn you!" Trevin ordered.

The charger took the stream in one leap. With a jarring thud he landed on the other side and tore up the hillside. Branches slapped at Trevin, the horse stumbled several times and shouts and frightened whinnies chased after them. "Come on you miserable scrap of horseflesh," Trevin growled, hugging low, urging the beast forward and smiling to himself. "Run!"

"What the bloody hell happened?" Webb yelled, but his voice was muffled over the sound of the charger's hoofbeats and heavy breathing. Trevin didn't hear the response, but grinned grimly to himself at the thought of besting the man who had sworn to kill his son.

Gwynn glanced over her shoulder. It had been hours since Trevin had left her on his fool's mission and her heart beat with a steady rhythm of doom. His silly plan could have turned against him; mayhap even now he was Webb's prisoner, beaten and bloody, forced to reveal Gareth's whereabouts. At that thought she clucked to the horse, forcing him from a slow walk to a quick trot. The moon was low, the air chilly with a wind that cut through her damp cloak and tunic. She'd met few travelers this night, only a lonely friar upon a donkey and a farmer driving a team of oxen struggling with a heavy wagon. Both meetings had been hours before, when darkness was new.

With icy fingers she touched her lips and remembered Trevin's kiss, so hard and firm and hot. A deep ache settled far below her stomach and she called herself a dozen kinds of a fool for the sinful want only he seemed to be able to inspire within her. Whether she liked it or not, she was a wedded woman once again and though her marriage vows were falsely given in exchange for her son's life, they were nonetheless considered sacred by God and church.

What foul luck she had.

Had she learned nothing in thirteen years? Her traitorous body even now remembered the touch and feel of a young thief's hands. Hands that trembled as he stroked her breast, fingers that were warm and steady and knowing. Now that boy was a full-grown man, mayhap a murderer but surely the father of her only son. He was a man to avoid, an outlaw baron whose castle was stolen in a game of chance. Oh, wayward, wayward heart!

Far in the distance, hoofbeats rang through the night, as if the rider were trying to outrace Satan himself. Trevin. Surely he'd finally caught up with her. Or was it someone else? One of Ian's men? A robber or other criminal escaping justice? Her mount was tired and she couldn't outrun a fresh horse, nor would she want to if the rider proved to be Trevin, yet there was no place to hide, no cover of building, bridge, nor woods in this section of rutted road. Though the moon was but a slit behind thin clouds, the fields on either side stretched into the gloom.

From the sound, only one rider approached, so Gwynn pulled up her hood and slid her dagger from its sheath. Should the lonely horseman be someone other than Trevin, she would be ready.

Glancing over her shoulder she saw a dark form approaching, a rider hunched over the shoulders of a huge destrier. The steed was mud-speckled and lathered and even in the darkness, Gwynn recognized Trevin's tall shape. He rode easily, as if he'd spent his entire life upon such a magnificent animal.

Her stupid heart leapt and Trevin's smile, a slash of white, caused an answering twitch in her own lips. Ah, he was a handsome one, she couldn't deny it. Even in the darkness, his eyes shone bright, his dark jaw was hard and square, and his shoulders wide and muscular. He drew back on the reins and his horse, blowing loudly, fell into step with hers. "Did I not tell you I would return?" he asked.

"Aye."

"You doubted me." His voice held a note of jest, as if he were pleased with himself.

"Always."

" 'Tis a mistake to underestimate me, Gwynn." He let out a laugh that echoed across the barren fields. "Sir Webb discovered that tonight. Now, not only is he half crippled—"

"That be Gareth's doing."

"Was it?" Trevin's laughter again rippled across the night-shrouded countryside. "Good. Now, the dark knight has no horse." Trevin patted his steed on his sweaty neck.

"So Webb will be more determined than ever to find us and Gareth," she said, failing to see any humor in the situation. "I'm afraid all you've done is make him a more treacherous enemy, Trevin. Now, 'tis certain he will not rest until he's captured our son."

"He won't get the chance," Trevin assured her, but the smile fell from his face and his countenance turned fierce as a cornered wolf. Gwynn shivered as a gust of wind swept over the land and chilled her to her very soul.

God help us, she silently prayed, but felt the knell of doom ring deep in her heart.

Chapter Six

"You helped her escape!" Ian pounded a fist upon the table in the great hall while that spineless worm Father Anthony shivered and shook in front of him.

His mazer of wine spilled, red liquid splashing onto the scarred oaken tabletop. The man was a buffoon.

The hounds, miserable animals, had been sleeping near the keep's door. At the outburst they jumped to their feet and began barking wildly.

"Shut up!" Ian ordered and both animals circled and settled back to their positions, letting out disgruntled woofs as the priest, fool that he was, licked his lips anxiously.

Ian turned his attention back to the pathetic excuse of a man before him. Were it not for the fact that Father Anthony was a man of the cloth and respected by everyone in the castle, he would have flogged a confession from his lying tongue.

"I know n-not of wh-wh-what you speak, m'lord," the good priest insisted, sweat sliding down the sides of his face, his Adam's apple bobbing nervously, his beringed fingers playing with a heavy gold cross suspended from a chain upon his neck.

Ian wanted nothing more than to clasp the links of that chain in his fist and choke the fool. Instead he motioned for the page who was quick to wipe up the mess and refill his cup. "Do not lie to me, Anthony. Need I remind you 'tis a sin to lie?" He lifted a skeptical eyebrow and watched the skinny man squirm deep in his vestments. "No one left the castle that night but the soldiers and you. All soldiers, except one have been accounted for. Somehow the thief managed to disguise himself as one of my men and soon we will find the missing sentry's body."

That thought rankled as well, for it meant either the men he trusted to guard the castle were bloody fools or there was a traitor in their midst. "As for the lady, she made her escape with you."

"B-but, my lord, the guard, he ch-checked the coffins."

Ian's head throbbed, his legs where Trevin's sword had sliced into his shins ached painfully and the mortification of being played for an idiot by the likes of Trevin McBain confounded him. This stuttering idiot of a liar did nothing to help his disposition. "Now," he said with false patience, "you may tell me the truth in here alone and be saved the public humiliation of a trial." He sipped from his cup. "You will not win."

"But—"

"The sentry who checked the coffins that you carted to the graveyard now says he can't remember if he saw all the bodies."

"But he opened each casket!" Father Anthony argued. "There was the miller, Bartholomew, and Brenna, and the little girl, Kate. You must believe—"

"What I believe is that you were a loyal and trusting servant of my brother, but that your allegiance to me as the new baron lacks sufficient . . ." he looked toward the high ceiling, where years of smoke had darkened the trusses, searching as if he expected to find the correct word in the dusty rafters, ". . . well, let us say portent."

"Please, m'lord, t-t-trust me." Father Anthony knelt on the other side of the table, his Adam's apple bobbing nervously. "I am but your faithful servant."

'Twas sickening, this display of false loyalty. "There are ways to test your devotion, you know."

Anthony gulped.

"Would you drown in the river if held under, or would your faith save you? Could you walk along a bed of coals and your skin not be burned, or, if you were unfaithful, would—"

"Please, you m-m-must believe me, Lord Ian. I am a true servant of Rhydd."

He was near the breaking point and Ian was relieved. He hated to see a man of the cloth grovel.

"We'll see what the guard has to say." Ian snapped his fingers and motioned to a knight standing at attention near the door of the keep. "Call in—"

The door flew open, banging against the wall and sending the dogs into a barking frenzy. Sir Webb, his face flushed, his dark eyes flashing was fairly shivering with rage.

Now what? Ian wondered, knowing instinctively that Webb was not the bearer of good news.

The dark knight strode into the great hall. "M'lord," he said through clenched teeth, then cast the priest a look that would melt the strongest steel. "I needs to have words with ye."

"And I with you." Ian waved off the priest. "I'll deal with you later."

"Th-th-th-thank you, m'lord." Father Anthony, sweating and scurrying away like an insect, took flight. Muttering to himself, he disappeared up the stairs.

Ian braced himself for what he expected was a

round of bad news and a bevy of excuses. "Where is the boy?"

"We found him not."

"I assume you took the trouble to look."

"He's a slippery one, he is."

"Right." His headache pounding, Ian took a swig from his mazer. "What of McBain?"

"Disappeared as well," Webb growled, rubbing the shoulder where he'd been stabbed. "With, I fear, my best horse."

"Wait a minute. Were you not to take a search party out and then, peel off so that you could put an end to the boy's life? I expected you, and your party, to return with a few corpses and another wound for your trouble." Ian struggled to his feet and his legs burned with sudden pain—fresh, hot, and angry—that screamed up his shins and festered in his knees. He sucked in his breath and glowered at the knight in whom his brother had devoted so much trust. "You have failed me."

" 'Tis only a delay."

"You were paid."

"Not yet enough," Webb said, unmoved.

Wincing, Ian fell into his chair and ground his teeth against the pulsating sting that the thief had wrought. "Do not dare to say that you have not at least returned with my wife."

Webb's lips lifted into a sneer. "She, too, has vanished."

Ian's eyes closed for a second. Cretins. He was surrounded by moronic, simpleminded Cretins. He saw a movement in the curtains that separated this room from the hallway and wondered who was listening in the shadows. "Lady Gwynn has not vanished," he said, motioning to the crevice where whoever was hiding lingered. "She is somewhere. Hiding. Searching for her child."

"Mayhap with the thief," Webb admitted. Quietly he walked around the table. "Though they left not together, we found a lame horse near the mill where mine was taken and tracks of two animals as well as boot prints, some belonging to a fair-sized man, the other much smaller, belonging to a woman."

"So you're telling me that my wife is with Trevin of Black Oak." He had expected as much, of course. Gwynn had been aided in her escape by McBain, but he'd been told that they had somehow left the castle by separate means and he'd hoped that they were not together. Jealousy spurted through his blood. For years he'd waited for her—his brother's wife who had so callously slept with another man and borne a child whom she'd portrayed as being Roderick's spawn. A lying whore, she was, but a beauty he'd wanted for as long as he could remember even when he'd been married to that watery-eyed lass, Margaret. What a cold fish she'd been, lying and not moving as he'd entered her. Her bed had been like a tomb.

But with Gwynn things would be different. She was a fiery one, his brother's wife. Ian's crotch tightened in anticipation. He could not wait to bed her. He would watch her eyes round as he penetrated her fiercely, claiming her as his own, feeling her soft body close around him. He would take her over and over again, in as many ways as he wanted and each time he'd feel a renewed power in her submission.

Mayhap Trevin, the thief, could watch her taming.

Webb opened the curtain and found a woman cowering in the alcove. Frannie the weaver. Brown hair, doe-soft eyes, teeth a little too large, and small lips. "Why are you not at your loom?" he asked.

"Forgive me, Lord Ian, I am but checkin' these curtains. The mistress . . . she, er, she told me we would be needing to clean these or replace them .. and I was wondering how much velvet 'twould take . . ."

Ian didn't believe her for a minute. There were many servants loyal to Gwynn within the castle walls, freemen and peasants who would gladly turn on him if she but gave the word. "You may take the measurements later," he said. "And should you breathe a word of what you overheard here, good woman, your days here would be numbered."

She gulped. "But, m'lord, I—"

"Do not test my patience."

With a quick curtsy, she turned and, heels clicking, scurried away.

"A spy?" Webb asked.

"Mayhap." Ian stroked his beard. He felt the undercurrents of dissatisfaction in the castle, had heard a few servants gossiping that he'd forced Gwynn to marry him, that he'd banished her son. He would have to tread lightly for he didn't relish the thought of an uprising.

"M'lord"—Webb's voice brought him out of his troubled thoughts—" 'tis tricked I was," he admitted. "And it cost me my best charger. But now the outlaw has not only stolen a horse from Rhydd but kidnapped the baron's wife. Surely there should be a price placed upon his head."

Ian glared at his brother's most trusted man. In truth he despised Webb, for the dark knight had ruined his plans in helping Roderick find freedom that Ian had paid for dearly. Keeping Baron Hamilton in gold had been costly, but Ian had been assured that Roderick would never escape. Until Sir Webb had ruined his plans. 'Twas lucky that fate had stepped in and the baron's false son had run him through, killing Roderick and ensuring Ian's rule. "You will be paid well for your trouble, Sir Webb, I've told you as much. But you've failed me. I wish you to kill the boy, capture the thief, and bring my beloved wife back to me." The smile he pasted upon his face was cold as death. "Is that too much to ask?"

"Nay, m'lord," Webb said, but his eyes flashed in anger and Ian realized that the dark knight liked taking orders from no one, including the new master of Rhydd. Webb could, for the right price, turn against Ian.

"Take fresh horses and rested soldiers—ten of each—and find the traitors. Deal with them as we have planned. Leave the rest to me. As soon as I've healed enough to ride, I will lead an army to Black Oak and lay siege upon the keep of the bastard who dared defy me and made my wife a traitor to her own castle." He rubbed the bandages on his legs and winced at the pain.

Trevin of Black Oak had been bold enough to wound him twice. The scar running down the side of his face had never disappeared and now, this new ringing pain in his legs. "Trevin McBain will be captured, tried, and proved to be a murdering kidnapper. The gallows will be too good for him." Ian warmed to his thoughts. "I'll see him drawn and quartered, his entrails spilled and his head cut off to be displayed from the north tower where all in the castle, including my wife, will be reminded of the price of disloyalty."

He motioned to a page with stringy hair and a bad complexion for yet another cup of wine. His legs felt a little better. The pain pounding through his brain had dulled. Time was, as it always had been, on his side. He just had to remember to be patient. 'Twas difficult. Very difficult.

" 'Tis daft you be," Gareth said as he watched the old man draw stick figures in the dry soil near the mouth of the cave. He was strange with his one eye, need for drink, useless cane, and gnarled fingers. He talked of curious images, of bloody links of a chain, of a future of ruin, of visions seen through a sightless eye. Daft. That was what he was. Mindless.

"Nay, child. Hush and keep that infernal dog away from me." The pup was playing, romping through the thickets, startling winter birds and growling at unseen prey scrambling through the underbrush.

"Boon is no trouble," Gareth muttered, his stomach grumbling in protest.

"Hush, child, ye disturb me thoughts."

The pup, ever curious, bounded over to the magician and grabbed at the ragged end of his cloak. Snapping firm jaws around the muddy hem, he pulled backward, nearly toppling Muir in the process. "By Pwyll, ye're a wretched little cur. Get away."

"Pwyll's a demon," Gareth protested.

The pup growled and backed up, shaking his head swiftly from side to side, ripping the old cloth.

"I should turn ye into a toad, or a snake or tortoise, ye dumb mutt." Muir lifted his cane as if to strike the dog or cast a spell.

"Nay!" Gareth leapt forward, but the pup scrambled away, the tired fabric of Muir's cloak tearing. As the cane came down, Boon, tail tucked beneath his legs, dashed into the forest, only to turn and peek backward, his face nearly hidden by the fronds of a fern, the prized piece of cloth dangling from his mouth.

"Ahh, now see what he's done." Muir glanced at the sky and rubbed his forehead as if staving off a great pain. With a quick damning glance at the dog, then a longer look at the cloudy heavens and position of the sun, were it visible, he muttered, " 'Tis time we were off."

"I thought we were supposed to wait for your friend."

"Aye, but we've tarried long enough as it is." Muir's eyebrows collided over his scarred visage. "Unless we want to face Ian of Rhydd's wrath."

Gareth was glad to be away from the cave. Inside, the darkness seemed to close in on him and the dusty air was hard to breathe. Asides, he was tired of sitting and waiting, of trying to trap rabbits and squirrels who seemed far more clever than he suspected. Without his bow and quiver filled with arrows, he was a useless hunter. Even the fish in the stream escaped his hands. He whistled to the pup, who, still keeping a wary eye on Muir, crawled from the bracken, the scrap still hanging from his jaws.

The magician paid no attention to the dog. "Come along, come along," he said, as if, after days of inactivity, he was anxious to be gone. " 'Tis less than two days ride to Black Oak."

"Why must we go there?"

" 'Tis safe."

"Did you not say there would be a siege on the castle?"

"Aye, but 'tis not yet."

"How do you know?"

"I have seen it."

"Yea, yea, as you have seen so many things that make no sense through that bad eye of yours."

"All will be revealed in time," Muir said pointing

toward the cave with his cane. "Now, do not dawdle. We must gather our things and be away. There is fine food and drink at Black Oak."

Gareth's stomach squeezed at the thought of trenchers of gravy, sausages, a joint of venison, and banberry tarts. His mouth watered at the thought of jellied eggs, stuffed eel, and hunks of bread with butter and honey dripping onto his fingers. For a moment his hunger outweighed another more pressing concern, a thought that had nagged at him ever since escaping Rhydd. "What of my mother?" he asked as thoughts of sizzling meat and sweet pies disappeared. "Is she safe?"

"That I cannot say."

"Of course she is not; she married Sir Ian." Gareth frowned at the thought. He'd never trusted his uncle, had always considered him lazy and lustful. All too often Gareth had seen the older man leer at girls decades younger than he and though he'd been married to Margaret, he'd lifted the skirts of many a kitchen maid.

For as long as Gareth could remember he was uncomfortable around Ian and had known that the old knight had lusted after his mother.

"She married Ian so that I would not be killed." The idea galled him and since leaving the castle guilt had been forever his companion. "I needs know she is safe."

"That I have not seen," Muir admitted.

"Some visions you have, old man. Seems they only come when 'tis convenient for you."

"Let us not argue."

"She is married to a pig," Gareth said, wishing he could have the pleasure of running Ian of Rhydd through.

"Boy!" Muir's voice brought him back to the here and now. "Get on with it, would ye?" The old magician had flung a bridle over his horse's head. " 'Tis time."

Gareth helped the old man onto his nag and then with Boon bounding behind them, followed the plodding horse. Deep in his pocket, he rubbed a smooth stone for luck. As much as he wanted a hot meal and a softer bed than the pallet within the cave, he needed to know that his mother was safe.

The cave was empty.

Trevin used still-warm coals to relight the fire. Though there were signs that Muir and his young charge had recently occupied the place, it was now vacant except for a horde of bats that hung upside-down in the cracks and crevices of the roof.

Gwynn sighed in vexation. Her heart had been filled with hope that she would be reunited with her son, that she would see his young face again and know that he was truly safe.

Now, she was certain he'd been here, so at least he was alive. She noticed the pup's paw prints along with two sets of boot prints. They could be from someone else, she supposed, but chose to believe that Gareth had found the magician and they were on their way to safety—wherever that might be. She sent up a prayer of thanks and promised herself to cast another spell for his safety.

Overhead the bats returned, their wings fluttering as they found their roosts and close together, hung upside-down, creating a large undulating mass near the door and moving restlessly as the fire caught and flames crackled.

Gwynn rubbed her arms and told herself not to

worry. The bats and insects scurrying into the dark corners were creatures of the earth, nothing to fear. 'Twas men and weapons who were her enemies.

Hanging her cloak on a root that protruded through the ground, she slid a glance in the outlaw-baron's direction. Broad-shouldered, lean-hipped, he was taller than she by a head. His jaw, now dark with stubble was square, his features harsh, his eyes a bold blue that she'd found intimidating. There was an irreverence to him that beckoned her, a prideful intolerance to pomposity and arrogance.

A quiet man who had kept his dark thoughts to himself during their journey, whose countenance was often grim and brooding, he'd ridden without rest. His eyes had forever scanned the horizon and his mouth had been set in a line so thin and determined he appeared unapproachable, a man who needed no one.

Nonetheless, she had trouble believing him to be a killer. Aye, he had probably slain an enemy or two during battle, but she doubted he had murdered the old baron of Black Oak. Trevin McBain was ambitious, yes, and could have easily duped a drunken old man into losing his castle in a game of dice, but murder? She shivered and refused to consider him capable of tossing an old man off the wall walk to his death.

"Where is Gareth?"

"He and Muir and the dog were here"—he pointed to footprints and paw prints in the dust—"not long ago as the embers still hold some heat. Now, they are on their way to Black Oak."

"Or, after leaving here, they've been captured," Gwynn said, her darkest fears resurfacing.

"Muir would not allow it."

"Oh, and is he magician enough to vanish into a vapor and take Gareth with him?" she asked as dry moss and tinder caught fire, causing flames to crackle noisily and smoke to roll toward the blackened rocks overhead.

"You, too, dabble in magic."

"I claim not to be a sorceress." She watched the shadows play upon his bladed features and felt a restlessness deep within her. "I cast spells, aye, but they are more like prayers for good luck, health, good fortune. I draw runes hoping for blessings, but I cannot cause a person to disappear."

"The boy will be fine."

"How know you this?" she demanded as he settled upon a rock and stirred the coals with a long, charred stick.

"Because Muir raised me." He looked up at her and held her gaze for but an instant. In that heartbeat her mouth turned dry as the dust of the floor. She cleared her throat and shifted her eyes so that he was only in her peripheral vision. "I knew not my mother. My father—" He lifted a disinterested shoulder. "Who knows? 'Twas Muir taught me to slip a coin from a purse and slide a ring from a bony finger. 'Twas he who fed me and gave me a bed on which to rest. He bade me learn of the church as well as the ways of the old ones and never did he place me in danger. With him, I was safe."

" 'Tis different with Gareth," she pointed out as she sat on a flat rock next to the fire and warmed the soles of her boots. "Ian has proclaimed him a traitor and a murderer. Though he promised to only banish the boy if I married him, I have broken my word and, therefore, no matter how much magic your sorcerer may conjure, our son is in danger."

"You broke your word to Ian," Trevin said, his eyes darkening, "because he struck you."

"He is my husband," she said simply, the thought curdling her innards. How could she ever return to him? Allow him to touch her? Lay with him?

"Aye, and he would as soon kill our son as not." Trevin climbed to his feet and dusted his hands. "You are right. Gareth will never be safe until Ian is dead." He stared straight at her. "Nor, m'lady, will you."

That much was true, but she could always throw herself on the new lord's mercy and hope that there was some shred of decency in Ian of Rhydd's vile heart. "I will go back to him, appease him. Mayhap he will leave Gareth be."

"Nay."

"But, if it means my boy's life—"

Trevin crossed the short distance between them and grabbed her by the arm, hauling her to her feet. "Listen, woman," he said through lips that barely moved. "I will not have you place yourself in harm's way."

"I have no choice."

"There are always choices. Only weak minds settle for the first option." His gaze met hers again and she was lost. Her pulse pounded in her ears and she told herself to step away from him, to toss off the hands that clamped over her arms and yet she could do nothing save swallow hard. "You, m'lady," he drawled, "have always done what was necessary to get what you wanted. You slept with me to get you with child, you ruled Tower Rhydd as if you, a woman, were the lord, and when it served your purposes, you married your brother-in-law."

"To—to save my child," she said as he cocked his head and observed her as if seeing her for the first time. He was so close. So near. 'Twas far too danger-ous to let him touch her. His scent permeated her nostrils, his fingers were warm through her clothes, and her lungs felt as if they could not draw another breath.

"You, Lady Gwynn," he said in a voice that was barely audible, "are unlike any woman I've met."

She didn't know if he meant his words as a compliment or insult, but didn't care. Her heart was pumping wildly and she couldn't draw her gaze away from the hard set of his mouth. "And . . . and you, thief, you are like no other man."

"Aye." His breath fanned her face and teased her hair, the hands around her arms released only to clasp at her back and drag her even closer to him. "Oh, lady, how you vex me," he whispered, his voice tortured. "Would I had never met you." His head lowered and, for a heartbeat, he hesitated, his mouth hovering a breath above hers.

She licked her lips nervously and he groaned. "Damn you, woman," he ground out just as his mouth claimed hers. She should stop him, push him away, and yet she couldn't. Warm and supple, his lips molded to hers and a tingle whispered over her skin. Her head spun and through she knew she was playing with dangerous fire, that she had to break away from him, pull back from the sweet seduction of his kiss, she couldn't summon up the strength.

Years she'd waited to feel like this, for the magic of this man's touch. How many nights had she envisioned just this embrace? How often had she dreamed of his touch only to awaken alone, yearning and covered in a sweet, dream-induced sweat?

His tongue pressed anxiously against her teeth and willingly she opened to him, her mouth accepting the intimate intrusion as if they had been lovers for years.

Groaning, he dragged her closer still, bowing her back as he kissed her, hands splayed upon her spine, hips thrust forcefully against the juncture of her legs. She felt his heat, the hardness of his member, the pulsating pressure of his body so close to hers.

Let me be strong, she thought, but was ultimately weak. Desire stormed through her blood and deep within that most feminine part of her she began to ache. His tongue stroked hers and she wanted more; to touch him everywhere, to let her mouth and fingers explore his hardened body now that he was a man. Images of lying naked with him glided easily through her wanton mind and she wondered what would it hurt to have him, the only man who had known her, be with her again.

His fingers found the ties of her tunic and as the fabric parted, he kissed her throat with lips that were as gentle as they were firm.

Her breasts ached and her breathing nearly stopped as he kissed the top of one breast, exposed above the neckline of her tunic. Beneath the velvet, her nipple hardened expectantly, as it hadn't in so many years.

"You were wrong," he said, his lips leaving a hot trail against her throat.

"W-wrong?"

"You are a witch."

"Nay." Warmth seeped from her womb to run in a hot current through her blood.

"But you enchant me, little one. Far more than you should." With a sigh he lifted his head and curled his fists in the strings of her tunic. "There is no time for this and . . . and I want it not."

Disappointment welled deep in her heart as sparks drifted toward the ceiling of the cave. She felt the struggle within him, didn't understand why he held her possessively yet tried desperately to push her away. "But—"

"And you are another man's bride. My enemy's wife."

"In body but not in spirit."

One side of his mouth lifted in a cynical smile. "In the eyes of the law and church." His hands dropped and he stepped away from her, as if being so close was perilous.

"It stopped you not before," she reminded him.

"Aye, and since then I've been cursed."

"As have I." Suddenly cold, she reached for her cloak, flung it over her head, and wrapped the voluminous dark blue folds more tightly around her torso. Her lips still tingled from Trevin's kiss, her body was still warmed by his.

Eyeing her, he said, "As long as Lord Ian lives, you will be at his mercy."

Her spine stiffened and fury snapped her head up. "Make no mistake, I will be at no man's mercy, outlaw."

His grin held no mirth and, as if he were making a vow to himself, he proclaimed, "Do not worry. I will see to the new Lord of Rhydd and do what is necessary."

Fear slithered down her spine as she understood. "You mean to slay him?"

Trevin's eyes glittered ominously. "If needs be."

"Nay, outlaw, he is a treacherous man," she said, and grabbed his arm only to release it quickly.

"So am I." He winked at her, but beneath the glimmer in his eye, there was something more, something deeper and darker that he refused to confide. "Stay you here and wait."

"Nay—"

"I'll ride to the next village and listen to the gossip,

to discover if Rhydd's soldiers are on their way to Black Oak."

She eyed the interior of the cave with its scattered, bleached bones, bat droppings, and winged inhabitants. She was not one easily frightened, but the thought of staying here by herself was unnerving.

"I will be gone but a few hours and will return before the morning."

"You'll be captured."

"Trust me, Lady Gwynn. I have evaded far more clever enemies than your husband."

"But he has soldiers and—"

"Shh." Again he grabbed her. His lips found hers in a kiss that stole the breath from her lungs and caused her heart to beat in a wild, wanton cadence. Her knees began to crumple. "Wait for me," he commanded, then that same sense that something far deeper was bothering him, that he was holding back, rippled through her.

"What if you don't return?"

"I will."

She raised one eyebrow skeptically and he kissed her lightly on the lips again.

"Have I not gotten you this far?"

"Aye, you've managed to anger my husband, place my son in grave danger, dupe Ian, wound his most trusted knight, steal Webb's horse, and bring me to this . . . this—"

"Hiding place."

"—tomb. We are no closer to finding Gareth than we were on the night we left Rhydd."

"You are impatient, m'lady."

"I worry for our son."

"Fear not."

Oh, if only she could trust him, believe that he

would save Gareth. She kicked at a pebble with the toe of her boot. "So be it, outlaw. I will wait one day. But, if you do not return by nightfall tomorrow, I will leave."

"And go where?" he asked, tightening his belt.

"Heath Castle."

" 'Tis a long journey."

She tossed her hair from her face. "At least I'll not be cowering in a cave with only bats as my companions."

"You'll be no closer to finding Gareth."

"Mayhap not. But then again I told him to meet me at my sister's, and he would be there now had he made good his escape and not been captured by your magician friend."

"He is safer with Muir."

She wasn't certain in this gloomy hiding spot. The thought of staying here without Trevin was terrifying, but her pride forbade her from voicing her fears. "As I said, *m'lord*, I will wait until dark on the morrow."

He turned and walked to the entrance of the cave. "Trust me," he called over his shoulder as he disappeared through the boulders that guarded the cave's entrance.

Her heart sank as she heard the sound of hoofbeats fading into the distance.

Trust me.

Oh, sweet Mother Mary, if only she could.

Never had she felt more alone.

Chapter Seven

The old man was an idiot, Gareth thought, standing on his tiptoes on an overturned barrel as he peered through the slats of the tavern's window. Not a magician, not a sorcerer, not a wizard of any kind. Just a plain old fool of a drunk who rambled on and on about "the circle" with its broken links and blood-stains. 'Twas naught but a foolish man's chants and no amount of amulets or eyeing the horizon or pointing his stupid cane toward the heavens would change the fact that Muir was naught but a lowly thief.

As Gareth waited in the shadows, his teeth chattered and goose bumps rose on his flesh. The moon rose ever higher in the sky. The interior of the shabby inn was dark, the only light from a meager grouping of candles and the embers of a dying fire. Men clustered around tables, laughing and joking and Muir, curse his hide, buried his nose in the bottom of a cup.

'Twas certain Muir practiced the dark arts frowned upon by the church, though Gareth had seen no indication that the withered one was truly a magician. The only spirits he seemed to raise were those that passed over his lips from a cup, and the spells he tried to conjure were always a little mixed up and never seemed to work.

As for his prophesies, they were enough to scare

Gareth, though he would never admit as such. All that mumbling about a dark circle and links of a chain. Father to son and son to father, or some such blither-blather. The old man was daft, pure and simple, though his mutterings spooked Gareth just the same. All the gibberish of replaying history, of sons killing fathers made his blood run cold.

"Some magician," Gareth mumbled to Boon who paced at his feet, sniffing the ground and whining as if in full agreement. "If he's so clever, why can't he conjure up a cup of ale or wine instead of having to come here?"

Boon sniffed at a stack of crates near the back door. The stench of garbage hung heavy in the air and voices from the inn filtered onto the street where shops and inns lined the heavily traveled road. Horses snorted, cattle lowed, and even an occasional rooster crowed, though 'twas after dusk and the temperature was low enough to cause Gareth's breath to fog. "Come on, come on," he muttered as he witnessed the old man rub his head and hold up his cup for another fill.

" 'Tis doomed we be, dog," Gareth muttered and considered leaving Muir to his own devices. So what if the thief-baron wanted him to stay with the ancient one? With a limp and only one good eye, Muir was more hindrance than help. Asides which, Gareth was worried about his mother. If he had any brains or guts at all, he'd leave the drunk here, ride back to Rhydd on the horse, and run old Ian through. But the thought of actually killing a man—any man—caused ice to settle in his innards. The taking of a life wasn't as courageous and noble as he'd once thought and the memory of shoving his sword into a man's flesh, only to see the lifeblood seep out of him, caused Gareth's stomach to turn sour.

Coward. Would you rather your mother gave her life to old Ian? He shuddered and wished Muir would give up his lust for drink and get on with their journey. "We've cast our lots with a simpleton, I fear, Boon." However, angry as he was with the sorcerer, he felt a bit of fondness for the old man. Hadn't Muir fed him, found him shelter, and although nagging him all the way, assured him that there would be safety soon? Mayhap the old man wasn't so bad after all.

Boon whimpered. The pup was standing on his back two legs, his front paws stretched against the barrel. He yipped for attention, his tail whipping frantically in the air. " 'Tis a good dog you be, Boon." Gareth reached down and patted his dog's head. "But keep quiet. Muir will be along soon." He blew on his thumbs to shake off the chill and hoped he wasn't lying.

The thud of hooves caused him to lift his head and climb off the barrel. He sneaked through the alley to the front of the inn where he saw the band of soldiers approach. Riding double file and wearing the green and gold colors of Rhydd, they entered the town at a fast trot.

Sir Webb, his countenance grim as death, his mouth a seam of undeterred purpose, rode in the lead.

All the spit in Gareth's mouth dried. He hid behind a cistern and prayed that the pup, distracted by a rat scurrying along the fence, wouldn't show himself.

"Here." Sir Webb's voice boomed through the night and ricocheted through Gareth's head. "We'll take sustenance and rest, then make camp on the far end of town."

Christ the Savior! Gareth slunk in the shadows, his

feet moving swiftly as he made his way to the back door and slipped into the warm kitchen where a large woman, sweat dripping from her red face, plump fingers curled around the crank of a butter churn was seated on a stool. The paddles within the churn clicked steadily in time with the movement of her arms. "By the gods, lad, ye scared the devil from me, ye did!" she cried. "Who be ye to be slithering around the shadows like a snake off a cold rock?"

Gareth had no time for pleasantries but he hoped he didn't appear as frightened as he felt. "Please, good woman, would you be so kind as to send the old man with the bad eye back here?" he asked anxiously. Suspended on a hook over the fire, a black kettle of stew was simmering and giving off the heady scent of cooked mutton. Gareth's stomach rumbled.

"What?" She shook her head as she continued to churn. "Go get 'im yerself, boy. Can't ye see, I'm churnin' here? I'll not 'ave me butter go soft or sour."

" 'Twill not. Now, please," Gareth said, then jumped at the sound of snoring. He spun and found a scrawny man sleeping with his head propped against a stack of firewood.

"Ye're not hidin' from someone, are ye?" the woman asked, her bushy eyebrows slamming together as she rubbed the side of her face on her shoulder to wipe away her sweat.

Gareth shook his head. "Nay, but—"

"The sheriff, is he lookin' fer ye?"

There was no arguing with her. "No." Gareth walked to the doorway separating the back room from the rest of the tavern and opened it a crack just as Sir Webb, his mail chinking loudly, entered the room. Conversation stopped as the customers sipping ale looked over their shoulders to view the new patrons.

Gareth's heart dropped to his feet. He couldn't show himself as the dark knight would certainly recognize him. He swallowed hard as Muir lifted his good eye and stared at the soldiers filing into the establishment and calling for ale.

"Oh, wouldn't ye know it?" the fat woman grumbled at the sound of so many new voices. "Nary a soul all night and now an entire army barges in." She turned her head. "Will. Will, wake up, would ye? Get another cask and help Bess out front, we've thirsty men—in armor—from the sounds of it."

With a sharp snort, the snoring stopped for a second before continuing evenly.

"Will!" she said sharply, and with a cough the scrawny man awakened and hopped to his feet.

He took one look at Gareth and ran a hand over his eyes. "Who the devil are ye, lad?" His front teeth were missing and his skin was splotched.

" 'E's not sayin', so don't bother askin', jest git the damned cask and help Bess out front, would ye? Oh, fer the love of Zeus." She sighed and stopped churning, her paddle slowing. "I'll do it."

Frowning, she mopped her brow with the back of her hand, then wiped the sweat away on her apron.

Gareth's heart was knocking wildly in his chest as she pulled the door open further and stepped into the front of the tavern. "What can I get fer ye, my good men?"

"Ale. Fer all who wear the colors of Rhydd." Webb's voice boomed.

"Good. Good. 'Twill be but a minute while me husband opens another cask."

With shuffling feet and a few words, the soldiers climbed upon the benches near the fire. Elbow to elbow, they sat, leaning on the heavy table and stretching the crooks of their necks or joking among themselves. Gareth watched through the slit in the door and was relieved to see that Muir had the good sense to keep his face averted, as if he'd found the fire suddenly fascinating.

As the fat woman poured ale into cups, Webb rubbed his shoulder and scanned the room. "We be lookin' for Trevin of Black Oak," he said, wincing slightly.

Gareth took little pleasure in the fact that he'd wounded the dark knight. All he'd accomplished was angering Sir Webb and making him determined to hunt him down.

"Ye seek the baron?" She carried a tray of cups to the table and began setting them before the men.

"Aye, he's a murdering thief, that one. Have you not heard that he killed Lord Roderick and stole his wife?"

So, Muir was right. His mother was with the outlaw. Gareth didn't know whether to be pleased or worried.

"What say ye?" The woman slopped ale onto the table and was quick to wipe it up with the discolored hem of her apron.

" 'Tis said he cheated Lord Dryw out of his castle, then killed the old man when he protested. Threw him off the tower."

"That much, I already heard," the woman said as her husband, grumbling under his breath and laboring with the weight of another barrel brushed past Gareth. For a moment his view was blocked and when Will and the cask moved out of his line of vision, Muir was no longer near the fire, as if he had truly disappeared. Slowly Gareth inched away from the door, ready to sprint into the alley.

A horrifying yowl screamed through the night.

Feet and fur flying, a gray cat dashed into the kitchen and sped through the crack in the door. Boon, yipping wildly, streaked by, fast on the tabby's heels.

"Nay!" Gareth whispered, lunging for the pup, but the dog galloped into the tavern.

"Say, wha—?" Will sputtered as the cat ran between his legs.

Men laughed, a serving girl screamed, and the dog, still barking madly, chased the terrified cat until it climbed up the alewife's voluminous skirts. "Ouch, Sweet Mary! Puss, stop it! Get yer damned claws off me!" Ale sloshed, men laughed, Boon leaped up at the cat, his paws clawing at the ever-moving skirts. "You, mutt! Out with ye," the woman ordered, kicking at the noisy, jumping dog while the cat pounced from the woman's broad hips to a post. Puss scrambled upward to the exposed beams of the ceiling.

Boon, barking his fool head off, circled the post and jumped up and down.

"Cursed mutts. Always comin' in." The woman reached for a broom near the hearth and began swiping at the pup.

"Hey, ain't that the pup—?" Webb asked.

Gareth nearly died.

"Aye, from Rhydd. The lad's—"

Gareth gave out a sharp whistle and the dog stopped, turned, and ears cocked, fixed his puzzled gaze on the back room. "Come!" Gareth ordered from his hiding spot.

"Who goes there?" Webb's voice reverberated through the inn.

He wasn't about to leave his dog. "Boon!" Gareth held the door open but stayed in the shadows.

"It's the lad" another voice said. "He called that mutt of his Boon."

"Fer the bloody love of Christ, get him!" Webb ordered and Gareth scrambled backward, knocking over a sack of flour and spilling white powder on the floor. He nearly fell, stumbled against the hearth where the stew was boiling, and burned the back of his arm against the blackened pot as he unsheathed his dagger. How small the knife seemed when he thought of Webb's men, all of them with swords or maces and armor.

The dog barreled through the door. Gareth wasted no time. He was down the steps and running through the backyard. Behind him, he heard the sound of soldier's boots and rattling swords as Ian's men swarmed through the kitchen.

"Wait!" A voice, soft as the wind and vast as the sea commanded. " 'Tis not the lad ye want."

No, Muir! No! Don't do this!

Muir! Gareth's footsteps faltered.

"Take me to Ian of Rhydd and we'll barter."

"What? You, old man?" a strong voice hooted.

"I am a magician."

"Bah! And I'm King Edward."

Laughter roared through the inn as the men hesitated.

"Lord Ian will speak with me," Muir insisted. "Or I shall call upon the Morrigu, the Great Mother—"

"Get out of me way, ye one-eyed pagan fool. We'll hear no talk of the warrior goddess 'ere."

Gareth spun and ran through the yard, along a pebbled street to a small opening in a fence. With the dog racing behind him, he slipped through the crack, scraping his leg, sprinting in the darkness, away from the main part of the town. Behind shops, under dark stairways, past closed doors, he ran. Chickens flapped their wings and clucked from their coops, other dogs barked, and Gareth stumbled over stacks of firewood and kettles used for washing.

His lungs burned. His head throbbed. His legs ached.

But he couldn't stop.

He heard the men behind him, boots pounding in the mud, curses ringing out, voices fading as he zigged and zagged through the town and into the surrounding forest. His breath seared his lungs, his legs ached, but still he kept going. He didn't know which direction he ran, but found solace in the woods, for there were trees to climb, bushes for cover, trails that wound in differing directions. He stumbled over roots and low branches, but kept on through the darkness, knowing he was losing his pursuers as their voices and footsteps became more distant.

Cramps tightened the muscles of his calves and he had to stop, his stomach gurgling. Gasping for breath, he suddenly retched and hung his head.

Please God, save me. Save Muir. Save Mother.

His head swam. He couldn't think.

Please, help me. Please.

He fell into a wet pile of leaves and waited. What could he do? Muir was certainly caught, for the old man had no spells to make him vanish, and now Gareth was alone in the gloomy forest with only a hungry dog and a bad sense of direction for companions.

"Great," he muttered, sick at heart. "Just bloody great." He had several choices, none of them worth the time of day. He could try to free Muir by chasing after the soldiers, but then he would put himself at risk, or he could try and find the bastard who, according to the wizard, had kidnapped his mother—the murdering thief.

And where would the man be going? Most likely

back to his ill-gotten castle. As would the soldiers. 'Twas a mess to be sure. He closed his eyes and envisioned his mother's face. Never had he thought he would miss her. Never would he admit to caring so deeply for her. He was, after all, nearly a man.

But he had to save her. As she had saved him.

And what about Muir? Do you not owe him your life as well?

He covered his face in his hands and tried to think. He would save the old man, of course he would, but first he would find his mother, and if that meant facing the outlaw, so be it. If, as Muir implied, Trevin was returning to Black Oak, then by a pig and a portal, Gareth would be waiting for him.

" 'Twas like a bad dream, I tell ye," Bess insisted as she spoke to Trevin in the shadows behind the inn. "And the soldier's they be lookin' fer ye and that wife ye stole." Bess, who worked at the inn, was a sweet thing with a small waist, large breasts, and hips soft enough to comfort an ailing and needy man, but Trevin wasn't interested. Nor had he ever been, though he'd known her for years. "I pretended not to recognize yer name," she said, "and most of the louts, when Sir Webb's back was turned, they were only interested in gettin' their 'ands up me skirts."

"Some things never change, Bess," Trevin said.

"Now, fer you, m'lord—" She smiled coyly and Trevin sighed.

"Tell me of the lad."

"I saw no boy—only the one-eyed man who started talking as if 'e was daft, I tell ye. Babbling on and on about the chain, father to son, son to father, blood to blood, or some such nonsense. Now, Lizzie, she's the cook, she seen a youth in the kitchen, but 'e and 'is

bloomin' 'ound got away. Tore off down the back
alley, like 'e'd seen a ghost, Lizzie says.''

"He got away?" Trevin felt a ray of hope.

"As far as I know, but the old man, the magician,
he wasn't so lucky. Sir Webb, he 'auled 'im away, tied
and bound like a roebuck on a huntsman's staff."

Trevin's back teeth ground together. Muir and his
cursed lust for ale. Now he was captured and the
boy . . . oh, for the love of St. Peter, the boy was God-
only-knew-where and wandering around the forest. At
least he was alive. "Thanks, Bessie," he said as the
voluptuous miss leaned forward, offering him a moon-
lit view of plump breasts rising invitingly above a
square neckline.

" 'Tis many a favor I'd do fer ye, m'lord," she
intoned.

"You've done enough." He handed her a coin and
her lower lip stuck out fetchingly.

"I'll 'ave none of yer money, Trevin of Black Oak.
I knew ye when ye were a whelp of a lad, a thief and
no better than the lot of us."

"Who says I've changed?" He dropped the coin between her breasts and she giggled as he climbed
astride Webb's destrier. "This goes no further, Bess."

"Aye, I've never seen ye, ye black-'earted bastard,
and 'ere—ye asked fer food, did ya not?" She handed
him a cloth sack that smelled of baked bread.

"You're an angel."

"Oh, go on!" She blushed in the moonlight.

With a mirthless laugh Trevin yanked on the reins
and his horse wheeled. "Hiya!" The game horse broke
into a gallop. Trevin rode east through the town, hoping Bess caught sight of his leaving. Though he trusted
her, he wasn't going to let her witness anything that
might lead her to guess where he and Gwynn were

hiding. Who knew what hidden eyes had observed his tryst with her? Only God could guess how much she'd say if offered the right price or if she were threatened by Ian of Rhydd's blade. No, neither she nor anyone else lurking about this village would guess his destination by his direction.

With the moon as his guide, he rode past several farmers' fields before doubling back and skirting the town.

So Gareth was free, but where? And Muir, curse him, what had he been thinking, pausing for refreshment before making his way to the castle?

Eyes narrowed against the blast of icy wind that tore across the land, he spurred his mount onward. To Gwynn. At the thought of her and their last stolen kiss, his chest tightened. God in heaven, he'd never been able to get that woman out of his blood, not even while he was married to Faith. Guilt pricked deep into his brain like a thorn into flesh. His dead wife deserved a far better husband than he'd ever been. Faith had loved him and he had never returned the fervor of her passion. Because of Gwynn.

A woman who would sell her body to save her son. God help them all.

The road forked and he headed west toward the cave. The stallion's strides never faltered though lather sprinkled his coat and mixed with the mud splashing onto his chest and legs as he ran.

" 'Tis a fine beast ye be, Dark One," Trevin said urging the steed ever onward. Harsh thoughts tangled in his mind. He could do nothing for Faith; she was lost to him and to this world, but Muir, the man who had raised him, was another story.

Webb would return Muir to Ian who would probably try to torture the truth from the old man. But

Muir was nothing if not clever and when the spirits of the cup did not cloud his mind, he was a match for any man, even the new ruler of Rhydd. The aging sorcerer's magic did exist, but, Trevin had decided, it came with quite a bit of luck and sometimes, in the worst situations, had forsaken him completely.

There was no time to waste. Trevin would have to fetch Gwynn, take her to the safety of Black Oak, then with his company of men, return to Rhydd to free the wizard.

Which was exactly what Ian would be expecting.

Surprise would not be on his side. He would have to be crafty. He smiled as the horse labored on. Somehow he would best his old enemy.

One way or another.

Gwynn stepped into the stream and sucked in her breath. 'Twas near freezing and she felt her skin turn blue, but she only shivered for a second before walking into the deepening pool. She was determined to scrub some of the filth from her body. She'd spent days on the road, time in the cave, and the final hours before nightfall she'd been on her hands and knees, collecting herbs, berries, and roots. Though skilled with dagger, bow, and sword, her true strength came in the casting of spells and healing.

She had once laughed at Idelle and her pagan ways, but over the past thirteen years, she had learned the power of yew, ash, foxglove, thistle, and the like. She was a Christian woman, aye, and prayed to the Holy Father, but she, too, trusted the old ways and believed in Morrigu, the Great Mother and her gifts of the earth. In her struggle to find and save Gareth, Gwynn vowed to use any skill, spell, or weapon that might help.

All that mattered was her son.

Slowly she sank onto her knees. She bit her lower lip and closed her eyes as the icy water splashed the sensitive spot at the juncture of her legs. She sucked in her breath in a hiss and as her body numbed to the cold, she scrubbed, using the brook's current and a handful of moss to wash away the dirt beneath her fingernails, between her toes, and in her hair. The water was fresh, cleansing, and gave her clarity of mind.

What if Trevin didn't return? What if he had no word of Gareth? What, oh dear Lord in heaven, what if her son was already dead! Do not think such, she told herself as she tossed water onto her face and blinked against the drops that lingered on her eyelashes. Surely he was safe and well, ensconced in Black Oak where Trevin's servants would provide for him and his soldiers would protect the boy. Trevin would see that each sword and shield at Black Oak would be raised to safeguard his only son.

Though she did not yet completely trust the thief-turned-baron, she believed that he cared for Gareth. Why else risk Roderick, and now Ian's, wrath? Why ride in the darkness, stealing uniforms and horses and seeming to be concerned for her? She was not foolish enough to think that the thief cared a whit for her, nay, she was Gareth's mother, nothing more. He still considered her the self-centered bride of Roderick who had done anything, even cast aside her virginity, to dupe the old man into thinking he'd spawned a son.

'Twas a long time ago.

Before she'd been a mother.

Before she'd known the fear for a child.

Before she'd fallen in love with a rogue.

Her eyes flew open. Love? In love? Nay, her thinking was addled, her worries over Gareth clouding her mind. She loved Trevin not. He was but a means for her to save her son. Nothing more. She wasn't a silly ninny of a woman who would confuse love with lust.

Still the thought disturbed her.

She lay in the stream and let the water float her body in slow circles where the current played in a lazy whirlpool.

Trevin.

The outlaw.

She'd known him a short time and yet, she feared, she was beginning to trust him. Oh, foolish, foolish heart. He was a thief and mayhap a murderer.

And the father of your son.

Trevin of Black Oak was not a man to whom any sane woman would lose her heart. He was too gruff and grim, too brooding, and too self-important, always giving her orders. But only for a while. As soon as she and Gareth were reunited, they would leave the robber-baron in their dust. His thoughts of her and his son would be but a memory.

There was no other way.

She wasn't in the cave. Trevin held his torch aloft and searched the blackened interior, but aside from coals still glowing in the fire, there was no sign of her. "Damned fool woman," he muttered, disturbing the few bats that still hung from the ceiling and feeling a deepening ache in his heart, an ache he quickly ignored. He had no feelings for the woman. None.

Angry, he walked outside. Why did she leave? Had she not promised to wait? From the corner of his eye, he caught a movement near the trees.

He extinguished his torch in the mud. No reason to have an enemy spy him. Stealthily he unsheathed his dagger and readied himself for a fight. If Webb had found the cave and Gwynn. . . . Rage, as dark and wild as a devil's heart, pounded through his veins. He would kill anyone who—

He came upon her horse still attempting to pluck a few blades of glass that glistened silver in the moonlight.

Could she have been taken? Had Sir Webb and his band of cutthroat soldiers from Rhydd stumbled upon her? The thought hit him hard and for an instant terror seized his heart in an iron-fisted grip. Surely the men wouldn't have stolen her and left her horse.

Silent as death, he stole through the underbrush, searching the area until he heard the splashing of the stream and saw her body, white and pale, as she floated completely nude in the river.

His gut tightened.

A fire started to burn in his loins.

Quietly, he sheathed his knife.

Her white breasts rose above the waterline, their dark nipples pointing toward the starry heavens. Lower, the patch of dark hair was stark against her fair skin and caused a living, breathing lust to flow in his veins.

She was as beautiful as he remembered and he considered lying with her. 'Twould be sweet torture. But she was another man's wife, whether by choice or force, 'twas no matter.

As she was Roderick's wife when you last made love to her.

How easily she had bartered away her virtue, but he did not blame her. Surely she gave up her virginity in an attempt to save her life. Would not he have done the same?

He wanted her. Damn it, he wanted her more than

'twas sane. *Remember Faith and your vow to her.* Guilt
took a stranglehold on his soul. He'd never loved his
wife and felt a deep remorse. She'd died only days
after their daughter and she, with pain-racked eyes
and weak fingers had begged him not to give his heart
to another. She knew he would find solace in another
woman, she only had asked him never to give his
heart.

Now, he cleared his throat and Gwynn jumped,
water splashing, her hair falling into her eyes as she
attempted and failed to hide her breasts and legs with
her hands. "Wh—who goes there?"

"Cover up," he said, catching sight of her tunic,
chemise, and cloak dangling from the branch of a
nearby tree. Swiftly he retrieved them all. He was
about to toss the garments her way so that she could
dress, but she held up a hand.

"Wait. Just . . . just hold them and turn your back. I
do not wish them to fall into the stream and get wet."

If he hadn't been so worried about Gareth and
Muir, he would have refused to do her bidding and
enjoyed her vexation as he watched her walk proudly
and naked as the day she was born from the stream.
But there was no time.

"As you wish, m'lady," he agreed, for he understood the reasoning in her command. Slowly he
turned, holding the clothes outstretched as she
splashed out of the stream and snagged each piece
from his hand. Hazarding a glance over his shoulder,
he caught a glimpse of her struggling into her chemise
as it clung to her wet body. Her navel was an inviting
slit, her ribs, as she reached upward, visible slightly
beneath full breasts that would easily fill a man's hand
or mouth.

His cock thickened as moonlight washed over her

and the dark nest of curls above her thighs shimmered. She caught his glance and frowned as she tugged on her clothes. "Where is Gareth?" she asked.

"He escaped."

"I *know* that much. Where is he?"

"Not with Muir."

"What?"

He turned as she was cinching a belt around her small waist. "Muir was captured."

"Oh, merciful Jesus." She paled even more.

"But Gareth was not caught." He explained all that he knew quickly while she interrupted, peppering him with questions, worrying aloud, and generally becoming more and more anxious as the seconds ticked by.

"We must find him. Do you think he went back to Rhydd? To Black Oak or mayhap to Heath and Luella?"

"Do not worry. Wherever he is, I will find him."

"But where? Oh, poor boy." She wrung out her hair with her hands and paced at the side of the creek. "We must—"

"I said 'I'll find him.'" His voice was firm, his anger rising.

"Aye. As you said I was to 'trust you'? Was that not the last order you gave me?" She threw her hands toward the black sky.

"Calm yourself."

"Tell me not what to do, Outlaw," she shot back.

"Then hear me out."

"Why? She demanded. "So you can lie to me again? So you can tell me to 'trust you'?"

"So that we can find our son."

"Ha! Is that not what we have been attempting? I have listened to you, followed you, waited for you," she said, her face a mask of rage, his own temper wearing thin. "And to what end? You know not where Gareth is, if they've captured him, hurt him, or what's become of—ooh!"

"Hush, woman!" He grabbed her roughly and intended to shake some sense into her. But as his hands spanned her rib cage, his fury gave way to the sweet seduction in her eyes. "Curse you, woman," he growled, then kissed her. Long and hard and with all the pent-up desire that had been tormenting him for days, he covered her open mouth with his. Her lips were chilled, her flesh beneath her clothes trembled, and for a second he thought she might slap him. Instead she yielded, her body sagging against his, her lips returning the fever of his kiss as if she, too, had waited for just this moment to lose herself in him.

Though there was little time to spare, though the moonlight would soon give way to dawn, though she was the last woman on earth he should desire, he couldn't resist the sweet temptation of her lips, the pliant softness of her body, the urge to take and conquer this woman with her blistering tongue and gorgeous face.

She sighed into his open mouth and his tongue pressed ever forward, touching hers, rimming her lips, exploring the slick moistness of her mouth.

Heat invaded his blood and his cock stiffened in anticipation as he dragged them both to the ground with his weight. A dozen reasons to stop this madness seared through his brain only to be chased away by the hot, dark lust that burned through his body and seared his soul.

Trembling, his fingers fumbled with the laces of her cloak. Anxiously he drew the unwanted garment over her head. His lips brushed a kiss over her neck and his blood thundered in his ears. He wanted her. More than he'd ever wanted a woman. More than was right.

Remember Faith. That you loved her not. Because of Gwynn. Did you not vow on her grave that you would never . . .

She shuddered and whispered his name against his ear. His lips moved downward and discovered the enticing circle of bones at the base of her throat. She tasted of water, smelled of the forest, and felt warm and safe on this cold, dangerous night.

God help me.

One hand untied her belt. The other reached beneath the hem of her tunic.

"Trevin," she whispered. "Do not . . . oh, please—"

She arched against him as he slipped the tunic over her head, the damp chemise clinging to her skin. He saw two dark circles where her nipples pressed against the frail fabric and he lowered his mouth over one inviting breast, kissing and sucking, closing his eyes as desire overcame reason.

He needed Gwynn. He needed her now and the devil could hang any reason for not having her—even his own faithless promise to a dead wife.

Lying above her, he kissed her lips. One hand tangled in the wet strands of her hair, the other surrounded a breast. He felt a need as strong as life itself. To bury himself in her, to dance in the sensual rhythm of lovemaking as she writhed beneath him and called his name to the heavens, to spill his seed within the warm haven of her womb was all he wanted.

"Trevin," she said again and he lifted his head to kiss her once more. Her hands found the ties of his mantle and tunic and helped him toss the unwanted clothes aside. He shivered, but not from the cool night air, nay, from the heat that ran beneath his skin. Her fingers traced the cords of his muscles and the scars that marred his body. She quivered with need. He held back, for he didn't trust himself. When she reached for the laces of his breeches, he grabbed her hand. He could not. He would not.

This was madness.

"Nay, little one," he whispered and with all the strength he could muster fought the urge to take her. He strained against the fire in his loins. Slowly, he pushed up the hem of her chemise and lifted her legs over his shoulders. "Tonight is yours, love. So that you may forget."

"But—"

"Shh," he breathed against her and Gwynn no longer protested. She closed her eyes and sighed as he touched her, his lips creating a special magic, his tongue probing and lapping as she seemed to melt into a sea of sensation.

He smiled to himself for he sensed that for the moment he'd chased away her fears for their son.

And what of you, Trevin? What of the promise you made to Faith? He squeezed his eyes shut and forced aside the memory.

For a few moments in this inky forest all that mattered was the heat between them, the desire that held them fast.

He did not think about the morning.

Tonight would be hers.

Chapter Eight

"What's this?" Ian asked, as Webb, nudging an old man in front of him crossed the bailey to a corner where targets had been mounted. For the first time in days, the sky was a brilliant shade of blue and a weak winter sun struggled to give off some much-needed heat.

Ian, who had been sighting his weapon, lowered the heavy crossbow as the ancient one approached. He was hobbled, his hands bound behind his back and he stumbled across the uneven grass. He stopped a few feet away from the lord of the manor and raised his head to meet Ian's gaze. Ian recoiled in disgust. Webb's pauper of a prisoner had but one eye. The other was sightless and scarred. Who was this man and why did Ian feel the taunt of a hellish memory tug at his mind?

"We found not the boy, m'lord," Webb admitted. His shoulders were stiff, his mouth a grim line.

"For the love of Christ—"

"But this man, a magician he claims himself to be, was seen traveling with a young lad who looked much like Gareth."

Ian walked toward the two and regretted his quick movement as pain exploded up his legs. Damn Trevin of Black Oak. That bastard would roast in hell for all the trouble and agony he'd wreaked. "The *boy* escaped?"

"He was hidden, m'lord, but we found this one"—Sir Webb shoved the old one forward and he stumbled to one knee before finding his balance again—"with his nose in a cup at an inn. He calls himself Muir and will not speak of his companion."

"Did no amount of . . . persuasion loosen his tongue?" Ian asked while trying to place the ancient one. *Muir.* Had he not heard the name before? The magician—if that's really what he was—again seemed vaguely familiar and teased the corners of Ian's memory, never quite coming into focus. Had they met before? When? Why would he not remember such a vile, ugly visage?

Webb lifted a dark eyebrow. "I thought mayhap ye would like to do the persuading yourself, my lord."

Ian turned the suggestion over in his mind, but couldn't imagine flogging this pathetic pauper. Nearly crippled, he was, and half blind. Ian would find no satisfaction in whipping the already hunched back. "Mayhap, in time," he hedged, "but we will kill him not. If we keep him here, there is a chance the boy or some of his accomplices might return to try and free him."

"Aye." Webb actually grinned as a hawk circled high over the battlements. " 'Tis an opportunity too good to resist."

Thoughtfully, Ian rubbed the stubble on his chin. "Be ye a sorcerer, then, old man?"

"Some say." The wizard had the audacity to stare him coldly in the face, and Ian fought the urge to shudder at the hate he felt emanating from that one seeing eye.

"I care not what 'some' say. What say you?"

" 'Tis only magic if ye believe."

"Tangled words from a fraud," Ian said, then added, "or from bait, for that is what you are, old man, bait for your friends."

"Ye would be wise to fear my friends," he replied, unruffled and prideful though he stood in a dirty, tattered coat that dragged on the ground and was so ragged it hardly covered his age-bent shoulders. "And, m'lord," he added with no hint of a smile, "ye would be wise to fear me as well."

"You? *You?* Do you jest?" Ian laughed at Muir's audacity though he felt a niggle of fear. The sorcerer was too smug. Too arrogant. And ugly. "Look at you, old one, you've got one foot in the grave as it is. 'Tis not I who is tied like a trussed boar. If ye are able to conjure up some magic, 'twould be wise to start now." He motioned to a page standing near the target. "Retrieve the bolts!"

"In time. Trust me, m'lord," Muir mocked. "I will use my magic in time."

"You've run out of time."

Muir's eye held not a bit of warmth. "We shall see."

Though there was no reason to think it, Ian couldn't shake the sensation that the temperature within the bailey had dropped. 'Twas as if a cold wind had raced across the bare brass to swirl around him and yet the air did not move.

The page returned with the bolts and once again Ian picked up his crossbow and pointed it toward the tarp that had been painted to look like a soldier, then spread across a pile of hay. "Take him away," he ordered the guards, tired of the uncanny look in the old man's eye. "Lock the wizard in the dungeon, but see that no harm comes to him. I wish him to stay alive."

"Aye, m'lord," a soldier, a skinny man named Harold agreed as he shoved Muir's thin shoulders. "Come along now."

Nearly falling, Muir turned to cast one last bone-chilling look over his shoulder. " 'Tis sorry ye'll be, Ian of Rhydd. Very sorry."

Though he knew not why, the lord felt a sudden and nameless fear.

Why she listened to him, she didn't know, but Gwynn, for once in her life, hadn't argued and had ridden with Trevin to Black Oak Hall. She'd hoped that Gareth would be waiting for her and, as their horses galloped through the crumbling portal of the bailey, she knew she'd been foolish. Gareth would not have come here without the magician.

So where was he? On the road to Castle Heath? Returning to Rhydd? Please, God, keep him safe, he is but a boy.

Black Oak Hall was nearly in ruins, though there were efforts, it seemed, to fix the chipped mortar in the walls, and replace rotting beams in the huts propped against the great hall as well as rethatch sparse roofs.

"Lord Trevin returns," a watchman yelled from the highest tower and Gwynn, glancing upward, shivered as she remembered the story, that the castle was cursed, had fallen upon bad times. Was that the turret from which Baron Dryw had fallen—or had been pushed—to his death?

"Lord Trevin!"

" 'Tis good y'er home, m'lord."

"Make way, make way."

Voices, echoing the guard's words, clamored with excitement. The farrier left his forge burning brightly, carpenters laid down their hammers and saws, the armorer who had been cleaning mail in sand brushed off his hands and loped across the bailey. As it was just past midday, the keep, smaller by far than Rhydd, bustled with workers and animals, peddlers, and a band of musicians.

Trevin reined to a stop and Gwynn, slowing her own mount, felt lost, as if she were alone in an unfamiliar land. She searched the faces staring up at her hoping against hope that she would spy her boy, but no where in the gathering crowd was there any boy resembling her son. Her heart dropped. Where was he? Captured with that simpleton of a magician? Rotting away in some dungeon at Rhydd? Lost or hurt in the forest? Set upon by outlaws or wolves?

Stop it, Gwynn! Gareth's a clever boy. Have faith. With fierce determination, she hiked up her chin, swallowed back her fears, and stiffened her spine.

Trevin slid off his mount and tossed his reins to a bug-eyed page who eyed Webb's charger warily. The horse tossed his great head and snorted as the nervous boy led him away.

With strong hands, Trevin helped Gwynn from her saddle and gave the reins to another, even younger boy with strawlike hair that stuck out in ungainly tufts and a smile missing more than one tooth.

"Thank the Good Lord for your safe return, Lord Trevin," a scrawny priest welcomed. He was a foot shorter than the lord of the castle and completely bald, the only hair on his head being a reddish beard. Freckles spattered his face, crown, and neck.

" 'Tis good to see you again, Father." Trevin clasped the man's bony outstretched hand.

"And you as well."

"M'lord!" A steward strode forward, his boots squishing in the wet sod of the bailey. He was as tall as Trevin but without an ounce of fat or muscle upon his bones. "Welcome home," he greeted warmly. "You're looking well and that steed"—with appraising eyes he glanced to the stables where Webb's charger was tethered and already being groomed—"he will make a fine addition to the herd."

"Won't he?" Trevin replied with a half smile, his eyes glinting in blue devilment. "I borrowed him from . . . an old friend."

Gwynn let out a puff of disgusted air. Old friend? Webb?

"Borrowed? As in permanently?" the steward asked, reading the baron's thoughts.

"Most likely."

Oh. They are used to the outlaw-baron and his thieving ways, Gwynn surmised. Funny, but she didn't think of Trevin as a thief any longer, but then she was being silly. Just because he'd kissed her to the point of her nearly losing consciousness was no reason not to see him for what he truly was.

"We were worried when you didn't return. Sir Gerald said you would arrive soon, but I admit I had feared the worst."

"No reason, Emerson," he said. To the steward and the others who had crowded around them, he added, "I'd like you all to welcome Lady Gwynn of Rhydd. She is my guest and will be treated as such. Whatever she wishes is hers."

"Welcome, m'lady." The steward bowed grandly. "I'm Emerson and pleased to be at your service."

Gwynn nodded, though she had no time for pleasantries. *Where was Gareth?* Scullery maids, alewives, gong farmers, farriers, and carpenters were filling the bailey. Children followed after their parents, boys and girls with freshly scrubbed faces, or runny noses as the air was cold but, of course, Gareth was not among them.

"The lady has come here looking for her son, a boy by the name of Gareth. Twelve years old with black hair and blue eyes, about so high—" Trevin held his hand at the level of his shoulders. "He was probably traveling alone, mayhap without a mount."

"I've seen no unknown lad," Emerson responded, his brow furrowing in concentration as he shared a glance with another man, a soldier, as if for confirmation.

"Nor I, m'lord," the knight with curling blond hair agreed. "I've stood guard at the gate as well as the west tower. No boy of that description, save Jake, the armorer's son who we've all known for years, has been to Black Oak."

" 'Tis true." A fat woman with hips that seemed to float beneath her tunic and a dingy white scarf wrapped around her head approached. Her hands were chapped raw, her apron splattered with blood. A girl of three hung on her leg, peering at Gwynn with curious, wary eyes.

"You know me, m'lord, I'm the eyes and ears of this 'ere castle and if old Mary ain't seen the lad, he 'asn't been 'ere." She gave a clumsy curtsy and shook her head. "Sorry, m'lady, but I've seen no boy who looks like yer son."

"Nor I," the priest agreed.

Bone tired, Gwynn wanted to break down and cry, or shake the living hell out of Trevin and demand that he find their son, but she stood as she was, dirty but proud, a mother worried sick for her boy. Her heart was heavy, her muscles ached, and she longed for the peace of mind that had eluded her ever since she'd heard that Roderick had escaped and was returning.

'Twas only days ago and yet she felt as if weeks had passed. She was tired, hungry, and irritable.

The whisper running through the crowd of peasants and freemen was that no boy matching Gareth's description was hiding within the crumbling walls of Black Oak. Gwynn's hopes fell onto the cold, sharp stones of reality that Gareth was captured or lost or worse. *Dear God in heaven, was it possible that he had died and she was unaware of the tragedy?* Her heart twisted painfully. Surely she, who had brought him forth into this world, would feel the rending of his life if he'd died.

Even Trevin's broad shoulders seemed to slump a bit, as if he, too, were realizing how futile their search might be. He took Gwynn's hand and led her toward the great hall. "Come. We'll eat and rest, then I'll make plans and find the boy."

"*You'll* make plans? *You'll* find him?" she repeated, her eyes narrowing. "Make no mistake, *m'lord,* I will not be left behind. If there be a plan to save Gareth I will be a part of it."

"It may be dangerous—"

"Think you I care? We are talking about Gareth, Trevin. My son!"

"And mine."

The door to the great hall opened as they climbed the stairs. Inside the interior was lit with hundreds of candles and wall sconces. A huge fire in the grate crackled and popped, giving off warm golden light that reflected on the whitewashed walls and caught in Trevin's eyes. For the first time in days, Gwynn felt warmth against her skin.

Servants scurried about, knights stood at their stations, pages walked swiftly along the corridors. Already a table was being prepared with wine, apples, cheese, and loaves of wastel.

"I knew not when ye'd be back, m'lord," a man with great jowls and silvering hair said. "If ye but give me a few minutes, I will have a feast for ye the likes of which ye haven't seen since the Christmas Revels."

Trevin waved off the man's concerns. "Do not worry, James," he said as he held a chair for Gwynn positioned next to his upon a raised dais. Gratefully she sank onto the seat. "As hungry as we are, we will eat what you've prepared and think it the best in all of Wales."

The cook's chest puffed up in pride. " 'Twill be, I swear. But for now, please, enjoy this bit of nothing, then rest a little, but the time ye've slept and changed, well . . . all will be ready." He clapped his hands and several pages scurried out of the great hall through a back door. "I've already ordered water heated and hauled to your chamber as well as to the lady's room."

"Good, good." Trevin settled into his chair—the lord's chair—a carved oaken piece that she suspected had belonged to the previous baron. He leaned low on his spine, and sliced cheese, apples, and bread, which he offered to her. As they ate and drank wine, Trevin listened attentively to problems that had occurred in the keep. The master builder was concerned about the wattle and daub walls being washed with lime, the carpenter was unhappy with his latest apprentice, the steward was certain that someone in the kitchen was stealing spices, and the armorer was worried that there wasn't enough steel to make the weapons that were sorely needed. There were other squabbles as well, but Gwynn hardly listened as she bit into a slice of tart apple. She was too tired to think of anything but her lost son and his rogue of a father.

Trevin would forever be a mystery to her. An accomplished outlaw, he could steal a man's horse from beneath his nose. A reluctant ruler, he nonetheless listened to the troubles and problems within the castle walls with a just ear and clever mind. A considerate lover, he could make her think of nothing save the touch and feel of him. And now, his new role, that of father, one he seemed to savor.

As men and women from the castle stopped in to welcome him back, meet the lady, or give him news, gossip, and complaints about the travails of Black Oak, Trevin listened, though he, too, appeared anxious, his skin tight over his cheekbones, his lips thin and bracketed with deep grooves.

Gwynn couldn't help but stare at him. How had she come to care for a man she didn't trust, didn't really know? Why did her silly pulse leap each time he looked her way? Did she not have enough problems, worrying about Gareth's safety? She could not, would not be distracted by this outlaw baron. Yet, she couldn't help but appraise from beneath the sweep of her lashes.

Aye, he was a handsome man. His hair, black as the night, fell fetchingly over eyes the shade of a summer sky near dusk. His skin was dark, as was Gareth's, and his smile, when he reluctantly offered it was a crooked slash of white that had, she supposed, melted the hearts of many a maid. Had not she herself been blinded by his black-hearted charm? Had she not let him undress her and touch her and kiss her in places only a husband should know of?

She felt a blush steal up her neck and in that moment, Trevin glanced in her direction, his eyes holding hers for half a heartbeat. Her lungs were suddenly too tight, her breath lost somewhere in the back of her throat. 'Twas as if, in that single instant, he could read her mind and see the wanton path of her thoughts.

She turned her attention to a loaf of white bread and sliced off a slab. What was wrong with her? She couldn't be around him without thinking of their love-making. Even riding in the saddle, watching his stiff back as he sat astride Webb's stallion, she was reminded of his touch. Between Gareth's whereabouts and Trevin's kiss, she thought of little else.

Conscious that he was watching her, she slathered her wastel with butter, then drizzled honey over the slice. What was she thinking? She couldn't allow images of Trevin's body to distract her. All she should be considering was the safety of her son. Nothing else mattered. By the time she'd finished the bread, her fingers were sticky and she licked them, only to notice Trevin's eyes regarding her in silent amusement. Embarrassed, she accepted the wet cloth and bowl of warm water from a page and refused to meet the glimmer in his gaze.

After more apologies and promises from the cook of a feast "like no other ye've ever seen" to be prepared for a later meal, Gwynn was shown to a chamber near the priest's quarters. A fire had been lit, the room was warm, and a tub of water with lavender-scented steam rising from it had been placed near the foot of the bed.

The bath looked like pure heaven.

A gap-toothed girl with red ringlets and freckles bridging a pert nose was wringing her hands near the tub. "I'm to bathe ye, m'lady," she said with a curtsy she hadn't yet perfected. "Me name's Hildy and if there's anything ye need, ye're but to ask me."

"Thank you." Gwynn decided to make a friend of this silly lass who seemed as if she'd never attended to a lady before. Though she knew she should insist upon being with Trevin every instant, demand to be a part of any plans he had to save Gareth, she couldn't resist the thought of fragrant, warm water running over her skin. With Hildy's help she stripped off her dirty clothes and sighing in contentment, settled into the hot water.

"Oooh, I've longed for this," she admitted. Her skin tingled and she used the scented soap to clean her hair and fingernails. As the moist heat enveloped her, she was reminded of her last cleansing and Trevin coming upon her while she bathed in the creek. All too vividly she remembered the magic of his lips and how possessively his hands had been on her body when he'd kissed her so intimately.

The silly little maid clucked on, talking about everything and nothing all at once. "—the baron, Lord Trevin, I, um, I thinks he's a good man no matter what some of 'em say."

"And what is that?" Gwynn asked, rotating her neck.

"Well, y'know, that 'e killed Baron Dryw just to keep the castle and he married Lady Faith to make certain that 'e didn't lose it. 'Tis a pity about her, fer she loved 'im, that she did. Never believed that 'e killed her father and always 'oped that 'ed' learn to love 'er back, poor thing."

"He loved not his wife?" Suddenly the twit had all of Gwynn's attention.

"Who knows?" Hildy lathered Gwynn's hair with fingers that were surprisingly strong. "She didn't think so and that was what mattered."

"But still she loved him?"

"With all her poor 'eart." Hildy took a pitcher from the shelf near the fire and filled it with water from the tub. Slowly she poured it over Gwynn's soapy curls. "She thought that bearing 'im a babe would turn his 'eart to her, she did, but then, ah, well, the baby came backwards and the midwife couldn't save it—a girl, Alison, they named 'er. Lady Faith"—Hildy cleared her throat and blinked rapidly—"she . . . she bled to death still 'oldin' the poor dead little lass in 'er arms. 'Twas pitiful." She took the time to make the sign of the cross over her breasts and water from her hands sprayed and dripped with her rapid movements.

"Yes . . . yes, it was," Gwynn agreed, horrified by the story but touched by Hildy's adoration of Trevin's wife.

"The baron, 'e blamed 'imself, if ye ask me."

"Why?"

"Because 'twas the bloody truth." Hildy lowered her voice as she wrung the water from Gwynn's hair. " 'E never loved Lady Faith, you could see it in his eyes. If ye ask me 'e's not capable of love. 'E's a looker, aye, and a decent man most of the time, I s'pose, but 'e's got a heart of stone, that one. I pity any woman who's foolish enough to give 'im 'er 'eart."

"So do I," Gwynn admitted.

"When Faith and the baby died, 'e . . . well, 'e became even more unhappy, or so it seems." She glanced up at Gwynn. "I tell ye, sometimes I think there be a curse cast upon Black Oak." Shaking her head, Hildy stacked towels on a stool near the tub. "I'll be right back, m'lady," she said as she made her way to the door. "The Baron's ordered ye clean clothes."

"Kind of him," Gwynn said under her breath. She bathed until the water cooled and closed her eyes as Hildy came and went, laying out dresses upon the bed, then cleaning Gwynn's shoes and boots with a smooth cloth before setting them near the hearth to dry. A dozen scented candles burned, the fire crackled, and Gwynn, for the first time in days, felt a sense of contentment. If only Gareth were here and safe, she could find some peace here at Black Oak.

With Trevin? Peace? Remember, he's an outlaw—some think a killer. All he wants from you is your son. Nothing more. You are only the woman who brought forth his heir. She didn't want to believe her nasty thoughts. Had Trevin not loved her thoroughly the night before, giving rather than taking, offering pleasure rather than demanding it? Because he wants you to trust him, to fall into his trap of seduction, so that you'll be lulled into the very sense of peace you're experiencing. *Don't be fooled, Gwynn, Don't let any man manipulate you again, especially not a rogue like Trevin of Black Oak Hall.* Remember what Hildy said—that he was incapable of love, that he didn't even love his wife.

But then had she loved either of her husbands?

The water finally grew tepid and reluctantly Gwynn toweled off before choosing a lacy chemise and a velvet and brocade gown the color of wine. The dress was heavy but warm as it hugged her breasts and fitted easily over her hips before sweeping the floor.

" 'Tis beautiful ye be, lady," Hildy said in awe as she wound ribbons through Gwynn's still-damp hair.

"Did this dress belong to the lord's wife?"

"Aye." Hildy handed her a braided silver belt that slid easily around Gwynn's waist, then stepped back, clasped her hands together, and sighed. "The lady never wore it as she was with child during the time it was sewn and then, poor dear"—again Hildy deftly made the sign of the cross over her own chest—"she had the babe and died. 'Twas a pity, sure and simple.

She was a kind one, was Lady Faith. True of spirit and soul. She was there that day, y'know, the day that her father fell to his death."

"She was?" Gwynn asked, cringing at her own curiosity.

"Aye, walking though the gardens. Lord Dryw and Sir Trevin were up on the wall walk, arguing loudly, and then, suddenly, it looked as if they 'ad come to blows and the baron pitched over the edge, right through the crenels and landed in the bailey just short of the old well." She shook her head and scowled, then crossed herself yet again. " 'Twas a sad day for all of us."

"Sir Trevin was with the baron?" Gwynn clarified.

"Aye." Hildy nodded her head and her springy curls danced around her face. "But 'e did not kill the lord. 'E did not.'Twas an accident." She was arguing with herself, as if it was she, not Gwynn, who needed convincing. "Even Lady Faith, she believed him, elsewise would she have married the man who killed her father? I think not."

"You saw the accident?" Gwynn asked, swallowing hard.

"With me own two eyes. First the lords were talkin', then arguin', then fightin', y'know, kind of shovin' each other, and then . . . then the baron he cursed Sir Trevin, told 'im, 'e'd see 'im in 'ell. Then . . . then . . ." her breathing was uneven, her eyes focused on a distant image only she could see, ". . then he tumbled through the crenels and let out a horrible scream." Closing her eyes, she shuddered as if she could feel the thud of the body as it landed. " 'Twas awful, m'lady."

"It sounds so."

"Lady Faith, she . . . she never got over it, but

married Trevin anyway. Cursed, I tell ye. We all be cursed by a hex that no one can break.''

"Hexes are meant to be broken," Gwynn said, as much to appease the superstitious girl as anything.

"Not 'ere at Black Oak. I know. I've been 'ere since me poor ma birthed me and I've seen death and ghosts.''

"Ghosts?"

Hildy nodded. "Aye; they walk the curtain wall and I've thought 'twas one of them undead who shoved the baron to 'is death. The devil, 'e never sleeps, ye know.''

"I've heard," Gwynn said dryly.

"Yea, and sometimes methinks 'e lives in the very dungeons of Black Oak. Why else would Baron Dryw's life be taken or Lady Faith's? And little Alison, why should she not be born to grow up, eh?'' She cleared her throat. "The baron, Lord Trevin, there isn't a day 'e be 'ere at the castle that 'e doesn't visit the grave.''

"Of his daughter?" Gwynn shivered.

"And 'is wife. 'E may not have loved 'er while she walked this earth, but now, me thinks, 'e misses 'er sorely. Oh, 'tis a sorry lot we be, 'ere at Black Oak.'' She sniffed loudly, then asked, "Think ye that ye can lift the hex that's been placed on us all?''

"Me?"

"I've seen yer 'erbs, m'lady, and there is a rumor about that the mistress of Rhydd is a sorceress.''

"I claim not to be anything of the kind."

"But ye will 'elp us, won't ye?" She bit her lower lip and kept her gaze fixed on the floor. "Ye see, 'tis not just fer meself I ask, but fer the babe within me.'' She rubbed her belly with gentle hands. "I be with child.'' She smiled and blinked. "But I 'ave no 'usband

and I pray that the curse of Black Oak is upon me not. I . . . I would not want to lose my babe as Lady Faith did."

"You will not. You are young and strong."

Hildy shuddered inwardly and shook her head, tossing the curls about her face. " 'Tis not enough. There 'ave been three babes born this year past who 'ave not breathed a breath of life. Others 'ave died in their cradles, not yet seeing their first summer." She was pale as a new moon. "I want only the best for my little one. Surely ye, a mother, can understand."

"Aye." Of course she could.

"Then, please, m'lady, use whatever magic you 'ave to put an end to the bad spell cast over this keep."

"I—I'll try. But I cannot promise 'twill work."

" 'Tis enough," Hildy said, brightening.

Shaken, Gwynn smoothed the folds of Lady Faith's dress. Not only was she wearing another woman's gown, but had kissed that woman's man as if he were her husband. She felt suddenly like a traitor to a ghost she'd never known in life. The story Hildy had spoken was bone chilling and yet she had to know more about Black Oak and Trevin, the father of her child. "So tell me," she encouraged as she stepped into a new pair of boots that Hildy had scrounged up, "of Muir."

"Oh, 'im!" Hildy waved a hand in the air. "No one knows if 'e's a sorcerer or nay. True, 'e seems to see things out of that bad eye of 'is and some of 'is spells appear to work, but then there's times when 'e's in a stupor and doesn't make a lot of sense, if ye ask me. 'E and the baron, well, they go way back, came 'ere together, they did, but to me way of thinkin' Muir's just plain odd. 'E didn't bother castin' any spells to scare away the curse, let me tell ye."

"You don't trust him?" Gwynn asked.

"Oh, 'e 'as a good enough 'eart, I s'pose, but 'alf the time methinks 'e's as daft as the town idiot."

This was the man in whom Trevin had entrusted Gareth's life? But then what did Hildy really know?

They talked on and Gwynn rested a little, dozing off on another woman's bed before a knock on the door signified that dinner was ready. "I'll be 'ere to serve ye, m'lady," Hildy said as Gwynn started for the door. "Lord Trevin asked me to be yer personal maid during your visit."

" 'Twill be short, I'm afraid."

The girl's sweet face folded in upon itself. "But the baron, 'e said ye'd be stayin' a fortnight or so—"

"Did he?" Gwynn gathered her skirts in one hand. "Well, he was mistaken. I'll be leaving soon to look for my son." She swept through the door and silently added, *And no one, not God Himself, or the damned baron of Black Oak is going to stop me!*

Hurrying along the corridor, causing the candles to flicker and smoke as she passed, Gwynn startled a cat who let out a yowl and scrambled out of her path. Down the stairs to the great hall where Trevin was already seated, she flew. He lifted his gaze at the sound of her steps and for the span of a short breath she was caught in the seductive blue of his eyes. Her feet faltered a step, her willful heart hammered a quick double-time for a second. A knight, the blond one known as Stephen, helped her to the main table.

Most of the guests were seated upon benches positioned at an angle below the dais supporting the main table. Heads turned toward her and curious sets of eyes watched her as she took a seat next to Trevin's.

"My lady," he said with a cock of one dark, insolent brow. " 'Tis breathtaking, how you look."

She flushed and lifted her chin. "Thank you, my

lord." Smothering a smile, she added, "May I say the same to you?"

He snorted a laugh. "You may, Lady Gwynn, do anything you wish." His smile was positively wicked and her stupid heart pounded even more wildly. His hair was freshly washed and attempted to curl, his square jaw freshly shaven, his eyes dancing a mischievous blue in the candlelight. He wore fresh clothes, all black, trimmed in leather and studded with silver. He looked dark, dangerous, and more outlaw than baron.

"The dress suits you."

"Does it?" She cleared her throat and was lucky to find her voice. " 'Tis the first thing here that does," she teased, wondering why she would bother to flirt with him. She eyed their guests but aside from a few curious glances, no one seemed to be unduly interested in them or their conversation.

One side of Trevin's sensual mouth lifted. "Hildy did not please you?"

"Nay, she's a good lass, but—"

"The chamber was not to your liking?"

"The room was fine, but I'll not be a prisoner here, *m'lord.*"

"Never."

A page filled their cups with wine.

"Good, then I'll be able to leave at will and search for Gareth."

He didn't reply as the cook, James, chose that moment to enter, leading servers with heavy platters of food. He'd not been lying about a feast of the highest order. Trenchers of brawn, pheasant and gravy, salmon, heron and eggs, tarts and pies, and a stuffed peacock with his quills attached were carried to the head table. Again, Gwynn shared a trencher with

Trevin and was treated as if she were, indeed, Mistress of Black Oak Hall. Serving maids and pages attended to her every need, bringing her warm wet cloths to clean her fingers, offering her wine or ale, asking if she would prefer salmon to eel or peacock to pigeon. As quickly as she finished eating one course, another, as savory as the last, was brought in.

Trevin ate heartily, as if he'd not seen food in the span of a full moon, and she, though worried sick about her son, couldn't resist the scents of spices and the taste of hot, fresh food.

Musicians played and acrobats performed as if the meal were a special event and most of the guests seemed genuinely glad for Trevin's safe return. Yet, behind the smiles and good cheer, lurking in the shadowy corners of the castle, buried just below the surface of the jubilation, Gwynn sensed a current, an invisible stream, of ill will. Not all in the castle seemed to trust their lord. Gwynn, as she picked at a joint of venison, wondered at the strain she sensed existed within the ancient walls of Black Oak. 'Twas almost as if the ghost of old Baron Dryw hid in the darkest corners of the keep.

A shiver, soft as the footsteps of a specter, climbed up her spine. She told herself that she was being silly, that Hildy's claims of curses and ghosts had colored her feelings for the castle, but she couldn't shake the sensation that something was wrong, very wrong, at Black Oak Hall.

After the meal, as pages were clearing the tables and the dogs were scrounging for scraps that had fallen into the rushes, Trevin remained in his chair and spoke with those who worked and lived under his rule. There seemed no rules about who could approach him. Everyone from the hound master who had lost his best bitch to illness, to the beekeeper who was concerned about the size of the straw skeps, appeared to need a word with him.

There were those who kept their distance, of course, and Gwynn wondered if they were the men and women who did not trust him, who thought him to be a thief, a cheat, and a murderer. How many knights and soldiers thought him the killer of Lord Dryw? Would they take up their swords against him or steal into his room in the dark of night to slit his throat?

She shuddered at the thought, but glanced at him again. A strong, agile man, he was all sinew and bone, muscle and fierce determination. Surely he could see to his own safety.

He turned, his eyes catching hers for an instant, and she looked quickly away, embarrassed at her wayward thoughts. The disturbing part of her own inner struggle was that she was beginning to care for the thief, not only because he was the father of her child, but because there was a part of him that touched her in a way no other man had. 'Twas foolish, of course. Feeling anything for him other than suspicion was dangerous. As Hildy had warned, Trevin of Black Oak was not the kind of man to whom a woman should be losing her heart.

But, curse it all, she was.

Chapter Nine

" 'Ere ye go, ye one-eyed bastard!" The guard, a squat, burly fellow with black hair growing profusely upon his arms, cast Muir's cane into the cell, then locked the door. "Now, I'll 'ave no more whinin' from the likes of ye."

"Thank you," Muir said and hid his smile. He'd been complaining about not having his cane ever since being tossed into the dungeon. 'Twas an ugly place. Water seeped through the walls and pooled on the floor covered with dank, sour straw. Rats, beady eyes reflecting the orange glow of a few torches, scurried through the cages where emaciated men barely survived. Muir had learned most of the inmates were newly incarcerated, those who had dared question the new baron's right to rule, and already they were in sorry shape.

The guard turned back to his chair and table where he was busy sharpening knives on a whetstone. The scraping of metal against rock was rhythmic and most of the inmates sat as if in a trance, neither speaking nor moving about.

Muir waited until the guard was bent over his blade and the candle that served as his only illumination showed his face set in deep concentration. Only when the magician was certain the sentry had forgotten him did he move to the darkest corner of his cell and with steady fingers unscrew the false bottom of his staff. From its hollowed-out center, he pried moss and stones, amulets, berries and herbs, a candle and, most importantly, a knife so small it could be hidden in a man's palm or if the owner was very careful, inside his mouth—a tiny, perfect little blade that was able to pick locks as well as slice through flesh. Muir smiled to himself and hid the knife in a special pocket sewn into the sleeve of his ragged cloak.

He replaced the rest of his possessions quietly and decided to wait until the time was perfect to make good his escape. First, he would gain information, listen to the gossip of the castle and discover what exactly Ian of Rhydd had planned. Then, he would disappear, but not before he relieved the baron of a few jugs of his finest wine.

Satisfied that things would turn out well, he closed his eye for a short nap only to feel a searing pain burn through his brain. "Jesus, Lord have mercy," he muttered between clenched teeth. His sightless eye stung in an eruption of pain that caused him to double over and clutch his face.

"What now?" the guard demanded, scraping back his chair.

" 'Tis nothing," Muir lied, hoping to stem the ache that burned as if he were being branded.

"Then shut up!"

"Aye."

The vision hit him hard. With the gale force of a storm. He saw all too clearly the images of boy and pup stalking through the forest. Gareth and his infernal whelp. The boy wandered easily through the thickets, the dog at his heels, and all the while murky shadows drew nearer, following the lad with a deadly

certainty that made Muir's heart stop. Just as the darkness attempted to cover the boy, Muir heard him cry
out and chains rattled sharply, showing themselves in
a coil like that of a labyrinth, blood dripping between
the rusting links. Father to son and son to father.

"No!" Muir cried, realizing that the old secret was
about to be revealed, that all he'd worked for his entire life was going to be destroyed. Oh, Morrigu and
Cerridwen, let this happen not!

"Shut up, old man, or ye won't live long enough to
see the gallows!"

"Aye, aye," he managed to whisper and wished for
a long, calming draught of ale. Clutching his cane as
if it were the staff of life, Muir rested his back against
the cold stone wall as the pain subsided.

There was no hiding, no sliding away from destiny.
Fate had seen to it that Gareth's future was placed
squarely upon Muir's stooped shoulders.

'Twas certain that if he didn't find a way to conjure
up a bit of magic—a miracle no less—he, Trevin, Gareth, and Lady Gwynn were doomed.

'Twas time the tables were turned, Gwynn decided as
she sneaked from her room and through the dusky
corridor to the lord of Black Oak's chamber. She hazarded one quick look over her shoulder as she climbed
the short flight of stairs, for she could not allow anyone in the keep to know her plans.

As she passed a dark, empty alcove, she felt a cold-
ness emanating from the spot, as if an invisible tem-
pest had cut through her to chill her blood. Was the
castle truly haunted as Hildy had insisted?

'Tis naught but a silly girl's imaginings, she chastised
herself, but shivered just the same.

She reached the door to Trevin's room and hesi-

tated. Earlier, as the meal was cleared away, Gwynn
had overheard Trevin speak in hushed tones to two
of his most trusted men. Sir Gerald and Sir Stephen
were to meet him in his room before the moon had
risen over the west tower. She, complaining of a pain
in her head, had made her way to her own chamber,
insisted that she was a private person and would have
no chattering maid sleep in her quarters with her.
Only after Hildy had disappeared down the stairs, had
Gwynn slipped into the empty corridor.

"God be with me," she whispered.

Once inside the room, she closed the door softly
behind her and paused to scan the large chamber.
Tapestries hung upon whitewashed walls and a spoked
chandelier with unlit tapers was suspended from a
high, domed ceiling. A fire crackled cheerily in the
grate and sconces held candles that had burned low
but offered a soft golden glow that played upon the
walls and ceiling.

The bed was low to the ground and offered no hiding place beneath it. A bench, three-legged stool, and
a writing table were arranged near the hearth. A wardrobe stood against the wall, but she dare not hide
within it as surely Trevin might take off his mantle
and hang it within. She eyed the ornately carved cupboard and decided if she were to hold her breath in
tightly, she could hide behind the heavy piece. 'Twas
a small space to be sure, the wardrobe too massive
for her to move, but if she inched her way in, she
would be able to hear what happened in the room
and once Trevin had fallen asleep, sneak away.

There was no other place to stow herself, so she
edged behind the wide wardrobe. A mouse scurried
from beneath her feet and cobwebs clung to her face
and hair, but she was able to press her back against

the wall. Her breasts were crushed by the oaken backing of the cupboard, her lungs constricted, her nostrils
filled with dust. She let her breath out slowly, found
she could breathe just barely, then waited as the
sounds of life in the castle filtered through the windows and crept up the stairs. Soft conversation, rattling dishes, chinking armor, and the ring of hammers
kept her from falling asleep on her feet. Once in while
a dog barked or an owl hooted. Doves and pigeons
fluttered to their roosts as life in the keep slowed.

After what seemed like hours she heard footsteps
on the stairs before the door creaked open. Swords
and spurs clanked and male voices she barely recognized heralded the lord's return.

The bench scraped against the stones of the floor
as a group of men, none of whom she could see, settled near the fire.

"Tomorrow we leave to find Gareth," Trevin said.

"And what of the lady?"

"She stays."

Gwynn bit her tongue, though her blood boiled.

"Knows she this?"

"Nay, but, Stephen, a woman would only slow us
down and we need speed and quick wits."

"Aye, m'lord," a third voice interjected. "If there
be battle we must not worry over her. She would only
be more trouble than we need."

"I think she will not like this." Stephen sounded
worried. " 'Tis her son."

"A woman knows not what she wants," the third
man said.

Gwynn's fists curled so tightly she felt her fingernails bite into the soft flesh of her palms.

"True enough. A woman is foolish thing." Trevin
sounded smug and Gwynn's temper soared to the

heavens. To think she'd actually thought she was falling in love with the stupid thug! "She will stay here and wait in case the boy returns."

"We will ride to Rhydd?"

"Aye, but we'll split up; one party will be the decoy to lure Rhydd's soldiers in the wrong direction, the other will actually scale Rhydd's walls and save Muir."

"The magician?" A snort of disdain. "Why save his flea-ridden hide? Did he not lose the boy?"

"Do not forget," Trevin said sternly, "Muir raised me. I entrusted him with the lad and if he's held prisoner, 'tis my doing, as surely as if I'd led him to the dungeon myself. I'll not have his death on my head."

The others grudgingly assented and they made more plans, talking and arguing while Gwynn stewed behind the wardrobe. Oh, how she wanted to leap from her hiding space and tell all the men, especially that arrogant Trevin McBain, thief, liar, and seducer, what fools they were, that a woman would only aid them in their quest. Gwynn was as good a shot with an arrow as most men and though a sword was too heavy for her to swing for hours, she was dangerous with her little knife. Asides, she used her wits more often than her muscle to get what she wanted. Trevin, though he knew it or not, could use her to help him find Gareth.

She couldn't hear all their plans, though, as more often than not their voices were low and muffled, muted by the other sounds of the castle.

The fire popped and sizzled, dogs barked outside, the wind rattled through the slats over the windows, and every once in while there came a harsh rap upon the door. Each time there was a knocking upon the worn oak planks of the door, Gwynn's heart pounded in trepidation for she feared that someone had looked into her room, found her missing, and was alerting the lord. She strained to listen and bit her lip. None of the disturbances were about her, however, and eventually Trevin's soldiers took their leave.

Thank the Lord.

Their footsteps dulled and the door of the room closed firmly.

Gwynn, hardly daring to breathe didn't move a muscle.

A lock clicked.

No! Where did he keep the key? Was she to be locked in this room alone with him?

Sweat dotted her scalp and her palms itched. What was she to do? Wait until morn when she would surely be found missing?

Think, Gwynn, think! She had no choice but to wait until he was fast asleep, then she could search for the key, unlock the door, and sneak silently back to her room. In the morning he would discover that someone had been with him and left his door unlocked, but she had no other option. This chamber was far too high for her to dare to leave by way of the window. If she jumped into the bailey, she would surely break her neck.

Dear God, help me. She was not going to be left here at Black Oak, treated like a well-kept prisoner while her son might be in danger.

The minutes ticked by and she heard Trevin unbuckle his belt and remove his boots. The sounds brought images to her mind that she forced back but she felt the cupboard doors open as he hung his tunic and breeches upon a peg therein. Sweat collected on her brow, palms, and spine as his scent reached her. She let out a long breath when the wardrobe doors finally shut and his footsteps over the rushes indicated that he'd crossed the room.

Please let him sleep long and hard, she silently prayed as he tossed a last chunk of wood onto the fire and then, she assumed, dropped onto the bed.

Now, all she had to do was wait.

An insect of some kind walked along the back side of her neck. She couldn't move, didn't dare scream, so endured the passage of the bug as it crawled over her shoulder and along the neckline of her bodice before thankfully taking its leave. Her fingers were curled into fists and she closed her eyes, concentrating on the sounds emanating from the bed. Was that steady, regular breathing she heard or the soft moan of the wind? Did the lord snore slightly as he rustled under the covers or was the noise only the trick of her imagination willing him asleep. Did Trevin drop off easily or did he toss and turn, vexed as the hours of sleep eluded him?

What did it matter? In the morn he would discover that someone had been lurking within his chamber and made good his escape. Certainly he would consider her a suspect. What then? Would he change his mind and instead of keeping her a spoiled, guarded guest, lock her in her room or worse yet, angrily toss her into the dungeon?

Nay. She had only to remember the way he'd touched and caressed her. Surely he wouldn't cast her into a dank, horrid corner of the castle.

She rested her forehead upon the back side of the cupboard as her legs began to ache from standing in one position. Oh, Lord, she couldn't stay here all night. Squeezing her eyes shut, she hoped to hear any noise to indicate that someone was about, but the castle was quiet and aside from an occasional muffled cough or rustle of mice in the rushes or wind sighing through the turrets, she heard nothing.

'Twas now or never.

Slowly she inched sideways, barely making a sound aside from the hammering of her heart. She peered from behind the wardrobe. The room was dark save for the embers glowing in the hearth.

Trevin lay on the bed, unmoving, his clean-shaven face in shadowy repose, golden light gleaming against his shoulders and catching the swirling, dark hair that grew across his wide chest. Her abdomen tightened at the sight of him, for the blankets had shifted and covered only a small section of his body. One strong, muscular leg was exposed all the way to his hip and Gwynn felt a familiar fluttering in her stomach. She dragged her eyes away from the enticing curve of his buttock and turned toward the door.

One step. Two.

"Leaving so soon?"

Oh, Sweet Jesus no! The sound of his voice stopped her cold.

"Why, Lady Gwynn, did you hear every detail of our plan?"

Dear God in heaven, give me strength.

"Did you not think I spied you cowering behind the wardrobe like a thief caught in the act?"

Slowly turning to face the bed, she saw the sparkle of amusement in his eyes, the slash of white as he grinned in bemused satisfaction. Oh, how he enjoyed mocking her.

"Well, now, *m'lord,* it seems we are even."

"Are we?"

"Aye. I caught you hiding in my cupboard years ago and now you've found me out."

He stretched lazily and the mischief brewing in his

eyes warned her that there was more trouble heading fast in her direction. " 'Tis true enough except for one small detail."

Whatever it was, it sounded dangerous. "I know not what you mean."

"Well—" He swung both legs out of the covers and stood. She gasped and forced her eyes to stay focused on his face for he was naked as the day he was born, his manhood visible in a thatch of dark curling hair. "—as I recall, I was forced to bargain with you, was I not?"

Oh, merciful God! Her pulse was thundering, her blood racing. Her throat was dry as desert wind in summer, her blood as warm as a vat of water left neglected on the fire. "You . . . you broke your part of the bargain," she reminded him.

"After thirteen years."

He was standing directly in front of her, so close she smelled the maleness of him, felt the heat of his body, noticed a trace of desire in his gaze.

Help me, she thought, knowing she was already lost.

"If I remember correctly, lady" he said in a voice that seemed lower in timbre than she remembered, "to atone for my having eavesdropped on your conversation with the old midwife, I was to spend three days in your bed."

Oh, God. She swallowed hard.

"Now, what say you? Would it not be only fair if we were to strike a similar pact?" He lifted a finger and traced the curve of her jaw.

She shivered, her insides warming, but managed a condescending smile. " 'Twas a different time, different circumstances. Had I not got with child my husband would have had me killed."

"If he'd not been conveniently imprisoned." He

lifted her hair from her neck, leaned forward just a bit, and pressed his lips to the sensitive spot behind her ear.

Her knees turned as soft as Cook's pudding and she closed her eyes. "Imprisonment is never convenient."

"Nay?" His lips were warm and oh, so, seductive as they moved against her skin. Desire awakened deep in the deepest part of her.

"Nay."

"How would you have explained the babe? Surely he knew that you were not carrying his child as you were a virgin when you took me to your bed."

The same question she had refused to answer so many years ago. He tugged on the neckline of her dress and kissed her bare shoulder. A deep lust stole through her blood. " 'Tis of no matter now." She cleared her throat, ignoring the passion he, and he alone, stirred within her. "I should take my leave—"

"Not yet, love."

She closed her mind to the endearment as she knew in her heart that he'd said the same words to dozens of women. She shouldn't fall into his seductive trap and yet when his arms surrounded her and he tipped her face up to his, she didn't stop him, couldn't find the strength to deny what she wanted so desperately. As he pressed her clothed body to his naked legs and chest, she felt all her resistance fall away.

Desire, her long-hated enemy, dared sear through her brain as well as the most intimate recesses of her body. Please, God, if You be listening, help me. Give me the strength to stop this madness.

But God turned a deaf ear to her pleas.

The laces of her dress gave way easily, the heavy fabric parting to drop in a wine-colored pool on the floor. Strong hands spanned either side of her rib cage, warm fingers searing her skin through the sheer fabric of her chemise.

His lips found hers and she sagged against him. Though she knew that what she was about to do was a sin; that in the eyes of God and the church she was a married woman, she could not find the resistance to stop the course of their twined destinies. Her pulse pounded, her breath was shallow, and all she knew was the touch and feel of this one harsh man.

Oh, Trevin, do not hurt me.

His mouth was hot, hard, and insistent. His tongue pressed against the seam of her lips and she opened to him, felt a thrill of anticipation as his tongue darted and played, plundered and danced with hers.

She welcomed him, tasting and touching as passion ruled her soul. Her arms wound around his neck, and her breasts, deep within her chemise ached for his touch.

"Oh, woman, what am I to do with you?" he said on a sigh.

Anything and everything crossed her mind, but she held back the words and kissed him until she was breathless.

With a moan, he dragged her closer. One callused hand lifted her leg to his waist and already melting inside, she felt his manhood pressed hard against her mound.

Don't do this Gwynn. Think! Consider Gareth! Remember that you are another man's wife! Know that nothing good will come of lying with the thief. And yet she was unable to stop herself. Her hands explored muscles as corded as thick rope, an abdomen as hard as a shield, chest hair coarser and springy to her touch.

He groaned against her ear as his weight dragged them both downward to topple onto his bed. Firelight played upon the angles of his face, accentuated the scars crossing his shoulders and back, and sparkled in his hair and eyes.

Lying atop her he kissed her eyes, her throat, her cheeks. "Ah, Gwynn," he whispered, his breath whispering across her body. " 'Tis beautiful you are." He kissed her breasts, first one, then the other, through the lace of her chemise until the fabric was so wet it was sheer against her skin. Tongue, lips, and teeth caressed her. Hot. Wet. Hard. She moved against him, wanting more as desire pulsed wildly through her. Faster. Hotter.

"You be so sweet, a temptress, to be sure," he said as he rimmed her nipple, so dark against the fine lace, with his tongue. Licks of desire swept through her, tingling her skin and creating a moist yearning deep in the most feminine part of her soul.

"And you . . . you be a smooth-tongued rogue."

"A rogue is what you want, Lady Gwynn." He lifted his head and stared at her with eyes a dusky shade of blue. "Say it."

"Nay, I—"

He kissed her nipple again, drawing hard, suckling as if he were but a babe. "Say it," he whispered across the breast.

"Nay."

"Oh, woman." He lifted the hem of her chemise and as he found her lips with his mouth, he discovered the rest of her with one strong hand. Fingers touched and probed and heat spiraled deep in her moist, intimate cavern. Sweat slid down her spine and she began to move, the wanting deep within her urgent and untamed. "Tell me you want me."

She licked her lips and he groaned before kissing her again. His hand moved. She bucked upward. He caught her and slowly let her down again. Her breath stopped in the back of her throat as he touched her in a spot that sent tingles through her body. As firelight turned his skin a deep shade of gold, she nodded. "Aye, thief, I want you."

"And I want you, love," he admitted with a scowl. "More than I've ever wanted a woman. 'Tis cursed I be with the want of you and I fear I'll be forever damned."

With one strong hand, he yanked the chemise over her head and settled his length to hers. Hard muscles collided with her softer flesh and the torment in his eyes faded. "The devil take tomorrow, may this night last forever," he whispered as he kissed her again and while holding her close, parted her knees with his. Gwynn stared up at him as he touched her with his manhood, gently prodding, not quite delving deep, causing her to lift up her hips.

Perspiration dotted her body. Need burned bright at her core. Still he teased, just gently nudging, but not quite entering as she writhed with the want of him.

"Trevin . . ." Her voice was but a desperate whisper. "Trevin . . . please," she begged, hating the sound.

"For you, love." With a single thrust he drove into her. Her heart pumped. Her lungs burned. The walls of the castle seemed to shift. He withdrew slowly only to plunge into her again. "Trevin!" Her fingernails dug into his shoulders and she moved with him. Slowly at first, then faster and faster, until she couldn't breathe, didn't think, was lost in the wonder of making love to him.

The years spun away and she was giving him her virginity once again, rising to meet him, whispering his name, holding on to him as if he were the only man in this world.

"Gwynn . . . Gwynn . . . Faith . . . forgive me . . ."

With a triumphant cry that shook the battlements and echoed through her heart, their souls collided and they were joined as if forever. His seed spilled into her and though she was married to another man, she knew in her heart that this thief, who had won his castle in a crooked game of chance, was the only man she would ever truly love. Even though as he'd loved her, he'd cried out his dead wife's name.

Chapter Ten

The embers of the fire had burned to naught when Trevin slipped quietly from beneath the covers. Gwynn rolled over and sighed softly. He froze, expecting her eyes to flutter open but she began breathing in a gentle rhythm again. His heart ached at the sight of her, asleep and innocent in his bed, her hair tangled and falling in red-brown ringlets over her smooth, bare shoulders. Thoughts of their recent loving—hot and wild and sinful—seared through his brain and it was all he could do not to take her into his arms again.

He'd only feigned sleep and as she'd snuggled against him, her naked body nestling to his, he'd struggled to stay awake and let her sleep, for he was determined to leave her.

He resisted the urge to bend down and kiss her forehead, or climb back into his bed and love her thoroughly again. But there was no time and before he left the keep, as was his custom, he had one more duty to accomplish.

Without donning his clothes he unlocked the door and slipped out of his chamber into the cold of the hallway. Quickly he ducked into another room where, without any noise, he threw on his tunic, breeches, mantle, and boots. As quietly as a cat stalking prey he hurried down the dark stairs.

Outside there was muted activity in the bailey. Armor, food staples, and tents were already packed into carts. Oxen were being yoked and some horses had been saddled and stood nervously waiting, their breaths fogging in the cold night air. Seven of Trevin's most trusted men were riding with him while Sir Bently, who was still recovering from a nasty wound received on a hunt for a wild boar, would stay at the castle and keep his eyes on Gwynn. It was Bently's distasteful duty to restrain the lady and keep her safely within Black Oak's walls. Trevin didn't envy the man his task.

Several of his men had collected near the stables, choosing their mounts and checking saddles, bridles, and weapons.

"All is nearly ready," Sir Stephen said. He thumbed the edge of his sword to test its sharpness. The blade glistened pure silver in the moonlight.

"I will be but a moment."

"Take yer time," Sir York said, yawning. A big man with a blond beard and round belly, he was tightening the cinch of his mount's saddle and was in no hurry to leave the comforts of the castle.

Trevin ducked behind the stables, through the outer bailey and motioned for the guard to open the gate. Rattling and clanging, the portcullis was raised. Trevin walked briskly up a well-worn path leading to the cemetery where pale white tombstones and wooden crosses marked the graves. His footsteps didn't falter as he wound his way to Faith and baby Alison's grave.

Pain tore at his heart and guilt, as always blackened his soul. He knelt on the damp moss and grass and closed his eyes. How had he come to this? From thief to outlaw to ignoble baron? Half the people under his rule thought him a savior, the rest considered him a demon who had heartlessly stolen an old man's castle, then killed him, and married his only daughter.

Pride kept his backbone stiff, fury clenched his fists, and remorse tightened his jaw.

He envisioned Faith as he'd last seen her, weary and in pain, still holding a babe that had been dead for two days. "Do not love another," she'd begged, agony showing in her eyes. "Trevin, please do me not the dishonor." She'd clutched at his arm, tears drizzling down her hollow cheeks. "I loved you. Dear God, how I loved you. Please . . ." She'd coughed and choked and he'd drawn her into the circle of his arms. "Vow to me, Trevin, that you'll never love another woman. Swear it."

"I swear. On my life, Faith. I will never love another."

He'd believed those words. Had known deep in his heart that he wasn't lying. But now, Gwynn of Rhydd had caused him to doubt all that he'd held true. He swallowed against a throat clogged with emotions he'd tried to bury.

"Forgive me," he said, as if his dead wife and child could hear him. "I . . . I tried, and . . . I failed. Both of you." His throat worked as he thought of his only daughter, born without taking a breath and the woman who had given her life to bear him an heir. "I am but a man, Faith," and the admission tore at his soul, for he'd betrayed her and the vow he'd made. "I did love you, you know," he said, glancing up at the moon and shaking his head at his own folly. "I just didn't know it until you were taken from me."

He thought of those dark days after her death, the loneliness and regret that had shredded his heart, the pain in his soul for the child who he would never swing in his arms or let ride upon his shoulders. He'd never known Alison, but he missed her sorely and it was her death that had led him on his quest to find his son. He would not lose another.

"I did not mean to lie to you," he said to Faith. "I never meant to love another woman, I thought I was incapable, but . . ." He let his words drift away on the breeze. Did he love Gwynn? Was it possible? Or was he confusing love and lust?

Reaching into the pocket of his mantle, he found the small pouch he'd put there days before. He untied the little purse and shook its contents into his palm. The ruby ring winked darkly in the night. "Curse you," he said, examining the jewel that he'd had with him all these years. Why? He'd told himself that he'd kept the ring for luck, that it was a symbol of his freedom for the coin and jewels Gwynn had given him so many years before. It had given him the means to ascend from lowly stable hand and thief to knight and eventually Lord of Black Oak Hall.

A station he regretted.

His fingers wrapped around the cold, heartless stone and wondered at the course of his destiny. "I miss you, Faith," he admitted, for the first time, since her death. "But I cannot live a lie."

So what was the truth? That he loved Lady Gwynn of Rhydd? His jaw hardened and he dropped the stone into its pouch. No. For the rest of his days he would love no one, not even the beautiful mistress of Castle Rhydd. Their lives seemed forever entwined because of Gareth, but he would not be foolish to lose his heart to the woman.

He slipped the pouch into his pocket and glanced at the black sky where the moon and stars shone bright. A breath of cold wind, as ancient as time, touched his cheeks. It was time. Renewed of purpose, he strode back to the castle. His new mount, Dark One, Sir Webb's charger, was waiting impatiently for him, pawing the damp ground, sidestepping whenever anyone came close to him.

Trevin touched the horse's quivering hide. With a grim smile he silently gave the signal for his small band to ride out, away from Black Oak Hall and toward Rhydd to find his son.

Casting one final glance over his shoulder to the keep where Gwynn was sleeping soundly, he felt another needle of guilt pricking deep into his soul. He'd tricked her, but then, hadn't she schemed to do just the same to him? Hadn't she been lurking in his chamber, eavesdropping on his plan to rescue Gareth? She deserved to be held captive for a few days.

After all, 'twas for her own good.

"Shh!" Gareth whispered into Boon's cocked ear. " 'Tis soon we'll both be able to feed our faces." Forlornly the little pup whimpered. Gareth's own stomach rumbled from lack of food and his legs ached from trudging for hours upon the deserted road. His last ride, on the back of a farmer's wagon, had been long ago and not for the first time did Gareth give himself a hearty mental shake that he'd left old Muir's horse back at the tavern. He'd been scared to the point of losing all the spit in his mouth and that explained why he'd run so fast and far.

It couldn't be because he was a coward. Not him. Or was it so? Doubts crowded through his mind that was already filled with guilt and remorse. Oh, what a selfish brat he'd been. If given one more chance to make amends with a mother who had spent all her life caring for him, he would take it. He thought of the times he'd crossed her, lied to her, sneaked out of the castle, and scared her out of her wits.

But he'd make it up to her. He would. If he just got the chance.

He should have flung himself into the foray at the tavern and tried to save the magician. Instead he'd fled like a fearful old woman. Well, he'd surprise them all, he thought as he carried the pup toward Rhydd. He hoped to be within a mile of the castle by dawn, sleep most of the day away in a hiding spot near the creek, then sneak into the castle just as the sun was setting and the guard was changing. He had enough friends within the castle walls to protect him until he found a way to save the old man. Surely Tom would aid him, and Alfred, the hound master and . . . well, there were sure to be others. Aye, his plan would work and he would avenge himself. He had to.

"I'll run old Ian through," he boasted to the pup though he didn't feel quite as sure of himself as he sounded. Even with a silver cast of moonglow, the forest was spooky. Leafless trees raised their spindly, crooked arms to the heavens and bracken and berry vines, lifeless and skeletal, hid all manner of creatures that he felt watching him with nervous eyes. As for killing a man, he'd done that once and felt not a speck of satisfaction for taking another's life. 'Twas not noble.

Again his stomach rumbled. Oh, to have a joint from one of Jack, the cook's, fat pheasants, or a slice of sweet pie, or a sizzling sausage. Even pottage, which the peasants ate, would go far to easing the emptiness in Gareth's belly.

"We'll find something soon," he told the dog and knew he'd have to rob a farmer's henhouse once again for fresh eggs or chickens for poor Boon. Though Gareth had been able to pluck a few winter apples from the barren trees, the dog ate not the fruit and his ribs had begun to show. "When we get back to Rhydd, I promise you, you'll have the finest scraps from the lord's table." The pup, as if understanding, wiggled against him.

The night was clear, the air brisk, the forest silent. Gareth wondered of his mother—what had happened to her? And the old magician, was he already dead or held fast in one of Rhydd's dungeons? Trembling, Gareth pulled his mantle closer over his chest. He hoped there was still time to save Muir and for the first time in his twelve years, he wished he'd paid more attention and listened as his mother and old Idelle had cast spells or drawn runes in the mud. He could use all the help he could get, even if it came from pagan rites.

Soon he heard the rush of water and knew he was approaching the river that ran past the castle. His heartbeat quickened in time with the increased pace of his footsteps. *Rhydd.* 'Twas odd how he felt about the castle in which he'd grown up. He'd enjoyed living there as the son of the baron, but now that he was no longer blood kin to Roderick, knowing that his mother had deceived everyone in the keep as well as Gareth, he felt a desire to return to his home and quieter days. Though he could not.

He reminded himself that he was banished. Being found anywhere near the curtain walls would spell certain death. Ian, whom he'd thought of as an uncle for all his life, was a cruel, heartless man; the thought of the black-hearted bastard being wed to his mother caused a foul taste to crawl up his throat. To rid himself of it, Gareth spat and Boon let out an excited yip.

"Nay! Hush!"

The trees gave way to brush and Gareth paused. Situated on a hill, looming dark and foreboding, stood Rhydd. A fortress. The keep of a cruel interloper. The only place Gareth had ever called home.

Tomorrow he would render his own personal attack against the current baron. He would sneak past the guards and— He jumped as he felt the tip of a cold steel blade press against the back of his neck.

He dropped the dog.

Boon let out a disgruntled "woof" as he hit the ground.

Gareth nearly lost all the water in his bladder.

"Well, well, boy," a nasty male voice intoned. "Who are ye, or should I guess? Don't tell me now . . ."

Gareth reached for his dagger.

"I wouldn't." The point of the sword pricked his skin. He froze. "That's better. Now be a smart lad, will ye? There's still a chance ye might live, Gareth of Rhydd, but, 'tis a slim one, to be sure. I, for one, will not be wagerin' on yer miserable hide."

Bam! Bam! Bam!

Ian's head reverberated with the infernal pounding. Too much wine. That was it, he'd drunk far too much wine.

"Lord Ian!" Again the horrid racket.

"Go away!" he grumbled.

"But, m'lord—"

"Hush, man!" opening one eye slowly, he glared at the door to his chamber and tried to still the dull roar drumming through his brain. He wiped a hand over his face and stretched in his bed when he caught sight of the lovely wench lying, drunk, upon the covers of his bed. Her skin was white and flawless, her hair a fine flaxen hue, her eyes—now closed—wide and blue and she could ride a man half the night, but, by the saints, she wasn't as smart as the tired old gong farmer and the ox he used to pull his cart of manure from the bailey. She hadn't stirred throughout the racket.

The sentry wouldn't give up. "Lord Ian, if you please—"

"Bloody hell, what is it?" Ian demanded as he climbed from the bed, threw on a black robe that had once been his brother's, crossed the room in three swift, painful strides, and flung open the door.

"I hate to bother ye, me lord," the rail-thin sentry apologized, his Adam's apple working when he caught a glimpse of the girl on the bed. " 'Tis the boy—Lady Gwynn's son. One of the soldiers found him lurking in the woods and—"

"Where is he?" Ian demanded, his headache suddenly forgotten. He nearly smiled. Could it be that his luck had changed?

"Downstairs in the great hall—"

Ian wasn't listening. He shoved the man out of his way and flew down the curved stairs though his legs still pained him and the robe billowed behind him like a mainsail in a brisk wind.

Finally!

The object of all of his wretched searching and nightmares had, indeed, been captured and now stood shivering in front of the fire. The new captive held on to a pathetic dog as if to life itself and flinched whenever one of the guards touched him or tried to get him to move.

"Leave me alone, ye dirty curs," he growled, though Ian thought his bravado was forced. The boy was so scared he shook.

Nonetheless Gareth still seemed to have some fight left in him. All the better. Ian cinched the belt of his robe and couldn't help grinning. "Well, well, well, look what the cat dragged in."

" 'Twasn't a cat, but an ass who hauled me in here," Gareth shot back.

"Pretty harsh talk from the boy who killed the baron."

The brat had the audacity to lift his head and hold Ian's furious gaze with his own. Though the boy was dirty and skinny and held on to the damned dog as if he thought he could protect the wriggling little beast, the cocky little son of a bitch still acted as if *he* were lord of the castle.

"You're in trouble, boy."

Gareth didn't reply.

Sir Webb and another soldier, a weasly looking man with bad skin, guarded their young charge with their swords drawn, as if they thought the urchin had a chance at besting them or outrunning them.

"Where did you find him?" Ian crossed his arms over his chest and circled the bane of his existence. Oh, 'twas sweet pleasure to have finally caught another one of the traitors. First the magician, now the boy, next the thief? Or that Jezebel of a wife of his?

"Lurkin' about in the forest, 'e was, m'lord," the scarred-faced soldier replied. "He seemed interested in that sorcerer, prob'ly came back to try and free 'im."

Gareth's jaw tightened defiantly. Apparently the guard had guessed the boy's intent.

"I figured ye'd want to see 'im."

"That I do." Ian let himself have the satisfaction of a smile.

"What shall we do with him?" Sir Webb frowned at the boy as if Gareth had manifested himself as Lucifer.

"I'd say hang him in the morning, but that might not be wise."

"You'd better kill me quick," the whelp had the guts to say. His blue eyes flashed courageously and Ian couldn't help but feel a tad of respect for him. "Elsewise I'll hunt you down and run you through with your own sword!"

"Will you?" Ian laughed at the boy's ridiculous sense of nobility. "I don't think so."

To prove his point, Gareth spit on the rushes at Ian's feet.

"Bastard!" Webb backhanded the boy and sent him reeling against the wall. Gareth's head snapped. His bones crackled. The pup gave out a pained yelp and fell to the floor. Paws scrabbling, he ran to a table and cowered beneath it.

Blood drizzled from one corner of Gareth's mouth but he managed to stay on his feet as he wiped his lips with the back of his hand. Smiling, he spit again. This time the bloody wad landed on Webb's boots.

The dark knight grabbed him by the collar. "Listen, ye thankless little brat," Webb warned in a low whisper. "I'll gladly kill your dog, then, after ye watch him die, I'll tan his spotty hide and pick the meat from his bones."

Gareth turned a sick green color.

"Believe me, I wouldn't think twice about killin' ye as well. 'Twould do me heart good."

Gareth blanched but he met the soldier's harsh gaze with nary a glance away. "Rot in hell."

"Nay, son, that be yer privilege."

"Let him go," Ian ordered.

Webb, after a second's hesitation, released his grip on the boy.

Gareth stumbled backward a step and wiped the

blood from the side of his face with the back of his hand. If looks could indeed kill, Sir Webb would have keeled over on the spot.

Turning his harsh gaze upon Ian, he asked, "Where's my mother?"

"Know you not?" Ian scowled. He'd hoped the boy would have information about where Gwynn was hiding.

"Nay, but I think you do." His blue eyes simmered with hate and for an insane second, Ian of Rhydd, experienced dread. This boy was the son of the outlaw. "So tell me, 'uncle,' where is she?"

" 'Tis a good question." Ian's eyes met Webb's for a second and he shoved his hands deep into the pockets of the black robe.

"He was alone," Webb explained, his cohort nodding.

"Unfortunate." Ian's mind as already turning toward the future and how he would recover his wayward wife. "However, she'll come looking for him." He hooked a thumb in Gareth's direction. "Just as this one crawled back here for the magician, the lady will come searching for her son."

"Aye." Webb licked his lips and grinned wickedly. "See, boy, 'tis not so bad. You want to see your mother and she'll return for you. You be the bait."

But Ian's thoughts weren't finished. "McBain will no doubt join her," he thought aloud, bile climbing up his throat as he considered the slippery thief who had lain with Gwynn so many years before. "For some reason, he seems to have decided to claim the lad."

"Claim me?" Gareth repeated. "What mean you?" Obviously confused, he dabbed at his bloody lip with the edge of his sleeve.

"Oh, did you not know?" Ian asked with feigned

innocence. He was only too glad to give the lad the bad news.

"Know what?" The boy was wary.

"That you, pretender to the throne of Rhydd, were spawned by a common thief?"

The boy shook his head. "Nay—"

"Oh 'tis true."

Horror dawned in the boy's blue eyes as he put the hidden pieces of his life together. "But my mother— she would not have—" He shook his head with surprising calm. "I'll listen to no more of your lies."

"Think on it, lad." Ian enjoyed watching the naive whelp's features twist in disgust as he considered the means of his conception.

"And you thought you were of noble birth, eh?" Webb added with a snort. "As fer yer mother, who knows what happened? Either she's a whoring slut who would spread her legs for the common man or she was compromised by the thief."

"Liar!" Gareth lunged, flinging himself at the knight, but Webb was ready. With a hefty shove, he heaved the kid onto the table and pressed his weight onto the boy. "Come on again, lad. I'll give ye more," he promised.

Gareth rolled to his side, his head hung over the edge of the table. He retched violently, his entire body convulsing. Had he anything in his stomach, Ian was certain he would have vomited the vile mass onto the rushes. As it was he clutched his guts and fought tears of indignation. "Nay," he said, over and over again. "Nay, nay, nay."

Straightening, Webb laughed wickedly and Ian suppressed his own urge to grin from ear to ear. At last his plan was beginning to work.

"You're a murderin' bastard," Gareth flung out recklessly.

"Careful, boy. Remember who was born with no sire," Ian said, then turned to Webb. "Take him down to the dungeon and make sure that everyone in the castle knows that he's being held until I decide when he'll go to the gallows."

Gareth paled.

"My pleasure."

"Oh, and see that a messenger is sent—nay, a traitor who is wounded, would be better—to Black Oak Hall with the news that Gareth of Rhydd is imprisoned here and sentenced to die." He slid the boy a glance. "That should send your mother running to save you, don't you think?"

"Go to hell."

Ian laughed. "You'll be there long before I arrive."

The lad straightened and sucked in his breath, but wouldn't give Ian the satisfaction of begging for his life. Instead he glowered at the lord of the castle as if Ian were but a useless insect he would like to squash beneath his boots. "I be not dead yet."

"Nor will you be until my wife returns."

"She is not—"

"Oh, yes, son. She is married to me. Legally. And she'll return. For you."

Gareth's eyes darkened in the same manner that did Trevin's of Black Oak. "And she will save me."

"Against all my men? I think not," Ian said but felt a premonition of dread crawl up his backside.

One corner of Gareth's mouth lifted into a hard, determined smile, another reminder of the thief. "Think again, for you know, she will punish you a thousand times over if any harm comes to me, Boon, or Muir."

"Oh, and how will she do so?"

" 'Twill be a simple matter," Gareth said, spitting blood onto the floor. "Remember, Lord Ian, she is more than a woman and much more than my mother."

"Is she?" Ian asked, bored with the conversation. His headache was returning and he had many more hours in bed with the wench, though she was as dull as one of Father Anthony's sermons. "We'll see."

"Aye, that you will."

"Take him away. He speaks nonsense." Ian stretched the muscles of his shoulders and considered a time when Gwynn would warm his bed. Oh, by the gods, then his revenge would be sweet.

"Be forewarned," Gareth said boldly as two guards slipped gloved hands beneath his armpits, dragging him forward while a third rounded up his dog. "My mother will not stand for this."

"What can she do about it?" Ian was tired of the boy's veiled threats.

"You don't want to know," Gareth warned, craning his head so that he could meet Ian's tired gaze. "But forget you not that she is a witch."

Ian shook his head and felt a weary sadness for the boy who believed so passionately in his mother. "Nay, child, Lady Gwynn is nothing more than a whore and a cheap one at that."

As soon as Gareth was out of earshot, Ian turned to Webb. "Now, see that one of the knights loyal to the lady, Sir Reynolds, mayhap . . . nay, Charles, Sir Charles would be the one. Make sure that he knows that Gareth is about to be hanged."

"Tonight?"

"Aye," Ian said, walking to his chair and staring into the dying coals of the fire. "Make a racket, talk about it, pretend that you are drunk, if it comes to that, but see that Charles awakes and hears the news. Then keep the castle gates open and follow him. 'Tis my guess he will ride to Black Oak Hall."

"You want me to sneak into the castle," Webb said, his eyes lighting with a gleam of satisfaction.

"Nay. Follow him closely so that you see where he goes, then wound him so that the lady and thief understand that the boy's plight is serious."

"Gladly."

Ian held up a hand. "But kill him not. He must get the message through."

"Aye, my arrow flies true. I will be able to give him a mortal wound that will sap out his life slowly."

"You were supposed to kill the boy before and make it look as if you were wounded yourself, yet you failed me."

" 'Twill not happen again," Webb vowed, sliding his jaw to one side. "I rarely fail."

"See that you don't."

Webb rubbed his beard, creating a scraping sound that irritated Ian. "Are you sure you do not want me to follow Charles and kill not only him but the others as well?"

Ian shook his head. "Death will come to those who deserve it," he said, "but I want to face my wife and the thief first." His muscles tensed as he considered them together. They had been lovers in the past and, he suspected, were again. "My justice will be slow and damning," he said, savoring the words. "Trevin of Black Oak will die knowing who it was that killed him."

Gwynn stretched languidly on the bed, memories of making love to Trevin still weaving in warm, sensual ribbons through her mind. Ah, 'twas sweet heaven to lie with him. Smiling, she slowly opened her eyes and reached out a hand to touch his warm body, only to have her empty fingers stretch and touch the cold far side of the bed.

Her eyes flew open and she sat bolt upright.

She was alone.

The bed was empty save for her.

Cold certainty settled into her heart, for she knew as surely as the sun would rise again that Trevin had duped her.

The fire had died and the lord of Black Oak's chamber was cold as a cistern.

"Oh, for the love of Mary." She pounded a fist against the covers, for she'd been played for a fool. He'd left Black Oak just as he'd planned. Without her.

"Thieving, black-hearted, son of a dog!" she muttered as if he could hear her. She threw off the blankets. While she'd been caught up in the rapture of making love to him, he'd used her, over and over again, until she, spent, had fallen asleep in his arms.

Oh, what a ninny she was. To forget her fears concerning Gareth, to wash away her worries of Ian, she'd let herself be caught in the sweet seduction of the outlaw. "Stupid, stupid, girl!" she chastised as, shivering, she flung on her clothes—well, Faith's clothes—then quickly finger-combed her hair and used water from a basin placed near the now-cold grate to splash over her face. Angrily she shoved open the door to the corridor half expecting a guard to place himself in front of her and order her back into the room, but the hallway was empty.

Good. She'd not be held prisoner; not by any man and least of all by Trevin of Black Oak. The nerve of the man seducing her, luring her into bed, then tempting her with sleep.

Was it any different from how you treated him in years long past?

Stomping her foot in frustration, she startled a cat that scurried out of her way. She was down the stairs in a matter of minutes and stopped in her own chamber where her boots and cloak were waiting. She didn't have time to change into her own clothes, laying clean and dry upon the end of the bed, but she searched for her weapon, the dagger in which she placed so much trust and discovered it, along with her pouch filled with the herbs, berries, and roots she'd gathered for the casting of spells, missing.

"Curse and rot your wretched hide, Trevin McBain," she muttered as she tossed her cloak over her head. Still lacing the mantle, she made her way downstairs and hoped beyond useless hope that she had misjudged him and that Trevin was still in the castle, that she had jumped to the wrong conclusion. Mayhap he was in treasury checking the keep's records, or eating a midmorning meal in the great hall, or walking through the bailey discussing supplies or repairs or the selling of oxen with the steward.

Aye, and mayhap you be a simpleton!

In the great hall, pages were setting the tables onto their legs and dragging benches into place. The cook was shouting orders, and servants darted through the hallways and up the stairs.

Gwynn ignored them all and nearly ran into the priest near the courtyard door. "Oh, Father Paul," she said, quickly crossing herself. "Could you tell me where Lord Trevin is?"

"The baron? Did he not tell you?" Paul's graying eyebrows became one and his lips stretched over his gums. "I believe—yes, I'm sure that the steward told me—the baron was leaving this morn with a band of soldiers—his best. Was he not searching for your son?"

"Yes . . . yes, I think so," she said, angry all over again, though she attempted to hide her true feelings. "He has already departed?"

"I know not," the man admitted. "I only assumed—"

"Aye," she said, turning to the door. There was a chance that she could catch up with him.

"We should pray for their safe return."

"Of course."

The priest brightened. "Good. I"ll see you in the chapel and there will be no more of this talk"—he fluttered his fingers nervously—"of devil worship."

"What?"

He leaned closer to her, as if he expected the very walls to hear his next words. "There is no reason to deny it, m'lady. 'Tis said that you practice the dark arts."

"Nay," she said quickly. "I am but a Christian woman, who prays to our Father as well as enjoys the gifts of the earth He gives us." There was no reason to explain to this man of the cloth that her spells and runes were but another means of trying to save her son, that she would attempt anything, aye, even bargain with the devil himself, if 'twould keep Gareth from harm. "Peace be with you." She reached for the handle of the door.

"Oh, there ye be, m'lady!" Hildy's voice preceded the rustle of her skirts as she hurried down the stairs. "Good mornin' to ye, Father Paul," she added crossing herself with the speed of a lizard scurrying to the safety of tall grass. "Lord Trevin said that I am to be yer maid and I fear I've failed ye as I've been tendin' to the dye vats this morn." She held up her hands and showed that the flesh on one arm had turned a bright shade of blue. "I splashed a bit as I was turnin' the cloth and old Mary, she was passin' by and told me to get back to me task. As if she can order anyone around," Hildy sniffed. "She's but a butcher's wife and has not the skill or patience for the dying of wool."

Gwynn had not time for the little maid's prattle, but she was trapped.

" 'Tis of no matter," Father Paul said, waving away Hildy's wounded pride with a flip of his pious wrist. "You must tend to your own business, which is, as you say, attending to the lady."

"I need not a maid," Gwynn argued as precious seconds ticked by.

"But Lord Trevin said—"

"I don't care what he said," Gwynn cut in.

"No, of course not, m'lady, I didn't mean to say that—"

"Do not worry yourself." Gwynn managed a smile for both priest and maid. "I will let you know when I need your services, until then you can go back to the dye vats or whatever other task is yours."

Leaving Hildy standing with her mouth agape and the priest gently shaking his head as if he saw within the mistress of Rhydd the very vestige of evil, Gwynn gathered her skirts and made her way outside.

Sunlight danced over the bailey. Geese honked loudly, flapping their great wings as they scattered by a pond where boys were busy trying to catch toads. Other, older youths hauled sloshing buckets of water from the well to the kitchen while girls, giggling and laughing, collected eggs in baskets or gutted fish in a trough near the kitchen door.

"Hurry, ye wretched snails!" the cook hollered. "I can't be boilin' pottage without water, now, can I?"

Gwynn ducked down an alley behind the kitchen where the scents of smoke and drying herbs vied with the warm odors of baking bread and the sizzle of venison. Two women were separating milk from cream while another milked a cud-chewing spotted cow.

Around the corner she dashed, her heart in her throat, her eyes searching the bailey, but nowhere did she see Trevin. Face it, Gwynn, he used you. Pure and simple.

She passed the garden and spied the stables at the far side of the inner bailey.

"Hey! Not now!" the candlemaker yelled at boys lugging pails of animal fat into his hut. "By the gods I've got no more room fer it this morn . . . oh, put it in the corner and be off with ye."

Clutching her cloak more tightly around her throat, she made her way to the stables where she surveyed the horses and with a sinking sensation realized that not only was Sir Webb's charger missing, but the horse she'd ridden—Trevin's steed—as well. Blast the man! He'd tricked her rather than the other way around as she'd planned. Well, she wouldn't stand for it and as she eyed the horses in the stables and those who were penned in the outer bailey, she mentally chose which one she would steal, a fiery-tempered dappled animal who appeared sound and swift.

Now all she needed was a little help to make good her escape and that 'twould be a simple matter.

But first she planned visits to the apothecary, the kitchen, the armorer, and finally the candle maker to replace the items Trevin had stripped from her. 'Twould take a little time, but she would soon be off to find her son.

She rounded a corner and nearly ran over the hefty knight known as Bently. "Oh."

"M'lady," he said, favoring his right arm that was in a sling from some hunting injury. "I've been looking for you."

"Have you?" The worry lining his brow gave her pause. "What can I do for you?"

" 'Tis my duty and my pleasure to be your personal guard."

"My what?" she asked, smelling a trick.

Two youths—a boy and girl—rolled a hoop as they raced by. Laughing, they yelled and hollered as they ran past and a dog dashed yapping at their heels.

"Your guard, m'lady."

"I need not someone to watch over me." Quiet fury seeped through her veins.

"The baron, he asked me, to—"

"Do not trouble yourself, Sir Bently. As Lord Trevin must have told you I ruled a castle by myself. Now, if you'll excuse me—" She bunched her skirts, but the man was persistent and wouldn't be deterred.

"I cannot. 'Tis my obligation to be with you and protect you."

"While I'm inside the castle?" she asked, wanting to strangle the man who had so recently loved her.

"Aye."

"And if I choose to go out?"

His gaze shifted away for a second before returning to hers. "The baron, he thinks it would be safer for you to stay inside."

"Does he? But that's impossible."

"Nay, m'lady, 'tis the way it must be."

He actually had the decency to look sorry, but Gwynn, anger invading her blood, wasn't fooled so easily this time. She sensed that he was a man who could not be moved. His mission was to see to her safety and she didn't doubt that he intended to do just that. She had no option but to pretend to agree.

"Fine, Sir Bently, though I like it not. I will wait until the baron returns and take up my, what would you call it, not my imprisonment or captivity, surely"—the guard winced a little—"but mayhap we'll refer to it as Lord Trevin's questionable hospitality."

"Thank you," he said and his eyes told her he didn't believe her entirely.

She would have to be patient and time, she feared, was running short.

" 'Tis nearly time for a meal and Cook's outdone himself again."

"Good." She forced a smile though it pained her. "If I might change into a suitable dress—"

"Surely, Lady Gwynn."

"But you'll stand guard at my door?"

He was solemn as death. "Aye. As the lord ordered."

"Then, Sir Bently, let us not tarry," she said, side-stepping a puddle and eyeing the gate where the port-cullis was open, but soldiers watched those who entered and departed with ever-sharp eyes. Damn that black-hearted McBain! When she caught up with him, Gwynn silently pledged, he would rue the day he thought he could outsmart her.

Chapter Eleven

"Why did you not tell me?" a voice in his dreams asked.

Muir snorted and turned over, then felt young fingers gripping his shoulders and digging into his old muscles.

"Wake up, would you?"

Muir stirred, his body aching. Who was bothering him? Slowly he opened his good eye to stare into the face of Gareth of Rhydd. His heart stopped for a second. By the gods, would nothing go as it should? "What the devil are ye doin' here?"

"A better question would be how did a magician let himself get caught and thrown into a dungeon?" the lad asked, eyeing his surroundings and shaking his head at the dark, damp interior of the prison.

"There are some things, boy, ye do not know about my magic," Muir grumbled.

"There seem to be things *you* do not know. It appears to get you into more trouble than it rids you of."

Muir stretched and felt his spine pop. Ach, what he would give for a pint. "Have ye not heard that patience is a virtue?"

"Patience?" the boy repeated, kicking at the filthy straw and sending an old piece of bone scuttling across the floor. "How can anyone be patient while rotting away in a prison?" He turned suspicious eyes on the old man and added, "Asides, *magician,* you lied to me."

"I tell only what is true."

"Then who is my father?"

Muir opened his mouth and shut it again.

"Is he Trevin of Black Oak?"

So the truth was out and the cursed prophesy was starting to reveal itself.

"Hey, quiet down!" the guard grumbled from the chair where he had been dozing. Other prisoners glared at Gareth from their cells, but said not a word as the argument continued.

"Can you not speak, eh?" Gareth whispered. He paced from one end of the small cell to the other. "Why did you not tell me that the thief and . . ."

"Killer? Is that what's troubling ye, boy. Listen to me, Lord Trevin murdered not anyone including Dryw of Black Oak. Hear not idle gossip, Gareth, lest you become the subject of wagging tongues."

"Oh, and you be a good one to talk." Gareth flung his hands upward as if in supplication. "You lied."

"To protect you."

"Little good it did."

"Because you returned," Muir guessed.

"Aye, I was an idiot."

Muir liked the boy despite all his impudence. "So ye came back to save me, did ye?"

"Yeah, as I said, a fool I be."

"And an insolent pup who is feeling sorry for himself."

Gareth sniffed and rubbed his nose with his dirty arm. There was blood on his chin and anger burning bright in his eyes. "They have Boon, too. Sir Webb plans to kill him."

"Oh, for the love of Saint Peter. Sir Webb won't harm the pup," Muir said, seeing that the boy was truly disturbed. "As for us, we'll be free soon enough." He cleared his throat and fastened his good eye on the sentry. "Fear not, for I will get us out of here."

Gareth rolled his eyes. "Oh, so now that I am here, you can suddenly make iron bars bend and stone walls disappear."

"Aye, in a manner of speaking." Muir couldn't help but smile as he thought of the little knife still tucked into his secret pocket. "Truth to tell," he boasted, "I can do even better."

"Can you now?" the boy scoffed, clearly disbelieving.

"Have a little faith, Gareth. We will be out of here afore too long."

"One minute is too long." Clearly the boy had no trust and Muir, despite his bold words, didn't blame him.

" 'Twill be me 'ead if Mary finds out I went against the lord's wishes." Hildy placed a basket of eggs on the edge of the bed in Gwynn's chamber.

"By bringing me these?" Gwynn asked, raising an eyebrow. She had no time for the maid with her silly superstitions. Sir Bently had been her shadow and she had to find a way to detain him as she carried out her plan.

"Not the eggs, m'lady." Hildy quickly scanned the room with her eyes as if she expected to find someone, mayhap one of her ghosts, to be hiding in the corners. Satisfied that she and Gwynn were truly alone, the girl lifted a few speckled eggs from the basket and moved

the linen liner. Hidden beneath the cloth were the
herbs and dagger that had been taken from Gwynn's
chamber. "I thought ye might need these . . . fer the
spell."

Gwynn was surprised at the simple lass's ingenuity.

Proudly Hildy lifted her chin. "Lord Trevin, he ordered all yer weapons taken and Mary—ye know
which she is, the fat 'un who s'psed to be 'elpin' 'er
'usband with the butcherin' but she's got 'er big nose
in everyone's business, that she does, thinks she can
tell us all what to do. Well, anyway, she told me to
take away anything of yours that might 'ave to do
with the devil and the castin' of spells. Was after me
like a 'ound on a wounded rabbit, so to get her off
me back, I stole yer things, gave them to Mary, then,
when she wasn't lookin', swiped 'em back again."

Gwynn couldn't believe her good luck. "Won't she
ask you for them?"

Hildy grinned. "Not fer a while. She thinks me a
silly girl without a brain in me noggin and I, I lets her
think whatever she wants. 'Tis easier that way. Right
now she suspects her own boy Elwin of doin' the deed.
" 'E's a mean one, Elwin is, always givin' 'er trouble."

"I see," Gwynn said, less interested in the snits of
the peasants and servants than she was of her own
plight.

" 'Tis important that ye get rid of the curse on this
keep and I wasn't about to let old Mary thwart ye."

"Good thinking," Gwynn said, but her own
thoughts were running ahead to her escape. If Hildy
were more clever than she first guessed, Gwynn would
have to tread cautiously. "Now, with these things
you've returned to me and a few more I bartered from
the apothecary and candle maker, I think I've got all

I need. But, we have to have privacy and, 'tis best for the kind of spell you want cast to be done in the forest."

"The woods?"

"Aye. 'Tis more likely Morrigu and Owein Ap Urien will hear us if we be in the solace of the forest, especially if we are close to water." She lowered her eyes and added a small lie to enlist Hildy's help. "Asides, you told me of the ghosts that walk the walls of Black Oak. We needs to be far from the castle walls if we are to keep the ghosts from interfering with our spells."

"Oh." Hildy nodded and bit her lower lip, as if she believed every word. "But if Lord Trevin finds out that I helped ye . . ."

"Do not worry about him. I will see to the baron. You only needs worry about Sir Bently, Mary, and the rest of the servants who might notice my leaving. I have a plan."

"A plan?" Hildy's eyes narrowed suspiciously.

How much could she trust this girl? After all, despite her worries for her unborn child, Hildy was loyal to Black Oak. But time was fleeting by and Gwynn had to hurry if she were to catch up to Trevin.

"If I am to save your babe and the unborn of others in this castle, I must cast my spell while the ghosts and demons of this castle sleep, while the sun is high."

Hildy nodded her head but didn't seem convinced.

"Lifting a curse is not an easy task."

"Nay, I s'pose not."

"So I will need your help while I steal one of the baron's horses."

Hildy's mouth rounded and her eyes widened.

Again she glanced nervously over her shoulder. "Oh, no. 'Tis one thing to dupe Mary about a few 'erbs and weapons that weren't 'ers to begin with, but steal from Baron Trevin . . . I cannot."

" 'Twill save his castle from the dark powers you say reside here."

"I know . . ." Hildy rubbed her lips nervously with the tips of her fingers. "But—"

"And 'twill save your child."

Again the girl hesitated and her forehead wrinkled. Absently she touched her flat abdomen. "Could . . . could ye also ask that a man fall in love with me and give me babe a name?"

"Which man?"

"Why the babe's father. Sir 'Enry."

Henry? The young knight with shaggy brown hair and sad, distrustful eyes. He was Hildy's lover? Gwynn had seen him only once and thought him a pitiful excuse for a knight, couldn't understand Trevin's faith in the boy, but now, she had no time to argue. "Consider it done," Gwynn agreed impatiently, "as long as you allow me the time to get away from Sir Bently."

"And steal a horse. Oh, m'lady, 'tis mad ye be."

Gwynn ignored Hildy's worries. "Are you with me?"

The girl hesitated, then nodded. "I'll do what I can."

"Good." Gwynn breathed a sigh of relief. She was anxious to get on with her plan for as the minutes passed, Trevin was getting farther from this castle in the search for their child.

One way or another, she intended to join him.

*   *   *

"We'll camp here for the night." Trevin swung off Dark One at the edge of a river that cut swiftly through the deep hills. A clearing at the edge of the forest would provide room for the tents as well as accommodate the ox cart. His horse waded into the shallows, lowered his head, and drank.

The men who rode with him dismounted while Sir York, driving the lumbering spotted ox, found a place to leave the cart. As he unharnessed the beast, Trevin watched his men work together. Ralph and Henry would take their bows and quivers in the search for fresh meat. Stephen and York would set up camp. Winston would tend to the horses while Nelson stood guard and Gerald scouted the road between the camp and Rhydd.

Everything was in place, so why did he feel so restless, as if something was amiss? His muscles were tense, his teeth on edge, but there was no cause for his worries. The supplies were plenty, the weapons strong, the animals and men healthy and yet . . . he felt anxious and sensed that there was danger. Mayhap that was why he had not shared his plans with his men.

Or mayhap it's the Mistress of Rhydd who vexes you. He plucked a reed from the water's edge and chewed upon it as he watched the men moving quickly about their tasks, but he was distracted with memories of Gwynn lying warm and naked in his arms.

Deciding that he was borrowing trouble, he helped in pitching the tents and watering and feeding the ox and horses and pushed all wayward thoughts of Gwynn aside.

Henry, the least capable of the lot, returned with three rabbits, which they skinned and gutted, then roasted over the fire. Gerald hadn't returned by the time the meat was roasted and again Trevin, as they sat near the fire and picked at the meat, felt a niggle of distress. He sliced a loaf of bread all the while searching the shadows, listening over the roar of the river for the sound of hooves.

"He should be back," Ralph said, as if reading Trevin's thoughts. A thoughtful man, he was prone to worrying. "Gerald. What takes him so long?" He bit into a shank of rabbit.

"Mayhap he ran into Ian's men," York remarked.

"Nay, he'll be here." Stephen skewered a piece of meat with the tip of his knife, then slid it between his teeth. "Have patience."

"On this fool's mission?" Henry scoffed. He shook his shaggy head and watched sparks rise to the heavens. "If ye ask me we all be lucky to be alive."

"Well, nobody's askin'," York said and several men chuckled.

Henry raised a pious eyebrow. "Wait and see," he warned softly. "I go now to pray."

"Good. Take yer time." York shook his head as Henry ducked into the woods. " 'E takes this life far too seriously."

"He's young," Trevin said.

"And green. Why 'e comes with us, ah, well, m'lord, 'tis your battle."

Trevin shook his head and took the jug. "Nay, 'tis all our fight. We all have reason to distrust Rhydd and the baron who rules there."

"Amen," York agreed.

"Aye. To Ian's death!" Winston muttered. "He and that dog of his, Sir Webb."

Ralph snorted, "Death to them all."

Trevin lifted the jug to his lips and swallowed. The hearty ale seared a path down his throat to settle like fire in his belly. He passed the jug to Ralph, then wiped his mouth with the back of his hand.

The men as they joked and grumbled, laughed and continued to pass the jug. Henry returned and several others took their leave to relieve themselves. There was a bit of discord, but they seemed well suited.

"I'll take first watch," he said when the jug was empty, bellies filled, and the fire burned low.

"Nay, m'lord, 'tis my duty," Nelson insisted.

Trevin agreed and slept uneasily, tossing and turning on his pallet, worrying for Gwynn and Gareth and wondering if he was able to help them. Near dawn he heard the hoofbeats, hard and steady, pounding through the forest.

"Who goes—" Nelson demanded as Trevin stepped out of his tent.

Breathing hard, lathered and covered in mud, Gerald's horse raced into the camp only to skid to a stop. " 'Tis bad news I bear," Gerald said as he swung from his saddle and Nelson grabbed the reins of his charger. "Trouble on the road." He was gasping for breath, his face splattered with dirt.

"What trouble?" Trevin demanded.

"I was on my way to Castle Rhydd when I spied a knight, his tunic stained scarlet with blood, riding the opposite direction, toward Black Oak. An arrow was lodged deep in his shoulder and another in the beast's flank. I called to him, but he heard me not and clung to the saddle for fear of toppling over. I know not who he is but he wore the colors of Rhydd and was kicking the horse like a wild man, so that the animal would continue to run."

Trevin scowled. "And then?"

"I rode back here as fast as the horse could run. I know not what happened, m'lord, but I fear we may be walking into a trap."

The worries that had been with Trevin since the onset of his mission turned darker and more dangerous. They were but one day's ride to Rhydd, and two days to Black Oak. He rubbed the tension from his muscles as the sun began to rise. "Stay here,' he told the small band of men. "Wait for me. I'll be back and we'll continue our journey."

"Where are you going?" Stephen asked, rubbing his eyes as he stretched out of one of the tents.

Trevin had walked to the line where the horses were tied and found the reins of Dark One. "I know not, but I'll be back."

"And if you're not?" Henry asked, his dark eyes suspicious.

"Return to Black Oak in three days. Until then, wait." He threw the saddle on his stallion's back, then sent up a prayer for Gwynn and Gareth's safety. Fear threatened his soul, but he pushed it far away.

Neither Gwynn nor her son would come to harm. He would see to it.

And what if you fail? His mind teased as he tightened the cinch, then climbed astride. He wouldn't. He would save his son and the woman who bore him or die trying.

"Y're sure this was your father's best horse?" Orwin, the stable master of Black Oak, was short and squat, an ox of a man with dull little eyes sunk deep into his head and arms as big as hams. The beast in question was running in circles on a tether that Orwin held in one meaty hand. With his other he snapped a whip and the horse clipped from a walk into a trot.

A boy of about six or seven watched the horse being put through his paces and nodded at the question. "Aye, this one, Paddy, he be a good horse. Pulled me dad's wagon, he did."

Hildy and Gwynn approached, staying close to the stables and away from the bite of the whip and the blast of wind that blew across the short grass of the bailey and brought the first clouds of the day. Gwynn was at her wit's end. It had been two days since Trevin had left and there had been not a chance for her to escape, nor the means.

"You know, yer mother, she's supposed to give the baron the best animal ye've got for heriot."

" 'Tis a bad tax, me ma says."

"But the law."

The boy, pigeon-toed and plain, nodded, though Gwynn decided he knew nothing of taxes or laws or heriot. All he understood was that his dad was gone and now the lord, the thieving, murdering lord of Black Oak, was taking his mother's best horse. Gwynn felt more than a second's misgiving. The boy's mother was right. Heriot was a bad tax. "Paddy here"—the lad said, motioning to the sickly looking nag—"was me dad's mount."

"Humph." Orwin, turning and keeping the leash taut, clucked and the animal reluctantly increased his stride into an uneven canter. "I'll have to see the rest of his horses. There, ye be, ye old nag." He slowed the animal to a walk and finally to a full stop. With practiced hands he examined the horse, running fingers along the gelding's back, then carefully prying open his mouth. "Tell yer ma I'll be needin' to speak with her. If this gelding"—he took his fingers from the horse's maw and hooked his thumb toward the sorry-looking nag—'is the best, as ye say, 'tis a pitiful herd ye have."

With a shrug, the lad took the reins of his horse's bridle and climbed astride his bowed back.

"Now, m'lady, sorry fer the wait." Orwin wiped his hands on his soiled breeches. "How can I be of service?" His smile exposed crowded, yellow teeth.

"I need a horse." Gwynn decided to be firm and insistent. Though she intended to steal an animal if necessary, she'd try first to coax one from the stable master.

"Do ye?" Stains from sweat darkened the green of his tunic and though it was a breezy afternoon, perspiration dotted his upper lip and ran along the edge of his jaw. "Beggin' yer pardon, m'lady, but Lord Trevin himself told me you were to stay within the castle walls."

She'd anticipated this, but Trevin's orders boiled her blood just the same. "So I've heard, but 'tis foolish for me to stay. If it's the horse you're worried about, I'm a good horsewoman. I'll take care of the baron's steed."

" 'Tis not the horse that concerns me, m'lady. The lord, he said—"

"I'm not his prisoner," Gwynn cut in swiftly. She was tired of excuses to hold her at Black Oak. She'd been polite and hadn't wanted to offend Sir Bently, James the steward, and priest, or anyone else who tried to make her at home at the keep, but the truth of the matter was, she could stay no longer. "I may come and go as I please."

"Nay, nay, I know that. The baron, he was clear about that, said you were his guest." Both his eyebrows raised, as if they were one. "Said that Sir Bently and Hildy, here, were to see after ye."

"And a good job they 're doing," Gwynn agreed. "Now, if I may have a saddle, bridle, and the gray horse . . ."

The man was used to taking orders, but was still unsure. "Baron Trevin, he told me that ye'd try to . . . well, leave the castle."

Gwynn lifted her chin and stared down her nose at the man. "As well I should. If I were a prisoner, would I not be locked away in my room or a dungeon?"

"Aye."

"And did not the baron tell everyone to see to my needs?"

"Yes, but the lord, he was afeared for your safety. Said that there were men at Rhydd who would want to do ye harm."

"How can they harm me if they be at Rhydd?" She smiled beguilingly though she had to grit her teeth. Who was this man—this stable master—to tell her whether or not she could leave the castle? Even while she was married she could do as she pleased. Because *your husband was held hostage.* Nonetheless, she had been her own overseer for the past thirteen years and wasn't about to let some servant determine her fate. Soon enough, when she had to face Ian again, her destiny might change, but not before. She held her head a fraction higher and was about to order the man to prepare her mount when the sound of hoof-beats pounded through the bailey.

A trumpet sounded.

"Open the gates, for Christ's sake," a guard ordered to the gatekeeper.

"But 'e bears the colors of Rhydd—"

Gwynn's head snapped up. Her heart turned to stone.

"For the mercy of the lord, open 'em. 'E's wounded, 'e is!" the guard cried. The portcullis rattled open and a horse and rider flew into the outer bailey.

"Who's that?" Hildy asked as she turned. "Oh, m'God, 'e's bleedin', 'e is."

"Oh, no!" Dread cast its horrid net over her soul. She recognized the rider as Sir Charles, the one man in whom she would have entrusted her son's life. Blood poured from a wound in his shoulder and his horse, lathered and wet with sweat, stumbled. The shaft of an arrow protruded from one flank and a dark purple stain ran in a hideous rivulet down the animal's back leg.

"Sweet Jesus!" Gwynn whispered, then more loudly, "Charles!" She sprinted across the bailey, her skirts flapping behind her, her slippers sinking into the soft, wet loam. "Get the physician," she ordered Hildy. "And . . . and my herbs. Now!"

"But, m'lady, d'ya think—"

"I said, 'Now!' "

Charles's normally robust skin was pale as death and his left arm didn't move. Blood crusted on his tunic. He toppled from the saddle and into Gwynn's arms. "Sir Charles," she whispered as she lay him on the damp ground. "Oh, nay, nay!" He barely breathed and his eyes, as he stared at her were like glass. "Charles, listen to me, I know you can hear me. You are here at Black Oak Hall and safe. Do not let go. Hang on, please . . . Charles . . . Charles?"

"L-lady Gwynn?" he asked, his voice a rasp.

" 'Tis I."

Charles had been with her for as long as she'd been

mistress of Rhydd. He'd stood at her side and spent long hours with Gareth, teaching him how to use a bow and arrow or hoist a sword or read the sky for the weather. He'd been her champion as well as her friend. She couldn't lose him. Wouldn't.

"Listen, for 'tis news I bear . . ." He coughed, his chest rattling, pain causing his face to blanch, his features to twist in agony. Though he looked at her, she was certain he was sightless.

"Shh. Save your strength."

He coughed again as peasants and servants hurried forward. Mary's harsh voice barked orders. "Give 'im room, would ye? Lousy clods. Make way. And some-one—you, Orwin, do *something* with that poor 'orse, would ye?"

"Where is the physician?" Gwynn nearly screamed as clouds covered the sun.

" 'Tis Gareth," the wounded soldier said, clutching at her arm desperately.

"Gareth?" Her blood ran cold.

"Aye . . . at Rhydd . . . in the dungeon . . ."

"No, Charles. You are mistaken, 'tis the pain speaking," she argued, though she had no reason to doubt him. "Gareth . . . Gareth is safe!" *How would you know?*

"M'lady, 'tis true. He . . . he will be hanged."

"Oh, God." Fear gripped her insides and she could barely breathe. She wanted to tell him he was lying, but could not.

"He . . . he is w-with the old one . . . the magician . . . I had to tell . . . to tell you, but I was discovered by Sir Webb. 'Twas . . . his arrow that wounded me . . . another that found the stallion . . ." His voice faded with the rising wind.

"Charles! Charles!" Scared to the very pit of her soul, she held him close, felt his blood flowing onto her dress as thunder rumbled over the land. "You must not let go!" *Dear God, save this man and save my boy. Do not let him die!*

Vestments caught in the wind, Father Paul ran through the crowd and upon spying the dying man, fell to his knees. "Our Father who art in heaven . . ."

"I found 'im not!" Hildy pushed her way through the throng. "The physician be not in his quarters and no one in the castle knows where 'e's hidin'. A bloomin' fool, 'e is, if ye ask me." Breathless, she handed the basket of eggs, now cracked and running, to Gwynn.

Though she wanted to give up, to fall into a puddle of tears and lift her fist to the heavens in frustration, Gwynn gritted her teeth and managed to gather her courage. Someone had to see to the wounded knight and then to free Gareth. "Sir Charles is to be taken to the great hall—the solar," she ordered and two men whom she'd never seen before stepped forward and began to gather the wounded knight into their arms. "Careful. Please." To Hildy, she added, "I will need hot water and clean towels, candles, and red string."

"Aye," the lass said as the two men carefully carried a moaning Sir Charles into the keep. "You," she whirled on Sir Bently. "If you plan to follow me, make yourself useful. See that the horse is attended to and watch for any more wounded." Grimly she added, "Charles may be but the first."

"Yes, m'lady."

The stable master urged the fallen stallion to his feet.

"Ah, 'e's a beaut," Orwin said, more interested in

the new addition to Black Oak's stables than the plight of the soldier.

Gwynn, mindless of the crowd that had gathered and the first drops of rain beginning to fall, pushed her way through the curious people to the great hall. She thought of Gareth in Rhydd's dungeon. *Dear God, keep him alive, please. And if that magician is worth anything, may he cast a spell and find a way to escape.*

Where was Trevin? Did he know of Gareth's plight? Her heart ached, but she could not worry, not until she was certain Sir Charles was being tended to.

In the solar Sir Charles was stretched upon a table, the life forces seeping from him with every second. He had lost conscious thought and when Gwynn leaned close to his ear and whispered his name, he didn't move.

" 'Twill be all right," she assured him, though she doubted her own words. "Rest easy, Sir Charles." Father Paul entered and shook his head. "Do not lose faith," she reprimanded him crossly. "We'll not be hearing last rites."

With the help of two women, Gwynn stripped Charles of his tunic and saw the gash, a fresh, gaping wound that sliced through his skin and flesh that was scarred from battles that were waged in the protection of Rhydd and the mistress of the keep. Guilt pricked at Gwynn's soul. How much pain had this proud man endured while protecting Castle Rhydd as well as her honor?

" 'Tis deep," one of the women said, gently touching the wound and shaking her head.

" 'Twill be fine." Gwynn swabbed the cleaved skin clean of blood and dirt.

" 'Tis mortal," the second one argued with a sad cluck of her tongue.

"We know that not. Come, no more of this talk. We must stitch him." Gwynn had seen to wounds before and though Charles's cut was severe, he was a strong man. While the priest crossed himself and, closing his eyes, knelt in a far corner and prayed for Charles's soul, Gwynn washed the wound with the hot water and towels Hildy had carried into the chamber, then began stitching.

" 'Tis too late, I fear," the girl said, but Gwynn would not listen to Hildy's concerns. Carefully, she sewed Charles's muscle, sinew, and skin together, then washed her hands.

"You may want to leave now," she said to the priest as she reached into her basket.

"Why . . . oh, nay," Father Paul said when he saw her withdraw her knife and candles. "You will not call up the spirits in this house, m'lady."

"I will do what I must." She leveled a glare at the man of the cloth and he sighed, imploring her with worried eyes.

When she refused to give in, he let out another long-suffering sigh and fingered his rosary. "I'll pray for your soul."

"As I will pray for yours."

While the ashen-faced priest and the women within the solar looked on, Gwynn lit candles and dusted the air with herbs for healing. Softly she chanted a spell, then tossed bits of apple, rose, and wild cherry onto the flames of the tapers and the fire burning on the hearth. "Save this good-hearted man," she asked, twisting knots in a red cord and tying it carefully around Charles's shoulder.

"Please, Lady Gwynn, do not use the dark powers here!" Father Paul beseeched again.

"I only asked for help."

"But use of the dark arts is forbidden. Please, I beg of you again, do not blacken this Christian keep."

"I seek help wherever I can find it," Gwynn snapped and laid her hands upon Charles's chest. Closing her mind to the priest's request, she concentrated only on healing, on letting her energy flow from her palms into the source of his pain. In her mind's eye she saw the wound from within, felt the heat and cold where Sir Charles ached.

When her energy started to fade, she said, "I bid you well, Sir Charles."

He did not move, but she sensed the lifeblood that had been flowing out of him was staunched. Her legs were weak, her body drained as she pocketed her dagger and herbs. While the priest dropped to his knees near the window and the women tended to the wounded soldier, Gwynn slipped through the open door.

On the stairway she met the physician, taking the steps two at a time and breathing hard. "The patient?" he asked.

"Is alive. In the solar." She pointed the way and leaned against the cool stone walls of the stairway as candles flickered in a dim, honey-colored light. There was nothing more that she could do for Sir Charles, brave knight that he was.

But she could help her son. Before Ian had the boy hanged.

Thank God fate had given her a new opportunity to escape.

While the keep was still abuzz with Sir Charles's

arrival and Orwin was trying to save the wounded charger, Gwynn planned to leave Black Oak and ride to Rhydd. Sir Bently was busy elsewhere and Hildy, too, was no longer attached to her.

She thought of Trevin, but decided to stay as far away from the outlaw as she could. Not only could her heart not be trusted whenever he was around, but he had seduced her, then imprisoned her in this very keep.

Her willful heart ached for she feared she would never see him again, but there was no time to be lost. Nay, she must ride to Rhydd alone. Once within the keep she would throw herself onto Ian's mercy. Bile rose in her throat, but she swallowed it back. She could endure anything, even sharing Ian's bed, if he would but let Gareth go free.

"Be with me," she prayed, needing strength.

Her first concern was to find a horse. The gray came quickly to mind, but Gwynn wouldn't be picky as long as the animal was fleet and sure. As she hastened down the remaining steps, she sent up another prayer for Gareth's safety and her own ability to steal one of Trevin's horses. That thought warmed the cockles of her heart.

No one accosted her as she made her way through the great hall and opened the door.

Outside the day had turned to night with the cover of clouds. Rain pelted from the sky and slanted with the harsh fury of the wind. Girls hastily tried to take down laundry that had been strung near the herb garden. Boys hunched their shoulders against the wind and rain as they drove sheep into pens at the far end of the inner bailey while Gwynn, ducking through the shadows, hurried past.

In the stables, Orwin was tending to the wounded horse, talking more gently than Gwynn would have guessed. Several boys who helped him with the herd were caring for the other palfreys, chargers, and jennets in the stables and there was no chance she could take one of them without being caught.

Her heart plummeted as she backed away from the stables and squinted through the storm. At the corner of the mason's hut she stopped short as she spied not one, but two horses tied to iron rings at the farrier's shop. The smith was at the forge, his back to the animals and before Gwynn thought twice she strode boldly forward. Her hands fumbled slightly but she managed to untie the bridle of a dun-colored gelding. His black mane and tail caught in the wind, his ears pricked up as she approached. He let out a soft nicker as Gwynn, without the aid of a saddle, swung across the animal's wet back.

The farrier didn't look up from his work.

Heart pounding, Gwynn pulled her cloak and hood more closely about her face and though one guard shouted at her as she rode through the gate and under the portcullis, she ignored him.

"Halt there, you!" he yelled.

"Hey! Wait! Was that the lady?" Sir Bently's voice rang from the western watchtower.

"Oh, for the bloody love of Christ!"

"If that be her, the baron 'e'll skin us alive!" Bently sounded frantic and Gwynn experienced a pang of guilt that she immediately pushed aside. "Move!" Gwynn ordered, leaning forward. "Run like the wind!"

The horse responded. His strides lengthened. His hooves pounded the road. Through the rain he ran, passing travelers, oxcarts, and wagons. Flinging mud with his hooves, neck stretched forward, he galloped, the wind forcing Gwynn's hood off her face, catching in her hair and causing her cloak to stream behind her like a banner. "Run," she ordered the horse. Would the soldiers follow? Oh, Lord, she hoped not, for not only would she be trying to outrace the knights of Black Oak, but she could be leading them straight into the waiting army of Rhydd. Even now Ian's soldiers could be on this very road. "Run! Run! Run!"

If she were smart, she would take to the little-used paths and trails winding through the fields and hills that separated the two castles. She could use the forest as cover and still, if she rode day and night, be able to reach Rhydd sometime the day after the morrow, albeit not before dusk. Not that it mattered. She had no plot to save her son other than offering herself and her undying loyalty to Ian and though the thought galled her, she swallowed back her foolish pride. 'Twas worth the sacrifice if only Gareth were allowed to live.

And what of Trevin?

"Black-hearted bastard," she growled as the rutted road, empty and scattered with puddles, stretched into the forest. How could she have been so duped by his lovemaking? At the thought she felt a tug on her heart and an answering pull deep in her womb. How could he love her so thoroughly, then heartlessly leave and hold her hostage in his own keep? Oh, when she got her hands on him, she would place them around his thick neck and . . . and what? Strangle him? Shake some sense into him? Or kiss him until both their knees were weak?

She had been foolish to give herself to him, to have lain in his arms, dozing and waking over and over again to the warm inspiration of his kiss and the scorch of his naked skin upon hers.

True, he had been her only lover. Oh, she'd slept with her first husband, shared his bed, and wondered at his cold nuzzlings.

Despite her vocal dismay and arguments, her father had bargained with Roderick of Rhydd, much as he would have negotiated the sale of a prized destrier.

She'd left her home and on the day of the wedding her husband had informed her that he expected her to bear him many sons. That night and for several weeks thereafter she'd shared his bed, attempted to submit to the foul act, and was subjected to Roderick's passionless kiss and cold hands. Aye, he'd mounted her, but never had his member held an erection, never had he been able to penetrate her. He'd blamed her, forced her to do despicable deeds that had failed to make him hard.

On the day he'd left to do battle, he'd tried again, insisting that she shame herself by kneeling like a dog so he could take her from behind. She'd suffered the indignity only to feel him fail yet again. He'd slapped her hard across her bare buttocks, then left, telling her that should she not deliver him the heirs he wanted, she would regret it.

His meaning had been clear. He had two dead wives who had foolishly not borne him children.

'Twas no surprise when Idelle, in Gwynn's chamber thirteen years before, had revealed that she wasn't with child and yet she wouldn't believe it. 'Twas only luck and Trevin's mercenary streak that had brought him to her chamber. 'Twas that first afternoon when she'd lost her virginity to a thief that she'd learned of lovemaking and had yearned, over the years, for more.

Trevin, blast him, hadn't disappointed her. If anything, his touch, now that he was a full-grown man, stoked the fires of her passion more readily than before. Despite her anger, she knew that she would never feel for another man the intensity, the lust, damn it, the love, she felt for him.

'Twas her very private secret. No one, especially not the thief-baron himself, would ever know the feelings buried deep in her wayward heart.

Through the rain she rode never seeing a sentry or knight from either castle.

Sometime during the night, when her fingers were frozen around the reins and her legs numb from the ride, the clouds parted and the showers that had followed her like a hex evaporated into the darkening sky.

Jewel-like stars were flung across the black heavens and a lazy crescent moon hung low in the sky, offering some meager silvery light.

Her horse was tired, lather and mud darkening his gold coat, and she, too, felt a weariness settle deep in her bones. Though the urge to ride onward, to keep going until she was at the very battlements of Rhydd, was strong, she had no choice but to rest.

" 'Tis good you've been," she said, stroking the horse's thick neck as she reined him to a walk.

At the edge of a stream, she dismounted, letting the horse drink as she washed her face and hands. Her back ached, her legs wobbled from hours in the saddle and yet she opened her pouch and tossed dust into the air for Gareth's safety.

"Now for you, Hildy," she said, as if the girl were with her. Carefully she drew runes in the creek bed, then cast a spell that she hoped would dispel the curse Hildy was certain had been leveled against Black Oak

Hall. The girl was silly, of course, but worried for her unborn child.

"Be with them all," she prayed to a God who had seldom listened to her as she led her horse to a tiny glade where winter grass offered him some feed. Once he was tethered to a young sapling, she found her own shelter under the spreading branches of a long-needled pine tree.

The ground was dry, old needles offering some cushion against the hard earth. Pulling her cloak about her, she ignored the pangs of hunger in her stomach and the foolish longing she felt for Trevin. She had only to think of their last night together to remember the way her skin tingled at his touch, the warm possession of his mouth molding to her lips, the heady sensation of strong male muscles pressed urgently to hers.

"Stop it," she mumbled. She needed to sleep, to prepare for the next day when she would have to face Ian of Rhydd. Her husband. That thought rankled her sourly, but she was reminded of Gareth and her heart turned to ice. He could not die! She would do anything, *anything* to save him.

She had no time to think of the lying bastard who had loved her so thoroughly, then left her without a word.

Slumber came easily. She was listening to the jangle of her horse's bridle as she plucked at grass, the sigh of wind through the branches overhead and the croak of a solitary frog when consciousness gave way to dreams.

Only much later as an exposed root poked into her back and she shifted did she hear another sound—the crackle of a stick being broken and the soft tread of boots. Fear shot through her blood. Instantly awake, she seized the dagger from its sheath.

"So, the lady awakes," a familiar male voice said. Her heart jolted.

Trevin of Black Oak, damn his lying hide, strode out of the shadows. Tall and imposing, he crossed his arms over his chest and glowered down at her. "Why is it, woman, that I'm not surprised you disobeyed me?"

Chapter Twelve

"I'll take no orders from you." Gwynn scrambled to her feet. Her pulse throbbed. Her heart thundered and she wanted to shake the very life from the man who dared stand before her. "How did you find me?"

"Luck," he admitted with a smile that was a jagged slash of white that flashed in the darkness. Dressed in black, a new beard shadow roughening his chin, Trevin glared at her with eyes as dark as midnight and she was reminded of looking into those very eyes while he had made sweet, slow, sensuous love to her. For the express purposes of lulling her into trusting him. Oh, what a simpering fool she'd been.

"Luck," she repeated, taunting him. "Like the kind of luck you had when you won the castle from Lord Dryw?" He didn't bother to answer and she stepped closer to him, her fury mounting as she remembered each incident of mortification she'd faced at being held hostage, for that is what it was, at Black Oak Hall. "You . . . You had no right to try and keep me prisoner!"

" 'Twas only to keep you safe." His voice was low, like the sea at the turning of the tide.

" 'Tis not your concern, *my lord.*" Gossamer clouds scudded in the heavens, partially hiding the stars, and the forest seemed to close around them as if they were the only two people in this world. "I-I can take care of myself."

"Can you?" A dark eyebrow cocked insolently and he stared at her so long and hard she could suddenly barely breathe. Her abdomen tightened, her diaphragm pressed hard against her lungs.

She heard the sounds of the night, the hum of insects, the soft hoot of an owl and the rush of water as it tumbled over a creek hidden behind the thickets of oak and fragrant pine. Oh, what cruel fate that he could turn her thoughts to such a jumble when they had no time, no time at all to rescue Gareth.

"Have I not for the past thirteen years?" she managed to demand. "Not only did I look after myself, but our son as well all the while ruling a castle."

"Yea, and now you are a bride who has run from her husband, our son is banished and might face death, and your castle is in the hands of a man who is your sworn enemy."

"All because of you!" She would not let him turn this all around. 'Twas his fault as much as hers. She tossed her hair from her eyes and one side of his mouth lifted in amusement as he extracted a long needle from the tangled curls. His fingers grazed her cheek and all the spit in her mouth disappeared. Fierce but tender. Threatening but gentle. So was Trevin the outlaw.

Her stomach did a slow, sensual roll and for a second she thought only of kissing those hard, blade-thin lips and tumbling to the ground with him. But she could not. There was too much at stake. "Do you know that Gareth has been captured?"

"No." His countenance was instantly grim.

" 'Tis true, Trevin. Though he was sorely wounded, Sir Charles rode to Black Oak and told me that our boy is now captive. It seems both he and your magician friend have been cast into the dungeon." Her heart was heavy with the thought of her son lying in the rotting prison beneath the towers of a castle he'd known as his home.

Trevin's jaw tightened and his eyes glittered with a seething, deadly rage. "One of my men saw a wounded man wearing the colors of Rhydd riding to Black Oak. He also spied Webb, who we think attacked him."

"Aye, Charles said as such. No doubt Ian ordered Charles slain to prevent him from reaching me with the news of Gareth's imprisonment." Gwynn shook the pine needles from her hair and fingered her dagger.

"So it seems." He glanced at the night black heavens, then back to Gwynn. "Worry not. I will free both Gareth and Muir."

"Nay," she said, for as angry as she was with him, she knew that if he were to face Ian, Trevin would meet his end and the thought of his death, of never seeing him again was a torment she could not bear. "I will go. Ian will bargain with me."

"Bargain?" He snorted.

"I will offer myself as trade."

"What makes you think he will honor a bargain made with a woman who has already pledged herself to him?" Trevin rubbed the muscles of his neck and his eyebrows were drawn together, his eyes narrowed thoughtfully.

She'd considered this herself and had no answer. "I think . . . at least I hope that he will want to please me."

"And if he does not?" Trevin asked.

Her gaze locked with his. "Then I suppose I will have no choice but to rely upon you, thief."

Trevin leaned down so that his gaze was level with hers, his breath warm as it touched her skin. "Make no mistake, woman. No harm will come to our son," he vowed.

"How can you be certain?"

"Your husband is not foolish enough to risk my wrath." His nostrils flared in the darkness. "Asides, he is using our son as a lure." Trevin's gaze met hers again and in one heart-stopping second she was lost to him. "He dares not harm him as it is you he wants."

"And you."

He took her hand and pulled her away from the tree. "Nay, m'lady, Ian wants me dead—or alive so that he can make a spectacle of killing me."

"Then I will give myself—"

"He will not get the chance," Trevin vowed.

"But—" The vision of Trevin bloodied from Ian's sword was too much to bear. "—you do not know him. He may be much older, but he is quick with a sword and knife."

"Not quick enough, m'lady," Trevin promised. He wrapped a strong hand around the nape of her neck and drew her head closer to his. "As long as I live and breathe, you will never give yourself to that cur."

"But for Gareth—"

"Shh. Know you this," he vowed, his breath whispering across her face. "I will never let you down, Gwynn of Rhydd. Nor will I let you place yourself or our son in danger. If you have faith in nothing else in this world, believe that you can trust me above all else."

She swallowed hard and tried to slow the heat rushing through her blood. But he was too near, too male.

The quietly disturbing scents of musk and leather mingled with the rain-washed smell of the forest. She felt his heat, knew a gnawing primal lust that was beginning to burn through her veins. "I—I can't."

"Try," he murmured, his lips brushing hers ever so gently.

Oh, God, was that her heart knocking so loudly?

"Please, Trevin . . . oh, nay . . ."

With pale moonlight caressing his face, he took her into arms as strong as barrel staves and pressed cool, insistent lips to hers. She felt a desperation in his kiss, a wild need that pierced her soul.

There was no time for this madness; she could not place her faith in a man who would sneak away from her bed and hold her hostage. She could not, would not . . .

Resistance fled.

Her chilled, ready lips parted as if of their own accord. His muscles strained as he kissed her, as if though he wanted her, needed her, he, too, was battling his desire.

All too willingly she accepted his tongue, warm and wet, as it entered her, touching, searching, playing with hers.

He trembled violently and she was lost to him yet again. Knowing she was making a mistake, she leaned against him and wound her arms around his neck.

"Sweet Jesus," he whispered. "Forgive me."

His weight dragged them downward and Gwynn closed her mind to the doubts that sped through her mind. Aye, this was wrong. Aye, she might regret the glorious act for the rest of her life, but nay, she would not stop it from happening. Tonight might be the last night they would ever be together, the last time she would feel his kiss, the last moment she would ever

feel his welcome weight upon her. Without another
doubt, she closed her eyes, drew from his strength,
and felt this dark, unforgiving night wrap around her
as she gave herself to the only man she had ever loved.

"I hate the bastard." Gareth rocked back on his heels
in this hellhole of a prison and glared at Muir. Cold,
beaten, and hungry, Gareth wanted the truth.

The old man stirred but didn't waken.

"And I think you be a lying one-eyed fool."

"Say . . . what?" The old magician, lying on his
side, stretched and opened his eyes.

"Trevin of Black Oak. The murderin' thief. I hate
him. He be *not* my father." Gareth wasn't going to
believe any such poppycock. So his father wasn't the
baron. Fine. He didn't need a sire. He'd gotten along
well enough so far without a father . . . well, except
that now he was being held prisoner in a rotting dungeon and scheduled to be hanged.

"Ah, boy, Trevin's a good man." Muir was quick
to hold up a hand when he saw the protests forming
on Gareth's tongue.

"I don't see how," Gareth growled as the guard,
keys clanging, opened up the cell door. Rats scurried
through the filthy straw.

"You. Old man. The baron wants to 'ave a word
with you." The guard belched and scratched at his
protruding stomach while Muir struggled to his feet
and, wincing, stretched his back until it made a series
of pops. "Come along now."

Gareth saw the ghost of a smile pass over the sorcerer's lips. "Find out about my mother," he begged,
"and Boon." He held onto the grimy bars as Muir,
led by the guard, was shepherded out of the dungeon.
'Twas a horrid place with rats and mice crawling

through the holes in the crumbling walls and a stench
that reeked from rotting food and urine.

If his mother could see him now she would keel
over. Better that she never know. Oh, Mother, he
thought, I've failed you. He'd never expected to miss
her, had often thought her bossing was a bother, but
oh, what he would give to have his blissful, naive life,
when he was considered the son of the baron, returned
to him.

"Fresh straw for the prisoners," a voice called down
the stairs and Gareth's eyes rounded when he spied
Tom, the butcher's son, hauling a bundle of straw
upon his back. "Where do ye want it?"

The only guard left in the dank chambers was
seated upon a bench under one low-burning torch.
"Anywhere," he muttered. "Who cares? Their sorry
lives are worth naught."

Tom, clumsy with his burden, unloaded his bundle
near Gareth's cell and as he untied the twine he whispered, "God's eyes, Gareth, how did ye get caught?"

"Does not matter."

"I always said you be a fool." Thick fingers fumbling with the twine, Tom glanced over his shoulder.
Assured that the guard wasn't looking, he slid a small
handful of straw between the bars, then straightened.

"What of Boon?" Gareth asked softly.

"I know not."

"Hey! What's going on?" The guard, realizing there
was conversation between prisoner and laborer reeled
and glared at Tom with suspicious eyes.

"Nothing. The poor sod's wanting me to get him
some of cook's sausage for him. Ha!" Tom spit on
the floor, then turned and made his ungainly way up
the steps.

"No talkin', y'hear me?" the guard grumbled, his gaze moving suspiciously from cell to cell.

Gareth didn't answer, nor did he touch the small bundle of straw that lay so near his fingertips. Only when the sentry's attention was drawn to another prisoner, did Gareth's fingers search the dried bunch to find a slingshot fashioned from bone and leather. There were no pebbles within the bundle but 'twas not a problem as the stone walls of the dungeon were crumbling and the mortar chipping away in bits and pieces. Ah, Tom wasn't such a bad lad after all, Gareth thought, his fingers curling possessively around his newly gained weapon. He couldn't wait to use it against some of the brutes who had hauled him in here.

Let anyone dare lay a hand on him. The fool would be lucky if he didn't lose an eye for his efforts.

"I know you." Ian stroked his chin carefully as he sat, one leg crossed over the other in his chair. The great hall was nearly empty, but the tantalizing odors of seared meat and spices lingered in the smoke-scented room. A wooden mazer dangling from the fingers of Ian's one hand held wine, and the sweet perfume of fermented grapes teased Muir's nostrils almost to distraction. A few guards were stationed near the doorways but they seemed disinterested in their lord and only snapped to attention when a fetching lass swung by. "We've met somewhere."

"Everyone within the kingdom has heard of Muir," the magician said sarcastically. Oh, for a mere sip from the lord's sweet cup. " 'Tis my powers that set me apart from the rest."

"Do not jest," Ian ordered, rubbing thumb and forefinger together. " 'Tis just at the edge of my mem-

ory. I cannot remember where or when, but I will."
His lips flattened over his teeth as he concentrated.
"In time."

Muir kept his expression bland for 'twould only
cause harm if the new lord's memory suddenly returned and he recalled the damning truth. 'Twas years
before, aye, when both Muir and Ian were young men.
Guilt settled in his bones for 'twas they who had
started this horrid bloody chain. "I see not why you
keep the boy in the dungeon," he said.

"He's a traitor. He killed the baron."

"Nay, nay." Muir shook his bald head. "He's but a
lad who was foolishly protecting his mother's honor."

Ian snorted and to Muir's disappointment, drained
his mazer. "Honor?" He shook his head and the veins
in his face became visible with a slow-burning rage.
"There is no honor or virtue in being a thief's whore."
Wincing as he stood, he withdrew his sword and studied the long, shiny blade as it reflected the gold shadows of the fire. "But I will deal with her as well. She
will be here soon, for I sent her a gift—a bloody messenger with the news of her son's imprisonment."

Muir felt a dull ache in his bad eye.

"The thief will follow."

Pain, swift and sharp, pierced Muir's brain. He doubled over and clutched his eye. Not now! He could
not have a vision now, but sure as he was born, it
came, in full view he saw Trevin and Gwynn together,
riding toward Rhydd.

Toward Ian's soldiers.

Toward the gallows.

Toward death.

He could summon no spit in his mouth and his heart
seared as if it had been burned.

Ian's voice came as if from far away. " 'Tis only a

matter of time and then, old man, revenge will be mine."

Nay, 'twill be mine, Muir thought as pain ravaged his body. And you, Lord Ian, will pay for all your sins.

Trevin cursed himself up one side and down the other. 'Twas a fool he was and there was no doubt of it. Levered upon one elbow, he stared down at Gwynn, still slumbering, unaware that dawn was casting its first gray light through the forest. A solitary winter bird had begun to warble its lonely song as dew drenched the boughs of the surrounding trees.

She was a beauty. No doubt of it. Her skin was white and pure, her hair in red-brown ringlets framed an oval face with a strong nose and pointed chin. Fine, curling lashes brushed the tops of high cheekbones that were a soft peach color. Her lips were parted, her breath regular, and he knew that beneath the cloaks that had been their blankets her naked body was firm and wanting, a glorious place of pleasure and sanctuary.

A place you vowed never to visit.

He gritted his teeth, his jaw growing hard. Never had he felt this way for a woman, but this one, with her fiery temper and quick tongue, had somehow wormed her way under his skin. He could not seem to get enough of her and though his member was sore from all the times he'd entered her, still he wanted more.

Gently he brushed aside a wayward curl from her cheek and wondered why she was forever on his mind. 'Twas not because she was beautiful, others were so. Nor was it because she was the mother of his son, again, other women could have borne him children if he so desired. Nay, there was more to it. She intrigued

him with her forest-green eyes, quick smile, and fertile
mind. She was brave to the point of being foolhardy,
outspoken for a woman, even of her station, and a
person who seemed to believe not only in God but in
the Earth Mother and magic as well.

Not that Trevin blamed her. Often times, it seemed,
God turned a deaf ear to prayers. Had he not seen it
himself when Faith and baby Alison had passed on?
Guilt took a stranglehold of his heart and squeezed
with iron-clad fingers. He should have loved Faith; but
he had not. Though he'd been true to her and never
lain with another woman, he had not cared for her
with the same intensity that he felt for this sharp-
tongued female.

Even though Gwynn was married to another.

Oh, fool that he was, he seemed unable to stop
bedding her while she belonged to his enemies. First
she'd been Roderick's wife—well, at least in name.
Now she belonged to Ian. Christ, Jesus, could he not
be with her while she was between husbands? Mentally he kicked himself from one side of Wales to
the other.

He knew of false marriages. Had he not married
Faith out of guilt for winning her father's castle, then
watched in horror as he'd flung himself to his death.
His attempts to save the old man had been futile and
had turned on him. Many who lived within the walls
of Black Oak and had watched him wrestle with Dryw
had assumed that Trevin had pushed the old lord
through the crenels to the cold stone courtyard rather
than believe that he'd tried to save the drunken fool.
Either way he'd lost and, as atonement, he'd married
Faith. 'Twas his fault she'd lost both father and home
and he needed to assuage his guilt.

But loved her, he had not. At the birthing of their

daughter, he felt close to her and had wrapped comforting arms around her when the baby had refused to draw a breath. He'd held Faith and the stillborn babe as she'd cried and tried to help her accept the loss of their child. She had refused.

He hadn't been able to save her, either. As Faith had lain upon her deathbed, he'd vowed he loved her but she'd looked at him with sorrowful eyes and shook her head.

"Do not lie to me, Trevin McBain," she'd said, lifting a weary hand and stroking his hair.

"I would not."

"Oh, you be fond of me. Aye, even care for me a bit," she'd said with a weak smile, "but do not shame us both by a lie."

He'd kissed her cold lips and she, still holding the dead child had begged him to never love another.

Vow to me, Trevin, that you'll never love another woman. Swear it.

He'd sworn upon her grave that he would never marry again, never pretend to love another. He'd managed to keep that vow until this morning as he gazed down upon the one woman who could bring him to break that oath.

Another man's wife.

Even now he wanted to wake her with a kiss. Instead he fought the powerful urge to take her yet again, and angry at fates, shoved his legs through his breeches and threw his tunic over his head. He would not think of their lovemaking again, for it only clouded his mind. He needed a clear head and aside from that he had a new problem—what to do with her. He was not surprised that she'd duped his sentries; many of them were untrained and disloyal. He'd taken his best men from the castle, aside from Henry, the boy he'd knighted out of obligation.

"Lady," he said, his voice rougher and deeper than was usual as he gently shook her shoulder. "Awaken. 'Tis time we meet with the others."

She stretched and smiled up at him, her eyes, when they opened, green shot with silver. "Mmm. Oh, m'lord," she said with a naughty wink, "have you not the time to kiss me again?"

"Nay, we must away—"

" 'Twill not take long," she cooed and he was undone yet again. Cursing his weakness, he hauled her into his arms and kissed her as the sun crested the eastern hills. Her warm, sleepy body molded to his and he knew deep in the darkest part of his soul, he was lost to her. He would have this one last union, for there would be no others and when she realized how he plotted to thwart her, she would be furious with him and never have want of his kiss.

'Twas bittersweet, this loving, and he kept his eyes open as he watched the sunbeams turn her hair to fire. Forever would her image be burned into his brain for 'twould be the last time his gaze caressed her flawless skin and never again would he sense her breath catch in her throat, feel the soft whisper of her fingers searching through his chest hair to discover his nipples, or experience the slick sensation of her tongue slide intimately over his skin.

Almighty God, he would miss her.

But he had no choice.

"We must help them, I tell ye," Idelle insisted. She paced in the small chapel and skewered the priest with a look she hoped would make him squirm. Some man of the cloth he was, always having a page flog him until his back bled—'twas addled.

"I cannot go against the lord's wishes."

"Why not? Oh, a fool ye be, Father Anthony."

" 'Tis not God's will." He wiped a gold chalice with his sleeve, then placed it into a cupboard with silver and gold crosses, goblets, and leather-bound tomes.

"Do ye think 'tis God's will that Lady Gwynn's son be locked away like a criminal?"

"He's a traitor. He killed the lord." A great sadness stole across his face. " 'Tis the law." Father Anthony locked the cupboard and tucked the key in the deep pockets of his vestment.

"And ye, being a priest, are bound by higher laws, are ye not? Are not God's covenants more dear than earthly decrees and possessions?" She stared pointedly at his carved, locked cupboard.

"Who are y-you to lecture me, woman? I know of your dark arts. Have I not turned a blind eye when you mention the names of the pagan gods? 'Tis said you cast spells and chant not the prayers of the church, but rave of devils and demons and the like. 'Tis time you came forward, daughter, and c-cast away your evil ways."

Idelle stood toe to toe with the priest. Her eyes might be weak, but her heart was not. " 'Tis not evil I worship, Father, but all things good and wise. I have faith in the Christian God, aye, but there is magic in the earth, wind, and sea that I will forever use. Asides, we have no time to argue about good and evil, for we both know what they be. We are talking of a youth, Father Anthony, Lady Gwynn's boy and of an old man who is dying."

"The magician."

"Aye."

"He, too, practices that which is forbidden. I prithee, Idelle, s-s-search your heart. L-l-look to God."

"And I prithee, Father Anthony," she said, her milky eyes focusing upon him, "look to your own soul. Who are ye to point a pious finger? I know of ye, Anthony, as I birthed ye to yer poor dead ma. I've watched ye grow from a lad to a man and I, too, have turned a blind eye to all that ye've become."

He swallowed hard. "I-I d-d-do not know wh-what you mean."

"Sure ye do, Father." Idelle, through the clouds in her eyes, noticed his Adam's apple twitch nervously. "Now, think of the good of Rhydd, the people within, and especially Lady Gwynn and her son."

"I—I will pr-pray on it."

"Do so." Idelle deftly crossed herself and genuflected at the altar, then she turned quickly and left the fool of a priest. He was a sorely troubled soul, one who could not look into a mirror without cringing. She only hoped he would search his heart, for she desperately needed his help if she were to free the lady's boy.

The last of the complaints had been heard and Ian's head pounded. The arguments were petty. One peasant argued with his neighbor over the size of his land, a starving farmer begged forgiveness for poaching a stag in the woods, and the cook whined on and on that the steward wasn't keeping stock of the spices and that the multure, fee for milling grain, wasn't enough to keep up with the demand of flour for bread. 'Twas too much for Ian and he wondered how Roderick, then Gwynn, had kept everyone in the castle at peace. Though he'd watched her over the years and offered his advice, even overseeing some of the work, Gwynn, in her husband's absence, had managed to rule Rhydd as well as raise that confounded boy without any outward trouble. Nor had he, while she was in charge, sensed any of the simmering rebellion that he now felt existed within the keep.

He stood and stretched, ignoring the pain in his legs. His wounds were healing and soon he would bear only scars from Trevin of Black Oak's sword.

"Bastard," he spit out as Webb, who had watched the lord dealing with his villeins from his post near the door, approached. "Have you news of my wayward wife?" he asked, knowing the answer.

"Nay. She be a slippery one."

Ian could not disagree.

"As she's with Trevin of Black Oak, she is even more difficult to find."

Ian saw the amusement in the knight's eyes and knew that Webb was not alone in his silent laughter at the new baron being cuckolded.

Most people in the castle, himself included, believed that Gwynn was with Trevin. Was he not the father of her child? Had he not lain with her years before? Her marriage to Roderick hadn't stopped her from bedding the thief, so surely her vows to Ian, given as the result of a bargain for her son's life, would be taken no more seriously.

He wanted to put Sir Webb in his place, but bit back a sharp retort, believing, as always, that he who gets the final laugh enjoys it most, and no one, not the thief or Ian's whore of a wife would get the better of him.

"You are a soldier," he said slowly to Webb, "one who managed to help my brother escape a prison where he'd been held for years. Surely a mere slip of a woman and a common thief are not so clever as to elude you."

The light of cruel merriment in Webb's gaze faded. " 'Tis only a matter of time."

"Good." Ian lifted a lofty eyebrow. "I would hate to think my trust in you was ill placed."

"Nay, m'lord," Webb said stiffly, but hesitated. "However, there is the matter of payment."

"Payment? For what?"

"Recovery of the boy." Webb's lips tightened a bit.

"I did promise that you would be paid, did I not?" Ian stroked his chin. "And, I suppose that even though the lad did practically walk into the keep, that you should have some reward."

The tension in the dark knight's face relaxed a bit.

"I will see to it," Ian said with a nod. "but since the task proved easy, I want you to do more for me."

"More?" Webb's back stiffened and Ian waved away his doubts. "Worry not, I said I will pay you for Gareth, and so I shall. 'Twas our bargain. Now I want you to ferret out the traitors within the castle. Trevin and the lady could not have escaped without help. Listen to the gossip, have our trusted men search through the hiding spots here at Rhydd, watch everyone more closely, and find out who would pledge his fealty not to me if the truth were known."

Webb leaned upon his sword. "Have you anyone you do not trust?"

"I trust no one." Motioning for two mazers of wine, he waited until a scrawny page had done his bidding, then sat with Sir Webb at the table. "Start with the old woman—the midwife—who attended to my wife."

"Idelle?"

"Aye. Though she is nearly blind, she sees all." Ian swirled his cup. "Then, look to the freemen. The butcher has distrust in his gaze, the carpenter is too silent, and the mason is a brooding, gloomy soul."

"Think you they are enemies?"

"Mayhap." Ian took a sip and let the wine slide down his throat as he swirled his cup. "But there are others as well, soldiers within our army who would take up arms against me if there were a choice between my wife and myself."

"What of the priest?" Webb asked.

"Father Anthony?" Ian scowled. There had always been something that bothered him about the man, but he could never put his finger upon what the trouble was. "Nay, he's a coward, to be sure. Spineless and jumpy, but he was loyal to my brother and would dare not defy me." He thought hard for a second, but dismissed Webb's concerns. "Worry not of him."

"Lord Ian!" A guard approached. "We found Sir Keenan naked as the day he was born, dirty and stumbling around the forest."

"Sir Keenan?"

"The knight who was missing on the night when Trevin of Black Oak escaped," Webb said, his hand upon his sword.

"Aye," the guard agreed.

"But he is alive?"

"Barely. He collapsed afore we got him through the gate. He babbles like the village idiot and says nothing but nonsense. We-we carried him as far as the atilliator's shop, for the old man is his father."

Ian's mouth drew into a hard, unforgiving line. "I will see Keenan now. Mayhap he will remember what happened that night and know who the traitors were who helped the outlaw escape." 'Twould be sweet vengeance to discover who was disloyal to him, sweet vengeance indeed.

"When I find out who the traitors are, I will see that they are punished to within an inch of their miserable lives." He drained his mazer and slammed the empty cup onto the table. Looking at Sir Webb, he added, "When I'm through with them, they'll wish they'd never been born."

Chapter Thirteen

"Trust you the atilliator?" Webb asked as they strode across the bailey. Fog was settling over the river and blanketing the castle in its filmy mist.

Ian slid a glance at the dark knight. "Did I not say that I trust no one?"

" 'Tis wise."

Though life in the castle seemed to go on as usual, there was an undercurrent of disloyalty, as dark and murky as a whirlpool, that Ian sensed swirled maliciously along the paths and alleys of Rhydd. 'Twas nothing he could see, just a feeling that there were those that would like nothing better than to slit his throat.

But who?

The gong farmer was mucking out the stables and nodded as they passed. "Good day, m'lord," he said, smiling widely as if he didn't know that he reeked of manure, as if he were innocent of anything close to treason.

Sheep bleated from the pens. A pig squealed in protest as the butcher's son managed to get a rope around its thick neck. Hammers rang loudly. The wheelwright mended a cartwheel and the carpenter shored up a truss supporting the roof over the roosts of the game birds that were kept alive until the cook needed them.

They nodded, said a quick, "M'lord," in greeting and went about their tasks as if nothing was wrong. Were they loyal, or just good actors? He didn't know. But he'd find out. One way or another.

With Webb beside him, Ian strode past the armorer's hut where the burly man was sharpening swords upon his whetstone. The screech of metal upon whirling stone screamed through the bailey.

As he finished each weapon, the armorer passed it to his son who polished the sharpened blades until they gleamed bright and deadly. Both man and son nodded to Ian, but did not meet his eyes. 'Twas a bad sign. Very bad. "Look hard at those two," Ian whispered to Webb. Was the sword maker loyal to him or to his Judas of a wife?

Ever since Gwynn's escape Ian had felt distrustful, dangerous eyes upon him and glacial stares from those who questioned his reign. Even among the servants in the kitchen and laundry there was a quiet, though ever-present dissention, a current of disloyalty that seemed to slither along the walls and hide in the shadowy corners of the castle, pooling and turning, waiting insidiously so that it could, when he least expected it, destroy him.

'Twas unsettling and he slept not only with his sword at his side, but a hidden blade beneath his pillow. He heartened himself with the knowledge that all the ill will would dissipate once Gwynn was returned and took her rightful place at his side, the mistress of Rhydd.

If she did.

The door to the atilliator's hut was open and inside, upon pegs were broken crossbows in various need of repair. The room was small and close. Parr, the man responsible for making crossbows, was a tiny man whose small stature belied his strength.

"Ah, m'lord, 'tis glad I be that ye came to see the fallen warrior," he said, nodding and rubbing the knotty fingers of one hand with the other. Paid well for his skills, it seemed unlikely that he would betray the lord, but Ian withheld judgment as his eyes adjusted to the dim light.

Sir Keenan lay on the table. A dirty blanket had been tossed over him, but beneath the old rag, he was pale as death and quivering, his eyes wide, spittle sliding from one corner of his mouth. "Nay . . . nay . . . oh, Christ Jesus . . ."

The physician, aged and stooped over, was peering into Keenan's glazed eyes and shaking his head. "He is near gone, m'lord."

"Well, do something. I needs speak with him."

" 'Tis naught to do but force water over his lips and wait." The shriveled man clucked his tongue and frowned, his forehead wrinkling in deep, worried furrows. "Sir Keenan? The lord, Ian of Rhydd, he is here and needs a word with you."

"Nay . . . no . . . no . . ." he continued to whisper through blue lips.

Ian had seen enough. "Keenan! What the devil happened to you?"

The man didn't glance in the lord's direction, just stared at the dusty beams over his head though, Ian suspected, he saw a vision known only to his eyes.

"Keenan, wake up!"

Still the man shivered and shook and didn't answer.

"He has cuts and bruises and this—" The physician's balding pate wrinkled as he lifted the blanket to show the soldier's chest where three large, even gashes ripped through his skin. The blood was dried, the wounds festering. "Mayhap a bear, or wolverine or other beast."

Webb slid his sword from his hilt. "There are ways to make him speak."

"Nay. He is lost. Put that away!" He motioned to Webb's weapon. Though patience had never been one of Ian's virtues and his temper was near the breaking point, he knew that Keenan would not awaken with a blade at his throat. To the physician, he said, "As soon as he wakes, send for me—no, better yet, move him into the great hall and keep a guard with him. I'm to be called immediately when he stirs."

"Aye," the physician agreed, "but I fear—"

"Where was he found?" Ian was in no mood for excuses or explanations.

"A mile away from the castle, wandering around in circles."

Ian sighed. "We will learn nothing more here. We must wait until Sir Keenan awakens."

"*If* he awakens," Sir Webb clarified and Ian's foul mood only worsened. 'Twas as if the devil himself was his enemy rather than a mortal man—nay, a lowly thief. *Have faith*, he silently told himself as he returned to the great hall. 'Twas only a matter of time. Sooner or later Trevin would return and then, by God, Ian would be ready for him.

"We'll split into two groups." Trevin, fingering his dagger squatted near the fire where two ducks and a rabbit were roasting on a spit. Fat dripped and sizzled on the coals, flames sparked and flared, and smoke curled upward through the leafless branches of the trees to the winter-blue sky.

His band of soldiers, eight men in all, gathered around him, and gave Gwynn a wide berth. She'd noticed their elevated eyebrows when Trevin had brought her to the camp, caught glimpses of shared glances and expressions ranging from amusement to disapproval as Trevin explained that she'd tricked Sir Bently and escaped the gates of Black Oak.

"The first group will be led by you, Gerald. Take Henry, York, Winston, and Nelson." With his knife, Trevin motioned to each of the men. "You will be the decoy party and will lead Ian's soldiers on a wild-goose chase away from the castle."

"Ye will not be with us?" Henry asked, obviously confused.

"Nay."

"Then why will they follow us?"

"Because they will believe I am with you. You cannot let Ian's soldiers get too close because one of you will be riding my horse—the steed that belonged to Sir Webb—and as you will all be wearing helmets, it should not be difficult to lure them away from the castle. They will think I am the rider upon Dark One.

"What if they do not follow?" Winston asked, pondering the situation and twisting the end of his mustache.

"Believe that, above all Webb will want his horse. 'Twas a bitter humiliation to lose such a steed and Webb is a prideful man. Now, once Ian's army has left Rhydd and given chase to you, the rest of us will enter the castle."

"Including the lady?" Sir Henry wasn't happy at the thought.

"Aye. She will be with me." Trevin's gaze locked with that of the younger man to quell any further arguments. "But we will need further deception," he said to the group at large, "one of you must dress as a woman."

All motion stopped. Sir Winston's fingers held firm to the end of his mustache.

Henry had been scratching his head. His hand stayed atop his crown.

Nelson had been picking his nails with his knife and cut himself at Trevin's words. "I must've heard ye wrong, me lord?" he said, sucking the blood from the pad of his thumb.

York had been whittling and the curls of pine wood dropping from his knife halted.

"I mean it. Ian's men will be looking for Gwynn so one of you will don her cloak."

"Nay." Henry shook his head. "I ain't dressin' up like no lass, you can count on it. Come now, m'lord, ye must be joshin' us."

" 'Tis no joke."

"Oh, me sweet mum!" Henry rolled his eyes to the heavens as if his dead mother could hear him.

All of Trevin's trusted men raised their eyes to stare at Gwynn with a mixture of awe and disgust. She wrapped her arms around herself as eight pairs of eyes appraised her mantle—which was a deep blue—nearly black—and trimmed with white fur. 'Twas distinctive, to be sure, and the new baron of Rhydd had seen it often enough.

"Won't they think you kept her at Black Oak Hall rather than risk her getting wounded or seized?" Nelson asked.

"They could," Trevin agreed, then one side of his mouth lifted in his crooked, devilish smile. "But Ian knows her well. He would expect her to escape from my capture just as she slipped through his fingers and the very gates of Rhydd. A woman who hid herself in a coffin to escape will do anything on her quest."

"A coffin?" Henry was horrified, his face white as a new moon.

" 'Twas empty, eh?" Ralph asked.

Gwynn's voice was strong. "Nay, Sir Ralph, I hid beneath a corpse of another woman."

Henry jumped to his feet as if he'd been bit. "Ach! A dead woman? Mother of Mary." He shuddered, then, as if sensing the others thought him a coward, he cleared his throat and calmed a bit. " 'Tis . . . 'tis clever ye be, m'lady."

"Thank you, Sir Henry." She didn't believe him for an instant.

Trevin swallowed a smile. "So. 'Twould make sense to think that Lord Ian will be looking for his wife."

At the word wife, Gwynn cringed. How could she be married to one man and love another? This past night, beneath the pine tree, she'd made love to Trevin time and time again, quivering in anticipation of his touch, reveling in the ecstacy of his embrace, crying out his name as the night birds cooed and dawn crept over the eastern hills.

Now, she looked away from the censure in his eyes and pretended interest in the charred meat sizzling over the fire. Using one of Trevin's gloves to keep from burning her fingers, she lifted the spit from the flames. Upon a flat stone, she cut the birds and rabbit into quarters, then let the men use their knives and hands to claim pieces of the small feast.

" 'Twill not be that bad," he told his men as they settled back on their haunches or upon rocks or roots from the surrounding trees. "The lady's cloak is large enough that one of you could throw it over your own clothes and use the hood to hide your face."

"But what of our helmets?"

Trevin's jaw tightened at Henry's question. "He who wears the cloak goes without his helmet."

"Ahh."

This was the man who had got Hildy with child? Gwynn wondered. Between the two of them, did they have but one working brain? Gwynn held her tongue but thought the girl was better off without such a mindless self-serving man as a husband. Why Trevin had chosen him to come on this journey was a mystery to her for the soldier—not much more than a boy— was willful, stubborn, prideful, and dim. A bad combination in Gwynn's estimation.

She picked at her joint of rabbit as the men, eating and passing a jug of ale around the fire, discussed at length how they planned to thwart Rhydd's soldiers. As the hours passed and the ale flowed, each soldier in the group retold his own story, why he held a personal grudge against Ian or Roderick or Rhydd.

Nelson's nose flared as if he smelled a foul odor when he told the story of his sister, who, at a tender age, had been raped by Sir Webb. York's tale wasn't any better. His entire village had been pillaged by Ian and a band of Rhydd's soldiers long ago, while Roderick was still alive. A few years back, Henry as a youth had been spying upon one of Ian's men as he'd cheated at a game of chance. When Henry had been foolish enough to speak up, the cheat had lost his wager and his pride. Later he'd taken the time to beat Henry and leave him for dead.

And so it went. Each of Trevin's men was not only on a mission for his lord, but was also seeking his own personal brand of revenge.

At least they were dedicated to their cause, Gwynn thought, though she was anxious to be off. Trevin had explained that they were to wait and arrive near the gates of Rhydd as the sun was setting and twilight made seeing difficult. As the fire dimmed and the ale wore off, Trevin kicked dust onto the coals. He spoke in a whisper to Stephen and Gerald, the leaders of the two groups of soldiers and though Gwynn strained to hear what he was saying, no words reached her. Stephen nodded and picked at a glistening amber flow of pitch that ran down one of the fir trees that ringed the clearing. Squinting hard, Gerald scratched at the stubble of his beard.

When they were finished discussing whatever it was that was so private, Trevin cleared his throat as he spoke to the rest of the men, "There is something you should all know about me and the lady," he confided.

Gwynn's head snapped up. What now? Her eyes met Trevin's and she knew in an instant that he intended to tell them the truth of Gareth's conception. *No. Not now.*

"The boy we are trying to save, Gareth—"

"Nay, Lord Trevin," she cut in, then crossed the short distance between them. Desperate to keep their secret, she touched his arm. " 'Tis not the time."

" 'Tis long overdue." He drew his arm away from her fingers and eyed each man in turn. Gwynn braced herself and pride kept her chin lifted though she felt the slow warmth of humiliation crawl up the back of her neck to color her cheeks.

The forest was strangely silent. Pale sunlight dappled the ground. "The boy who we are trying to save, Gareth of Rhydd, is my son."

No one moved for a second. Henry's Adam's apple worked and he avoided Gwynn's eyes.

Trevin pocketed his knife. "The lady and I knew each other long ago and I allowed Gareth to be claimed by Lord Roderick. 'Twas a lie. One I have oft hated and one I should have renounced long ago, but Lady Gwynn and I struck a bargain and thought it best that Gareth know not who sired him."

Ralph let out a soft whistle.

Winston kicked at the dirt with the toe of his boot. Stephen grinned as if pleased.

Gwynn wished the earth would open and swallow her, so that she would not have to suffer this embarrassment. Surely all the men would realize that Gareth was conceived while she was married to another and though her vows to the other man were not her choice, though her father had sold her like a prized rooster, she had sworn before church and state that she would be Roderick of Rhydd's bride and as such be forever faithful to him. No one here would understand her reasons.

Trevin's band of soldiers were uncomfortable. York fidgeted. Nelson cleared his throat. Others shifted and looked away. Only Sir Stephen raised his eyes to search Gwynn's face.

"I, for one, pledge my life to find the lord's boy and keep him safe." He stood and flung his sword into the soft ground. The blade stuck. " 'Tis my honor to do so."

"Mine as well," Gerald agreed. He jabbed his sword into the earth. "I will not rest until the baron's boy is returned to him and the lady."

"Aye!" Winston's sword joined the others, as did Ralph's, Nelson's, and York's.

Only Henry appeared to have misgivings. He eyed Gwynn and chewed on the side of his lip. His hand sweated enough that he had to rub it on his tunic. "I—I, too, pledge myself to ye, Lord Trevin," he said, swallowing with difficulty as all eyes were upon him.

"But you are troubled."

"Aye." He nodded and puffed out his chest. " 'Tis the lady. m'lord. I like not riding with a woman to do battle, I trust them not."

Trevin's smile was cold as death. "I assure you, Lady Gwynn can ride as well as any of you. Her aim with a bow and arrow is equal to most soldiers'."

Sir Henry's expression said it all. He didn't believe her capable of anything other than spinning, embroidery, or bearing children.

They had no time for this. Gareth's life was dependent upon this motley group of soldiers, including Sir Henry. "Mayhap the knight would like a demonstration," she said, keeping her anger under control, though, in truth, she would have loved to slap the upstart. "Sir York. May I borrow your quiver and bow?"

"Nay, nay, 'tis not necessary," Henry said. " 'Tis not that I doubt the lady's accuracy with a weapon but . . . but . . ."

"Say it, man, we have not all day!" Trevin said.

" 'Tis said she's a witch, m'lord." His eyes were round with worry.

"What?" Trevin asked.

"Aye, that she practices magic and the dark arts, and calls upon demons and . . . prays not to our Father." Quickly, he crossed himself, as if he expected Gwynn to level a curse upon him and send him to the pearly gates this very instant.

"Did not Muir also call up the spirits?" Trevin asked.

"Only when they came from a cup of ale."

At this some of the men tittered.

" 'Tis true," Gwynn said, stepping closer to Henry and smiling coldly. She was tired of the young knight's whining. "I am a witch." 'Twas time to teach the fool a lesson.

Trevin muttered something about stupid, hard-headed women under his breath. "Please, m'lady, do not—"

"But he's only heard the truth and if he returns to Black Oak he will learn that I worked my magic trying to save poor Sir Charles from a mortal wound. He will also know that I stopped outside of the castle walls and tried to remove a curse that some of the people within Black Oak's walls believe has been leveled against the keep. Aye, Sir Henry, I scribble runes in the sand. I chant spells and pray to the Holy Father in the hope that someone, whether it be Morrigu or Mary, is listening and will help me in my quest to save my son."

"But—" Henry licked his lips. " 'Tis a sin."

"Enough of this!" Trevin hissed.

Gwynn wasn't deterred, she stood close enough to the young knight to smell his sweat. "I have never yet cast a spell to harm anyone, but you surely test and vex me Henry of Black Oak, and if you do not help Lord Trevin and me in our quest for our son, I might be tempted to try out a few spells known to cause warts to form, or an eternal itching to consume a man's body or . . ." She paused as if to think and noticed that all the knights had become deathly quiet as they stared at her with worried, skeptical eyes. ". . . there is one that causes a man's cock to shrivel and become useless for all his days. Let me see, I will need the wishbone of a drake. . . ." She reached toward the burned, picked-over carcass of one of the birds.

Sir Henry gasped and not for the first time Gwynn wondered how this simpleton had become a knight.

Stupid, easily goaded, and without courage this boy/man was surely unworthy of his title.

"Here we are," she said, lifting the bone in question and holding it close to the lad. "Now with a little thistle and Saint John's Wort and—"

"Nay!" Henry seemed about to lose control of his bladder.

"Enough of this teasing," Trevin cut in. "We have serious business to attend to." He sent Gwynn a glare that would slice to the core of a lesser woman's heart. "You, lady, will stop your silly incantations and Henry, you will accept that Lady Gwynn will ride with us and ride well. You are to defend her, to protect her, to honor her, and most of all allow her to use her weapons, whatever they be."

"But if she starts callin' the spirits and—"

"*Whatever* they be," Trevin repeated, his voice ringing through the surrounding hills. "Now, do you all understand our task?"

"Aye, m'lord."

"Yea."

"As ye wish."

They were all in agreement, it seemed, and even Henry nodded and pledged himself to the duty at hand. Trevin eyed Gwynn and she, though her back was stiff as a flagpole, acquiesced. " 'Tis nothing I want more than to free my son."

"Good. Let us break camp. Sir Gerald and his men will lead the soldiers off through the woods and to the north. After the commotion has died a bit, we will enter by way of a peddler's cart."

"You have this wagon?"

"Aye." Trevin and Stephen exchanged a quick, mysterious glance that bothered Gwynn. "Bought and paid for. 'Tis waiting for us." He kicked more dust over the coals and, satisfied that the fire was extinguished, motioned for all his men to pick up their weapons. "Let us be off!"

The peddler's cart wasn't much to look upon. Mud caked the spoked wheels and the few wares displayed had seen better years. Tin and silver trinkets, dusty furs, and bolts of cloth that had begun to fade were some of the items for sale.

The donkey harnessed to the wagon had a dull, winter-shaggy coat and listless eyes that surveyed Trevin's band of men without any interest. Ears turned backward, one back hoof cocked, he dozed in the afternoon breeze.

"Whatever you paid for this, 'twas too much," Gwynn whispered to Trevin as she pulled on the reins of her horse and surveyed the rig.

"Ah, m'lord, I had about given up on ye." The owner of the wagon was a rotund man with a girth as wide as the cart's wheel. His tiny mustache and pointed little beard appeared out of place over his thick jowls and he reminded Gwynn of a hog with his tiny sunken eyes and short nose.

She changed her mind when he grinned, showing off perfect teeth and those tiny eyes glimmered with merriment as he gazed upon Gwynn. "M'lady," he said, taking off his hat and bowing so low as to nearly sweep the ground with one hand. "Me name is Fitch and 'tis my pleasure to meet ye."

"As it is mine to meet you, good sir," Gwynn said, noticing for the first time that his thumbs were crooked and barely moved as he gestured.

"I hear ye are on a journey to save yer son. Godspeed to ye."

"Thank you."

He handed Trevin the reins of the cart. "And ye, m'lord, know how I feel about Sir Webb. If I can be of any assistance in cutting out that devil's wretched heart, I'd be glad to ride with ye."

"The cart and ass are good enough," Trevin said. "Thank you, Fitch."

"No thanks I need, m'lord. Just your assurance that this good earth will be rid of the likes of that viper."

"Rest assured."

A trade was made—two of Trevin's horses for the wagon and donkey and the peddler rode off. Only when he'd rounded a bend in the road did Trevin turn to his band. "Now, 'tis time. If our plans go awry and you are captured, remember there are those at Rhydd who are true to Lady Gwynn and myself. You can trust Richard the carpenter, and Mildred who brews ale."

"Aye, and Idelle who is a midwife," Gwynn added.

Trevin looked each knight in his eyes. "If you are caught, I will save you. 'Tis my vow."

"What if ye be the one who is captured?" Henry asked.

Trevin's smile was wicked. "Do not worry."

"But—"

"Do not try and save me, for I will fight my own battle. 'Tis enough that you have come with me for my son's sake and to save Muir's hide." He eyed the lowering sun. " 'Tis time."

"Oh, fer the love of Saint Jude," Henry grumbled as Gwynn removed her cloak and handed it to the smallest of the knights. Grudgingly he donned the mantle, pulled the hood over his head, and peeked sheepishly from its shadowy, fur-lined depths.

"Oh, ain't ye a cute thing?" York teased and winked at Henry.

"A rare beauty, 'e is, er, she is," Winston agreed and hooted.

"Enough!" Trevin's voice brooked no authority, but he could not hide the devilment in his own eyes. "Now, Sir Gerald, be off with ye. Make haste."

"Come along," Gerald said, clucking to his mount and riding away.

"Ye, too, sweetie," York stage-whispered to Henry and was rewarded with a glower.

"Leave me alone, ye big braggart." Henry gathered up his reins and guided his horse after Sir Gerald's.

"Oh, I like a lass with spunk, that I do—" York's voice faded as they rode away and a flock of birds flew overhead.

"They joke when they should be serious," Gwynn said.

"They are good men."

She didn't doubt their intentions nor their dedications, just their judgment. "God be with you," she whispered as the last of the group rounded the bend. Her worried heart sank. How could she possibly trust this band of ruffians, and not even particularly bright ruffians, to accomplish Trevin's plan? Gareth's safety was at stake, if, indeed, he was still alive, and the thought that his future depended upon duping Ian's men with the likes of Sir Henry made her blood turn to ice. Nay, she could not count on those buffoons for anything.

"Do not worry," Trevin said, as if reading her mind. "All they needs do is provide a distraction."

"I pray to God that they can do it," she said fervently, sending up a prayer before climbing off her horse.

"We will leave the horses here with you, Sir Ralph," Trevin ordered. "You are to take them back to Black

Oak with news that our mission has failed and we have been captured if we don't return by morn."

The knight seemed about to argue, but held his tongue. "Aye, m'lord," he agreed.

"Stephen, you will take off your armor and wear the clothes Fitch left behind." He reached into a side panel of the cart and found a filthy pair of breeches and stained gray tunic, which he tossed to the blond knight. " 'Tis your job to convince the guards at Rhydd that you are truly a peddler. As no one in the castle has seen your face before, 'twill not be a difficult task."

"What of us?" Gwynn asked.

Trevin's smile was positively evil. "You and I, m'lady, shall ride in here." He reached beneath the rig, unlatched a metal bolt, and displayed the false bottom of the wagon.

"What is this?"

"Fitch is more than a peddler," Trevin replied.

She should have guessed. She eyed the dusty, hidden compartment. "He's a thief like you."

"And a smuggler of cats and men or pieces of gold. Aye."

"Why does he hate Sir Webb?"

"Did you not notice his hands? Sir Webb was the man who broke his thumbs and told him he was lucky that they were not cut off."

"He was caught stealing?"

Trevin nodded. "Aye, A loaf of bread for a starving child."

"Oh." Gwynn had new respect for the rotund man whose features resembled a pig ready for slaughter.

"Don't misunderstand. Fitch would steal from a poor man as well as a rich one. He is truly a criminal."

"But his heart is good."

Trevin lifted a shoulder. "Most times, though some might disagree." He motioned to the dark compartment beneath the floor of the cart. "We have no more time for gossip," he said. "Come, m'lady, your coach awaits."

She hesitated. Something felt wrong about this. Very wrong. Yet, 'twas a clever way to enter the castle unnoticed and she had no choice. She had to trust Trevin, for he wanted only to save their son as much as she did.

"Hurry and slide to one side as there must be room for me as well."

Gingerly she crawled under the wagon and slipped into the tiny, dark confines of the wagon. Dust swirled around her and she sneezed. Trevin followed her beneath the wagon, but instead of climbing inside, he swung the door shut.

Thunk.

It was suddenly dark as night.

"Nay—"

With a clunk, the bolt slid into place.

"Trevin!" She pounded on the sides of the cart as she realized that she was trapped. He was abandoning her! Oh, for the love of Saint Peter. He couldn't be doing this. Wouldn't! No! No! No!

" 'Tis for your own good."

"You demon! You can't do this! For the love of God—" She kicked and pounded, furious with herself for trusting him and burning with rage that he would trick her. Again.

His voice was muffled but she heard him say, "Take her back to Black Oak and stand guard at her door. 'Tis your duty to keep her safe."

"Nay!" Tears of frustration burned behind her eyes. What a fool she'd been. How many times would she let this man dupe her? "Trevin, please, I needs go with you. For Gareth." She thought of her son in that dark horrid dungeon. "Do not do this!" she begged. "Trevin!" She kicked hard and pounded until her fists began to bleed, but to no avail.

Did Trevin not know that Ian would kill Gareth if she did not return to him? Was he willing to gamble with their son's life. "Curse and rot your hide, Trevin of Black Oak, let me out!"

"As you wish, my lord," Sir Stephen said as the wheels creaked and started turning. The cart jostled in the rutted road.

Gwynn gnashed her teeth and fought her stupid tears. Whether she liked it or not, she was on her way back to Black Oak Hall. Away from Trevin. Away from Gareth. Away from any hope of ever seeing her son alive again.

Chapter Fourteen

"What the devil are you doing?" Gareth asked, his voice filled with horror. The old man had truly gone daft, for he'd smoothed away the straw on the floor of the dungeon and somehow—Gareth wasn't exactly certain how he'd accomplished this—Muir had begun to bleed from his finger. Chanting words that made no sense, he let the blood flow onto the floor in a snakelike pattern that coiled evilly.

"Shh." Muir grimaced and squeezed harder as he continued his task while the goosebumps on Gareth's skin began to rise. From the bench near the stairs the sentry snored loudly, his mouth open, his head bent forward as he dozed.

"I like this not," Gareth whispered.

"Nor do I, but 'tis necessary."

"Why?"

"Do you want to escape this dungeon? Aye or nay?"

"Aye, but—"

"Then pretend to be asleep and have no more questions," he ordered and added under his breath, "Silly, miserable youth." The drops of blood continued in their coiled labyrinthine configuration until the old man was satisfied.

"Now what?" Gareth asked as Muir sighed and sat on the floor, his back propped against one wall.

"We wait."

"For what?" Gareth was confused and he didn't like the old man talking in riddles.

"Until 'tis discovered."

"And then?"

Muir smiled. "Then, my boy, ye will see magic unlike any ye've ever seen.

"From you?" Gareth snorted in disdain. "I doubt it."

Muir's good eye was fast upon him. "You will see."

Gareth was sick of the riddles, the talk, and no deeds. He had his own way out of the dungeon and it didn't take chants or spells or scribblings in blood. Nay, with his slingshot he'd be able to wound more than one guard, dash up the stairs, and breathe fresh air again. He wasn't going to listen to Muir's silly ramblings and boastings that were naught. "I'll believe it when it happens."

"So be it," Muir said and closed his eyes. "Before this night is over, son, your mind will change."

Gareth snorted in disbelief and yet he felt a breeze, cold as snow, upon the back of his neck though there was not a breath of fresh air in this dank pit. Shivering, he ignored the old man's advice and rummaged through the filthy rushes for another stone to add to his growing pile. The addled wizard could believe in sorcery or pagan gods or demons for all Gareth cared. He, more practical, would depend upon his quick wits and his weapons.

His callused fingers encountered a chipped bit of daub from the wall and he smiled to himself as he pocketed what would become another pebble in his growing arsenal. Aye, whenever the soldiers came to take him to the gallows, they'd be in for a surprise. He'd give them a damned good fight.

*   *   *

His head plumped by pillows, Ian glanced down at his flagging member and cursed silently. Why couldn't he find hardness with his comely wench? Her skin was dark, nearly swarthy, her hair jet black, her eyes, wide with fear, a deep shade of blue. He'd forced her to straddle him and she'd complied, but still he felt no welcome warmth or tightening of his crotch.

"Damn it all to hell." He shoved her off him and scowled darkly. Though he'd lived nearly five decades he had the body of a younger man and very rarely could he not take a woman. Usually when that unlikely event had occurred 'twas because he'd consumed far too much wine.

Not tonight. This evening he'd swallowed hardly a drop as he'd waited for news from Black Oak Hall. Surely Sir Charles had reached the keep long before now. Aye, he'd been wounded, but he was a strong man and Ian was certain he would have made the trip. As foolishly loyal as the man was to Gwynn, he would have staved off death until he found the lady. Only then would he have dared give up his soul.

So, Gwynn, if she was at the keep as Ian suspected, would have heard that her precious son was imprisoned. She wouldn't think twice but would make haste to return either to beg for Ian's pity and oh, that thought was pleasant—or try to devise a way of helping the lad escape. Either way, Ian's wayward wife would return.

He couldn't wait.

But what of Trevin—the Outlaw Lord. Ian's muscles tensed at the thought and he shifted in the bed. The thief could not be ignored. No doubt he, too, would return. Ian planned a surprise for that one. For the

humiliation of stealing his bride, the man would pay
with his life, but first, as vengeance for the agony he'd
inflicted in Ian's legs, Trevin of Black Oak would suffer, long and hard, in full view of everyone in the
castle. Especially Gwynn.

The thief would be an example to anyone who considered going against the new ruler. There were others
as well, men and women, servants and peasants who
were more loyal to Lady Gwynn than to their new
lord. They, too, would be publicly destroyed.

As would the boy. Gareth could not be allowed
to live.

Yea, Ian thought, gazing at the tapestry of a great
stag that hung near the fire, all he needed now was
patience and a little relief.

"Touch me," he ordered roughly to the woman in
his bed.

"M'lord?" the wench asked, her voice soft as a
doe's breath.

"I said, 'Touch me' and be quick about it."

Biting her lip she reached under the covers of the
bed and he felt her fingers, young and nimble, surround him. He closed his eyes willing an erection, but
still did not respond. By the gods, what was wrong?

"Stroke!"

She gave off a soft mew of protest.

"Just do it."

She began her ministrations and he sighed. 'Twas
as if a weight were pressed onto his chest. All this
worry about his traitorous wife, her son, and the
damned thief caused his head to pound. Oh, when he
got his hands on that woman who had wed him. . . .
At the thought of Gwynn he felt the first stirrings of
desire course through his veins. Uppity, she was, the

little snipe. Oh, when he finally took her, 'twould be pure ecstasy for him. He would not hold back, but mount her like a stallion and make her scream out of need. He knew how to satisfy a woman, but with Gwynn, 'twould not be a mating for pleasure, but a challenge, a show of power. He would make her squirm and beg and then plunder her body.

Mayhap the thief would get to watch their fierce coupling before he was put to death.

His cock began to throb though the girl had the touch of a blacksmith and worked with leaden hands. With Gwynn 'twould be different. And he would make her pay. For lying with the thief she would have to atone with her hands, her lips, her entire body. That thought, of her doing his bidding, whatever he wanted, caused him satisfaction.

He glanced down at the girl in his bed and for a split second he remembered another woman, so long ago it seemed as if 'twas someone else's wife.

That one, too, just past girlhood had raven hair and eyes as bright as sapphires. Comely and tart, she'd been the sister of a man who had interfered when Ian, much younger then, had made his advances known. The woman had declined and he, randy from a recent battle, had refused to take no for an answer.

"Yes, yes," he said as the wench in his bed continued to rub him, but still the old memory wrapped around him like a shroud. His breathing was ragged, his chest ready to explode, but he could not forget that other act so long ago.

'Twas in a forest, where the girl had been gathering mushrooms. Ian had spied her and the brother and wanted her. When she'd refused his lusty advances, he'd had no choice but to take her by force, using his dagger to encourage her into submission.

The brother, a slight man with a fierce countenance had jumped him from behind and in the ensuing fight Ian had used the knife he'd held at the woman's throat to hobble the man. One cut to the leg, another to the arm, and a final blow to the face. He'd fallen then, screaming, his hands over his wounds, blood streaming through his fingers. The woman had been hysterical, but, as her brother lay bleeding to death, Ian had mounted her. The rest, robbing her of her virginity and spilling his seed into her, had been easy.

He'd left that particular village feeling strong and powerful. A true ruler. It hadn't mattered then that his brother, the eldest, would inherit Rhydd. He'd proved himself not only as a warrior, but as a man.

Now, years later, the ghosts of his past haunted him and though the girl in his bed was scared but willing, he could not hold a damned erection. There were too many distractions and the truth of the matter was, he decided as he rolled away from the girl and motioned her to leave, he would not be satisfied until he could have his wife.

And have her he would.

"We cannot stop now," Sir Gerald insisted. "We be but an hour's ride from Rhydd."

Henry wasn't going to be bullied. "I needs to piss."

"Ye should have thought of it afore."

" 'Tis nervous, I be." Henry pulled up on the reins and with Gwynn's cloak around him, he climbed off his steed. As they had ridden ever closer to Rhydd, the air had seemed to become thicker and damp with a soft shroud of fog. " 'Twill take but a minute."

Sir Gerald glowered from beneath his helmet, but he raised his hand, silently imploring the rest of the small party to halt. "If anyone else feels an urgency," he invited, but the rest of the men waited as Henry hid behind a small copse of fir and oak trees, bundled Gwynn's long mantle, unlaced his breeches, and let loose a long stream.

Finishing, he took a chance, ducked further into the woods where the foliage was dense and dark and there, where needles and dry leaves littered the ground, Henry dropped to his knees. Crossing himself quickly he tried to rally his courage, for his was a quest that was as dangerous as it was difficult.

He had not long been a knight and never would have become one had not his father died in the saving of Lord Trevin's life. At the memory of his slain father, blood pooling around his body, Henry's stomach twisted and the same sour taste that he'd experienced on that horrid day again crawled up his throat.

Lord Trevin, in an act of gratitude had knighted the slain soldier's only son and, Henry feared, already had begun to realize that he'd made a mistake. Though he fervently wanted to please the new master of Black Oak, Henry could not. The new lord was not worth the dung of his father's destrier.

Did not Lord Trevin consort with a married woman?

Did not he trust her though she practiced dark arts and pagan magic?

Had he not killed Lord Dryw?

Had it not been for Trevin would not his father be alive today?

Had he fathered a child of another man's wife?

Henry spat and felt pain pounding behind his eyes. Trevin of Black Oak, a thief by trade, was not a man to whom Henry, nor his trusting father, should have sworn his allegiance, his fealty, or his life. The new lord of Black Oak was but a fraud, a man who kid-napped another man's bride, a man who cheated at a game of dice to win a castle, a man who had a murder-ing black heart.

A crow flew overhead cawing loudly.

"Forgive me, Father, for I have sinned," Henry whispered, his heart hammering wildly as he prayed in the wisping fog. He thought of Hildy and the fact that she was with child—his child. He should not have lain with her and yet she was so comely, warm, and soft. She offered sweet haven when his life was so confused. "Help me in my efforts to serve Ye. Be with my unborn child and sweet Hildy. I vow, if I am victorious in my quest, I will marry Hildy and give my son a name and forever be Your devoted servant."

"Hey, Henry!" Gerald yelled from the road. "Are ye not finished?"

"Aye about," he said, angry that his prayer was interrupted.

" 'E even pisses like a woman. Takes all day," Sir York observed with a chuckle and Henry's blood boiled.

He'd show them all. More swiftly than he wanted, he ended his prayer and stood, dusting the stupid woman's cloak he'd been forced to wear. Another hu-miliation he had to stomach at the hands of Lord Trevin. Well, not for long.

He appeared from behind the trees and York, astride his destrier let out a long, low whistle. " 'Tis beautiful ye be, lass," he said.

"Yeah and what would ye know of beautiful women," Henry retorted with a swagger as he ap-proached his horse, "when every one ye've ever been with 'as been ugly as a vulture?"

"Fortunately there 'aven't been many," Sir Winston added with a smirk, his mustache twitching.

"Enough of this nonsense!" Gerald eyed them all gravely. "We have not the time. There is much to do and nightfall fast approaches."

Henry swung into the saddle. His hands were sweaty on the reins, his mouth dry as wormwood, his heart racing. He, too, had much to do before the coming night and he was ready. 'Twould be sweet vengeance to prove Trevin of Black Oak the murderin' bastard he be.

Gwynn's legs had lost all feeling and her back ached as she bounced and jostled inside the dark compartment. How many times would she let Trevin play her for a fool? If she ever got out of this cursed box on wheels, she'd find a way to get even with him.

Would you? that pesky voice inside her brain demanded. *Remember his lovemaking, remember the way you felt as he kissed you, remember how easily he bent your will to his.*

Never again, she vowed as one cartwheel hit a rock and swerved slightly.

"Oh, Gareth, I fear I have failed you," she muttered, then gave herself a quick mental kick. She couldn't give up. 'Twas her duty to save her son and no one, not even Trevin of damned Black Oak was going to stop her. Somehow, some way she had to trick Sir Stephen. That would be difficult, for, of all of Trevin's soldiers, he seemed one of the smartest and most loyal.

She pounded upon the flooring of the cart. "Sir Stephen! Please. Stop!"

"Nay, m'lady," he replied, over the creak of wheels and rattle of the peddler's wares.

"But I need to relieve myself."

"Then ye best be doin' it in there."

"Please, do not make me soil myself."

He didn't reply.

"I could cast a spell on you and force you to do my bidding."

He chuckled. "Aye, so ye say."

"I jest not."

"Neither do I."

So he wasn't superstitious. Damn the fates.

"Ye may as well sleep and not waste yer breath on me," he said, "because unless Satan himself stops me, I'll see that ye be safely to Black Oak."

There had to be another way. For the dozenth time she let her fingers skim the interior of the compartment, from corner to corner, over the rough boards, picking up slivers for her efforts. She discovered where the bolt was driven into the false bottom, but it was secure and all she received for her efforts of trying to move it were bloody fingers and broken fingernails.

She closed her eyes and concentrated. She was in a box—a wooden box made of planks fastened together. Atop the box was the floor of the cart and above that foldaway shelves and cupboards holding the peddler's wares. Nay, she could not find a way through the upper flooring.

She couldn't give up! Nor could she rely on silly luck.

Again she searched the base and this time her fingers traced each board. Under one of her shoulders, she felt a knothole large enough for three of her fingers to delve through. If she moved slightly, the hole would allow a little light into her dark coffin, but not much as dusk was shadowing the earth. Craning her neck, she was able to see the axle that ran between the two front wheels. If somehow it could be broken . . . she still had her dagger, but there was no way for her to reach through the boards, and aside, the knife was too small to slice through a solid oak rod.

But there had to be a way.

Think, Gwynn, think! You're a clever woman. You ruled a castle in your husband's absence. You found a way to stay alive when Roderick threatened your life if you didn't give him a child. You tricked Sir Bently and the guards at Black Oak into letting you go free. Certainly a simple wagon can't trap you!

Notion after silly notion entered her head, only to be discarded. Night was falling swiftly and with each turn of the wheels she was being hauled farther from her son. Farther from the man she loved.

Though she was furious with Trevin for deceiving her, she still worried about his safety. If Ian discovered him, he would be tortured and killed. Ian of Rhydd was not a kind man nor a patient man. Even if she returned to the castle and threw herself upon his mercy, she didn't know if he would let Trevin and Gareth go free.

But 'twas the only chance they had.

Again she eyes the knothole. She forced three of her fingers through the small space. The fourth would not fit. She reached into her pouch, withdrew her dagger, and discovered it, too, would fit. But still it was a useless weapon . . . or was it? Perhaps if she . . . Her mind spinning with a new idea, she used her tiny knife to start ripping her tunic. First one strip, then another and another which, with pained fingers, she laboriously tied together in tight knots. "Holy Mother, please let this work," she whispered as once the tunic was completely destroyed and she was shivering with the cold, she tied one end securely to her dagger, which she used as a weight. If she could drop it through the knothole and it would catch on the ground, there was a chance that the cloth strips would wind along the axle until they reached the wheel whereupon the torn pieces of fabric would wind in the spokes and clog the wheel so badly that Stephen would have to stop the cart.

And then what? Still, he would not open the hatch. Nay, she was doomed to return to Black Oak.

Nonetheless she let her knife drop. It hit the ground, bounced upward, and caught around the axle. Slowly her handmade rope began to slide through the knothole, winding as she'd hoped upon the axle. She rubbed her arms to keep from freezing and felt a change in the pace of the donkey as the wagon slowed.

"Come on, come on," Stephen yelled to the beast. "Hey, what—" The cart began to turn in a circle. "Straighten out, you stubborn beast."

Gwynn crossed her fingers.

"What in the name of Saint Jude?"

The wagon slowed to a stop and bounced as Stephen hopped onto the ground. "What's the matter with you?" he asked the donkey. "Oh, for the love of Christ. What the devil?"

"Sir Stephen, please," she said. "You must let me out."

"After what you did? By the gods, you might've ruined this cart and then where would we be?"

"I . . . I had to get your attention."

"By disabling the wagon? God's eyes, m'lady, what does that help?"

"We need to save Lord Trevin."

There was silence.

"Please, just listen to me, I beseech you." She didn't bother masking the desperation in her voice. "My husband . . . the Baron of Rhydd, he'll kill Lord Trevin if he but gets the chance."

"He won't."

"You don't know Ian," she cried. "Please, we must save him and Gareth. I can do nothing from here or Black Oak Hall." When he didn't respond, she added, "I know the lord thinks he's saving me, that I would only get in the way, but you must believe me, I've lived at Rhydd for over thirteen years and I know the castle like the back of my hand. I can save Trevin and Gareth."

"You're but a woman—"

"I was the mistress of Rhydd. I ruled the castle alone. I have servants, soldiers, and peasants within the walls of the keep who would do my bidding if only I can get to them. Trevin knows not who is ally or enemy. Please, we must hurry. There is little time."

"I cannot go against the baron's wishes."

"Of course you can when 'tis to save his very life! Sir Stephen, I know you to be loyal, aye, but smart as well. Please, I implore you, open this hatch," she ordered. "I would offer you coin, but I know you be a noble man who would be offended. However, whatever it is you desire, I will grant it to you. All you need do is let me escape."

She felt the shift in the air; knew he was weighing his options. Fiercely loyal to Trevin, he nonetheless wanted to help him.

"You and I—together we can aid the baron in his quest. What good is it for you to dress up like a peddler and spend two days' journey upon the road when you could be taking up your sword and fighting Black Oak Hall's sworn enemies?"

"I cannot listen to your prattle—"

" 'Tis not prattle, Sir Stephen. Tell me, how would you feel if the lord and his son died and you were busy driving a donkey and a woman away from the battle?"

Again silence.

"Sir Stephen, have you thought of it?"

"Aye—"

"Is not the lord's life worth his wrath?"

"Oh, by the gods, I should be bathed in hot oil for this," he grumbled, but she heard a wrenching of metal and a loud click as the bolt gave way, the hidden door opened, and fresh air invaded the dark interior of the box.

Gwynn didn't waste a second. She dropped to the ground before he had time to change his mind. Cold air rushed across the earth and brought goose bumps to her skin.

"Oh, for the love of God. You've got no clothes— m'lady, please!" Stephen stood and worked the latches on the top of the cart. Averting his eyes, he dug through the wares and came up with a leather tunic with metal studs that looked as if it were made for a small boy. "Here, until we reach Black Oak—"

"We go not to Black Oak," she corrected, as she drew the tunic over her head and cinched a small corded belt around her waist. He found a hat as well as she tied her hair onto her head before donning the hat. She eyed the peddler's cart with a scowl. "Can the wheel be fixed?"

"Aye." Stephen bent on one knee, sliced the tattered strips of fabric away from the axle, and after cutting her little knife free, handed the dagger to her. "Your weapon, m'lady."

"Thank you."

"Now," he said, straightening and wiping his hands on his too-small breeches. "I will take you back to Castle Rhydd and accept my lord's ire even if he banishes me, but I want your promise that you will do as I say and stay out of danger." His blue eyes were troubled.

"I swear. Except that I must talk to Ian."

"With me," he insisted. "Elsewise I will take you to Black Oak Hall if I have to carry you over my shoulder like a sack of flour."

"But—"

"Do not argue, m'lady. I fear not your sharp tongue, your little dagger, or your spells of nonsense. Nor do I fear Lord Trevin's wrath or Ian of Rhydd's blade, but I will not go against my lord's wishes without your oath that you will obey me and, when we meet up with him again, the Lord of Black Oak."

The words stuck in her throat and Stephen stood as if rooted to the earth of that very spot in the road. He folded his arms over his great chest and waited. "What will it be, Lady Gwynn? Back to your hiding spot in the cart and on to Black Oak, or will you do as I ask on our way to Rhydd?"

"I have no choice."

"Then say it."

"I, Sir Stephen, will do as you ask." 'Twas a lie, but a small one, just a fib, to assure her that she would have a chance to save Gareth.

"Do not cross me, m'lady."

"I will not. Now, come, let us be off. There is no time to waste!" She climbed onto the driver's bench and Stephen, grumbling under his breath that he was the worst kind of fool, climbed aboard and took up the reins.

Night had fallen, they were hours from Rhydd and Gwynn worried her dagger in its hilt. What if they were already too late?

"Swear to God, Sir Webb, they were out there. Five, maybe six of 'em. all wearin' the colors of Black Oak Hall." From the watchtower where they stood peering through the crenels the guard made a sweeping gesture toward the forest where a thick mist was beginning to rise.

Webb eyed the young sentry as if he'd gone daft. "Why would they show themselves? If I were to try and sneak into another's keep, I would disguise meself so as not to warn me enemies."

"I know not," the young man said, his thick eyebrows butting together. He was a serious lad with dirty-blond hair, dark eyes, and a crooked nose. Webb had never known him to lie or make up stories, but then times were strange and as the lord had pointed out, no one was to be trusted. Not even this snot-nosed soldier. "I know what I saw and there were half a dozen men and a women—aye, 'twas a woman's cape, like the lady's."

"Lady Gwynn's?" Webb asked, more interested.

"Aye. I've seen her wear it afore—deep blue with fur—white fur lining it."

"She would come this close to the castle? Why take the risk?" Webb fingered the hilt of his sword and stared at the darkening forest with its eerie, shifting blanket of fog. Though the soldier had no reason to lie, Webb smelled a trap. "Prithee, what else did ye see?"

"Your destrier."

"What?" Every muscle in his body tensed.

"The black with the off-center splash of white down

his nose or his damned twin," the boy sentry insisted. "Swear on me poor mum's grave that the leader was ridin' 'im."

Anger, hot and dark, shot through Webb's veins. The damned thief had made him look a fool at the mill that night by stealing his favorite mount and now he was parading the beast, flaunting the fact that he'd bested Webb. "And the woman in the cloak was with him and his band of men?"

"Aye." The youth's head bobbed up and down faster than a chicken plucking up bugs. "I don't think they thought they'd be seen as 'twas nearly dark and the fog, it was shiftin' in, but my eyes are keen."

"So they are." Was it possible?

"Could they not be going to make camp in the forest nearby until they are ready to attack?"

" 'Tis a small amount of men," Webb thought aloud as he rubbed his chin.

"And a woman," the sentry reminded him. " 'Tis truly what I saw."

"And they rode toward the river?" Webb sighed. 'Twas a cold night and fog, damp and cloying, had begun to roll over the curtain walls and into the bailey. The thought of chasing through the woods and coming up empty-handed again wasn't appealing, not when there was a cup of ale and a game of dice to be had. This sighting of an enemy army could be naught but a young guard's overexuberance. "Did you see any of the men close up?"

"Nay," he admitted, "but the mantle the woman wore was Lady Gwynn's, I be sure of it."

"Or like hers."

He lifted a shoulder and had the decency to look worried. "I thought the lord would want to know."

"Aye. That he will," Webb thought aloud and considered how much of a reward he would pocket if, indeed, he captured Trevin of Black Oak as well as the lady. 'Twould be well worth giving up a cup of wine, warm fire, and a game of chance.

Asides, his interrogations had gone badly. The mason had known nothing, the carpenter had been close mouthed with a hard glint in his eye. An odd one, that. As for Mildred, the alewife, she had been scared, to be sure, but her mouth hadn't been pried open and Parr, the atilliator, had seemed innocent. Webb hadn't tortured anyone, not yet, and though it bothered him not to inflict pain, he preferred to use the whip or brand or knives only if other means were not effective. He'd planned to speak with old Idelle on the morrow and that wasn't a pleasant thought. The midwife gave him the chills. Those near-blind opaque eyes saw far more than a normal person's. The chants she whispered as she moved about the keep caused his innards to turn to pudding.

She was a daughter of Satan and there was no doubt of it.

"Find a replacement for your watch, I want ye to ride with me and show me where the bloody bastards went. I'll get the others." Webb said, as there was no other option. Mayhap the thief was foolhardy and desperate to save his son. Certainly the lady would risk anything for the boy. Aye, 'twas possible that Ian's plan was working.

Webb hurried into the turret and took the stairs leading ever downward. He'd wake up the houndmaster to ready the dogs, and take a dozen of Ian's best men. If the thief was stupid enough to ride up so close to the portals of Rhydd, Webb would personally drag him before the lord and if the lady . . . Webb's thoughts strayed into perilous territory when he considered Ian's wife. Unlike any woman he'd ever seen before, she was beautiful, smart, and sharp-tongued. Webb usually liked women who were pretty and stupid, willing to do whatever he wanted without too much of an argument, but Gwynn of Rhydd was the exception—a fiery challenge. He wondered, not for the first time, what she would be like warming a man's bed, then, as he shoved open the door to the outer bailey and stepped into the damp mist, he pushed those wayward thoughts aside.

She was Ian of Rhydd's wife, lady of the castle, and Webb would think of her as such. Nothing else. To do otherwise would spell instant death.

Instead of the thief, it could be he who would end up dangling by the neck from the hangman's noose. Webb had worked too hard and too long to let his eager cock determine his fate.

But he had to remain cautious. There was a chance that the sentry was mistaken, that there was no small army from Black Oak, or, that he'd mistakenly identified a group of travelers as enemies, or . . . was it possible? Could the sighting be part of Trevin of Black Oak's plan to lure some men away from the castle and ambush the lot of them?

Webb glanced over his shoulder as he made his way to the kennels and some of the hounds began to bark. Was it his imagination or were there enemy eyes already watching his every move?

Curse it all. He'd never felt a moment's fear in his life, until he'd come across that slippery thief with the cold blue eyes. Christ, the thief caused a blade of dread to twist in Webb's guts.

The sooner the bastard was caught and brought to Ian of Rhydd's swift justice, the better.

Webb's mind worked feverishly as he awakened his

men—his best soldiers. Some would ride with him, the others would stay, awake and alert, to defend the castle.

Trevin of Black Oak wasn't going to outsmart him and make Webb appear the fool again. 'Twas time to even the score.

Chapter Fifteen

The fog was a blessing he hadn't expected. It rose from the river, enveloped the castle, and provided Trevin with a cover he might not have otherwise found in the shadows of Rhydd's watchtower. He grinned to himself as, with a clang the portcullis rattled open and two files of Rhydd's best soldiers mounted on steeds worthy of battle galloped through. They carried torches that burned bright in the night but gave off small illumination in the gloom.

"Ride, you bastards," he muttered softly and spied Webb's stiff back as the dark knight rode upon a pale charger. The company seemed to be made up of Rhydd's best soldiers, but nowhere in the small army did he spy the lord of the manor. So Ian of Rhydd was still within the curtain walls.

Good. Trevin wanted to deal with the baron personally.

Before the guards had a chance to lower the gate, he slipped into the bailey. Like a wolf slinking through a dark glen, he made his way unnoticed to the carpenter's hut and silently sneaked inside.

"Richard?" he whispered as his eyes adjusted to the dark interior. " 'Tis I—"

"Yea, I know who ye be," Richard said from his bed jammed into a back corner of the shop. "Be quiet, will ye, or we'll all be killed." Tools lined the walls and the scent of sawdust and raw wood was heavy in the air.

"Richard?" The carpenter's wife, Maggie, rolled over as he climbed out of bed.

"Shh, wife. 'Tis only Trevin."

"Ach. The baron, y'mean. I *know* who he is and what trouble he brings to this house," Maggie grumbled over a yawn. "Whether ye be a thief as I knew ye years before or all high-and-mighty Lord of Black Oak. 'tis a dark cloud ye carry with ye, Trevin McBain."

"Hush!" Richard ordered.

"Hush, yerself. Here I am, with child now, and Trevin, oh, excuse me, his lordship, comes in and ye're ready to lay down yer life. Haven't ye suffered enough?" She sat up in the bed, held the covers around her ample breasts, and pouted. "I needs ye, Richard. I love ye."

"Aye, and ye hate Lord Ian as much as I do."

Maggie, sighing theatrically, fell back to the pallet. "Oh, all right," she groused. "What do ye want me to do?"

"Pretend that nothing is amiss," Trevin said, his voice low.

" 'Tis a miracle ye want from me then."

Richard turned and reached for a tunic hanging on a peg. As he did Trevin saw his back, white skin marred by dark, ragged welts.

"You've been flogged," Trevin whispered, fury burning through his veins.

"Within an inch of his life. Because of you, McBain," Maggie was anxious to tell him. "Sir Webb that devil was on a tear. Lookin' fer spies, he was."

"Worry not," Richard said. "Sir Webb first came sniffin' around, just askin' questions, of not only me, but others as well. When he found out nothin' he resorted to . . . stronger measures." Richard found his sword and strapped it onto his belt. "I kept me tongue quiet, as did everyone, even old Matilda when they threatened to burn her fingers one by one. She's a tough old hen, I'll give her that. Now, my friend." He looked up and grinned in anticipation. "What have ye got in mind?"

" 'Tis time to take the castle away from the lord."

"Oh, is that all?" Richard mocked.

"Nay, we need to free Muir and Gareth as well."

"And did ye bring an army to help ye?"

Trevin shook his head. " 'Tis only I, but Lord Ian's best soldiers have ridden out of the castle to be led on a merry chase."

"So, then, have ye got a plan in mind?"

"A simple one," Trevin said.

"From you, would I expect more?"

"Be sure this plan, 'tis one that works," Maggie mumbled from beneath the covers.

"To be sure," Trevin agreed. "Now we need to quickly round up the men to take over the great hall and the dungeon."

"Gladly," Richard said and Maggie, from the bed, sighed dramatically.

"Be on your guard," she advised, her eyes shining in the dark.

"Always," Trevin vowed as he opened the door a slit and stared through the crack. When he was certain the sentries weren't looking, he and Richard would launch his personal attack to save his son.

"Good work." Gerald held tightly to the reins of Dark One as the charger sidestepped and snorted, nervously shifting in a tight circle.

"Here they come." From their vantage point on a hill, Trevin's men could barely discern the looming darkness of Rhydd. Shrouded in the fog, the fortress was black except for two columns of torchlights shining weakly in the gloom.

"Like a dog to a bitch in heat," York said and Henry watched, his heart beating rapidly, his body bathed in a cold, worrisome sweat.

The five of them sat astride their mounts waiting to lead the warriors from Rhydd through the forests and hills. But Henry had his own plan, a scheme that didn't include racing along the edge of the river to disperse on differing trails through the woods while Ian of Rhydd's soldiers stupidly split up and followed their lead.

"Now!" Gerald said as the lights shone brighter. He kneed the black stallion and snorting, the beast took off. Tail aloft, hooves clanging on stones, the charger raced through the dark trees. Winston, York, and Nelson took up their reins and their mounts, too, raced through the underbrush and damp mist.

"Guide me, Father," Henry prayed, trailing behind, his steed's gait an easy canter along the wide path. The sound of the river, water rushing through the canyon met his ears and he told himself to have faith. He was doing that which was right. Remember your father, how he died needlessly, taking an arrow meant for the outlaw-turned-baron. Remember Lord Dryw. A good man. An able leader. Murdered by Trevin. His breathing was labored, sweat running in his eyes, Lady Gwynn's mantle billowing over his bay's rump as he slowed his horse, fighting as the animal tossed his great head, anxious to be part of the ever-fleeing herd.

"Hold back," he said to the horse as the trees gave

way to a strip of rocky shore that bordered the black, racing water. The others had already urged their animals onto the sandy beach, hoping that their pursuers would catch glimpses of the small army before each rider turned into the dense foliage once again. Nelson's mount splashed along the river's edge, York's hugged close to the trees, Gerald and Winston rode together in the middle of the sandy strand. Henry hung back, his trepidation mounting as wisping trails of fog separated him from the others. Certainly this was the right thing to do—the most noble of acts. Or was it?

His throat ached in fear and for the first time he doubted the wisdom of this one, rash act. Hoofbeats sounded behind him. Men's voices, unfamiliar voices, caught up to him. He swallowed hard and sent up another prayer. "Please, Father, keep me safe. Let me follow the courageous noble path worthy of—"

"Hey! There's one!" he heard as he wheeled his mount.

"Do not harm me," he yelled. "I am with you."

" 'Tis the lady—" one of the riders, dark and ghostlike as he appeared in the haze, yelled.

"It don't sound like 'er."

"Use caution. She is not to be harmed." Webb's voice boomed through the fog. Bobbing lights burned ever more brightly. "Stay your weapons!"

Soldiers on huge horses emerged from the mist to surround him and his nervous stallion.

Henry began to tremble. "Do not harm me for I wish to join you," he said as he tossed off the hood of Lady Gwynn's mantle. "The lady is not with us as we—the other four riders and I—are part of a decoy mission."

"Decoy?" Webb thundered, his mount mincing as it approached.

"Aye. Trevin and the others, the lady included, stayed back and planned to take the castle."

"Four of them?" Webb asked.

"There are others inside; those not loyal to Ian of Rhydd." Oh, he hoped he'd not made a horrid mistake in throwing in his lot with Lord Ian and this surly knight.

"Why, pray tell," Webb said, guiding his horse so close to Henry that the beast's hot breath shot down his leg, "should I believe that you've turned traitor?" His face was wet from the mist and glowered darkly in the dim, flickering light of the torches. "Could you, too, not be part of a trap?"

"Because I tell the truth. I—I am Henry. Sir Henry." Why wouldn't they believe him?

"You be a knight?" One of the soldier's laughed and another joined in. Henry squared his thin shoulders and tried to hold up his wobbling chin.

"Hush!" Webb glowered at this company and his face took on the visage of Satan incarnate. "Tell me, Sir Henry, why ye have turned against the man for whom you ride?"

Sweat trickled down Henry's cheek and settled in the sparse hairs of his beard. "I trust him not. He killed Lord Dryw and . . . and my father lost his life saving that of the outlaw." His reasons, nay his convictions, sounded feeble and unfounded.

"Ye expect me to believe you?"

"Aye." Henry nodded quickly, his eyes darting as the soldiers seemed to draw nearer, evil messengers from hell getting ever closer. His horse tossed his head nervously and Henry had to fight every instinct he had to kick the steed and try to race away from the sinister forces he suddenly realized were at work here. " 'Tis . . . 'tis the truth I say, Sir Webb. This be not part of a trick. If . . . if ye do not believe me, ye can take me hostage, but please, please trust me, Trevin is at this moment inside the gates of Rhydd. He will not rest until his son is free and Lord Ian is dead."

"What of my horse?" Webb asked, his countenance menacing.

" 'Tis ridden by one of Trevin's men, part of the deception, as is this mantle of Lady Gwynn's."

"Where is she?"

"We left her with a peddler, but . . . but I think Gerald, one of the knights, said that she was to be returned to Black Oak by Sir Stephen, another one of Trevin's knights."

Slowly Webb unsheathed his dagger. Leaning forward in his saddle so that his face, a mask of dangerous fury, was within inches of Henry's, he whispered, "Listen to me, *Sir* Henry, I will trust ye for a while. We'll return to the keep and if I find that ye have deceived me, I will personally cut out yer lying tongue and throw it to the dogs, do ye understand?"

Henry nearly fainted. He swayed in the saddle. "Aye. Aye. but 'tis the truth I speak," he managed to say as Webb leaned back, pulled upon his white steed's reins and the animal, rearing, wheeled and nearly fell against Henry's mount.

"To Rhydd," he said and Henry felt a moment's relief. "And you"—he pointed a gloved hand at a burly giant of a knight—"Sir Patrick, make certain our prisoner does not escape."

"Prisoner?" Henry said as someone slapped his mount's rump and the edgy horse leaped forward. "Nay, Sir Webb, I am not a traitor to Rhydd."

"Nay? A man who turns his back on his lord is not to be trusted. This, I know."

"But—" *Prisoner? No, this was all wrong!*

"Ye didn't think ye'd be a guest, now, did ye?"

"I thought I would ride with yer men."

"Did ye?" Webb's laughter was dull and wicked. "You be a simpleton, then. 'Tis a miracle you be called a knight. Come! Once we secure the fortress, then we shall retrieve my horse and find the lady." He spurred his mount and the white stallion took off like a shot, galloping fearlessly into the thick darkness.

Henry, astride his steed, was swallowed in a sea of horses, soldiers, and torches. Though he felt betrayed, as if he'd cast his lot with the wrong madman, he had no choice but to follow.

"Help! Guard! Please, help me with the old one. He's . . . he's dead!" Gareth cried, banging on the iron bars of his cage with his fists.

"Dead?" the sentry, a behemoth of a man whose only speed was slow, asked. "Nay, he's just sleepin'."

"He breathes not! He . . . he has no heartbeat! Please call for the physician."

"If he be dead, then 'tis already too late." With a snort of disdain, the man climbed from his bench and lumbered through the murky darkness to the cell. "He looks fine to—what the devil's that?" Frowning, his heavy face distrustful, he opened the cell door and walked inside.

"I know not," Gareth said, eyeing the rune the Muir had bled from his own body onto the cell floor. "Did you not hear the old man rambling on and on and drawing on the floor?"

"Nay . . ." The sentry slowly shook his massive

head. "I listen not to the prisoners." He scratched his crown and his face pulled into a confused frown.

"Well, he did and then . . . then he lay down as if to sleep and died . . . I swear it!"

The guard didn't move, nor did he approach the old man who lay motionless on the filthy rushes.

" 'Tis the mark of the devil," the thickheaded sentry whispered, fear flaring his nostrils.

"No . . ."

The guard, rather than enter further into the cell as Gareth had hoped, backed out and closed the door with a clang. "I'll not be in any place where Lucifer sleeps," he insisted and a few of the other prisoners grumbled their agreement. "Hey—John, you at the top of the stairs. Go and get the priest."

"Why?" a voice yelled down.

"Do it and do it now unless ye want to find yerself in the maw of hell!"

"Go and get 'im yerself!"

"Gladly." Backing up the stairs he disappeared and Gareth kicked at the straw in disgust.

"He believed you not," he whispered, thinking Muir's plan to trick the guard had been feeble at best. "We needs to do something else."

The old man didn't stir.

"Did ye hear me?" Gareth asked, moving closer to the corner where the sorcerer slept. "We needs—oh, God." Muir was not sleeping as was the plan. Nay, he lay, not breathing, his one eye open and staring sightlessly. "Oh, no, no, no!" With footsteps as cold as an ogre's breath, fear crawled up the back of Gareth's spine and wrinkled his scalp. "Help!" he cried again, more loudly this time.

"Oh, shut up, would ye?" a ruffian grumbled from his cell.

"You shut up, Reginald," his cellmate shot back. "Help!"

Gareth's heart thundered, his palms sweated. He'd never liked the old man, not really, and yet he felt a horrid loss in this dank, close prison with its dripping walls, rotting straw, and hidden rats. To be in this dungeon, alone, without anyone with whom to speak was unthinkable and the sorcerer for all his faults was a good old sod. The world seemed to collapse upon him and Gareth realized the futility of his plight. He thought of his mother and tears burned the back of his eyes, tears he would never shed for 'twas weak to show how much he missed the woman who'd borne him.

All of his bravado failed him and though he tried to summon a drop of courage, he had but to look at the old man, his mouth agape, his chest not rising, his scarred eyes open and Gareth wanted nothing more than to climb through the damned bars and escape. His slingshot was tucked into his breeches and he had more that a handful of pebbles in his pocket, but he was so scared he could think of nothing more than getting away from the dead body.

"Hey, is the old sod really dead?" one of the other prisoners asked.

"I'll be buggered. Are ye sure?" another joined in. "Ain't 'e some kind of magician or somethin'? Maybe 'e's just in a damned trance."

"Aye and I be the King of England."

The men chortled and told more jokes, but Gareth didn't listen. He stared at the stairway and silently prayed for the priest, the guard, *anyone* who would remove the body.

It seemed like hours before he heard voices and

saw the dance of golden shadows from a torch playing against the bottom of the steps.

" 'Tis too late for last rites," Father Anthony was saying as he, grim faced, along with the guard and old Idelle entered the dungeon.

"This place be a disgrace," Idelle said, shaking her aged head as if she could see through eyes that had turned a milky white. "If the mistress was still in charge—"

"Well, she ain't and this is the way Lord Ian likes things," the guard said as he reached for his keys.

"Gareth, lad! Idelle's wrinkled countenance lightened with a grin. " 'Tis troubled I've been, knowing ye were here." She hugged him fiercely and again those dreaded tears came to his eyes. Idelle, so close to his mother, had always been good to him. "I've tried to come and see ye, but Lord Ian had forbidden it."

"Where is my mother?"

"Oh, would I to know," she whispered, kissing the top of his head before turning to Muir's still form.

"Look, there, on the floor!" The guard pointed at the rune Muir had created with his own blood. " 'Tis the mark of the devil, I tell ye."

"Nay," Idelle dismissed the man's fears. " 'Tis only a drawing about life."

The priest, trembling, made a quick sign of the cross, then leaned over Muir. "This poor soul—"

At that one of the magician's hands moved.

"Achh!" The guard yelled.

"Holy Father." The priest backed toward the cell's door and Gareth, heart beating faster than a rabbit's, yanked his slingshot from his breeches, loaded, and fired a piece of mortar. Ssst! Crack! The rock hit the sentry squarely on the back of his head.

"Ouch! Say what?" He turned just as another piece

of flying mortar shot into his forehead. "Ach! Stop!" Another shot. This one to an eye. "Stop it, ye've blinded me, ye filthy little bastard." With one hand over his wound, the other to his sword, the guard didn't expect another sharp stone to launch into his gut.

"Jesus, Mary, and Joseph, stop him!" He yanked out his sword but not before Muir jumped to his feet and imbedded his tiny knife into the guard's neck.

"Run!" he ordered.

Blood spurted and sprayed. The sentry swung wildly with his sword and Gareth took off like a startled colt. He didn't wait to see what happened to Father Anthony or Muir or Idelle. He ran up the stairs two at a time and threw open the door to the bailey where fog shrouded the keep. He slunk through the shadows, hanging close to the curtain wall and thankful for the mist that was his cover. Two sentries guarded the main gate and the portcullis was down. No escape there. He inched around the edge of the keep until he came to the kennels where the dogs, already restless, woofed softly at his approach. Alfred was nowhere in sight, so Gareth let himself into the pens and was nearly knocked over by Boon.

Tail whipping, the pup yipped and dance at Gareth's feet. "Hush," he ordered, picking up the wriggling mass. Most of the grown dogs, those trained for the hunt, lifted their heads, then lowered them again as they were used to the boy visiting at odd hours. He held his puppy close and felt the wild, erratic beating of Boon's heart. "Shh," he warned, trying to stay in the shadows.

Muir, the old goat, had duped him. Why hadn't he told him that he could put himself into a trance or whatever it was and appear dead? Gareth shivered as he carried Boon out of the kennels and sat behind the huge kettles used for washing clothes. He had no plan for escape, but knew it would have to be done quickly, before everyone in the castle was looking for him.

On his feet again, he made his way past the ferret kennels where the nervous beasts were pacing restlessly in their cages. Boon stiffened, but didn't bark as they passed only to stop at the end of the kennels and view the sally port where a sentry, a young lad from the looks of him, was positioned. He wore no helmet so there was a chance that Gareth could use his slingshot against him, but he had only one more pebble. 'Twasn't enough. He needed a pocketful of rocks and then he'd attack the guard and set himself free.

Once he was outside of the walls of Rhydd, he'd do as his mother had ordered him and head south. In a few days' time if he walked partway and caught rides on carts, he'd arrive at Heath Castle where his mother's sister Luella was mistress.

Except he had no money or jewels. Those his mother had given him before were with Muir. Gareth had nothing, not a single coin. Unless . . . He smiled to himself in the darkness. So his father was a thief, was he? Well, Gareth could be one as well. He'd steal a dagger from the armory, bread and apples from the kitchens, and a few jewels from the castle treasury, for unless Ian had changed things in the short time he'd become lord, Gareth knew where the spare key to the treasury was hidden.

Something was wrong. Terribly wrong. The sounds of the castle were different. In his sleep he'd heard men shouting, horses neighing, and the excited barks of the hounds. Ian had incorporated all these noises into his dreams, but now, though the fire had burned down and the torches were dark, he sensed another presence in his chamber.

He reached to the side of the bed where his sword was lying, but his fingers found only cold stone and thick rushes, no metal blade.

His heart hammered and he turned, expecting to find his dagger and its sheath near him on the pallet, but it, too, was missing.

"So you finally awaken."

The voice was that of his enemy. The thief.

"I thought I might have to slit your throat while you slept."

As Ian's eyes adjusted to the darkness he saw his nemesis, dark and foreboding, looking larger than ever as he stood near the window. In one hand was Ian's sword, in the other his knife.

"How did you get in here?"

"Through the front door."

"Guard!" Ian yelled, but Trevin crossed the room and was upon him, his own knife pressed against his throat.

"I've dispensed with those loyal to you," he said in a harsh whisper that turned Ian's blood to ice. "Now, I think you should get dressed and come with me."

Gwynn eyed the sky and wished for moonlight and a swifter means of getting to Rhydd. They'd traveled for hours, she and Sir Stephen, and finally they were near, though the tired ass lagged and 'twas only the reins slapping him on his buttocks that kept him plodding along.

The air here was dense with fog and cold enough to freeze flesh. Gwynn blew on her hands and hoped beyond hope that she was not too late, that Trevin was safe and Gareth . . . oh, if only he were alive and somewhere safe.

"Cannot we move faster?" she asked, not for the first time.

"Would that we could, but 'tis not possible.

Time was ticking by so quickly and Gwynn shivered to the marrow of her bones. She should never have let Trevin trick her so, never have trusted him and yet, furious as she was, her heart was with him and the few men he'd taken.

'Twas a fool's mission but she couldn't quell that little bit of hope that burned bright in her heart. Surely he was safe. He had to be. With Gareth. Oh, what she would give to see her son again, to embrace him. If only she could see them both one last time, she would be able to give herself to Ian and be his dutiful wife.

The idea was pure poison and it turned sour deep in her belly, but she would find a way to survive being Ian of Rhydd's wife, suffer any indignity he suggested as long as Trevin and Gareth were safe.

She sent up yet another silent prayer and somewhere in the forest nearby a wolf gave up a lonely cry. The donkey, so listless moments before, bolted and the cart rolled forward at a faster clip.

Rhydd was close now. She could feel it in her bones, but along with that welcome sensation was a dark fear that those she loved most in the world were in danger . . . or worse yet, neither had survived.

Gareth couldn't believe his good luck. His pockets bulging with jewels and coins he'd taken from the countinghouse, the puppy tucked under one arm, he dashed along the curtain wall, pausing behind a wagon to scan the bailey.

All the sentries were missing, away from their posts, and he had the vague feeling that something was amiss, something more than his escape from the dungeon. Was it possible old Muir had finally cast a spell that worked and all the guards had fallen asleep at their posts, or mayhap, after the fight and confusion in the prison could it be that the sentries were scouring the castle looking for him?

Gareth didn't stop to think too hard. All he knew was that the gatehouse appeared empty and though the portcullis was lowered, it was a simple matter of raising it and slipping through. It would take time and agility, for the minute the huge metal gate began clanging upward, the castle would be alerted. Then he would have only seconds to race down the stairs and dash through the gatehouse to freedom outside the castle walls.

Cautiously he slunk along the edge of the walk, squinting so hard through the fog that his head ached. His slingshot was tucked into the band of his breeches and in the hand not holding the dog, he carried a dagger.

He reached the gatehouse and holding his breath, slipped through the open door and up a winding staircase. He expected to run into a guard hastening down at any second, but heard no sounds and the torches and candles in the sconces on the walls had burned low, some mere embers that cast little light.

Heart thumping, he reached the winch room, then realized he couldn't open the portcullis without another man's help. "Damn," he muttered under his breath as boon gave out a yip and scrambled out of his arms. "Shh!"

"I wondered when ye were goin' to arrive."

Gareth froze, then watched in wonder as Muir,

cackling, appeared from a dark alcove. So the old man did have a little magic in him after all.

"Hurry now, boy. We have not much time. Grab that handle!"

Gareth did as he was told though he wondered at the old man's strength. The gate was heavy, meant for two stout men to reel it upward and yet there was no other way. If he and Muir and Boon were too escape, they had to open the gates.

"The prisoners have escaped!" A guard was yelling, his voice rolling through the bailey as Trevin, his sword still at Ian's throat, pushed his captive through the doorway of the great hall. No other men came running, and the few sleepy-eyed servants who appeared in the windows did not seem inclined to help the anxious sentry.

Trevin smiled to himself. Richard and the other men they'd gathered must have been victorious in their efforts of subduing the few guards and soldiers left in the castle. He leaned forward and said into the older man's ear, "Now 'tis time for you to smell the stench of the dungeon." Trevin prodded Ian with the tip of his blade.

The sentry, running toward the great hall was tackled by a clumsy lad no more than thirteen. They rolled on the grass until Richard, hiding behind a broken wagon, leapt forward and helped the awkward boy restrain the guard. "Sorry," the carpenter said, looking up and appearing sheepish. "We missed this one. Good work, Tom."

"The rest?" Trevin asked.

"Most have either sworn allegiance to you or are in the dungeon."

Ian's shoulders slumped as if a weight had been

placed squarely upon them. In the poor light, he appeared old and tired.

" 'Tis as it should be," Trevin said.

"Nay, 'tis not all good news. A few men loyal to this one"—he spat on the ground at Ian's bare feet—"escaped and the boy and sorcerer are missing."

"What?" Trevin's fingers tightened over his sword. "Missing?"

Richard nodded gravely. "I led the group into the dungeon, but the guard was already dead, the boy and Muir gone, and all that was left was a strange, bloody drawing on the cell floor."

"All for naught, thief?" Ian asked, one eyebrow lifting.

"Where are they?"

Ian shrugged. "I have no idea."

Trevin believed him, but felt a moment's fear. "Search every inch of the castle," he ordered his men but as the words escaped his mouth, he heard the creak and groan of ancient gears. Rattling like the chains of dying prisoners, the metal portcullis slowly raised. "No!" he yelled for just as the gate opened, the hollow, damning sound of hoofbeats rang through the bailey. "Close the gates!" he ordered, "For the love of Christ, lower the gate!" But it was too late. Through the fog he saw two figures, an old man and a youth, slip out the door of the gatehouse while, riding through the unguarded portal was a company of soldiers, torches held high.

In the lead, his sword drawn, the blade gleaming a malevolent gold in the light, was Trevin's old enemy.

Sir Webb, hatred distorting his features had returned.

The only object between him and the outlaw baron was Trevin's son.

"Gareth, run!" Trevin screamed. "Here, take this one!" He shoved Ian toward Richard and ran across the bailey, his sword raised, fury and fear pumping through his blood. "Run, damn it, boy, run!"

But it was too late.

"Get him!" Webb ordered. Two men jumped from their steeds. Another took quick aim. The dog, which Gareth had been holding, dropped to the grass and yipping, scuttled away.

"Nay!" Trevin vaulted a pile of firewood in his path, landed quickly, and didn't miss a stride as he ran. He was only fifty yards from the boy.

Thwack!

The first arrow hit Gareth in his leg. He screamed and the sound echoed in Trevin's heart. Writhing in agony, the boy fell. His slingshot slipped to the ground. With a whimper, the puppy ran further into the shadows.

Another deadly hiss.

Thud. The second arrow lodged in Gareth's shoulder. Again that horrid, shrill scream.

"Nay!" Fury, as black as a demon's heart tore through Trevin. He raced forward, his sword raised, the keening scream of denial he heard, torn from his own throat. He swung and one of the archers fell with a sickening thunk. Horses whinnied and reared. Men shouted. Swords flashed in the ghastly orange lights. Metal clashed. Grown men yowled in pain.

"Stop him!" Webb's voice thundered above the horrid cacophony.

An arrow hissed through the air, whizzing by his head.

Another sizzled as it passed.

"Trevin! Watch out!" Richard's voice. Somewhere nearby. Or far away. Men scrambled off their horses and in the midst of the soldiers, captured, his face white as death, was Sir Henry.

Thwang!

Pain exploded in his thigh. Trevin stumbled. His sword nearly fell from his hand. He forced himself onward. "Gareth!"

An archer sighted on his boy.

Trevin threw his sword. It hit the archer and sliced deep.

Screaming, blood spraying from his chest, the soldier dropped to his knees, clutching the weapon that was ending his life.

"Stop this bloodshed! In the name of the Almighty, I implore ye!" Father Anthony, robes flying behind him, descended through the dark bailey like a furious, avenging angel from heaven. "D-d-do not—Oh, merciful God!"

Trevin was at Gareth's side. His dagger was in his hand. "Stay back!" There were other men about. Some rushing from their huts, others taking up weapons. Whether for him or his enemies, he knew not. The torches reflected on the thick mist and in the wild eyes of the restless steeds and the flash of weapons.

Dogs barked, horses snorted, and in the distance he heard a baby crying. Men were shouting or screaming, the sounds jumbling in his mind.

An arrow hissed by his ear. Another pierced his shoulder. "Gareth, get up. Run."

" 'Tis too late," Muir, appearing through the fog was suddenly at his side. Gareth lay unmoving, blood staining his tunic.

"Nay. He will live and survive and—"

" 'Tis too late for all of us," Muir said.

"Never!"

Trevin reached under the boy, intending to carry

him to the keep. "Gareth, lad, rest easy. I will see to you," he promised, staggering as he lifted the boy and the pain of his own wounds burned through his muscles.

"Stop!" Ian's voice was cold as the bottom of a well. "Traitor. Murderer. Thief!"

Trevin pushed onward. The words were far and distant, their meaning unclear. A roar, like the sound of a mighty, tumbling waterfall, filled his head. If he could get Gareth to the keep, lie him on a bed, all would be well.

And what of Gwynn?

By the gods she was beautiful. If he could see her again. Just once. He fought the pain and the darkness that threatened his vision. The dull roar in his head grew louder, like the sound of the sea pounding the shore. *Gwynn, love, I will see that our son is safe. Remember that I love you as I have loved no other. . . .* With a shake of his head, he cleared his mind. He could not lose his senses, not yet.

"Did you not hear me?" Ian roared.

Trevin trudged onward, his legs heavy, his feet stumbling in the bloodstained grass. He would save his son. If he'd done nothing of purpose in his vile life, he would save his boy.

Sweat poured from his skin. Blood flowed from his wounds. Pain gnawed at his body and soul. Still he trudged forward. 'Twas not much farther.

"Run!" Richard yelled. "Trevin, please . . . all is lost! Save yourself!"

Ian, who had managed, with the help of the miller to wrest Richard's weapon from him, watched the fool carry his boy toward the keep. With each step Trevin of Black Oak faltered yet he kept onward, intent upon his mission, caring for a child he'd never really known.

The battle was nearly over. Webb's soldiers and weapons were strong; the insurgents—peasants and servants—were no match for trained warriors.

Ian turned to a marksman who had slain several men in the uprising. "Take care of the traitor," he said and watched as the archer drew back on his bow, aiming at Trevin's back.

"NAY! TREVIN!" A woman's voice, his *wife's* voice, shrilled. Ian turned and saw Gwynn, her face a mask of horror running through the bailey. Her feet were swift as she passed the soldiers who had managed to round up most of the traitors. She had just arrived in some sort of cart and was dressed in men's clothing, leather tunic and breeches. Her hair streamed behind her, tears ran from her large eyes and never had she looked more beautiful. "Stop this! Ian, I beg you, please—"

Trevin, hearing her voice, turned.

The archer released his missile.

True to it its mark, the arrow whistled through the air and lodged deep into Trevin's shoulder, only inches above Gareth's head.

"Nay, nay, nay!" she yelled, racing over the wet grass and through the thick mist, speeding closer.

The outlaw baron staggered. His son rolled to the ground and with one final look at the woman racing through the gloom, he fell.

"Trevin! Oh, no, no, no!"

She tried to race past him, but Ian would have none of it. This woman had humiliated him before. She'd run off with the thief on their wedding night, slipped away from him and caused him to be a buffoon to his own men. She was not to be trusted, never to be let out of his sight again. For all he knew she could already be carrying another of the outlaw's children in her womb.

That nasty thought curdled his blood.

Though he was nearly fifty, he was quick and he caught her. He reached for her arm and she, flying around empty carts and splashing through the edge of the eel pond, jerked her elbow away from him. As if his very touch repelled her.

Wicked little slut.

"Stop, wife!" he commanded and when she attempted to keep running, he tackled her, knocking her onto the muddy grass. Tears still pooling in her eyes, she tried to push him away and when his grip around her only tightened she pounded his chest with her fists.

He pinned her with his weight and grabbed her hands so that she could no longer strike him. So close he could smell the scent of heather in her hair, he heard his men surround them, knew that Webb and his soldiers were witnessing the taming of his woman. "Listen, you little wench," he breathed hard into her ear. "If you value the lives of your lover and your son you will get up and stand with me as my wife. You will find a way to repair your dignity as well as mine."

"I cannot."

" 'Tis your choice, m'lady," he said, seeing the righteous fury flashing in her eyes and feeling her breasts, beneath him, rising and falling with each of her shallow, indignant breaths.

"I would rather die."

" 'Tis not your life with which I barter."

Every muscle in her body stopped moving. Finally, he had her full, though unwilling, attention.

"If you do not do as I ask, I'm afraid, they'll both die."

"No!" She twisted, trying to catch a glimpse of her beloved and their child.

Her faith in the thief was enough to make a man sick, though he was awed by her courage and the fervency of her emotions. " 'Tis your choice, sweet," he said, trying to keep the snarl from his voice. "If you do not stand by me they will die, either by the wounds they have received this night or by having their necks snapped in the gallows as soon as they are strong enough. So make up your mind. Now. Just remember, their fates rest with you."

Chapter Sixteen

"Why not just kill 'em?" Webb asked as he picked at his thumbnail with the tip of his dagger. He leaned against the stones of the grate as servants scurried, eyes averted, in and out of the curtains and up the stairs. Guards were posted at all the entrances of the keep, ready for an attack, should one come from Lord Trevin's loyal soldiers at Black Oak. Though many of the peasants and servants were in prison, there were enough to run the castle and all of those couldn't be trusted. Not yet. There were dozens of pairs of eyes and ears that were watching and listening.

Ian sighed. He would have to be careful if he wanted to earn the trust of those whom he ruled.

A spark shot from the fire in the great hall and he kicked the dying ember back to the flames. It had been two days since the attack by the outlaw and he would like nothing better than to put an end to Trevin McBain's miserable life, just as he'd promised Gwynn. Nothing better. But he had to think in larger terms, about the future, about his wife, and his power. As for the boy, well, once again, it had to appear to Gwynn as if Ian were a forgiving man even though he'd shown his true colors on the night of the attack. He'd kicked himself several times over for her to see the hatred that blackened his heart.

Gwynn was the key. The sorry fact was that he was afraid he loved her. The image of her face, twisted in pain and fear as she'd raced across the bailey intent on reaching her child and lover had seared through his brain. He doubted it was possible that she would ever care so much for him. He'd once only wanted her submission, her taming, and cared not if she loathed him. Now he needed more. Not just her expressionless compliance, but her heart as well.

" 'Twould be easy enough to kill 'em," Webb said frowning as he cleaned each of his filthy fingernails.

"Aye, and then what? They will die anyway, but I needs not hasten it along. Let the midwife chant her spells and burn her candles." He fluttered his fingers in the air as if waving off a bothersome fly. "Allow the priest to pray and flog himself in atonement." That one, Father Anthony, was an odd man. Never had Ian seen a man so intent on doing himself physical harm. "Do not stop the physician from testing urine, or letting blood." He leaned forward in his chair and rested his elbows on the trestle table as he eyed the candles burning brightly within the ring of interwoven antlers suspended from the ceiling. Webb was an imbecile, who thought only of the moment at hand and Ian, though it was against his nature and would like nothing better than to slit the outlaw's throat, tried to be patient. "I want to rule with her at my side. For that she must trust me."

"Why?" Webb spat into the fire and sheathed his blade. He wiped his nose with his sleeve and eyed the lord of the manor as if he were weak. " 'Tis too late for trust, m'lord," the dark one snorted with a cruel laugh. He reached for the mazer of wine he'd left on a corner of the table.

"Do you not know it's never too late?"

"Oh, aye, and now ye'll be quotin' scripture or some such rot to me. Ah, Lord Ian, a fine and righteous and pious man ye be." He laughed again and Ian seethed, his neck growing warm. As soon as things at Rhydd quieted and he and Gwynn were ruling the castle amicably, he'd find a way to dispose of Webb. He was a good warrior, true, but he felt no bond with the man who had helped his brother go free after Ian had paid dearly to keep Roderick imprisoned. Webb would have to die for that mistake.

Ian leaned back in his chair and propped a boot onto a nearby bench. Today he was feeling his years. Five decades and no heir. 'Twas time to change that, if he could. Margaret had given him no sons, nor had any of the wenches he'd bedded claimed he'd fathered their children, and then there was the sorry fact that his wife might be pregnant. With the thief's issue yet again. Had they not been together, spent nights alone or only in the company of Trevin's men?

Anger surged through him, that same bloody anger that was fed by his hatred. He touched the side of his face, his fingers tracing the wound the thief had given him. Oh, how he longed to kill the bastard. 'Twould be so simple. Webb was right.

But Ian would have to be patient. If Gwynn was with McBain's child, then the babe would never survive the birth. Ian would see to it. He would not be played for the fool his brother had been. But until the child, if there was one, was disposed of, he could not chance bedding Gwynn. If she did get with child, how would he know whether it was his or the spawn of the thief's?

He had to wait.

Either she was pregnant or would, soon, have her time and the laundress would know. But there was no reason he couldn't hurry McBain's death along, was there? Who would know? Mayhap, for once, the dark knight was right. "I will think on it," he said. "Now, tell me, what of the magician?" Another burr under his saddle.

Webb scowled into his cup. "Disappeared."

"Impossible."

"He must've ducked out the gate before we closed the portcullis. In all the fighting and with that bloody fog, 'twas hard to see."

"He's here. I can feel it." Ian sipped from his cup and tried to dispel his thoughts about the old sorcerer. There was something about the old cripple and his bad eye, something he should remember . . .

He heard footsteps on the stairs and looked up to see Gwynn accompanied by two guards descending into the hall. Dressed in deep, red velvet, her hair braided away from her face, her chin lifted, she was as beautiful a woman as he'd ever seen. And she was his wife. A fleeting sensation of pride swept over him until he remembered she might be with child. A babe without any of his blood running through its veins.

"Wife," he greeted, standing and pulling out her chair. "Come, come, there is much we needs discuss."

"I want to see my son," she said, her cheeks two bright spots of color.

"And you shall, as soon as he improves—"

"Now!" she insisted. "I needs see him, touch him."

There was pain in her green-gray eyes and he knew he had no choice. If ever she was to trust him, to love him, he would have to accord her this one small wish.

He inclined his head. "I will see to it."

She stiffened for a second and distrust marred her beauty.

Ian glanced up at one of her guards. "When we are through here, the lady will visit her boy."

The ghost of a smile touched the edge of her lips. "And Lord Trevin?"

His patience snapped. Murdering the thief in his sleep sounded better all the time. "Nay. He, though being attended to, is a prisoner. The same as the others. As soon as he is well enough, he will be sent to the dungeon to await my judgment." Ian had to be careful. He wanted her trust and confidence, he hoped someday she would care for him just a little, but he refused to look weak. He reached into his pocket. "By the way, I found something of yours."

"Wha—? Oh, merciful God." Tears filled her eyes as she watched him twist the ruby ring in his thick fingers. She'd not seen it in thirteen years, yet she recognized the ring Trevin had stolen from her, the one she'd eventually given him in order to keep his silence about Gareth's conception. Now it winked in the firelight, dark facets sparkling as Ian placed the stone in her palm and she curled her fingers over it.

" 'Twas with the thief," Ian admitted and her heart tightened in pain.

In all the years they'd been separated, Trevin had never given away the ring, never sold it. Tears filled her throat. "Thank you," she said.

"Anything for you."

She saw a glimmer of love in his hateful amber eyes. "Then please, m'lord," she asked, her words tumbling out, "forgive those who rose against you. Do not seek vengeance against the carpenter, the alewife, and all the others who were caught in the fight. Have the gallows dismantled. Show some pity, some caring for those you rule and let the soldiers of Black Oak go free—"

"I cannot," he said simply. "Though it grieves me, lady, those who rose against me must be punished."

"But they did it for me."

"Then they will have to learn who the lord is. You are but my wife and though 'tis my every wish to make you happy, I cannot appear weak. Now, go, see the boy and"—he glanced up at the guards —"my wife may see the midwife who will attend to her from this moment on. She will no longer be locked in her room, but"—he added when she lifted her head expectantly—"for the time as it is, she must remain within the great hall."

Gwynn didn't know whether to thank him or demand more freedom. She opened her mouth, saw the set of his jaw beneath his silvering beard, and she nodded. "Thank you, m'lord," she said, still clutching the ring. If he were willing to concede her this much freedom, she would take it and plan accordingly.

" 'Tis nothing, Gwynn. I only ask that you believe I want to please you as I hope you want to please me." His benign smile was not to be trusted, for the gleam in his eyes reminded her that he'd lusted for her long and she knew him not to be a kind or forgiving man.

"Aye, m'lord."

"Take her to her son."

Heart pounding, she allowed herself to be led away by the guards. Finally she would be able to see Gareth, to touch his face and hair. If only she could do the same for Trevin. She ached to touch him again, to kiss him, to tell him how much she loved him. . . . She walked along a corridor to the western edge of the great hall and up the stairs. All the while she squeezed the dark ruby so tightly it nearly drew blood, then at the locked door in the towers, she slipped the ring upon her finger.

Gareth was in a small, windowless room resting upon a tiny bed. One candle burned in a sconce and the air was thick with the smell of death. For the first time she believed that she might truly lose her only child. Grief, ugly and creeping, gnawed at her. "Oh, Gareth," she said on a sigh as she fell to her knees and touched his forehead. His skin was hot, his eyes closed, and he moaned softly. Tears burned behind her eyes as she saw the blood-crusted bandages wrapped over his wounds, one in his chest, another in his thigh.

"I'm here," she said, holding his hand, now larger than hers, in her fingers. Please God, save him. Please hear my prayer. "Gareth, I will stay with you. But please, awaken." Her heart was heavy for he did not stir and the thought that he might never awaken tore at her. Guilt took a stranglehold of her throat and she wept, her tears staining his blankets and dropping onto his skin. "You have been my life, son," she admitted, "and you will always be."

Pain seared through his body. Every inch of his skin felt as if it were charred with red-hot coals and he couldn't open his eyes. He heard people, the priest, the old midwife, voices he didn't recognize, but Trevin knew he had one foot on the path to hell.

Gwynn. Where was she? Had she escaped? No. He'd failed. Somehow she'd returned to Rhydd and tried to save him and the boy. His head pounded. He'd failed Gareth as well. His only son; now, without a doubt, if not dead already, on his way to the gallows.

"He awakens." The priest again.

"Nay, he only stirs." Idelle's voice, as if from the far end of a corridor.

"Will he live?"

"He is strong of heart but who knows? His wounds were deep, and if he survives 'tis only to face the hangman's noose." Cold, brittle hands smoothed his hair from his face.

"Let us pray."

Idelle agreed and as he drifted in and out of consciousness, Trevin heard their whispered prayers for his wayward soul. He felt himself slipping away, but fought hard. He could not give up. Not while there was a breath of life in his body. Not while Gareth was alive and needed him. Not until he was certain Gwynn was safe.

"Ye must eat, m'lady," Idelle said as she eyed Gwynn's untouched trencher of brawn that lay, where she had placed it, upon a small table in Gwynn's chamber.

"I'm not hungry." Gwynn paced from one side of the room to the other, pausing to look out the window and cringe each time she viewed the gallows, hastily constructed and nearly ready should they be needed. Ian had savored the irony of having Richard, the wounded carpenter, oversee the building of the very structure that would eventually take his life. No amount of pleading from the carpenter's wife, or from Gwynn, could convince him to spare Trevin's accomplice. All the men who had taken up swords against Rhydd that night had been shackled in the dungeon, including Henry, who, it seemed, had been a traitor to Trevin's cause, though he was loudly complaining of his treatment according to some of the women who had taken food to the prison.

With the exception of Muir, they'd all been caught. The old man had vanished from within the fog-encased bailey. No one had seen or heard from him since and it had been days . . . long, sad lonely days that had bled into the other. She found her only solace in the fact that both Gareth and Trevin were alive, if only clinging to life.

She spent a large part of her days with her son, the rest here, in her chamber, for though allowed the freedom of the keep, she had not the heart to take up her duties as mistress to Lord Ian. She cared not about the herbs, gardens, nor the books or records nor the damned cloth that needed to be purchased. Nor could she stand the fighting between the cook and steward.

All that mattered were Trevin and Gareth. Somehow she had to free them both. There had to be a way. There had to! She clenched her fist and felt the ring upon her finger—the ruby. The depth and darkness of the stone gave her strength.

"But ye must think of the babe, if not yourself," Idelle said.

Gwynn knew the old woman was right, of course, there was the chance that she was starving a child, should there be one, growing within her. Ian suspected that she had made love with Trevin and as such, was waiting to see if she was pregnant before taking her to his wedding bed. He wanted his own heirs and wasn't about to be duped into raising another man's child as his own the way his brother had been. So she had some time; not much, but a little.

"Tell me again of Trevin."

"He grows stronger, aye, but does not wake. He is guarded at every hour and when 'tis time and he has healed, he will be taken to the dungeon where, along with the rest of his men, he will await his trial."

"You mean his death," Gwynn said, worrying the ring in her fingers.

"Aye."

"You are allowed to see him?"

Idelle nodded.

"Then you must take him a weapon, a—"

"He does not waken. 'Twill do no good."

"But we must save him."

"And risk Gareth's life?" Idelle asked, shaking her head, her half-blind eyes sad. "Do you not think that Lord Ian's retribution would be swift and sure if Trevin were allowed to go free?" She picked up the tray of uneaten food. "Let him go," she advised. "M'lady, Lord Trevin's destiny is now in his own hands."

"Nay—"

"Think of your son. His son. What would he have wanted?"

"Then you must help me. I have to see Trevin one last time." She was desperate. "Is there nothing you could put in the guard's food to make him drowsy? So that I could visit Trevin for but a few minutes."

Idelle hesitated. " 'Twould be difficult."

"But not impossible."

Slowly the old woman nodded. "Nay, not impossible."

"Then, please, Idelle, do it."

"Ye will not be able to leave this room unnoticed. Ye may rove free, but you are watched."

"I will go at night."

"A guard is posted at your door."

"I know the guard and his ways." Gwynn sensed the old woman weakening.

" 'Tis too dangerous. Ye will be caught."

"No. Bring me animal fat and I will grease the hinges and do not worry about the guard."

Idelle hesitated.

"Please, Idelle," she said firmly. "Do this for me."

With a shake of her graying head, the midwife rolled her opaque eyes. "As you wish, m'lady."

For the first time in a week, Gwynn felt a ray of hope pierce her dark soul. She wouldn't give up. She couldn't. Twisting her ring, she walked to the window and eyed the gallows—built squarely in the middle of the bailey for all to see. Richard was at his post, chained and guarded, as he instructed younger men to pound nails and shore up the posts that would eventually end his life.

Unless she did something.

But what? The question haunted her and kept her awake at night. Now the wheels were set into motion. She had a chance to see the only man she'd truly loved. Somehow she had to find a way to save him.

Think, Gwynn, think. You're a smart woman. You've ruled this keep. Your son and the man you love are dying. You have no time. Hurry!

"In the name of the Father and the Son and the—" The priest's voice stilled and he froze as Trevin skewered the man with a deadly gaze. "Oh—for the love of God, you live!"

"Shh!" He'd been waiting for days and now, as night was falling, he knew it was time to return to the living. He'd awakened to broth being spooned down his throat but had kept the presence of mind to feign the same deep sleep that had kept conscious thoughts at bay. He swallowed, but was unable to speak for a second.

"I am p-p-pleased that—"

"Hush!" Trevin ordered in a harsh whisper. "Give me your cross."

"What?"

"The cross!"

"Oh. Nay, I cannot—" Trevin's hand shot out and wound in the folds of the priest's vestment.

"If not for me or Gwynn, then for Roderick," Trevin forced through cracked lips. "I have heard your prayers, Father, when you thought you were alone and I know that you broke your vow of celibacy, but not with a woman." The priest nearly fainted, then slowly, his glance sliding toward the closed door, he lifted the chain supporting the heavy gold and silver cross that hung from his neck. With shaking fingers he handed the chain to Trevin who snatched the cold metal and stuffed it under the thin blanket covering his body. "Speak of this to no one and I will keep your secret."

"I—I—"

"Shh. Get out." Trevin closed his eyes and held on to the metal. At first he hadn't believed Father Anthony who, in his rambling prayers, had continually begged forgiveness for his own sins of the flesh with the lord of the castle. 'Twas no wonder Roderick had been unable to get Gwynn with child. He'd been in love with a man. The thought knifed through Trevin's innards and disgust brought bile up his throat, but he would not think of the two men together, nay, but concentrate on the fact that now he had a weapon. Cold metal filled his palm and he brushed his fingers over the pointed tip of the cross. Now, he had to wait.

But not for long.

Muir's old bones ached from hiding in a small space below the loom, a place Idelle had hidden him on the

night of the escape. He'd been brought food and water
and even a pint now and again while he'd waited,
hoping that the soldiers would believe that he truly
had vanished, or, if not that, at least think that he
scuttled away through the open gate.

But he would not leave Trevin. Not when there was
a breath of life in his old body or any in his young
charge's. For he still considered himself Trevin's
guardian and whenever that thought faded, he had
only to think of his sister, Cleva, and the cruel, ruth-
less soldier who had raped her. Muir, who had robbed
the man earlier, had tried to stop the travesty, of
course, had attacked the man as he'd unlaced his
breeches, but the soldier had been swift with his blade
and had swung fast, nearly killing Muir and leaving
him blind in one eye.

Muir, shivered in his hiding spot, little more than a
grave it was, with straw for a bed and rats for companions as, overhead, the weaver kept at her task, the
shuttle clicking loudly as the threads were woven.

He remembered the blow, strong enough to cleave
a man, but it had glanced off his hard skull, slicing
through his eye as he'd fallen and in that moment a
great light had seemed to glow in the forest. From
that moment on, he'd had visions, cursed as they were,
and he'd heard his sister's screams as the young soldier—brother to the lord, Roderick of Rhydd—had
mounted her, raping her over and over again while
Muir could do nothing to save poor Cleva.

Nine months later she'd birthed Trevin and, after
forcing her brother to promise to take care of the
baby who only reminded her of that one, violent, dark
act, had drunk enough hemlock to kill herself. There
had been nothing Muir could do to save her and he
had raised her son—Ian of Rhydd's son—as if the

boy had been his own. He'd sworn to his sister that he would never reveal the name of the boy's father or tell him how he'd been conceived. Only then had Cleva been satisfied. For all these years he'd kept his promise, but now, with the circle of fate ever tightening, he saw all his best intentions sliding away.

He banged on the false door with the hook of his cane and the clicking halted. The weaver, a stout woman with fair skin and merry blue eyes kicked off the rushes and opened the trap door. Fresh air flooded the small niche and filled Muir's old lungs.

" 'Tis time," he said and she, worrying her lower lip, only nodded. She was one of the few in the castle who were loyal to Lady Gwynn and detested Ian of Rhydd, yet had managed to escape prison.

"God be with you, Muir," she whispered as he ducked behind spindles of colored thread mounted on pegs near a back wall.

"He always is." His legs were cramped, his blood felt as if it were congealed and a tingling sensation in his feet and fingers made walking and holding his staff difficult, but as evening was soon approaching, he had little time to spare. His vision had come earlier and, if it could be trusted, an army was nearing.

None of the soldiers who guarded the roads leading to Rhydd had discovered the men as they sneaked through the forest on foot, but Muir could sense them approaching, had seen through his pained blind eye, that they slunk at night through the forest. They were the men loyal to Trevin—Sir Gerald, York, and the rest. Now, he had to do his part, which was simple. He would steal the keys from a guard, unlock the dungeon, freeing the men inside, then have them overcome the guards of the sally port and throw long ropes down the outside of the curtain so that more armed warriors could scale the walls and save them all.

The scents of warm bread and roasting meat hit him as he slunk behind the kitchens but he ignored the rumbling in his stomach. Barrels of wine were being rolled into the wine cellar and he licked his lips as he thought of the nectar within the oaken casks, but he kept to his mission. Now was not the time to give in to his lust for wine. There would be time for sampling the barrels soon. If all went well. If it didn't . . . then his thirst for the spirits would be forever quenched.

Gwynn watched the moon rise and waited until the sounds of the castle had muted and the farrier's hammer had stilled. The geese, ducks, and chickens had roosted for the night and the torches had burned down and were but smoldering. The gallows, skeletal and foreboding, were visible in the moonlight, so she looked not through her window.

Asides, she had a mission.

She cracked the door slowly and the old creak of hinges no longer squeaked as she'd greased them with sheep fat Idelle had stolen from the kitchen. Her boots, too, were soft and silent as she watched the guard at his post. He never dozed and took his job quite seriously, but she knew he could be distracted, and as she waited, her heart pounding, sweat dripping from her forehead, she saw the comely kitchen girl who met him regularly at night.

He spoke—a quick joke. The girl giggled and tossed her head as he approached. They embraced and for a heart-stopping moment Gwynn remembered making love to Trevin deep in the forest—his touch and the feel of his mouth upon hers. She licked her lips and once the two lovers were caught in each other, she slipped from the room, closed the door softly behind her, and took the corridor to the steps that ran to the back of the castle.

Heart thudding, she made her way through the hallways to the far tower of the keep, the one where not only Gareth but Trevin was housed. She'd asked about him, but the gossip that had returned to her had been in snippets and contrary. Some said he was hovering near death, others thought him stronger by the day, but never had he awakened. Idelle seemed to think that he might forever be in this state of near-death and that thought was the worst of all.

Let him live, she silently prayed as she climbed the stairs to the room where Gareth lay. No guard was posted at his door, so she stopped, walked noiselessly into the small room, and brushed a kiss across her son's forehead. "I miss you. The pup is waiting for you as I am, Gareth." Her throat swelled shut and she fought tears, as she did each time she visited him.

It pained her to leave him, but she had another mission tonight. Quietly she walked to the top floor of the tower, her back pressed against the wall as she climbed the stairs, for she feared that she would be spotted.

She hoped that Idelle's herbs had worked and the sentry was sleeping. She paused, straining to hear the sound of snoring, but the hall was silent. No sound greeted her and she hurried up the final steps only to send up a quick, silent prayer and round the final corner.

The guard was missing. No one stood at his post and the door to Trevin's room was ajar. For a moment her stupid heart leapt and she thought that he'd escaped, but as she inched forward and peered into the tiny chamber, her blood turned to ice. Trevin lay on the bed. Unguarded. Unmoving.

Her heart shattered. He was dead. Oh, no. "Trevin," she whispered, falling to her knees and taking his still-warm hand in hers. "Oh, love, no, no, no." Inside she was dying. How could she have loved him so long and never told him? How could she have regained him only to lose him all over again? Tears burned behind her eyes and fell onto his body, bare aside from the bandages that were wrapped over him. "I love you," she whispered, sniffing and holding him. "Forgive me, but I loved you with all my heart and love you still." Desperation tore at her soul. Grief raked through her body and her years ahead—alone, without him, seemed long and purposeless. She reminded herself that she had Gareth, that part of him would live on through their child and also that she might have another babe growing deep within her. "Trevin, please . . . please do not die. I need you, I—"

"Touching."

The voice curled with acrimony and Gwynn started. She turned and saw Ian looming in the doorway. But he was not alone. With him was the magician, hobbled it seemed, his hands bound behind him and the woozy guard as well, trying and failing to keep his eyes open. A small cry escaped her lips.

Hot amber eyes burned in anger. Ian shoved Muir into the chamber and ground his teeth together. "I tried to be patient with you," he growled. "I gave you freedom. I didn't kill your bastard of a boy, I—"

"You only stayed away from me because you thought I might be carrying Trevin's babe," she accused, standing up to him, glaring back at eyes as deadly as a wolf's. Tears ran down her cheeks and pain burned deep in her heart, but she wouldn't back down, not ever. "And I am with child." Her voice shook with pride and she hoisted her chin even higher. "My time has come and gone and I know that I carry Trevin of Black Oak's child in my womb."

The minute she said the words she regretted them.

"Whore!" Quick as lightning he grabbed her. "You vile, worthless slut, there's no reason to hold back any longer, is there? I've waited long for this—"

"Leave her be!" Trevin's voice rasped through the darkness.

Gwynn jumped back. Her heart soared.

Ian whirled and glared at the bed. "Dare you speak, thief?"

"Trevin?" The dead weight within her dissipated as he opened his eyes. She tried to reach him but Ian shoved her roughly aside.

"I should have done this long ago." A dagger glinted in Ian's hand.

"No!" Gwynn cried. The blade slashed downward. "Nay!"

Trevin's arm erupted from the covers. Metal met metal in a sickening clash.

"Oh, God, no—"

The sharp tip of Trevin's cross plunged deep into Ian's belly.

"Aaagh—" Blood poured from the wound. Ian staggered backward.

Gwynn screamed.

" 'Tis true, 'tis true, father to son and son to father—" Muir mumbled seemingly horror-struck as Ian reeled against the wall, his dagger falling from his hand.

"What?" Trevin asked, blood staining his hands as he pushed himself upright.

" 'Twas your destiny. Ian of Rhydd is your father."

"Nay!" Trevin bellowed, his face still white as death.

"Holy Christ . . . the girl in the forest . . ." Ian's eyes glazed over and he mumbled incoherently. "I . . . knew . . . oh, Christ in heaven . . . what have I done?"

"She was my sister." Muir's voice was flat and hard.

"Who?" Trevin asked, his eyes dark with a quiet, nagging certainty. "Who was?"

"Your mother."

"Nay—"

" 'Tis true," Muir insisted.

"You are my . . . son." Ian's face was slack, his breathing labored as he slipped to the floor. "My only . . ." His voice faded and he breathed his last rattling breath.

"Oh, God." Gwynn was shaking. Ian was Trevin's father. She was in love with the son of the man . . . but it didn't matter, she told herself firmly. Nothing did other than Trevin and Gareth's safety.

"I . . . can't believe." Trevin's face was twisted in pain. He moaned from the deepest reaches of his soul. "Nay. Nay. Nay! NAY!"

"Believe," Muir insisted.

"Never!"

"You must, Trevin, for it is the truth."

"It . . . it is hell," he whispered, painful white lines bracketing the corners of his mouth.

Gwynn, shaking off all the anguish that tore at her, flung herself onto Trevin, the only man she'd ever loved. "You live. Think not of anything else!"

"But, my father—"

" 'Tis of no matter." She held his face in her hands and rained kisses over his cheeks and lips. Tears ran in crooked paths from her eyes. "You live. Oh, Trevin, you live—"

"But—"

"Shh. Think not of the pain. Look at me." When he failed, she pressed harder on his cheeks. "Look at me!"

Slowly he raised his eyes and the torture in his eyes found hers. "You live! I—I thought you were dead. Now 'tis not the time to think of anything but living."

He swallowed hard, cast one last look at the dead man, and shuddered. "Aye," he finally agreed with a half smile as if he, too, could shake off the torment at least for the moment, "I live, and I shall, I fear, for a very long time." She kissed his face and shoulders and refused to think of the slain man so close at hand. When Trevin glanced once more at the corpse of his father, she kissed his eyelids, forcing him to think only of her.

"I love you," he said when she finally lifted her face from his.

"What?" She froze, hardly daring to believe what she'd heard.

"I love you, Gwynn of Rhydd, and I have for all of my life. From the moment I spied you in your chamber years ago, I lost my heart to you."

She felt as if her heart would break with love for this man.

With one finger he lifted her chin and stared deep into her eyes. "Why did you think I kept your ring for all those years?"

She shook her head. "I know not."

"Because every time I looked at that dark ruby that sparkled in the light, I thought of you, lady. Every time. Even when I was married to another." His eyes held hers. " 'Tis my curse to love you, Gwynn, a curse I will bear for the rest of my life."

"Oh, for the love of all that's holy," Muir said,

"would ye give up this silly talk and cut me loose? There's wine to be drunk."

Footsteps sounded on the stairs and Trevin jumped to his feet, grabbing Ian's knife and ready to slay whoever entered. He shielded Gwynn's body with his own. "Halt!" he commanded as Stephen's face came into view.

"Nay, m'lord, do not harm me," he said. "Gerald and the others have come and freed the prisoners. We have taken the castle. Sir Webb is behind bars, but Ian . . ." His gaze moved over the small room to rest on the still form of the dead baron. "Ah. All is well."

"Aye." Trevin's arm circled Gwynn's waist.

Stephen cut off Muir's bonds and the old man rubbed his ankles and wrists. " 'Tis time to celebrate, methinks."

Relief caused Gwynn's legs to buckle, but Trevin held her steady. He looked into her eyes and kissed her. "Now, take me to my son and"—he threw Muir a dark look that brooked no compromise—"I'll hear no more of this nonsense about Ian being my father."

"But—" Muir said.

"I said, 'tis never to be spoken again. But . . . I will want to know of my mother."

One side of Muir's mouth lifted. "As you wish, sire."

"Don't call me that."

Together Gwynn and Trevin made their way down the stairs to the chamber where their son lay as she'd left him, unmoving, white as death. "He does not hear me," she said, tears stinging her eyes. Oh, if only Gareth would rise up.

"I know what the lad needs. I'll be back soon." Stephen, none the worse for his days in the dungeon, left them alone for a few minutes.

Trevin looked upon his son and love crossed his features. "He will live," he predicted. "He has not stayed alive all these days only to die."

"I . . . I . . . I pray it so." Gwynn could not think of life without Gareth. Would God be so cruel to give her Trevin again only to steal her son's life? Her insides shriveled at the thought and she clung to the man she loved, the father of her boy.

Trevin's arm tightened over her shoulders. "Have faith." He kissed her slowly upon her lips and images of making love to him filled her head.

"I love you, thief," she whispered, her lips trembling into a bit of a hopeful smile.

He traced those lips with the pad of one callused thumb. "As I love you, Gwynn. As I love you."

Surely God would not punish them, give them this precious love only to wound them by taking their boy. And yet . . . *Have faith.* Trevin's words echoed in her heart and she vowed to trust in him, in God, and in the powers of all things good on this earth.

But Gareth didn't move.

Tears burned behind her eyes as Stephen returned with the puppy who wriggled in his arms.

The big knight bent down, allowing the pup to nuzzle Gareth and anxiously wash the boy's face with his slick tongue.

"Come, lad, your Boon needs you," Stephen encouraged.

Nothing.

Trevin's face was a mask of tension.

Gwynn bit her tongue and swallowed the tears that were thick in her throat.

"I love you, son," Trevin vowed.

"Oh, Gareth, please wake up," she whispered.

No movement.

The dog gave out a lonesome, pitiful howl and Muir sighed as loudly as the wind upon the sea. " 'Tis too late."

"Nay!" Gwynn wouldn't give up.

Boon yipped.

Gareth moved slightly. Or was it the torches casting hopeful shadows over his face?

"I need you," Gwynn said, hardly believing her eyes.

"Aye, and so do I." Trevin brushed the hair from Gareth's forehead.

The boy's eyes fluttered open for a second.

"Gareth?" Gwynn dropped to her knees and took one of his hands in hers. "Can you hear me? Gareth?"

"He will be fine," Stephen predicted, winking at Trevin as Gareth stirred and moaned from his bed. "But he'd fare much better if his mother and father were married, I think."

"Married?" Gwynn repeated.

" 'Tis only a thought . . ."

"But a good one." Trevin, his eyes glistening, lifted Gwynn to her feet and cupped her face between his big hands. "What say you, m'lady?" he asked, his eyes holding hers. In that blue seductive gaze, she saw her future, her love. "Will you marry me?"

She glanced at Gareth, breathing easier it seemed. Her boy. His boy. Their first. There would be more. Many more. If she could but trust her heart to him.

Had she any choice?

She tossed her hair over one shoulder. "Marry you, eh?"

" 'Twould be my honor if you became my wife."

"And mine, if you were to be my husband."

"Good, good, now. Let us celebrate." Muir was down the stairs, moving more quickly than anyone would guess a man who professed himself to be a one-eyed cripple should be able to travel. Stephen carried Gareth, the puppy loped behind and Trevin, holding Gwynn's hand, walked her to the great hall where Muir was already ordering pages to bring mazers of wine.

Once the cups were filled he lifted one in a toast. "To the baron and his wife, may they live long and prosper."

"Here, here," the voices of those who served them faithfully rejoined.

Trevin tipped the edge of his cup to hers. "To you, fair lady," he said and she laughed merrily. Life was as it should be.

"And to you, thief." Her smile was wickedly seductive. "You know, you stole my heart a long, long time ago."

"Aye, lady, as you stole mine." His arms surrounded her, his mazer fell to the floor, and he kissed her until she couldn't draw another breath. "May you never give it back."

Epilogue

Trevin stretched and felt his wife's body curling sensually against his. A cock crowed in the yard and already he heard sounds of the castle awakening. He'd learned to love his life here at Rhydd and a smile grew across his jaw, for he would spend the day hunting with Gareth.

His boy had survived his wounds and accepted Gareth as his father. With Muir and Boon as his constant companions, Gareth had gotten into his share of trouble, but no more than his father had years before.

He heard a giggle, then another, and lifted an eyelid. "Who goes there?" he demanded to a chorus of childish laughter. An impish blue-eyed face with a mop of dark curls poked from behind one side of the wardrobe, while a red head—the spitting image of her mother—eyed him from the other side.

Twins! His twins.

"What are you two doing?" he demanded, his voice fierce. The girls weren't afraid but ran forward, each throwing themselves upon him as he wrestled with them in the bed. With a yawn, Gwynn slowly opened her eyes.

"Get up! Up! Up!" they insisted.

"Demanding as your mother, you two are," he teased.

"And stubborn as their father." Gwynn hugged her girls and kissed their crowns.

Things had worked out well, he thought. The traitors had been dismissed, Hildy had married Henry and had come to Rhydd to be Gwynn's maid, and Trevin had finally forgiven himself for loving her. He'd made his peace with Faith, but he was still troubled by the fact that he was Ian of Rhydd's son.

He would never think of it again and concentrated, instead, on his own growing family.

"There ye be, ye little scamps!" Hildy scolded as she walked into the room. With her hands on her hips, she sighed and rolled her eyes. "Come along, now, and I'll show ye how we gather eggs."

"They'll break them all," Gareth said, sticking his head into room and skewering his father with an impatient look. "Are ye not coming? 'Tis nearly light. Muir is waiting . . . or he was when I saw him last, although he said something about tasting from a new barrel." Gareth shook his head and waved at his father to come hither. "We must hurry or he will not want to join us."

"I'll be along," Trevin promised.

The girls, laughing, hurried away with Hildy fussing and muttering under her breath as she shepherded them down the hallway.

"I will wait for you at the stables. Come, Boon." Gareth whistled for the hound, then left them alone. The door banged shut and they were alone for a few fleeting moments of peace.

Trevin reached for his wife. He kissed her neck and she snuggled against him.

"Have we time?" he asked, one hand cupping her breast.

She laughed deep in her throat. "I know not." Her eyes danced mischievously as she reached for him. "But I think if you are a true man, you can be quick to satisfy a lady, can you not?"

"I can only try," he said, teasing her nipple with his thumb.

"Then try, thief," she suggested as she kissed his lips and melted against him. "Try very, very hard."

Dear Reader,

I hope you enjoyed reading *Dark Ruby*, Trevin and Gwynn's story, as much as I did writing it. I love castles, magic, and courtship. Throw in some incredible warhorses, a few spells, an irreverent hero, and a feisty heroine and I'm in heaven.

Dark Ruby is my first tale from Topaz, but I'm planning two more in the near future. *Dark Emerald* is the next story and it will be followed by *Dark Sapphire.* All three stories are set in medieval Wales with the same components of danger, excitement, and, of course, love.

The next story, *Dark Emerald* is of raven-haired Tara, kidnapped as a toddler, raised by a forest crone some called a witch, and a woman who wants desperately to find her true parents and identity. She is thwarted at every turn by a rogue knight, darkly seductive Rhys, whose hidden past fascinates her as well as frightens her. Who is he and why does she suspect he is the key to unlocking the truth surrounding her own hazy past?

Following *Dark Emerald* is *Dark Sapphire,* the tale of Sheena, a woman with fiery red hair and a temperament to match. Daughter of a baron, she's never fit into the mold of lady of the castle and when falsely accused of murder, she steals away on a ship only to be held captive by Keegan, captain of the *Sapphire*. A hard-edged man who will let no one, especially not a strong-willed stowaway touch his heart, his intent is to ransom her back to the father from whom she ran. Unfortunately, for him, Sheena has the ability to melt the frost surrounding his heart and make him face the pain of his own tragic past.

Dark Emerald will be available from Topaz in the winter of 1998–99 and *Dark Sapphire* will be in your bookstores the following summer or fall. I hope you enjoy them both.

If you'd like a copy of my newsletter or have some comments on *Dark Ruby,* please write me at the following address.

Here's to many hours of happy reading!

Lisa Jackson
333 South State Street, Suite 308
Lake Oswego, Oregon 97034

Please turn the page
for a sneak peak at
the next book by
Lisa Jackson

Twice Kissed

coming soon from Zebra Books

Help me!

Maggie froze.

The old Maxwell House coffee can she used as a grain scoop slipped from her fingers. It hit the floor. Bam! Oats sprayed. Horses tossed their heads and neighed. Her legs buckled and she grabbed hold of a rough-hewn post supporting the hayloft.

Maggie, please! Only you can help me.

"Mary Theresa?" Maggie mouthed, though no sound passed her lips. Was it possible? After all these years would her sister's voice reach her? The barn was suddenly hot. Close. Sweat collected on her scalp.

It was Thane. He did this to me.

Thane Walker. Mary Theresa's ex-husband and the one man Maggie never wanted to lay eyes upon again.

"Did what?" This time she spoke out loud, though her throat was as tight as dried leather.

Maggie, please, don't let him get away with it. . . .

"Where are you?" she cried, knowing spoken words were useless. Squeezing her eyes shut she tried to throw her thoughts to wherever her twin might be. But it wouldn't work. It never had. **Mary Theresa, can you hear me?** *Can you? What did that bastard do to you?*

She waited.

Nothing.

A restless mare snorted.

"If this is some kind of sick joke . . ." she said, though her heart was pounding a million beats a second. "Mary Theresa, I swear . . ."

An anxious gelding stomped his foot and snorted.

Maggie trembled, the inside of her skin quivering as it always had when Mary Theresa contacted her through their own special means. Mental telepathy. Instinct. Magic. Witchcraft. ESP. Clairvoyance. She'd heard it all. Slowly she sank to her knees and rested her head against the post.

She concentrated, willing her breathing to return to normal. **Come on, Mary Theresa, come on. One more time.** Squeezing her eyes shut, she strained to hear, but the only sounds were the rustle of hooves in straw, hot breath blowing out of nervous nostrils, the scratch of tiny claws of mice scurrying between the barrels of grain. "Don't stop now," she said, her teeth sinking into her lower lip until she tasted blood.

Nothing.

"Damn you, Mary Theresa . . . or Marquise or whoever you think you are. Talk to me!"

The inside of the barn felt as if it was a thousand degrees. Perspiration broke out all over her skin, soaking her blouse and running down the sides of her face. "Mary Theresa—"

"Mom?" Becca's voice sounded far away. The door to the barn creaked open and a shaft of daylight sliced into the musty interior. "Hey, are you okay?"

"Fine," she forced out, climbing to her feet and dusting her hands on her shorts. She managed a weak smile, hoping it would mask her lie a little.

Becca's freckled face, with eyes a little too large and

a lot too serious for the age of thirteen, was instantly suspicious. "What were you doing in here?" She motioned to the pose. "Praying?"

"No—"

"You were on your knees, Mom. Did you, like, have a heart attack or what?"

"I was just feeding the horses and I, um, needed . . . a rest." Maggie cringed inside because the lie was so ridiculous, but what could she say? That her sister, whom she hadn't heard from in months, was finally contacting her through telepathy? She'd learned from the past that no one would believe her, especially not her nearly estranged daughter.

Becca eyed the empty coffee can that had rolled against a burlap sack of feed. "Right."

"I was. I just . . . well, if you want to know the truth—"

"That would be a change."

"Becca," she reproached, then held her tongue. The strain between them was palpable. Mother and daughter. How had they grown so far apart when they had once been inseparable?

"I—" Oh, God, how would she explain this—this connection she had with her twin? This weird way of communicating when it hadn't happened in years. ". . . just had a little spell."

"A little spell?" Rebecca repeated, nodding her head as if she had expected just such an answer from a mother she could no longer trust, a woman who had single-handedly ruined her life.

Frustration caused a headache to pound behind her eyes. She'd love to tell Becca the truth, but then her daughter would just think she was crazy. Anyone who had heard her try and explain about the weird connection she had with Mary Theresa did. "Yes. A spell. When you get older—"

"You're only thirty-seven, Mom. You keep telling me it's not exactly ancient."

Thirty-seven and sometimes it feels like seventy.

"Maybe you should see a doctor. Another one." Was there just the hint of concern beneath the sarcasm?"

"Maybe I will." Maggie bent down, picked up the can and found a push broom hanging from a nail. "Nothing to worry about." She swept with long, sure strokes, though she was still shaken. There was a chance she hadn't heard anything after all. Maybe she was just overworked—exhausted from the move and the emotional turmoil that she'd been through.

Becca lifted a thin adolescent shoulder. In a tank top and cut-off jeans, she showed off the beginnings of a womanly figure. "I, um, thought I'd go for a ride."

"It's kind of late."

"If you call eight thirty or so late. Geez, Mom, if you haven't noticed, it's summer. I'll take Jasper."

It was useless to argue. No reason to. Becca was right. "Just be back before it gets dark." She hung up the broom and scooped another ration of oats.

"No one's gonna get me here in the middle of no-where," Becca said as she pulled down a bridle. "It's not like when we lived in California, you know, in the middle of civilization."

"Just be careful."

"Always am."

"Take Barkley with you."

"He'll come whether I want him to or not, but he's not much of a watchdog."

"Just take him."

"Fine."

"And let Jasper finish his dinner first, okay?"

Becca rolled her eyes and let out a theatrical long-suffering sigh, but she did as she was told, leaving the bridle looped over the top rail of the stalls and even going so far as to grab the pitchfork and toss hay into the mangers. They worked in tense silence, the heat of the day and the argument simmering between them. It took all of Maggie's will power not to make small talk or criticize. **Patience,** she told herself. **The resentment will fade. Give it time. Lots of time.**

When Becca was in one of her the-world-is-against-me-and-it's-all-your-fault moods, anything Maggie said would only exacerbate the situation. She had learned it was better to hold her tongue. Besides, Becca wanted answers and what could Maggie say? **I heard your flamboyant aunt's voice here in the barn, even though she's thousands of miles away? Yeah, right.**

When Jasper had eaten his fill, Becca snapped on his bridle, walked him to the pasture and as the other horses filed out of the barn to the dusky evening, she saddled the gray gelding and whistled to the dog, an aging German shepherd with one mangled ear and a bad hind leg, the result of an old battle he'd waged and lost with a raccoon.

As if she'd done it all her life, Becca rode through a series of gates to the Forest Service land where scrub brush was interrupted by stands of jack and lodgepole pine trees. The countryside of this part of the Idaho panhandle was desolate and empty. Blue sky appeared to stretch forever only to be scraped by the spires of the Bitterroot Mountains to the east. She and Becca were alone. Just the way Maggie wanted it. As far from the city and all the painful memories of L.A. as she could get.

Arms folded over her chest, she watched her daughter ride into the surrounding hills, the dog, using only three legs, loping easily behind. Barkley had adopted Becca when they'd moved here nine months earlier. Both broken souls, Maggie thought anxiously, and ignored the first mournful cry of a coyote hidden somewhere in the distance. Though the temperature hovered near eighty, she shivered and rubbed the goose bumps that rose on her arms.

Night was an hour from falling, but the moon, a smiling crescent that shimmered in opalescent tones, had already risen though the sun was still undecided about settling into the western horizon. Cattle stirred and moved, chewing their cuds, swatting their tails at flies, lumbering without much grace in the lengthening shadows. The horses, a small herd of five without Jasper, collected near the stream that sliced sharply through the fields.

Yes, it was peaceful here, she thought. And safe. The nearest neighbor was half a mile down the road, the closest town not much more than a stoplight, grocery store, post office, and gas station.

Deciding to go inside, she yanked sheets that she'd been drying off the line that stretched from the apple tree to the corner of the front porch. As she unhooked a clothespin from the final sheet she heard the telephone ring impatiently.

"Yeah, yeah, I'm coming . . . I'm coming," she grumbled, tossing the bedding into a wicker basket and hauling it into the old ranch house just as the telephone gave up its incessant ringing. She lifted the receiver, heard a dial tone, and started to hang up only to stare down at the instrument. Who had called? If only she lived in the city as before so that she could check caller I.D. **Or you could buy a new battery for the answering machine and plug it in. You don't have to be a hermit.**

That much was true. She eyed the mouthpiece of the receiver, then placed the hand piece into its cradle. So someone had called. It could be one of Becca's friends. Though they didn't get many calls here, there were a few and just because she'd thought she'd heard Mary Theresa's voice was no reason to panic. **Just calm down.**

The truth was that she'd been hiding for nine months, turning her back on a world that had hurt her and her daughter one too many times.

Coward. Other people cope. Why can't you?

Could the caller have been Mary Theresa? It had been so long since they'd spoken, too long. . . . She picked up the receiver again and dialed rapidly before she let her pride get the better of her. The long-distance connection was made and she waited. One ring. Two. Three. Click.

"Hi, this is Marquise. I can't come to the phone right now, but leave a message after the tone and I'll get back to you as soon as I can. I promise."

The recorder beeped and Maggie steeled herself. "Mary Theresa, this is Maggie. If you're there please pick up . . . Mary Theresa? . . . Oh, okay, Marquise, are you there?" she asked impatiently, using her sister's stage name, hoping that if Mary Theresa was within earshot she'd put aside her petulance and answer. But she heard nothing. "Look, I, um, I got a message from you, at least I think I did, and I need to talk to you, so please call me back. I'm still at the ranch in Idaho." She rattled off the number, waited a heartbeat in the fleeting hope that her sister was listening and then hung up.

The sun had finally set and the cabin was suddenly stuffy and close. She opened the windows, glanced toward the mountains as if she could will her daughter's image to appear from the shadows and tried not to think about her sister's cryptic message. What had she said? **Only you can help me. It was Thane. He did this to me.**

Did what?

Maggie unloaded the dishwasher and ignored her computer, which had been waiting for her all day. She sorted socks, listened to the call of night birds and finally opened the front door, letting the screen keep the insects out as she hoped for the breath of a breeze. She felt nothing but hot, stagnant air. Snapping her hair into a ponytail, she felt her blouse clinging to her and she swiped the sweat from the back of her neck with a cold cloth. As the cabin grew dark she turned on the lights and thought about Thane. Sexy and irreverent. A lone-cowboy type complete with a Wyoming swagger and enough lines in his face to add an edge of severity to already harsh features. The kind of a man to avoid. The kind of man who attracted trouble. The only man who had ever been able to make Maggie's blood run hot with one cynical glance.

"Forget it," she told herself. She must've imagined the whole scene. She'd only thought she'd heard Mary Theresa's "voice" because it had been so long, so many silent months without a word from her twin. She walked to the fireplace and plucked an old framed photo from the mantle. It had been taken nearly ten years earlier when Mary Theresa, who had reinvented herself as simply Marquise, à la Cher or Madonna, was about to launch her own Denver-based talk show.

In the photo, the two sisters stood back to back, identical twins except that they were mirror images. Mary Theresa was left-handed, Maggie used her right, one side of Mary's mouth lifted more than the other, the opposite was true of her sister. One of Mary Theresa's pinkies turned inward—the right. On Maggie, it was the left.

Maggie felt a smile tease her lips as she ran a finger over the faded snapshot. She and Mary Theresa both sported auburn hair that curled wildly, but Mary Theresa's had been highlighted with gold and framed her face in soft layers while Maggie's had been scraped back into a functional ponytail. Mary Theresa had worn a black dress, a designer original, complemented with a strand of pearls, black hose and heels. She'd been on her way to a party with some once-upon-a-time celebrities. At the same frozen moment in time Maggie had worn jeans and a flannel shirt with a tail that flapped in the wind and had balanced three-year-old Becca on one outthrust hip. With the snow-shrouded Rocky Mountains as a backdrop, the two sisters braced themselves on each other, then swivelled their heads to grin into the camera. Bright I-can-take-on-the-world smiles, rosy cheeks, a smattering of freckles and hazel eyes that snapped with fire and stared into the lens.

It seemed like ages ago.

A lifetime.

She set the photo on the mantle, where it had been, between pictures of all stages of Becca's life as well as her own, then glanced outside. The evening was gathering fast, stars sprayed the purple heavens as darkness shadowed the land.

"Come on, Becca," she worried aloud as she

snapped on the light and stepped onto the front porch. Silently she hoped for some sign of Jasper galloping toward the barn. But there was no sound of hoofbeats, no glimpse of a dark horse appearing over the slight rise of the field. The clatter of a train rolling on far-off tracks, then again a howl of a coyote split the silence. She leaned one hip against the porch rail. An answering soulful cry, lonely and echoing, rolled across the land and put Maggie's teeth on edge.

Watching a moth beat the life out of itself as it flew against the single lightbulb over the porch, she fidgeted with her hair and wedding ring that she still wore on her right ring finger. It was a joke really, something she'd have to give up, but couldn't quite. Not yet.

First she heard the rumble of an engine, then the crunch of gravel as it was flattened by heavy tires. She looked down the lane and saw twin beams flashing through the night, the beacons broken by the trunks of trees as they passed, headlights of a truck that rolled to a stop not far from the barn.

"Maggie?" a male voice called as the driver cut the engine and stepped out of the cab.

Her throat turned to sand and her stupid heart jolted.

Thane Walker slammed the door of the truck and started toward the porch. **It was Thane. He did this to me.** Mary Theresa's voice haunted her and Maggie swallowed hard.

His slow western saunter had disappeared, replaced by purposeful strides that ate up the gravel-strewn lot that separated the house from the barn. With a countenance as harsh as the wind-swept Wyoming plains he'd once called home, his face was grim and set, his jaw clenched, his eyes, even in the darkness, drilling into hers.

"Thane," she said, not bothering with a smile as he stepped into the small circle of light cast by the lone bulb. "You're about the last person I expected to see here."

His lips flattened over his teeth for just a second. "I'm here because I need your help."

"My help?" She was already shaking her head and trying to stay calm. Just because she thought she'd heard Mary Theresa's "voice," was no reason to panic. But the fact that he was here had to be more than coincidence. Didn't it? She folded her arms over her chest. "You know, Thane, you've got a lot of nerve. After everything that happened between you and Mary Theresa, I can't imagine why I'd even consider helping you."

"Or because of what happened between us?" he asked.

She stiffened, felt a jab of undeserved guilt and refused to rise to the bait. "What's up?"

"It's Mary Theresa." He didn't bother to mount the steps, instead he stared straight into her eyes.

She hardly dared ask, "What about her?"

"I don't know how to say this but to do it straight out," he admitted, rubbing his hand over a jaw that was in dire need of a shave. "Brace yourself."

"Oh, God—"

"She's missing, Maggie. Been gone at least three days. No one knows where she is, but . . ." He looked away, then took a deep breath. "It looks bad."

"How bad?" She held on to the rail of the porch for support.

"Everyone's really worried. I was hoping . . . I'd

thought she might be here. I'm surprised the police haven't called you yet."

She felt the breath of something cold and sinister against the back of her neck. "You know Mary Theresa," Maggie heard herself saying, denial running circles in her mind. "This could just be one of her stunts. It's not like she hasn't run away before."

A shadow flickered in his gaze. "This time she doesn't have a husband to run from."

"For the love of God, Thane, listen to you. Mary Theresa is fine. She's just . . . hiding."

"But not here? Not with you."

"No—"

He looked tired. Weary. As if he hadn't slept in days. As if he really believed that this time Mary Theresa had gotten herself into thick, dire trouble.

"There's more," he said and his tone of voice—so flat and guarded—told her to beware.

"More?"

"The police suspect foul play. That she's been kidnaped or worse."

A soft cry erupted from her throat.

"No—"

He held her gaze with eyes that were, in the darkness, a dangerous midnight shade of blue. "I'm sorry, Maggie."

"Look, Thane, I don't want to hear this. It's nonsense. It . . . it just can't be. Mary Theresa is fine. She's in Denver and—"

"I was there. At her place. She wasn't there. Hadn't been for days. Yesterday she missed a meeting with her agent."

"She could just be out of town. You know how she is."

His teeth clenched and a muscle worked in the corner of his jaw. "The police will be calling."

"Oh, God." She shook her head. "Nope," she said with new determination. "You're wrong. Something's going on, sure, but—"

"Why would I lie?"

The question stopped her cold. She opened her mouth, then snapped it closed.

"Why would I drive all this way just to tell you a lie?"

Her head thundered as night descended. She felt detached as if she were watching a drama that she was a part of. "I-I don't know. You have before."

"Not about this."

"No, but—"

He grabbed her hand, held it in a grip that squeezed hard. "I didn't come here to freak you out, Maggie. I didn't come here to upset you or worry you. I just thought you'd want to know, to hear it from me. So, please, stop denying for a minute and hear me out."

He looked so beleaguered she half-believed him and then the pain began in earnest, the agony of what he was saying plunged deep into her soul. Tears burned in her eyes. "I don't want to hear this."

"And, believe me, I don't want to say it, but Maggie, you've got to listen. There's a detective with the Denver Police who thinks that she . . ."

"What?"

His lips turned down at the corners. "That she might be dead."

"Oh, sweet Jesus, no—" This was all happening too fast; Maggie was getting too much information, too much horrible information too quickly. Her stomach twisted and she thought she might be sick. "Why?

What would lead him to believe . . ." She swallowed back the bile that rose in her throat.

"I don't know. They haven't found her body, at least not that I know of, but they keep digging."

Tears rolled down her cheeks. "I don't believe you, Thane. This is all too crazy. Mary Theresa is alive, damn it! If something had happened to her, I would know." She hooked a thumb at her chest. "I would feel it."

"How?"

"I don't know, but I would."

"Because you're twins."

"Because . . . well, yes. She and I are close."

"You haven't spoken in years."

But I heard from her. Just a few hours ago. She called to me. Maggie started to utter the words, then held her tongue. She'd learned her lesson long ago. No one would believe her. Not the psychiatrists she'd visited, nor her parents, and especially not Thane Walker. Sniffing loudly, she ran a finger under her eyes to stop the tears. "I just think I would know. Don't ask me to explain it, okay?"

He hesitated, then shoved his hair out of his eyes with both hands.

"Is there something else?" she asked, determined not to let this man with his wild allegations get to her.

He frowned and nodded curtly. "Yeah."

"More speculation?"

"Maybe." His dark gaze found hers as he mounted the stairs and stood over her. "I might need your help."

"You?"

"Because of this. The investigator in charge—his name is Henderson—he thinks I had something to do with Mary Theresa aka Marquise's disappearance."

"No!"

A sharp woof heralded Barkley's arrival. Three legs moving swiftly, the shepherd tore into the yard and raced up the steps. The hairs on the back of his neck bristled, his fangs flashed an evil white and his mangled ear lay flat and menacing against his head. He growled low in his throat, glaring at Thane with suspicious dark eyes and looked as if he would like to tear into the stranger.

"Where's Becca?" Maggie asked, all thoughts of her sister quickly forgotten.

"What?" Thane asked, then commanded "Hush" to the dog who backed off but still snarled from beneath the old porch swing.

Maggie, fear turning her heart to ice, stared at the night-darkened fields. "Becca. She went riding about an hour or so ago. Barkley was with her . . ." Maggie strained, hoping to see the horse and rider and spying nothing but the small herd of horses and a few head of cattle, dark shapes shifting against the bleached grass. Why would the dog return alone? Goose bumps rose on her flesh. "I hope something didn't happen . . ."

The phone rang and fear congealed deep in her soul. Something had happened to Becca, she just knew it. But who would be calling so quickly? Oh God. Oh God. Oh God. She threw open the screen door and ran inside, snagging the receiver on the third ring. The door banged shut, and Thane, with the dog guarding him, stared through the mesh.

"Hello?" she answered.

"This is Detective Henderson with the Denver Police. Is this Margaret Elizabeth MacRae?"

"Yes."

"Your sister is Mary Theresa Walker, also known by the single name of Marquise?"

Maggie began to shake. Her blood turned to ice. Biting her lip, she stared at Thane's face and nodded, as if the detective could hear her. "Yes."

"I'm afraid I have some bad news for you, Ms. Mac-Rae," Henderson said solemnly. "It's about your sister. . . ."

SEARING ROMANCES

☐ **STEALING HEAVEN by Jaclyn Reding.** Torn from her bed by an unknown abductor, heiress Gilliam Forrester found herself in a forced marriage with a wastrel she devised. She would risk disaster itself to escape, and she did—only to lie unconscious on a country road waiting for death, or for a rescuer. The "Rakehell Earl" of Morgan, Dante Tremaine, was on his way home when he found an injured woman—and his destiny. "These lovers will steal your heart."—Catherine Coulter
(406494—$5.99)

☐ **SPRING'S FURY by Denise Domning.** Nicola of Ashby swore to kill Gilliam Fitz-Henry—murderer of her father, destroyer of her home—the man who would wed her in a forced match. Amid treachery and tragedy, rival knights and the pain of past wounds, Gilliam knew he must win Nicola's respect. Then, with kisses and hot caresses, he intended to win her heart.
(405218—$4.99)

☐ **PIRATE'S ROSE by Janet Lynnford.** The Rozalinde Cavendish, independent daughter of England's richest merchant, was taking an impetuous moon-lit walk along the turbulent shore when she encountered Lord Christopher Howard, a legendary pirate. Carried aboard his ship, she entered his storm-tossed world and became intimate with his troubled soul. Could their passion burn away the veil shrouding Christopher's secret past and hidden agenda?
(405978—$4.99)

*Prices slightly higher in Canada
